VICTORIA JANSSEN

THE
DUCHESS
HER MAID
THE GROOM
& THEIR
LOVER

Spice

THE DUCHESS, HER MAID, THE GROOM & THEIR LOVER

ISBN-13: 978-0-373-60526-2
ISBN-10:   0-373-60526-9

Spice and Colophon are trademarks used under license and registered in
Australia, New Zealand, Philippines, United States Patent and Trademark
Office and in other countries.

www.Spice-Books.com

Printed in U.S.A.

For Lorrie. Twenty-plus years of pie and helicopters, and counting.

CHAPTER ONE

The Duchess Camille's maid, Sylvie, draped a blue silk robe over her shoulders. Camille had to restrain herself from clutching it to her bare breasts. Normally, Camille had no particular emotion about being dressed or undressed by her servants— it was too common an occurrence—but today each touch made her flinch. Sylvie's anger made her tension worse, even when demonstrated only as a hint of roughness when tugging Camille's long, dark hair free of the robe. Sylvie hadn't yet cleansed the splotch of Camille's blood from the front of her own simple blue gown, and her long blond braid extruded messy wisps. It didn't help to know Sylvie was not angry at her, but the Duke Michel.

Across the room, the midwife finished washing in a porcelain basin painted all over with flowers no larger than a woman's thumb, the fierce jerks of her arms dripping water and imported jasmine-scented lather onto carpet so thick it swallowed the feet. The midwife's cropped hair glistened in the light of a dozen fat candles. They were surrounded by all the luxury one could want, except for safety.

Camille didn't dare give in to her own anger. She had denied it for so long that it had gone solid in her belly like a chunk of dirty glass. She felt sick with it, and weary down to her marrow. She would give anything to be alone for a few moments, to collect herself, but if she sent them away now, after the examination she'd just endured, she would reveal her weakness. She had already let slip her emotions once today, when the duke had told her Lord Alphonse was dead. In her distress, she had nearly revealed his mission, the mission which had led to his death. She would keep her dignity now, and with it her secrets.

Sylvie said, "I will fetch you a glass of wine, madame, and ice for your bruises."

"Sit," Camille ordered, unable to bear a continuation of Sylvie's earlier pacing of holes in the plush gold carpet. She glanced toward the washbasin, carefully avoiding her reflection in the nearby full-length oval mirror, its wide frame like a tangle of golden brambles. "Mistress Annette?"

The midwife was thirty years old at the most, and normally worked at the brothel in the town, caring for the diseases from which prostitutes suffered and helping to birth what children they might bear. She was a tiny woman with hair cut close to her scalp and a scar on her chin. For her surreptitious visits to the palace, she dressed in a baggy dun gown, a sparrow flitting into a golden cage and out of it again, unnoticed by any except Sylvie and Camille. Camille had never seen her elsewhere. She did not even know where Mistress Annette lived; Sylvie always fetched her, when she was needed. But she would—had—entrusted Annette with her health and life.

"You were not pregnant, Your Grace."

Camille did not allow herself to show any reaction, but all the same, Sylvie rose from her chair and returned to where Camille stood.

"Am I injured?"

Mistress Annette picked up a towel and dried her hands. "You are bruised," she said, as if Camille had forgotten the reddened swelling over her jaw and cheekbone, her skin broken from the impact of the duke's rings. Her left shoulder ached from slamming into the silken wallpaper of his private audience room; her hip and elbow throbbed from hitting the marble floor.

"There is no injury inside?"

"No, Your Grace." Mistress Annette set down the towel and stepped closer, until she stood within arms' reach. She said calmly, "He will kill you one day, you know."

Sylvie began to speak but Camille held up a hand for silence. "I could become pregnant. I am not too old."

Mistress Annette crossed her arms across her chest. "Your Grace, I am hard put to remember you are not just any woman. Because in this matter, you are certainly as unwise as any I've met."

Camille heard Sylvie catch her breath; ironic, as Sylvie was not afraid to speak her mind to her duchess, either. "If I give the duke an heir, he will have no need to find another duchess."

"His Grace has no bastards, but not for lack of trying. Not a one. If I were you, I would find another sire, and pass the child off as his."

Mistress Annette had never stated it so boldly before. Camille shook her head in refusal. She had married Michel, a younger son, and in becoming her consort, he'd become duke, with power over her. She could have protested her father's order to marry Michel and run away, but she had not, foolishly fearing the duchy would suffer without her. She had spoken the vows with her own voice. Once she had done so, she had a responsibility to her marriage, and a responsibility to her duchy's people. She had stood up to her mistake for over twenty years.

A few blows should not weaken her resolve so much. Except, this time Lord Alphonse had died. He'd been killed while trying to help her, not even knowing that the appeal he carried to Lord Maxime betrayed his duke. He'd been barely older than Annette or Sylvie. Sylvie might very well be next.

"Madame!"

Camille blinked as the room slowed and settled. Sylvie was holding her arm, fingers digging painfully into her bruised muscles. Mistress Annette ducked beneath Camille's other arm and supported her to her bed. The underside of the bed's canopy, blue and gold like the sheets and coverlet, bore appliquéd figures of men plowing fields and sowing grain, a transparent allegory to encourage the fertility of the couples who lay within. Except Michel had never taken her here; she'd always been brought to his chambers, or more lately, wherever he felt she would be uncomfortable and refuse his advances.

"He will kill you," Annette said again, without emphasis, as if stating the sky was blue. She laid the back of her hand against Camille's forehead, then her cheek. Camille closed her eyes; that single tender touch brought her close to shattering. "Sylvie, fetch blankets."

Nauseated and beginning to shiver, Camille said, "I'm only hungry. I didn't eat while Sylvie went to find you."

Annette tucked a pillow beneath Camille's feet. She repeated, "He will kill you. And you know what will happen then. He will rape this duchy, and then move on to the next, just as your father did."

Even now, Camille could not bring herself to say aloud that she had failed, that Michel had indeed won, even when it was true. She said, "You must leave the palace, before you're found in my apartments."

"Never fear, Your Grace. Unlike you, I have concern for my own skin."

Sylvie returned and spread blankets over Camille's feet before moving upward. "Madame, you need rest. Annette, what must I do?"

"Convince her to find someone else to get her with child," Annette said. "And have a care that he's healthy, and looks enough like the duke."

Camille was no longer allowed to ride, but she could still venture out onto the palace's high white walls and glimpse her horses from afar. Two weeks after Mistress Annette's visit, she strolled there, her two eunuch guards trailing behind. Kaspar and Arno knew when she was not in the mood for conversation; this cool spring evening, they did not even speak quietly with each other.

The breeze from outside was sharper up on the walls, and she smelled a hint of rain mingled with the grass and manure of the paddocks below. She slipped into an embrasure, concealing herself from anyone's view—anyone except her eunuchs, of course—and gazed toward the stable that held her mare, Guirlande, and all the others she'd spent so long cosseting, training and schooling.

The stableboy was riding Lilas, his body seemingly immobile atop her sleek back as she danced patterns into the loose dirt of the riding ring. Only his thick brown hair ruffled in the wind. Four years ago, the duke had forbidden her to ride, and since that day she had not been to the stables, nor near her horses, nor had she spoken to their keeper. But she had years ago watched the boy be trained to ride. She had ridden out with him, and she knew his posture and seat, even from this distance. Her Lilas was in good hands.

She wondered what he looked like now that he was closer to his man's growth. She remembered big hands, lush eyelashes and an engaging, open smile. He would be almost twenty now, and might have changed a great deal. It occurred to her that he was half her age. If she had borne a child in the first years of her marriage to Michel, the stableboy was the right age to be her son.

Sylvie had reminded her that the stableboy's eyes were blue. Like the duke's.

Normally, she would watch until she had caught at least a glimpse of each of her horses, and perhaps drawn in her sketchbook, but this evening she turned away and strode toward her own wing of the palace. The wall's stone felt cold beneath her thin slippers. Kaspar and Arno fell in behind her, their movements betrayed by the faintest chiming of their weapons; they followed her down the turret staircase, across a square of immaculate garden that replaced the old bare defensive area, and through enormous mahogany doors carved with the ducal arms, each door swung wide by a footman in the duke's livery.

Camille led her eunuchs past the locked door of her audience room and through a hidden doorway. The narrow secondary corridor leading to her suite of rooms was thickly carpeted in blue and gold, an agreeable softness to her cold feet. Camille did not allow herself to slow and appreciate the softly patterned gold wallpaper, the candles muted behind colored glass or the paintings of horses that adorned the walls. Sylvie would have dismissed the rest of the staff by now, and they would have less than an hour of privacy.

Kaspar and Arno followed her through the outer rooms and into her bedchamber where Sylvie waited, perched on the edge of a spindly, decorative chair that Camille had never liked. "All is as you wished, madame," Sylvie said, meaning that the suite was deserted but for the four of them.

For this meeting, they all should sit, Camille thought, for she asked more of her servants than duty. She looked to Kaspar and indicated the empty chairs. Kaspar grinned. "Perhaps not, Your Grace. I fear it would shatter beneath my weight." He was taller than most and twice as broad. Leather straps crisscrossed his bare, hairless torso, supporting a knife sheath that nestled between his shoulder blades. The knife's flat grip, she knew, had been etched and inlaid with silver filigree in her own crest. A short sword was strapped to each thigh atop his blue breeches, but those hilts were unadorned, wrapped in strips of dark blue suede.

Arno, the younger of the two eunuchs, said, "I would prefer to sit on the floor, Your Grace."

"Very well," Camille said. She took a chair. Even seated on the floor, the eunuchs were not so far below her and Sylvie. Once all were settled comfortably, she captured them with her eyes, giving each a smile. It was not only for herself and her own safety that she did this, but for theirs; it was only right that she pay them this respect. Then she said, "Of the men whom Sylvie has investigated, three were superior choices in terms of health, appearance and proximity to the palace."

"Madame," Sylvie said, "we could entice Lord Pierken from his estate. He has an interest in you." Kaspar sent her a quelling glance, and she made a rude gesture at him.

"I fear not," Camille said. "Remember, it's planting season." Also, Lord Pierken would not be content to simply impregnate her and depart. He would want something in return, more than she could give. She continued, "Of the three, Lord Gustave resembles Michel the most, physically. His temperament is not suitable, however. He is quick to take offense and convinced of his own importance. I dare not trust him to keep this secret. And he might require a longer-term liaison and a gift of political power in exchange for his seed, which I will not give."

Sylvie asked, "And Lord Jon-Petite?"

"I fear he is too old," Camille said reluctantly. "He has a son nearly thirty years old, and he has no other. He is my ally in the palace, it's true, and it would be easier to arrange meetings with him, but if he cannot serve the purpose the effort will be wasted." She had once considered him a friend, and though she rarely saw him anymore, she hated the thought of destroying their friendly relationship with her demand that he put himself in deadly danger to service her like a stallion. Also, she was not sure that Lord Jon-Petite's scruples would allow him to betray her husband.

Sylvie said, "That leaves only the stableboy!"

Camille glanced to Kaspar, then Arno. Their expressions remained impassive. She said calmly, "You yourself brought him to my attention as a potential candidate. He is young and healthy, he has the necessary hair and eye color and his mother came from Michel's homeland, so there is a superficial likeness of facial and body type. Best of all, he is loyal to me, yet will not feel entitled to interfere with my role as duchess. He is good with my horses. He is the best choice for this."

"But—madame—he is a boy! Nineteen years old!"

"All the more likely he's virile, then," Camille said. "You will bring him to me as soon as possible. His name is Henri." She swallowed the lump forming in her throat. Who was she to demand such a thing of him, when he'd given her nothing but loyalty? But if she did not do this, Michel would kill her, and she did not want to die.

"He will not understand the serious nature of this duty——"

"Sylvie, you will bring him to me."

If Sylvie truly thought the boy would not serve the purpose, she would never have included him in her list. She stiffly bowed her head. It didn't matter that she wasn't pleased. She would obey. Later, she would see that Camille had made the wisest possible choice. She need not fear having to exchange political favors with a stableboy. And if he cared for her as he did for her horses, she did not think he could betray her.

"Kaspar and Arno," Camille said, "this plan may fail. If it appears my imprisonment or execution is imminent, we must flee the palace. I rely on you both, and on you, Sylvie, to secure sufficient monies and supplies for a journey of some weeks. You three will accompany me. It is crucial that this activity be completely concealed from any in the palace or in the town."

"It shall be done," Kaspar said. "Where will we go?"

"We shall travel to the coastal protectorate, and there beg aid of Lord Maxime. He will keep us safe. He will not have forgotten that he and I grew up together, here in the palace."

"Lord Maxime?" Arno blurted out. "Your Grace, he would like nothing better than to make the protectorate a duchy again! What better way than to harm you?"

Camille eyed him coldly. "Harming me would change nothing. It is my husband who will not free the protectorate," she said. "He claims it is because my father conquered it and killed Maxime's father, and it is his duty to care for the land and its people. But the duke wants only the protectorate's income. Maxime will help me. Then we shall return here, and I will take what is mine."

True, Maxime would want favors from her. He would not help her out of pure charity; for the sake of his people, he could not. For the sake of her own people, she would only give so much. But he would help her, and then...then she would make sure that Michel never harmed anyone again.

CHAPTER TWO

Henri ran his hands over Guirlande's sleek hide, adding a final gloss to her grooming. As he ducked beneath the cross-ties which held her still, she snorted affectionately into his hair. Henri grinned and loosed the ties from her halter before moving on to Tonnelle.

"Boy!"

Henri whirled, wondering what he'd done—or not done—this time. A sharp-featured young blond woman stood in the open doorway of the stable, holding her skirts well clear of the straw. He'd spotted her once or twice before and assumed she was the lover of one of the senior grooms or perhaps of a courier. She wore a nondescript scullion's dress, but gestured as imperiously as an upper servant. "Leave the horse. Come with me."

"I have work," he said.

"It can wait. Her Grace wishes to see you."

At first, he was sure he'd misheard. He stood gaping. He hadn't seen the duchess in months, even from a distance. He'd even heard whispered rumors the duke had killed her in a wild rage, or that she'd been shut up in an asylum, gone mad from failing to bear a child. Perhaps she *had* gone mad. It was unheard-of for her to summon a servant as lowly as he. Had he misunderstood? Was he meant to meet with a steward? Still, it would be good to know at least if she lived, and how she fared. Perhaps this woman could give him news; perhaps he could give her a message about the welfare of the horses. Perhaps that was why the duchess wanted to see him; she wanted to personally question him about her horses. "What does she want of me?"

"That is for Her Grace to say. Come, boy. I cannot loiter here all day."

Henri kept his head down as he followed the maid through a servants' entrance in the palace's immense white walls, down a dim corridor, and through a fitted door into the ducal palace. Why had he been summoned? He could not guess if the purpose was good or bad. Or, he told himself, it might be good for the duchess, but bad for him.

The maid walked very quickly, without glancing behind to see if he followed. The floor was polished marble, a gray color that reminded him of winter ice. No one moved through the corridors, a circumstance Henri found chilling, as well; he knew the duke had nearly a hundred servants. Surely some of them would be about. Someone would have to clean this floor. And he knew a few footmen; they spent a great deal of time standing about in corridors, waiting for someone to need them. Where had the footmen gone? The only section of the palace that had no footmen was...but of course he could not be walking through the duchess's wing of the palace. She saw her servants in an audience room, off the main hall, the one everyone knew from when court was open to the public. This must be merely a different route there.

That still didn't explain the deserted corridors. The main hall would have even more servants than the duchess's wing. As the maid led him up a narrow stairway that smelled strongly of lemon and beeswax, he wondered how many bribes their privacy had cost, and why the bribes had been necessary. Then the maid stopped before a mahogany-paneled door inlaid in gold leaf, opened it and gestured for him to go through. Henri did so; she did not follow. The maid shut the door behind him and he heard a *thump,* as if she had leaned her back against it.

The room was incredibly bright from a chandelier bristling with lit candles and crystalline droplets of the clearest glass he'd ever seen. The light reflected almost painfully from the white marble floor. The walls were hung with tapestries in lush twining, leaflike patterns of blue and gold, dazzling his eyes and muffling sounds. He felt as if he'd stepped inside a jeweled box, like the one in which the duchess had kept the bridle ornaments for Guirlande. Though for all its intricate glamour, the room felt too still; its air had the faintest dusty smell of disuse.

He turned to his right, intending to examine the tapestry more closely, and saw the duchess, immobile as a statue. Truly the duchess, and not some functionary. His breath caught at her beauty and aristocratic bearing. She wore a crimson gown with a belled skirt and a low squared neckline that emphasized her bosom, and more jewels than he'd ever seen in one place at one time, even on a courtier riding to a party. Faceted blood-colored rubies were pinned into her long silver-streaked hair; more rubies dripped from her ears like tiny clusters of grapes. Her pale eyes fixed on him, and he fell immobile from the intensity of her regard. Henri was rarely noticed by anyone. Being noticed by the duchess was like being hit in the chest.

She'd noticed him before. When he was a boy, it had been she who sent her own riding teacher to tutor him as well, for those times when she could not be present to school her own horses. And one time only, Henri had provided cupped hands to boost her foot into the stirrup. He'd been about fifteen then. He still remembered the gold heel on her supple leather riding boot, beneath a lavishly embroidered skirt hem; he'd been afraid to look higher. She'd given him a copper. Only weeks after, she'd been forbidden to ride—it was said her riding astride had prevented her from conceiving an heir. She had never even borne a girl.

She was forty now, and probably past bearing, so it couldn't hurt for her to ride again, could it? She might defy her husband for such a freedom. Henri remembered how she'd stroked her horses' necks and pressed her forehead to theirs. He'd watched her, many times. She loved her horses, he could tell, and for that reason he loved her. Horses knew people. One horse might love her if she were cruel, but certainly not all of them. Henri had ridden all of her horses, and every one worked with him in perfect trust. He'd ridden one or two of the duke's hunters, as well; that had taught him that the duke was cack-handed and deaf to the animals' body language, for their actions were stiff and awkward. In contrast, the duchess's horses moved like silk.

"You look enough like my husband," she said. "It should be possible."

He couldn't mistake her meaning. The whispers, the rumors, they were true. Henri couldn't speak; one wrong word and she could have him caged in the city square and pelted with rotten fruit and rocks. But he couldn't run away, either, because the duchess had summoned him. She'd had him summoned and he hadn't fled, as any reasonable person would have done when the nobility took notice of them. If only he did not care. If only it did not matter to him if she bore an heir or if she died.

In this audience room, they were alone. If he were seen alone with the duchess, by anyone at all besides her loyal maid, he would die in the worst way imaginable. So far as he knew, the duchess was allowed no men in her direct presence without her eunuch guards—or without her husband, the duke, of course. Henri stared even harder at a porphyry medallion set into the white marble floor. The cleanliness and luxury made Henri's knees shake and his balls shrivel. He was probably already doomed, when he had done nothing to harm anyone, nothing but obey the duchess's maid who'd brought him here like a favorite riding hack.

"Boy? Do you understand what your duchess requires of you? I understand you know something of the breeding of horses, so you should be more than equal to this task." Her voice was low but commanding. He could not imagine defying that voice.

She approached him, and he shrank from her. Was he supposed to reply? His throat felt stuffed with old hay. Then came the unthinkable—a light touch to his hair.

"Look up."

Trembling, he did so, as if she tugged his reins.

"Please," she said. She might as well have been asking for morning ale. Her face was like a silver coin he'd once seen, cleanly cut lips and a long, straight nose, but this close he could see the bruises, carefully covered, along her jaw, and fine lines feathering from the corners of her eyes. Thick swatches of iron-gray streaked the ebony hair that fell past her waist. Her eyes, the cold gray of a winter sky, shone and swelled with water before she blinked, once, and transformed them back to metal.

His world shifted for a moment into some afternoon fantasy, glimpsed in sunlit dust sifting down from the hayloft. He would save her, and she would…have him killed, so no one would know what she had done? "Y-Your Grace," Henri said. Her gown exhaled costly spices he could not name. His own clothing was pungent from horses and leather and sweat. The maid had directed him to leave his muddy boots behind, so his bare, calloused toes curled against polished stone.

The duchess stood back from him, her skirts unfurling over her jeweled slippers. "If I do not provide an heir within the year, I will be killed, so my husband can take another wife within the bounds of law," she said flatly. "They will shave my hair and cut off my head. Do you understand? Answer me."

"Y-yes."

"I cannot protect you. I am a woman and my command to my husband's guards is not worth a copper coin." She paused. "Will you do this for me?"

For her. She would never humiliate herself like this, not to someone like him, unless she truly needed his aid. His mouth felt numb with fear as he nodded and knelt on the marble, searching in vain for another flicker of humanity in her pale, regal face.

Her crimson gown rustled as she paced to the door, like the caged crow in the stables. He scrambled back to his feet and followed. She had what she wanted of him, as the aristocrats always had what they wanted. It was their right.

How in the world could he even disrobe before her? Much less...less...

She stopped before the door and said, as if discussing her choice of gown, "It's best done now. My husband will send for me tonight."

Henri nodded again. What else was he to do?

The duchess opened the door a crack and peered out. She murmured to her waiting maid, then snapped the door closed. Henri twitched. "This way," she said.

He followed. A delicate wooden chair with a plush red seat and curving arms that ended in carved blossoms hid another door behind swaths of red fabric, embroidered all over with flowers in a deeper red thread. Henri expected darkness, but the corridor of red marble was lit by yellow beeswax candles, sweet-smelling and thick as his forearm, in gold sconces shaped as unearthly smooth disembodied feminine hands, braceleted in cruel red stones. He'd never seen so many candles in his life. Who lit them? Who trimmed away the drips? Ebony chairs lined the walls, each carved with more flowers and accompanied by its own little matching marble-topped table, for what purpose he could not imagine. Each table was bare. The duchess swept down the corridor without glancing at the paintings of flowers in gilt frames, the tapestries populated by gardens and ladies and fat babies, even the carved figure of the duke's head in white marble whose gaze, blind but all-seeing, made Henri want to hide his eyes. To his relief, he saw no guards.

He had to catch himself when she abruptly halted and withdrew a golden key from her bosom. Hastily, Henri averted his eyes, saw the dirty smear his hand had left on the pale pink wallpaper, and scrubbed it clean with a corner of his sleeve. The key scratched in the lock and the door swung open.

Henri scarcely saw the rooms they passed through now. He retained a blurred impression of fresh flowers and jewel-colored velvet, oval mirrors in frames as wide as his hand, overstuffed tapestried sofas with matching pillows, silver platters of fresh, shiny fruit, sinuous glass oil lamps perfuming the air. When the duchess finally halted, a square wood bed loomed before him, roofed in wood, canopied and curtained in fringed gold silk and piled with tasseled blue pillows—a bed wider than a prize stallion's loose box and half the size of the hovel where he had been born. Henri had spent his nineteen years sleeping on straw, his spare shirt for a pillow and rats scampering across his discarded boots. Now he was expected to service the duchess on a bed worth an entire village? Impossible. His cock dangled flaccid as an empty sausage casing. He didn't recognize his own voice when he said, "Stop."

The duchess turned.

"I—I want—" Henri swallowed.

The duchess gazed impassively at him. She said nothing. She did not have to speak, he realized. He was here; she'd got her way and apparently had no further concern for how the…act proceeded.

He would make her feel something. If he was to die after, then he wanted to die a man, not a silent slave. "I want you in there," he said as firmly as he could, gesturing toward the room before, a less frightening room.

To his surprise, the duchess retreated without comment, her skirts brushing his leg as she passed. Henri shuddered like a nervous horse and went after her.

This room was huge as well, but at least there was no bed. The duchess said, "If you give me a child, I shall reward you in gold coin."

Henri's cheeks flushed with shame. He was not a whore. As if gold would help him, if the palace guards caught him in her chambers. Gelding by hot iron was the first and least of what he would suffer. Delicious anger stiffened his cock, rasping it against his homespun pants, and he found he didn't care what she thought of him. He hadn't been asked to be her friend, only her stud. He could do as he liked with her. Anything. In this room, Her Grace the duchess was his to rule.

If he failed, would she find another to do her bidding? He couldn't bear the thought. He must not fail. For a little while, he must rule her.

"Remove your clothing," said Henri.

"I cannot. You must help me."

This problem had not occurred to him. He was not a lady's maid any more than he was a whore. However, the idea curiously excited him. "Bend over that sofa," he said. "No, over the back."

She did exactly as he asked. Bent over like that, her bosom swelled out the top of her gown, almost bursting free. Her face was hidden, but he could see bare white skin at the nape of her neck. Henri circled her, looking from all angles. Buttons bound her into her crimson gown. He'd never seen so many buttons on one garment. He imagined how many hours a seamstress might have spent covering those buttons, sewing them on and painstakingly stitching fabric loops to hold them. He imagined ripping the buttons off, letting them fly everywhere. Instead, he slipped them free down to her waist, then insinuated his hands down her bodice to squeeze enormous soft handfuls of breasts. Her breath hitched. So did his. Her buttocks twitched against his groin. He closed his eyes. Yes, he could do this; his body was brave. Reluctantly, he let go of her and returned to his task.

The gown pooled at her waist. He knew how to unlace a bodice and accomplished that task swiftly. Beneath lay a chemise of fine silk, softer even than her skin. The chemise was meant to be drawn over her head, but the thin silk tore easily and the sound of its ripping traveled straight to his balls. Beneath it she wore nothing. Henri feasted on her exposed vertebrae. He sucked on her neck until he remembered the consequences of leaving a mark and changed his strategy, just in time.

She was breathing unevenly, and he felt fine tremors under his hands. He examined her disarray as if she were a saddle he'd been given to polish, except that this saddle was his to ride upon. He dug his toes into the thick carpet, trying to decide what to do next.

"Hurry," she said.

He hesitated, then said, "No."

Stripping off his patched shirt, he flung it aside. His skin tingled, caressed by cool, perfumed air. The heavily embroidered fabric of her skirt crackled as he gathered up fistfuls, his calluses snagging on the nap. "I want you to stay here, like this," he said.

The duchess did not respond to what he'd said, so he lifted up her skirt—acres and acres of skirt—as if she was a kitchen maid. He finally crushed it as best he could around her waist, revealing another layer of thinner, stiffer skirts. He treated these perfunctorily, arriving finally at her drawers, no different from anyone's except for being fine red silk. Curious, Henri inspected with his fingers and found a perfectly ordinary slit in the fabric, no gold thread or jewels or even embroidered flowers. But beneath! Perfectly smooth! Was this a sign of her aristocratic birth, or——of course not. Stupid. She had an army of maids to cleanse and shave her.

The image of her and her maids was nearly too much for him; it resembled a painting that hung in the Dewy Rose. Henri stroked one finger down her slit and she quivered, like a horse flicking off a fly. Her steamier heat rose from within, so he could not resist parting her lush folds and sliding his finger deeper still. She was slick as melted butter, ready for him already. He excited her. More likely, he thought, the situation excited her, but who was he to complain? His free hand untied his pants' drawstring, and his cock fought free.

Booted feet rang in the corridor, blessedly some distance away. His feverish eyes lighted on a padded bench against the wall. He grabbed the duchess's arm and hustled her to it, holding his pants with his free hand, letting her gown fall where it would. She stumbled and stepped out of it, whispering, "I hear the guards! You must——"

The boots didn't slow as they approached. "Not for us," he said. They wouldn't dare. Not just before he entered her. The boots passed on. The duchess sagged, but only for an instant.

A neat pile of sewing rested on the bench he'd chosen, probably belonging to one of the women who served her. Henri swept it to the floor, all of it. She looked at him over her shoulder, her eyes icy; he took a deep, shaky breath and nudged the fabric carefully away from their feet.

He was relieved when she looked away from him again. She wore the remnants of her chemise and silk drawers with her earrings. Her slippers had disappeared somewhere along the way, but a heavy chain of brilliants collared her neck. He hadn't even noticed them against the splendor of her gown. Her hair, though mussed, retained its ornate style and jeweled hair ornaments. He could almost imagine her a ten-copper lay, playing at being duchess in one of the bawdy houses down in the town.

She drew the ripped chemise from her body, each arm flowing gracefully. He'd never seen skin so white and smooth. A rich attar of flowers rose from her bared, heated flesh, making him want to wipe his feet on the carpet and cower even as he possessed her. He shoved his pants down his legs; luckily, his cock remained undaunted.

Her hands loosened the string holding her drawers, and slowly, so slowly, dragged them down over lush hips and plump white buttocks. The body of a woman made to bear children, Henri thought, burning even more hotly.

Unable to wait an instant longer, he mounted her from behind in one deep push. She groaned deeply as if he'd struck her. Henri savored her cunt's scalding grasp as long as he could before beginning to thrust, short sharp strokes, each punctuated by his grunt and her gasp.

He heard boots again in the corridor, drawing nearer. The

duchess gasped, either with fear or because his calloused hands squeezed her breasts hard each time he withdrew. Henri didn't care about guards right now. He couldn't stop. He *wouldn't* stop. Blind to all but the bucking flesh beneath him, he crushed her into the bench, impaling her again and again. Her cunt squeezed his cock and he sucked in air. Seizing her hips, he ground into her as fiercely as he could, pressing her bud against the padded surface beneath them. Too hard; he should be more gentle, but she twisted and moaned, the sudden sound like fire down his spine. He jolted into her pulsing cunt, until she had drained him dry.

Afterward, silence. The sweat of his effort dried quickly, and he landed in cold and sticky reality. The sound of boots slowed and drew nearer.

Henri shuddered, then realized it was the duchess whose body shook. "Be still," he breathed into her ear. The boots clicked away, down the hall. Henri let out a slow breath and withdrew himself from her body.

He didn't want to just leave her with his seed drying on her thighs; he wouldn't do that even to a whore. The duchess straightened slowly but did not turn to face him. Henri said, "Turn around," but he couldn't muster the commanding tone he'd managed earlier.

She turned anyway, a woman with thick long hair obscuring her luscious breasts, clad only in a jeweled collar and silken stockings that tied at her knees, like an erotic painting. She did not move to cover herself, but stood tall and poised; even in bare feet she was slightly taller than Henri, he noted for the first time. "You have done well," she said. She did not smile.

Had anyone ever seen her smile? His anger was gone, spent. He felt only sadness as he looked at her.

Henri remembered the sounds she had made only moments earlier. He thought he had given her some pleasure, at least. "Will you tell me if you are breeding?" he asked, then glanced away, feeling heat creep down his neck. The whole duchy would know if she were breeding.

"Look at me."

Henri lifted his head. Her cheeks and chest were still flushed, and the air reeked of sex and sweat. Yet she still appeared untouchable.

"Yes, boy, I will tell you if I am breeding," the duchess said. "Now you must go. You've been brave, but it won't do for you to be caught here. The duke is jealous of his possessions."

He couldn't bear to leave her like this. "No." Henri took a step back and felt his pants under his heel. Slowly, he bent, picked them up, and stepped into them, all without turning his back on her. She was not looking at him. Her gaze rested on a portrait over the mantel, of three bay horses grazing among grassy hills.

The cloth of his pants felt coarse after the luxurious fabrics he'd ripped from the duchess's body. Staring down at his hands as he knotted the drawstring, he said, "Your Grace, if you are *not* breeding, will you tell me?"

"If I am not breeding, it will be no surprise."

Henri felt for his shirt on the carpet and finally located it. From inside its folds he said, "Will you come to the stables?"

"My husband does not permit—" She hesitated. "Yes, I will come to the stables."

Her voice was as calm as it had been before, but he fancied he could catch a trace of hopelessness. He reached for her hand without thinking, then let it fall before it reached her, afraid of giving offense. Perhaps he could persuade her. "Come at night. I would save you if I could, Your Grace. If you would travel away with me. You can ride. You do not have to die."

She crossed her arms over her breasts. Even nearly naked, she looked every inch a duchess. She said, "I do not think there is any escape from this life."

He'd never before thought of the palace as a trap. He wondered if she ever struggled against it. "I did not think I could…try to give you a child, either."

Her mouth twitched into an unconvincing smile. "We shall see, Henri. We shall see. Now, go. Sylvie will see you safely back to the stables."

Henri knew what *we shall see* meant. She'd set herself on a course and meant to stick to it. He'd heard that tone before, from his most stubborn uncle, who'd ended up dying at sea, food for sharks, all because he refused to make peace with his father over a woman whom he hadn't even married. Henri was in even less of a position to argue with the duchess. He might be good enough to service her, but she seemed unlikely to take advice from a grubby stableboy.

He lowered his eyes and quickly bowed before hurrying to the door. He would do better to forget about this, as soon as he possibly could manage it.

CHAPTER THREE

The Duchess Camille sat on the edge of her bed, the blue silk velvet coverlet caressing the bare backs of her thighs and the drawn-back curtains of the canopy brushing her bare shoulders. Under threat from Sylvie's eagle eyes and sharp tongue, a flurry of bathmaids gathered up discarded towels, bottles of bath oil and skin cream, razors and strops, polishing grit and all manner of perfumed oils and balms, which Laure had applied to her skin while Tatienne and Solange shaved her legs and pubic area. It was all very tedious. She had never been sure why it mattered, since no one ever saw her bare skin except the maids and her husband. She sometimes wondered if the rituals of adornment were meant solely to devour time for women more idle than she.

Camille was now grateful she'd let the boy take her in a sitting room and not her bedroom. Sylvie had set a rose-scented candle burning in the sitting room, which overwhelmed everything. If the bathmaids had noticed anything amiss, they had not spoken of it.

She closed her eyes for a few moments, welcoming the

spring chill as the perfumed bathwater dried on her body; she needed to return to reality before darkness fell and her husband called for her. If he called for her.

Now she was tired, and her body ached. Sylvie chased away the last of the bathmaids, summoned two footmen to haul away the tub, then returned to hover over Camille. "Madame," she said, in a much gentler tone than she'd used with her fellow servants. "You must eat. I brought you food while you were in the bath. See? All things you like. I prepared it myself."

There was a silver tray on her side table, filled with cubes of fresh bread, thin slices of sharp cheese, a ramekin of soft goat's cheese, a cluster of meringues and a juicy pear, laid out in a fan of slices. "Thank you, Sylvie. You may go."

"Madame, are you well?"

Sylvie had served Camille for too many years. Camille knew she was truly asking about the boy, and what she had done with him. Camille resisted asking Sylvie's opinion of him. She said, "I am perfectly well. I do not require your help to eat."

"Yes, madame." Sylvie bowed and departed. Listlessly, Camille picked up a slice of pear and forced herself to chew it. She would need all the strength she could muster. She did not want to face the duke. Not just now. But she must face him. Doing things she did not care to do were part of her duty.

Heaps of documents obscured the surface of her marquetry desk, tucked into a corner near shelves of weighty tomes inherited from her father and his father before him. In her anxiety over the duke's increasing impatience with her, she'd neglected her normal perusal of the financial and judicial reports, brought in daily by Lord Stagiaire's secretary. More than five years had passed since the duke had removed her from sitting in judgment, or even from reviewing cases, but she hadn't been able to stop herself from at least following the duchy's business in private. Lord Stagiaire had been her tutor once, and still maintained a confidential position with the king. Even if the duke found what information he'd provided and continued to provide to Camille, his status as an elder of politics would protect him.

Once, Camille had been able to throw herself into the work of researching precedents and alternative judgments. It wasn't how she might have chosen to spend her time, but it was worthy work, and she'd been well-trained for it. However, once she'd been denied directing or even witnessing the outcome of the issues she'd so carefully studied, her research had begun to seem more and more worthless, equivalent to decorative embroidery that would never be seen. Once she'd been forbidden her horses as well, she'd retreated into herself. The sight of her abandoned desk gave her a guilty stab. By giving up her studies, she'd done what the duke wanted. And here she was, trying to get herself with child!

She remembered hearing the door click shut behind Sylvie and the boy. No, not merely a boy, she corrected herself, but Henri, whom she'd taken into her body. If they'd been successful, he might be the father of a child she carried, and her child would not be fathered by some boy of no name. Camille tried to imagine having a child, seeing it grow and learn. Would it be a boy or a girl? A boy might be all that would keep her from death. She would never be able to tell it of its true heritage. That would be too dangerous. It would likely to be too danger-ous even to allow Henri to see the child. Perhaps he would not care. She had been told the lower orders did not care so much for their children, as they lost them so often. She had no way to find out if it was true. No peasant would give a truthful answer to his duchess. Perhaps Sylvie would know. She was very resourceful. Perhaps the midwife would tell her.

After her first year of marriage, Camille had summoned a midwife from the town for a careful examination, as she hadn't trusted the palace's male physician. Nothing had been wrong with her physically, nothing that the midwife could see, and she'd been told to expect a child in good time. Two years ago, in desperation, she'd summoned a second midwife, whom Sylvie found for her; that was Annette. That first time, Sylvie smuggled Annette in as a pageboy, and she'd examined Camille thoroughly, both inside and out. Cold as her manner had been, Mistress Annette reassured Camille that she'd suffered no dis-ease, and scoffed at the notion that riding astride could prevent pregnancy.

"Your husband's jism is more likely to blame, he wastes it so freely." Her scorn for the duke had been clear, and Camille was grateful for once that he had his own amusements and never visited the town's brothel; if he heard Annette's words, he would have her executed without a second thought. Camille had believed everything Annette had told her, but had not yet been desperate enough to try to find another possible father for her child.

Now she wished she had been. She had wasted far too much time in hope. How ironic that her own mother had given birth a mere ten months after marriage, though she had not had much to do with Camille afterward, leaving her to a wet nurse and having her brought down, suitably wrapped in velvet and a lace cap, for ceremonial occasions only.

Camille had no idea if she herself would be able to love her child. If she could not...how cruel, once it knew. To know you lived only to save your mother's life. If she lived past its birth, though, she might have emotion to spare for her child. She would at least try. She would not leave the babe to nurses and tutors while she shut herself away among her own amuse-ments.

Perhaps none of it would matter. She did not feel pregnant. How long would it take before she would know? She felt sure she would know, somehow, in her body, before she missed her courses or had any other physical sign. She tried to imagine how her child would look, and could only picture a smaller, rounder Henri, thick brown hair matted to his forehead, endearing snub nose, wide blue eyes surrounded by lashes dense and long as summer grass, an enticingly plump lower lip. If she was not pregnant— she could not think of that now. It was out of her control for the time being. To think of her own doom was just as dangerous as thinking the opposite. She had survived so far by living moment to moment to moment. She should think on the present.

She sat cross-legged on the bed and ate another slice of pear, then a fragment of cheese. She could feel the stretch in her leg muscles from her afternoon exertions. Her quim throbbed pleasantly, deep within. It had been a long time since she'd had sex. The duke did not seem to care if she became pregnant or not. A younger woman, and a more compliant one, would be infinitely more to his taste, and had been from the beginning of their marriage, over twenty years ago now. His ideal duchess would be a younger woman who never spoke and always smiled. No, Michel wouldn't notice the smile if the woman kept her legs open.

How unfair, to die because you were not a man's preferred toy. If he'd put her aside in favor of his concubines, even publicly, she might have endured, holding on to her dignity as the only blood heir to the duchy. Her people would have blamed the duke, not her. That was likely what he feared would happen, should she be both out of his favor and alive. Even though he ruled, he had not been born in the duchy. Her people would remember. They accepted him now, as he'd been crowned by her father. What would happen if Camille repudiated *him?* Of course, she could not do so while trapped within her suite of rooms. He could find her too easily, and close her mouth by opening her throat. She had already embarked on the safer course of convincing him he'd achieved the heir he needed to consolidate his position.

She lifted her hair in front of her shoulder and fell back onto her coverlet. The tasseled golden ropes binding back the curtains could symbolize her bondage here in the palace. Perhaps she should have insisted that Henri take her here, but he'd been so afraid, and so defiant of his fear, that she had done what he asked. It had been a small thing. He was doing her bidding, after all. She refused to remember her small moments of fear, when she'd thought she would not be able to convince him to take her.

He had surpassed her expectations. There was something to be said for vigor and enthusiasm when accomplishing a difficult task. Being fucked over a bench had been unexpected. Caught up in sensation for which she had not planned, for long moments she'd been unaware of her surroundings, lost in the intensity of being fucked by a partner whom she could not see.

If Henri had been the duke, she would have wanted to keep an eye on him. She would have been unable to relax even a fraction. As it had happened…she had been surprised by her own response. Perhaps because she had known she could stop Henri at any moment she chose? The duke's threats had always been present in the back of her mind, but for those moments with Henri, she had taken something for herself. How much risk would there be in summoning him again? It might take several tries before he impregnated her. If he failed, would she be able to remain hopeful, and find another potential sire?

Soon, she'd be expected to give herself to the duke. His pleasure would be at issue, and her life.

Until then, she had only herself to please. She lifted her hand

and ran it down her belly, pressing in lightly with her nail, then sliding her fingertip between the folds of her quim. She circled her bud, then pressed in. She twitched inside, as if in residual orgasm. She still had life in her, even after what had gone before. She rubbed herself again, sliding her other hand to join the first, using that one to massage her outer lips, pressing into the finger on her bud. Her arousal rose and spread slowly, like golden light. She thought of riding, she and her bay mare Guirlande cresting a ridge near the east boundary just as the sun vaulted over the hills, her groom and guards far outdistanced for a moment alone, a moment of peace.

She trembled into climax, each gentle spasm flooding her with another liquid wash of delight. When it was over, she slipped beneath her coverlet and linens, curled on her side with her knees drawn up, and coasted into a deep, satisfying sleep.

"Your Grace."

Camille blinked and stared up at the duke's chamber servant, Vilmos. He wore his usual blue livery trimmed in gold, and carried one of her heavy silk robes over one folded arm. His thick neck, pale hair and heavy features could give the impression of stupidity, though she knew he was crafty and perhaps more intelligent than his master the duke. His eyelids always looked sleepy and full; she could never tell what he was thinking, or how far his loyalty extended. Presumably the duke did not fear him, or he would never allow him into his bedchamber. If she were the duke, she would be more cautious.

Camille swallowed and said, with as much alertness as she could muster, "Where is His Grace the duke?"

"He is waiting for you below," Vilmos intoned. "I am to bring you and your escort."

So she was to be summoned like one of his concubines. Again. Vilmos would ensure she did not refuse. "I am ready."

He held out her necklace and earrings and waited while she put them on, then wrapped her impersonally in the red silk robe, knelt and inserted her feet into embroidered slippers, and led her through her rooms. Camille took a moment to be grateful that she wasn't being taken to the duke naked, as she had been on other occasions. She suspected that had been the order, but Vilmos had given her the robe for his own private purpose. She wondered what that meant about his relationship to her husband. Could Vilmos, perhaps, be coerced to her side? And if so, what would be the best advantage she could gain?

She glanced at Vilmos, but he appeared lost in his own thoughts. She knew the game of conspiracy, from her youth in the court of the king, but Vilmos showed no hint of it. She was building castles from sand. A single gesture of humanity did not mean Vilmos would betray her husband. Perhaps he merely pitied her as she grew older.

Kaspar and Arno awaited them in the corridor. Though their muscularity was less impressive than Vilmos's due to their castration at a young age, they were of a height with him and she immediately felt less vulnerable.

She held her head high as they walked through opulent corridors, past the occasional courtier or footman or maid, and once past a courtier and a maid copulating in an alcove with enthusiastic gasps, at least until they noticed Vilmos's steely gaze. Camille involuntarily stepped back against Kaspar as Vilmos shot out a meaty hand, seized the maid's shoulders, and dragged her free of her petrified partner with an audible sucking sound. "You," Vilmos addressed the man, one of the lesser land barons whom Camille affected not to recognize. "Leave."

Grabbing at his trousers, the baron backed away, eyes fixed on Vilmos until he rounded a corner and scuttled off. Vilmos clamped one hand around the maid's upper arm and with his other, tugged her gray dress and shift back down over her hips. "Marrine, you are late for your duties tonight," he said reproachfully, and dragged her along with their procession. One of her husband's concubines, Camille guessed. Marrine stood barely as tall as Vilmos's elbow and was thin as a wraith except for her exuberant bosom. Straggles of violently red hair escaped her sober gray cap. A red suck-mark was clearly visible on her neck.

Camille hoped Marrine had not recognized her. Why should she? Minus her gown and cosmetics, with her hair pouring down her back and Kaspar's and Arno's protective bulks blocking her view? Then again, why should she care? That would be less embarrassing than being shamed by her own husband. She didn't doubt the whole palace knew the duke's proclivities. The courtiers seemed to remain loyal to him despite how he treated his duchess. Perhaps it was simply easier to do so. If she had not rebelled, why should they? And how many of them knew for a fact how she'd been treated? If they were wise, they treated two-thirds of everything they heard in the palace as rumor.

Vilmos led them through a door flush with the wall paneling and down a narrow staircase lit by lamps burning perfumed, musky oil. Camille wrinkled her nose, then quickly repressed her reaction. She was obviously heading for another of the duke's outlandish scenarios. He planned to make her watch. Inwardly, she sighed. She did not have the stomach to watch his pale buttocks pumping over some pliant maid in a strange costume for the rest of the night. Unfortunately, she had little choice. Had the last one been a milkmaid or an extravagantly female version of a courier? No, there had been two. One in a blacksmith's apron and nothing else, the other wielding a bellows in ways Camille had found more humorous than erotic.

The stairs changed from carpeted wood to carved lime-stone. She had never traveled this passage before. Only servants and prisoners were obligated to visit the underlevels of the palace. She might be taken there if she were to be beheaded. Inwardly, she shuddered at the thought. Outwardly, she focused her gaze on Kaspar's big shoulders moving down the stairs ahead of her.

She heard a clanking noise as Vilmos drew out a bunch of keys to unlock the red door she glimpsed at the bottom of the staircase. She guessed they must be adjacent to the cool rooms where cheese was stored, and for a wild moment considered what erotic use the duke had found for the duchy's famed tart blue.

Camille entered the chamber, her guards swiftly positioning themselves at her shoulders. Vilmos had already dragged Marrine to the duke, who chucked her under the chin before he waved his hand toward a table heaped with furs. Vilmos lifted her as if she weighed as little as a broomstraw and deposited her there. Marrine did not fight him as he removed her cap and her red hair sprang free; she reached over her shoulder and began to unbutton her dress.

The duke strode over to Camille, reached out one manicured finger and hooked it beneath her jeweled collar. Camille took care not to jerk away; she did not want to be choked. "You've taken pleasure today," he barked. "I know it."

He didn't know for sure, or he would have acted much more swiftly and decisively. "You keep an army of concubines, Your Grace," Camille replied. "Do you begrudge me satisfaction? You've made no move to provide it yourself."

"Women were placed on this earth to please men," the duke said. His plump lips curved behind his silky gray beard, but his cold blue eyes did not change expression. "It has been a long time since *you* have pleased *me*." He snorted. "It is a pity you had the time to dress before Vilmos brought you to me. Would you have liked to parade the palace naked, I wonder? Would your lover have seen you?"

His finger still crooked beneath her collar, the duke stepped closer. His floor-length robe of dense velvet was trimmed all down the front in silky black fur. One step more and the fur brushed her robe, raising a nasty prickle.

"You will tell me who it is," he said. "I can make you afraid of me."

She *was* afraid. He held her life in his hands. He simply didn't want to see it. He wanted to break her anew each time, like a boy plucking wings off a populace of flies.

"I'll have an answer out of you, Camille."

"Yes, Your Grace," she said, hating herself for letting him bully her, but hating him even more.

His left hand rubbed up and down her cheek, his hot fingers squeezed by rows of rings. The set stones caught the light and glowed dully, angrily: ruby, emerald, topaz, amethyst. Square plates of gold interspersed with hunks of tourmaline banded his thick wrist. She stared at the stones rather than look up at his leering face. She could smell the perfumed oil in his beard and the cloves he chewed for his breath.

At last he released her collar. He trailed his finger down and squeezed her breast through her robe. Perhaps she was to be his vessel tonight. He had to fuck her at least once, in case she had managed to become pregnant that afternoon. She wasn't sure how she was going to manage that part. She closed her eyes, feeling her nipple draw tighter at the duke's manipulations. Given enough time to prepare herself, this could be bearable. Just once, and never again. Just once—nausea strangled her. She could not. She would do anything if she never had to see his prick again.

She stared at his hand as his fingers pressed painfully into the soft flesh of her breast. His other hand grabbed her shoulder, forcing her to her knees. "Have you learned to swallow a cock yet? I'm told a lack of breath is an effective incentive. Vilmos, perhaps you could hold her, so she may learn properly how to please me."

Camille couldn't help her flinch, a choked whimper escaping her lips. The duke shoved her away onto the floor. He traced his foot over her bare fingers, as if contemplating how best to crush them, then shifted and ground his toe into her quim. "You are less amusing than you once were," he said. To the air he said, "There is a throne for Her Grace. Secure her there."

A spectator again. Relief drenched her. Arno glanced at her apologetically as he strapped her arms to the ornately carved chair. He settled at her feet like a faithful hound, his shaven head almost touching her knee. Kaspar stood behind the chair, a looming shelter. She could feel the warmth of his body on the back of her neck.

Camille had a clear view of the cellar room, which was carpeted in plush red silk and hung with erotic tapestries she recognized as having once hung in the duke's bedchamber. She'd always despised them, because the women were always depicted being taken unwillingly, if one could guess from their stark facial expressions. An ebony table held a basin and pitcher; another held wine and cups. She could particularly see a side view of the fur-heaped table where Marrine reclined, naked and with her hips elevated on a pillow. A pile of cut roses on long, thorny stems lay near her. No costumes tonight, then, unless someone was to wear the flowers.

The duke unfastened his wide, jeweled belt and tugged it free. He draped it over one shoulder, the buckle dangling in front. His robe fell open, baring his naked body. He was thickening around the waist and sagging in the chest but his legs were still powerful. His prick hung turgidly; he stroked it as he lounged in a chair similar to Camille's, though his boasted a padded, embroidered seat.

Camille glanced at Marrine, then at the duke, unsure of his intentions. He was not inclined to restraint. She lifted her chin, anticipating a new threat to be faced.

"Vilmos," said the duke.

His servant turned, to face her, Camille realized. He wore knee breeches, stockings and flat shoes with his uniform jacket. He stripped open his jacket and pulled apart the halves of his shirt to reveal a massive chest. His chest hair was only fractionally darker than that on his head, and just as dense. Then he flicked open the buttons on his breeches and withdrew his prick, partially erect and already thick as Camille's wrist.

"Her Grace will accommodate you for a few moments," the duke said, smiling nastily. "Her mouth must be useful for something other than insolence."

Vilmos stepped out of his shoes, pushed his breeches down his hips, and stepped out of them as well. He padded over to her in his stockinged feet, one hand holding his cock. He stopped a pace away from her. Arno glared up at him. Camille said softly, "Arno," and he rose immediately, though without releasing Vilmos from his gaze. She heard Kaspar's hiss of warning from behind her. At last, Arno stepped back. He rested one warm hand on her shoulder, an unusual liberty, but one which she did not deny him.

Vilmos pressed his shins against her legs and held out his cock. He looked uncomfortable. He did not have the control she did. She would show the duke nothing of her thoughts.

Vilmos was so tall, she scarcely had to bend to reach him. Thankfully, he was clean, his hot skin smelling of chamomile soap. Had he known this would happen? If so, she appreciated the consideration.

In other circumstances, she might have enjoyed tasting so large a cock, but not in front of the duke. She opened her mouth and took him in, sucking hard and dipping her tongue into his slit to speed him along and deny the duke as much pleasure as she could. Vilmos swelled alarmingly fast; she pulled back once, but he pressed against her lips until she opened to him again. He began squeezing and stroking his own length while she licked and suckled at the crown; she could hear him gasping. Just as her jaw was beginning to ache, he tugged himself free of her mouth, his hands falling to his sides.

The duke lifted a ringed hand. "You and the maid will entertain me now."

Camille nearly laughed at his indifferent tone. She could see his prick nudging his belly, its head shiny with fluid. Had her submission aroused him, or Vilmos's unquestioning obedience?

She did not want to watch the duke. Pretending he did not exist, she turned to Vilmos and Marrine.

Vilmos cupped his hands beneath Marrine's thighs and pulled her legs loosely around his waist. She crossed her ankles and smiled like a dancer about to take the stage. He had powerful buttocks that clenched impressively as he guided himself into Marrine, or at least to a point just past the flange of his cock's head. There he stopped. Marrine squirmed. Her arms, which she had flung provocatively above her head, reached for their joined bodies as if to tug him forward.

Camille wondered if calling out advice was allowed. She suspected Marrine would have better luck being taken from behind. She also suspected this awkwardness was part of the show. What a show! She fought back a laugh. Would they follow with a trip to the menagerie? And where were the food vendors?

Vilmos drew back and thrust forward again, his hands shoving Marrine's thighs farther apart. At the peak of each thrust, he held still for a moment, and then pushed forward incrementally more. Marrine had uncrossed her ankles and her bare feet bobbed in the air. She was panting. Vilmos let go of her legs and held open her folds, rubbing her bud with his thumb as he continued his stuttered rhythm. Camille could see he'd penetrated a bit farther, and as she watched, he eased in farther still. His cock was dark maroon, shiny with Marrine's fluids.

Vilmos thrust hard and Marrine groaned, a surprisingly deep sound from so small a woman. The involuntary sound was shockingly arousing, a visceral reminder of her own afternoon with Henri. Camille's quim dampened as Vilmos sped up his efforts and, all at once, slid fully into his partner. After that, it didn't take long. Marrine slid among the furs with the force of Vilmos's thrusts, her fingers plucking at her own nipples. She groaned more loudly. Vilmos was silent, though his fingers kneaded Marrine's quim, thighs and belly with frantic grasping motions.

Camille breathed slowly, showing nothing, though her body wanted to writhe. Arno's hand tightened on her shoulder, and she glanced up at him in surprise. She had forgotten he stood there. He smiled at her, an expression she was not accustomed to seeing on the faces of her guards.

"Hurry!" the duke's voice commanded. Camille twitched in distaste. Vilmos redoubled his efforts. Marrine squealed as she came, then relaxed as she rode out his last few thrusts. She was smiling, and sensuously writhed her shoulders against the furs.

Camille felt no such relaxation. Her bones thrummed inside her legs and arms. Her palms itched. Her quim contracted uselessly around nothing; her clitoris ached for her to press upon it. She focused on Arno's grip on her shoulder. Gradually, she settled back in her chair. She did not want the duke to hear, or even see, her beg. She'd done so, before. Never again.

She heard a creak of wood as the duke stood. "My robe," he commanded Vilmos.

Vilmos moved quickly for so large a man, and with surprising dignity for someone whose cock flapped free. He drew the robe from the duke's shoulders and folded it over the back of his chair, while the duke went over to Marrine. As if inspecting a pastry, he prodded two fingers into her quim. She lifted her legs gracefully and clasped them around his neck.

The duke snorted. "I'll have none of your theatrics, girl." He reached up and gripped her calves, pulling them apart and down to his waist. "Vilmos! I require your service."

Camille thought she saw a flicker of annoyance on Vilmos's placid face, then it was gone. He bowed and returned to the naked duke. As the duke eased his prick into Marrine—whose smile this time seemed, to Camille, distinctly insincere—Vilmos warmed his hands beneath his arms, then laid them on the duke's pumping buttocks.

Camille blinked. She had seen the duke use two female concubines at once, or even three, for his amusements, but never anything like this. And Vilmos had no erection whatsoever.

She meant to look away. She did not want to watch the duke, and his eyes were fixed on Marrine's jouncing breasts, so he would not notice that Camille was ignoring him. But her curiosity kept her watching Vilmos, who had begun to trace his fingers down the crack between the duke's buttocks. When the duke stopped moving and abruptly called his name, Vilmos bent and ran his tongue along the path where his fingers had been. To Camille's astonishment, he then pulled the duke's buttocks apart and began to lick around his hole. She thought he might have dipped into the hole with his tongue, but was not sure.

"Enough!" said the duke, and began to fuck Marrine again. Vilmos kept his hands on his master's rear, his expression blank. When the duke stopped again and called his name, he worked two fingers into the duke's hole. The rest of his hand jerked, as if he simulated a spurting prick.

The duke resumed his fucking, but this time Vilmos did not stop what he was doing. After a moment or two, the duke let out a cry such as Camille had never heard from any man and sped up his thrusting. His face had reddened, and sweat dripped from the ends of his hair. She watched Vilmos's hand, and identified an upward stroke that elicited the duke's pleasured cries.

The duke came very quickly. That much, Camille thought wryly, had not changed. She was impressed, though, with what Vilmos had done. She had never seen such a thing before, and if she had been watching any man but her husband, she might have found it arousing to see a man penetrated as if he was a woman, and to know that his pleasure came from the hands of his penetrator. The idea of that sort of control excited her in a way she was sure the duke had not intended. She had momentarily forgotten her predicament.

It appeared the show was over. Marrine was licking the duke's prick clean, and Vilmos was washing his hands and surreptitiously rinsing his mouth with wine. Camille would have appreciated a glass herself. Vilmos brought a cup only to the duke, however.

"Your Grace," Arno said softly. "Allow me to remove this."

For a moment, she thought he meant her robe; then she saw

his hand on the fur-lined cuff which bound her arm to the chair. She nodded, hopefully with aplomb. Arno set to work on one arm and Kaspar on the other. They both completely ignored the activity on the other side of the room, which she supposed made sense, as they were eunuchs. For the first time, she wondered if any sexual pleasure at all was possible for them. They still had, she understood, their pricks, though their sacs were empty.

When her bindings were entirely removed, she stood, careful to let the blood flow back into her knees before she attempted to straighten. She said, in her most commanding voice, "Do you have further need of me, Your Grace?"

Her husband had drizzled wine from Marrine's breasts to her thighs, and was currently snuffling in her quim while she swatted at his flanks with a handful of the roses. He waved a negligent hand and said, "Vilmos, take her to her rooms and secure the door. Bring her back to me next week, and we shall see if she is more amenable." Then he returned to his concubine.

She was forgotten. Camille felt cold. The duke's treatment of her made it obvious that he no longer cared if she became pregnant or not. She was only a toy to him now, and one of which he would soon tire.

Her time was rapidly running out.

CHAPTER FOUR

By the time Henri finished mucking out Guirlande's stall and carting the soiled straw to compost, the moon was up. He stopped midway back to look at the stars.

Even a stableboy could be dazzled by the glory of the night sky. His heart slowed and swelled with awe. He couldn't touch the stars, but he had touched the duchess.

He sighed and trundled his smelly wheelbarrow back to the yard. He needed to stop thinking of his afternoon with the duchess, stop making it into more than it had been. She had used him. Hadn't she?

He couldn't deny that, secretly, he had wanted her for years. Desire had slowly replaced his earlier fantasies that she'd singled him out for equestrian training because he was somehow special. Now the danger was past, he didn't even mind she'd used him. There was no other way he could have had her.

How bovine he'd been, blurting out that he would help her escape. As if she would ever need *him* to rush to her rescue. Her maid was loyal, and her eunuchs. There would be others, too, greater than a stableboy. He wondered if any of them cared for her at all.

He took a last walk down the row of his charges, petting the noses of those horses still awake and eyeing him over their stall doors. He would have to be up early to school Tulipe in the ring, and Lilas needed to be conditioned on the longe line. Guirlande, he sensed, would be coming into season soon, and possibly Tonnelle also. That would mean a trip to one of the far-flung breeding barns and, for him, relative luxury. Not only would he be caring for far fewer horses, he wouldn't be assigned odd jobs, as when he was easily in view of the stablemaster and his chief grooms. He wouldn't be catching the associated random blows. Even better, the breeding barns were built in past days of unimaginable affluence, for a duke who had loved his horses, so the hayloft where Henri slept would rival— well, he had used to think it would rival the very bedchamber of the duke, but today he had been disabused of that notion. It didn't matter. Small luxuries were easier to enjoy.

He felt again the weight and smoothness of her dress as it sagged from his hands, inhaled the flowery perfume she'd worn in the crook of her neck. While he, Henri, stank of horse sweat and dung. She hadn't flinched from his hands upon her. Still, he hadn't dared touch her face, or kiss her lips. He wished now he had. Then he would feel they'd known each other, however briefly.

It was childish of him to expect so much. She was as far above him as the stars, and old enough to be his mother. It was true many men took brides much younger than themselves, so perhaps it wasn't so awful. Why not the reverse? He imagined her in his imaginary cottage, gorgeously gowned, rocking a cradle, and he laughed. More likely he'd be rocking the baby and changing nappies.

He turned away from Tonnelle and headed out the double doors, into the night. His body hummed. He couldn't sleep yet.

It was late, but not too late for a bath. Perhaps, afterward, he would indulge in something more. The Dewy Rose specialized in all sorts of relaxations, and he never spent much of his paltry wages, sleeping as he did amid the horses. Perhaps he would share some of his money with the girls of the Dewy Rose. He could afford one of the cheaper whores. For an hour, perhaps. He always allowed himself the possibility, though in the end he usually decided to save his money, knowing that if he was frugal, his own cottage would be real that much sooner.

He walked into the town, principal seat of the duchy. The streets were more active than the estate had been. Drunken revelers spilled from a tavern near the gate, coaches rattled over the cobbles, and a raucous game of dice devoured an entire alley. Most of the street whores ignored him. He looked like empty pockets. He was just as happy to be on his way unmolested. It hurt him to look at the streetgirls' eyes.

The Dewy Rose, a massive building of rough gray stone, towered three stories over the neighbors on either side, its white windowsills scrubbed clean daily and the shingled roof trimmed with decorative strips of copper. Its baths were cheap and popular. It cost extra, though, to climb the stairs with one of the girls, and cost considerably more for one of the young men Madame Hubert had imported from a desert land far to the south. He had glimpsed them once or twice, on his way to the baths: slender men with flawless skin and dark outlining around their eyes, wearing only long silken drawers, layers of necklaces and silver rings on their bare toes. The duchess might have bought herself one of those, through an intermediary. Except their skin was too dark for any child of theirs to pass as the duke's.

Torches crackled at either side of the grand front entrance. Henri shoved open the carved oaken door and was confronted by a giant elderly eunuch wearing a black robe. He silently held out one slablike palm, and Henri laid a quarter-copper there. The eunuch's hand closed over it; with his other hand, he jerked a thumb at the corridor beyond. Manic laughter swelled from the house's interior, mingled with the clink of goblets and knives and, faintly, a twinging harp.

The common room's doors were folded back to allow heat to escape, and to let the bath's patrons have a preview of the evening's entertainment. Henri had meant to pass straight by. He could not resist a look, though, to see if his memories of the room's appointments compared ill or favorably with those of the duchess's.

He could not see much of the furnishings. The long buffet table bore food on either end and a nude woman in the middle; two men in shirtsleeves were licking honey and wine from her belly and breasts. A couple copulated in the chair nearest the door. The woman, bodice pulled down to her waist, gripped the arms of the chair to raise and lower herself on her partner's swollen red cock, her white buttocks flashing as her minuscule skirt fluttered with each stroke. Henri gaped, amazed that they were allowed to do that in the common room, even in a brothel, until he saw a ring of watchers. This was some staged entertainment, like the two women arranged on a chaise by the fireplace, one daintily fondling the other, who plunged an ivory dildo into herself. One of the male whores was massaging her feet. She looked up, as if awaiting orders. Henri followed her gaze to the center of the room and saw the duchess.

He had seen that court gown at a distance, and the outline of her hair confined within its tiara was familiar to him from the coin he'd just placed in a eunuch's palm. The skin around his cock tightened automatically. Except—she could not be here. She would not be here. He looked closer, and of course the duchess was only Madame Hubert, was only a whore.

If he emptied his savings and paid her fee, he could have her. Well, almost. In a year or two he would have enough. For a moment he considered it; but it would be a mockery. He felt ashamed even for letting the thought cross his mind.

He hurried down the corridor and exited into the quiet rear yard. The bathhouse occupied almost the entire space; the narrow alley between its wooden walls and the tall fence had been planted with wandering roses. Their scent flooded his nostrils, clearing the indoor stench of perfume and wine and sweat, and sweetened the woodsmoke which rose from stoves at the rear. He followed a white gravel path to the entrance and pushed open the door.

The bathhouse was unusually quiet; he could hear water lapping and trickling. The pre-supper crowd had already departed, and visitors to the brothel would not yet have emerged for a sluicing before they returned home.

Henri stepped onto a rough straw mat in the narrow corridor running the length of the building. To his right was an alcove with hooks and benches where he hung his clothes and left his boots. The child who normally guarded belongings was sleeping on a pile of towels in the corner. Henri let him be; he had nothing of value to steal, anyway, except his boots, which were mired in horse muck. He took a towel from a shelf and entered the next room along the corridor. The floor in there was limestone, just rough enough to avoid getting slippery. The sluicing room held stools and stone bowls of soft, gritty soap, the cheapest kind. Smooth perfumed varieties had to be purchased separately; Henri always used what was provided. It did well enough.

He hung his towel and scrubbed off. His shoulder and elbow were scraped where one of the upper grooms had shoved him into a wall that afternoon for being late. He washed the wounds gently, but they had stopped bleeding hours ago and the bruises were emerging. He'd barely noticed them at the time, and if they'd known the reason for his being late, it would have been much worse. A few bumps and bruises were a small price to pay.

Pipes trickled warm water into flagons; when they overflowed, the water drained through a hole in the center of the floor. During peak times, the time saved in heating separate containers of water balanced out the waste of it, and the brothel didn't need to worry about their water supply running out since they controlled a natural spring, a secondary source of Madame Hubert's wealth. The duke had a spring, too, somewhere in the bowels of the palace. To lay siege to a place with its own pure water supply would be the purest folly; that was one reason he held so much power. Or so people said. Henri thought it would be easy enough to take the palace, from the inside. But the people inside the palace lived in luxury, and were likely well satisfied with their lot in life. They wouldn't want to tear it apart. Well, maybe the duke's servants weren't satisfied, but if he were one of them, he would go after the duke, not the palace. He'd want the palace for his own afterward. Any smart person would. A treacherous thought intruded: he would want the duchess for his own, as well.

Pouring water over his head, he didn't hear the bathmaid enter. He shook his wet hair from his eyes and startled at the quiet figure standing near the door. She was perhaps his own age or a little older, with short-cropped ebony hair over a beautifully-shaped skull. The short cut made her dark eyes seem even larger than they really were. He didn't often see this girl working in the evenings; usually it was the one-legged man, or the girl who never stopped talking.

She wore a thin shift that hung only to her knees. It clung damply to her small breasts and curving hips and a darker shadow between her legs. Sometimes the bathmaids worked in the nude, but Henri found her minimal clothing a thousand times more enticing. Her breasts looked like round peaches, just the size to cup in his two hands. She smelled of soap and roses.

He realized he was standing with his mouth open, soapsuds running down his legs, and a flagon dangling forgotten from his hand. He deliberately did not look down at his cock. It had risen as he handled it to wash, and he did not want to draw the maid's attention to it. She likely had to deal with lecherous men all day, every day. He did not need to add to that. He'd had a tumble already. With mild hysteria, he thought of explaining to her that he was having a bath because that afternoon he'd fucked the duchess.

She said, prompting, "Are you ready for the tub, sir?"

Henri nodded. He hurriedly reached to place his flagon on the floor, but she took it from him, chose a full one, and said, "Stand still. There's more soap."

Henri closed his eyes as she doused him, head to foot, twice more. The water trickling down his body could have been her fingers, small and chapped from constant washing. He didn't usually have this much trouble in the baths. Of course, usually the room was full of other men, and they would be dousing each other with careful courtesy. He wasn't used to being alone with a bathmaid, much less a pretty one. He tried to think cold thoughts, and his erection did subside a little.

The bathmaid wrapped his towel around his waist before leading him to the next room. He'd never received such a service before. Perhaps she thought he was someone important? Or just hoped for a good tip. Or thought he was too slow to do it himself, and she wanted him to be done and clear out. She said, "My name is Nicolette. Nico."

"Henri," he said. Or perhaps she was being friendly.

She smiled at him and said, "I know. I've seen you here." In the flickering lamplight, he watched the curves of her bottom move as she walked ahead of him and bent to turn a stopcock. Steaming water gushed from the pipe and into the copper tub. She tested the water and added cold water from a bucket, then tested it again. At her gesture, he climbed inside.

He'd worked hard all day, both before and after his visit to the duchess. The heat flooded his tired muscles like the rush of orgasm. "That's nice," he said, reaching out his legs and wiggling his toes.

"Let me wash your hair," Nico said. "Here, lean back onto this towel."

"I didn't pay for—" He hoped she would not get into trouble for offering a free service.

"It's all right," she said. "We haven't any other customers right now, and Suzette will tend to them if we do."

"If you're sure it's all right," Henri said, already tensing in anticipation of an unexpected treat. He leaned back.

"Suzette told me you work in the duke's stables?"

Suzette had to be the one who never stopped talking. "I care for the horses that the duchess rode," he said. "I hope someday she will ride them again."

"I do, too," Nico said. "I've always admired her. She seems so strong and dignified."

Henri tried to think of a neutral comment. "She rides beautifully," Henri said. "I'm lucky to learn from her horses."

"Annette—she's the midwife in the brothel—Annette has actually met her. In the palace, the duchess didn't come here, of course. I asked what she was like. Annette wouldn't tell me. She only looked sad. Annette never looks sad, that's one reason why we…why I…oh, no. You'll think I've turned into Suzette, if I keep on like this. You're a good listener. Close your eyes." She poured warm water over his head, then dabbed the drips from his face. She winnowed her fingers through his wet hair. "Your hair is so thick. It's a pleasure to handle. I miss my own hair, but working here, it's so much more convenient to keep it clipped. Madame Hubert requires it, anyway."

"Clipped…it suits you," he said. "I think so. I think it, it makes you look beautiful." He could feel a blush scalding his cheeks, but in the dim room he hoped she wouldn't notice.

"Thank you," she said. "You're very kind to say so." She dug her fingers into his hair again, this time after coating them with soap. The scent of lavender washed over him as she scrubbed his scalp and squeezed the soap through hanks of his hair. He had to work not to moan at the pleasure of it. Each scratch of her fingers seemed to shoot straight to his cock.

"Do you like this?" she asked.

"Oh, yes," he said. He felt drunk, only better, like being drunk ought to feel.

"Do you have time to stay a little longer?" Nico asked.

She'd sounded lonely when she spoke of Annette. "As long as you want," he said.

"Sit up, and close your eyes." She poured rinse water over his head, another hot rush of pleasure, then did it again, and again. Henri felt limp, except for his cock, which he could feel bobbing in the water like an eager puppy.

"Done," she said. Then, "I would like you to fuck me."

He began to turn around, but Nico put her hands on his shoulders, preventing him. "You're wondering why," she said.

This was true.

Nico began to massage his shoulders, digging strong fingers into the muscles by his neck, and he moaned. "You like that? Good."

He more than liked it, he had never felt anything so good in his life, except his cock inside a woman's slippery tunnel. He'd been ready to do anything she wanted after she'd washed his hair. He wasn't going to tell her to stop, though.

Nico said, "The bathhouse is going to get crowded again later. It always does, after the shows in the house let out. Then we get another rush in the morning. Right now, it's the only time there's any privacy, and then you came in, and I've seen you. You're always nice to us. Not like some others."

"Hmm?" Henri said. He was listening, but her massage was making him sleepy at the same time that it aroused him.

"You don't grab," she said. "I like that. So I thought, why shouldn't you get a reward? And why shouldn't I have a little something for myself? We can enjoy each other."

"Anything you want," Henri said. Surely he was dreaming. No other explanation made sense for a day like this.

"Let's go in the steam room, then. Have you ever tried it?" She gathered up his towel and a pile of others, tucking them under one arm.

"Costs extra," he pointed out, standing up slowly. His blood was having trouble reaching his head. It kept getting diverted and pumping into his cock.

Nico held out her hand and he placed his within it. It felt natural to do so. She was like him, she knew what it was like to work all day and then to want to relax. He squeezed her hand and she peeked over her shoulder and smiled at him. She had a wide mouth, almost too large for her face, but somehow just right with her long nose and big brown eyes. When she smiled, her upper lip crinkled and so did the corners of her eyes. He would have followed her anywhere.

The steam room wasn't very large. All of the walls were tiled, and running with droplets of water. Vapor poured into the room from a pipe near the floor. Through the billowing steam, he could barely see three wide benches placed against the walls.

He took a deep breath and nearly choked, the air was so thick. He began to sweat, or perhaps it was the steam on his skin. He couldn't tell. "Easy," Nico said, and then he could breathe, more deeply than he'd ever breathed before. The odor of crushed peppermint stung his nostrils. Relaxation flowed through him.

Nico spread the towels over one of the benches and all at once he understood their purpose. His cock, which had flagged a bit, recovered quickly. Nico turned to him and smiled again. "Would you help me with this?" She plucked at her now-sodden shift.

Henri palmed her breasts through the cloth first, sighing with her as he rubbed the wet fabric against her nipples. "I could eat them like apples," he said. When he realized what he'd said, he looked away in embarrassment, but Nico giggled and put her hands on either side of his face.

"You are sweet," she said, and kissed him. A droplet of salty sweat ran off her upper lip and into his mouth, and he swept his tongue after it, moaning low in his throat when she recipro-cated, suckling his tongue and making him think of what it would be like to have a mouth on his cock. He ran one hand over the soft spikiness of her cropped hair over and over, but the other didn't want to let go of her breast. He squeezed it rhythmically as they kissed, sure he'd found the softest thing in the world. It was funny that so soft a thing could make him so hard.

They stopped to breathe, slowly taking in the steam and letting it out again. He helped her drag her wet shift over her head, and then was lost again as he tasted the sweat on her throat and breasts while his hands traced her upper arms, petal-soft skin over muscles hard from labor. In return, Nico gripped and massaged his arms, his shoulders, his back. When her hands wandered down to his buttocks, he pressed his erection into her belly and thrust tantalizing, twisting strokes against her slippery skin.

His skin was wet, too, but felt as if it was on fire. He was going to come in a minute if he wasn't careful. He pulled away from her, sucking air, and walked toward the bench with the towels, Nico playfully backing toward it as well. The bench caught her behind her knees, and she sat, reaching out her arms for him.

Henri sat next to her and dragged her onto his lap. He had to be inside of her soon, but he couldn't stop moving against her for that delicious drag of wet bare skin on skin. He writhed against her with his hands, his face, his chest, his thighs. Nico straddled him now, her breasts on a level with his face. He buried his nose between them, where her scent and heat were strongest, and it was like being inside of her. He could feel her heart pounding, racing.

She shoved her belly against his erection, forcing it back against his stomach, and rubbing it between their two slick bodies. Little gasps escaped her, and he darted his tongue into her mouth three times, quickly. "Please, please let me fuck you," he said. Before he'd quite finished speaking her chapped hand wrapped around his cock and fed it into her cunt. She plunged down and he grunted from feeling her wet cunt lips slap against his balls.

Gripping his shoulders painfully, she writhed on his cock, as if she were trying to find purchase, sucking at him from the inside and then shoving her hips forward. He worked his hand between their bodies and let her grind against the heel of his hand, hoping desperately she would start to move up and down soon; at the same time, he never wanted her to stop this exquisite torture.

"More," she said. "More, more, fuck me!"

"Yes," he said. Bracing his feet on the floor, he thrust upward with enough force that she jostled on his lap. Soon she joined in his motion and rode him until he thought his heart would burst. She came twice, he thought; the first time he was concentrating so hard to keep his own control that he wasn't sure he really felt her inner flutters, but the second time was unmistakable; her cries rose and rose and then broke. He pumped into her a few more deep strokes and then he was spurting inside of her, his tension releasing in excruciating, ecstatic jerks, and even more wetness was trickling over his legs. He threw his head back against the wall, gasping, feeling as if he could sink into the wood bench. Nico leaned over to nuzzle his throat.

"You're so sweet, Henri," she said. "But I think you need another bath."

This time, Nico scrubbed him off, and he scrubbed her in return. Their toweling dry turned into an impromptu kissing game, and by the time they had rubbed each other's skins with oil, he wished he could stay even longer. But noises at the house were signaling an end to their evening together. He kissed her goodbye just inside the door, promised to return when he could, and hurried back to the stables, resolved that Nico was a very good reason to forget all about his imprudent dreams of the duchess.

CHAPTER FIVE

Vilmos ushered Camille personally into her rooms, indicating that Kaspar and Arno were to accompany her inside, instead of posting themselves to either side of her door as they normally did.

She wished they had not been so protective of her in the duke's presence. The duke's will was always supposed to supersede her own, even in the matter of her personal safety. They might pay for their loyalty later. She would have to take better care for their safety. Escaping the palace would be a good first step.

Vilmos stood, as if waiting. Arno turned his back suddenly and prowled the edges of the room. "Yes?" Camille said.

"Your Grace," Vilmos said, and inclined his head.

Camille lifted her chin. She might have sucked his cock, but she was never going to bring up the subject again, even if Vilmos felt the need to apologize. She'd had little choice. Neither had he. It was useless to dwell upon past humiliation.

Vilmos bent respectfully into a low bow, then departed,

locking the door behind him. She heard the bolts slide home, and the *clank* of the large iron hasp that bore the duke's seal.

With that final sound, Camille's knees weakened. She forced herself to stay upright. She might be safe while the duke was occupied with his private amusements, but…she no longer believed she would be safe any longer than that, even if she had gotten herself with child. She could no longer bear the thought of letting the duke fuck her, and if he did not, she would be killed as quickly for being pregnant by another as he would have her killed for being barren. She had been fooling herself to think that if she gave the duke what he wanted, he would let her live.

The clock on the marble mantel, a fantastically ugly creation embellished with golden angels and white-lacquered sheep and their shepherdesses, showed that the middle of the night had just passed. She felt as if days had gone by since she had summoned Henri to her audience chamber. How long would it be before the duke found a way to take her life? What would he do to her before he had her beheaded? Was it true that one could still see after one's head had been sliced off? She felt like a bird fluttering against the bars of its gilded cage. She picked up her sketchbook, then put it down. She rubbed her wrists, though they bore no marks.

Kaspar said, "Shall I call for a bath for Your Grace?"

He always spoke first. She had never noticed particularly, but Arno always deferred to him, perhaps because Kaspar was older. He was nearly thirty, she thought, while Arno had been delivered to the palace at eighteen and was now not quite twenty-three. She had asked Sylvie their ages; it was difficult to tell when they never put on a man's muscle, at least not in the way one was used to seeing.

"Where is Sylvie?" she asked. Baths were Sylvie's duty.

"Sleeping, Your Grace," Kaspar said. He stood at ease, his big hands resting on his sheathed twin swords. From this close, she could see the thin white scars that marked his forearms, old injuries from training with blades. His eyes were pale gray. "Shall I wake her?"

"No," Camille said. She wanted a bath, but not enough to wait for one to be prepared. She had to think. And Sylvie had slept little recently, instead spending most of a night and day finding Henri and arranging to bring him to Camille. She should let Sylvie sleep now, she realized, because they must escape the palace tonight, she and Sylvie and her eunuchs as well; she could not allow them to die because of her. To die in her service was one thing. To die for nothing was quite another.

Right now, her brain spun like the innards of a clock, getting nowhere.

Arno stepped forward and laid his hand on her shoulder. For a moment, everything in her mind stopped. His hand was so warm. She drew strength from it. He said, in his gentle tenor, "Please, Your Grace, let us put you to bed."

Kaspar added, "We will keep you safe."

Surely they knew that was impossible. "That is your duty," she said, to test his response.

"That is our duty and our desire," Kaspar said. "Do not doubt, Your Grace, that we will care for you to our deaths and beyond."

She could not protest his dramatic words; if she were killed, they would be killed as well. She nodded.

Arno added, before he let his hand fall from her shoulder, "You may ask anything of us. Anything we can do for you, we will. Let us serve you tonight."

Camille drew a deep breath. She could not delay any longer, nor did she care to do so. "The guards at the outer walls change in the hours before dawn. We will leave then, both of you and Sylvie and I, and we will——" She hesitated the barest moment, remembering Henri with a rush of affection. "The stableboy is loyal to me. He will help us to hide until we can go." If Michel discovered what the boy had done…and she was gone, and all her most treasured servants and horses…no. She could not abandon him to that. "The boy Henri will come with us, as well."

Kaspar knelt before her, touching his forehead to her foot. "As you commanded, all is prepared for a rapid escape. I will follow you, Your Grace."

"Arno?"

The younger guard knelt beside Kaspar. "Your Grace, I—I think I should not go. Not at first."

Kaspar sucked in an audible breath.

"Don't," Arno said, touching Kaspar's arm. Camille watched

the interplay keenly; Kaspar did not look at him. Because he thought Arno's plan unwise, or out of fear for his friend?

Arno said, "Someone will need to gather information, about pursuit. I could come to you later, on the road, or send someone I can trust. It is better me. You see, Vilmos will protect me. His mother was my mother's cousin. It is not his fault I was cut, and ever since he found me he has watched over me. Also, now he owes you something as well, and will speak for you among the palace guard. I would not flaunt my presence in the palace. I have friends in the town."

"Your Grace, he would be in grave danger from the duke," Kaspar argued. "It is true, Vilmos's loyalty to the duke is not strong, but—"

Camille's suspicions were confirmed. Vilmos was not utterly enamored of her husband. She said to Arno, "It is more risk than I should ask you to bear."

"It is your right to ask me to go to my death," Arno said. "I do not think this will be my death."

Camille thought. Kaspar was distressed, but Arno was correct. Arno's actions might save them all from death. She nodded, once. "Arno will stay. We will have Henri to help care for the horses on the journey."

Kaspar closed his eyes for a moment, then opened them. He bent and kissed her foot.

Camille and her guards packed the few personal items they would take with them; the rest would be retrieved from a hiding place outside the palace walls. They quickly finished, but nearly six hours still stretched out before they could depart.

Camille said, "We will let Sylvie sleep a while longer, then send her to the stables to find the boy. Until then, you must also rest."

"Your Grace," Kaspar said. "Let us serve you tonight."

Custom encouraged using eunuchs for sexual pleasure. In all their time together, Camille had never asked. She'd been loyal to Michel, even after he'd betrayed her a thousand times. This afternoon, she'd betrayed him with Henri. To do this with her eunuchs—one of whom would go into desperate danger for her sake—seemed suddenly to loom as an important mark of how she'd changed. Also, it would be better than lying in her bed alone, staring at the ceiling and worrying herself to flinders. She said, "Thanks to you both. I would like that, very much."

She let Kaspar take her hand and lead her to her bedchamber, Arno trailing behind.

Kaspar lit tapers on her nightstand and dressing table; after she sat down on her bed, Arno knelt and removed her slippers. The stubble on his skull glinted gold in the candlelight. He set the slippers aside but remained at her feet, his head bowed, the nape of his neck vulnerable.

When several seconds passed and he did not move, Camille said, "What is it, Arno?"

He shook his head, then bowed lower and kissed the tops of her feet, more sensually than Kaspar had done, warm damp pressure that sent tingles up her legs. She reached down and laid her palm on the crown of Arno's head. His skin was hot, his stubble like a cat's tongue and so pleasant to touch that she rubbed her hand over all of it that she could reach, ending with a tug at his ear. She sat back on her elbows. "Both of you, join me."

"If I may, Your Grace?" Kaspar asked. He indicated his weapons. She nodded, and he divested himself of his harness, laying his throwing knife on her night table and his swords on the carpet next to her bed. Arno did the same.

Her two guards did not completely disrobe; they never had done so in her sight, and she had not liked to demand that of them. Kaspar kept his loose trousers, and Arno his long drawers. She wasn't sure if their modesty was meant to protect them from her gaze or to protect her from having to see that they were not whole men. She thought of telling them that it did not matter, but then another reason occurred to her; perhaps they meant to reassure her of their intent. What they did was for her and not for them.

Kaspar untied her belt, pushed her robe from her shoulders, and lifted her in his arms, something he had never done before. He cradled her against his bare chest while Arno marshaled pillows into a nest, all without speaking. She wanted to turn into him—it had been years since she'd been held like this—but could not quite bring herself to do it and reveal her need. Just then, Kaspar's hand cupped the back of her head and pressed her face into his shoulder. She closed her eyes. His thumb rubbed the back of her neck, his fingers tangling in her hair. "A moment longer," he murmured.

His voice was lighter than a whole man's but comforting all

the same. What made him less than whole? The loss of his stones? She did not have a man's stones, either. And in many ways, Kaspar was a better man than her husband, though such a thing could never be spoken. She wondered if either eunuch truly cared for her. If not, their pretense was infinitely better than whatever the duke felt.

Arno took her from Kaspar's arms and laid her on the pillows. She sank into the pile of velvet and satin, so soft that she would have difficulty if she tried to struggle out, but she did not want to struggle. Her head lolled as Arno began to massage one of her legs, Kaspar the other, beginning at her toes and working up her foot to her calf. They both had considerable skill. Perhaps—probably—they did this for each other. Whom else did they have?

Her mind drifted, seeking refuge and rest in pure sensation. When her guards' hands reached her knees, Arno continued upward, his big hands squeezing the taut muscles at the tops of her thighs and sweeping his thumbs over her hip bones.

The bed shifted as Kaspar departed, only to return a few moments later with a ewer and bowl, and a cloth folded over his forearm. Arno slid his hands intimately close and pressed open her lower lips. Camille closed her eyes as Kaspar bathed her in rose water, teasing her tender skin with friction from the cloth and trickles of water. She shifted restlessly against Arno's hands, then tensed when the next pressure against her came from Kaspar's tongue. At first flinching at the intensity, she soon twisted her hips, seeking more. "Use your finger, please," she said. Kaspar's finger nudged at her opening and she swallowed a cry.

Arno bent close and licked the shell of her ear. "What is your desire, Your Grace?" he asked. "Command me."

"My breasts," she said. "Suckle my breasts."

Arno teased her nipples at first with light flicks of his tongue, but soon, in response to her arching back, pinched one between his lips and pulled, rolling her other nipple between his finger-tips. Each squeeze stabbed her belly, pleasure sharp as that of Kaspar's thick, calloused finger rubbing inside of her. She panted against the knots twisting her insides. "More," she said.

Arno palmed her breasts and squeezed. She balanced on a web of tension. Kaspar could not reach deeply enough to cut her free. She gasped for air and pushed into his hand, but could not come.

"Arno," she said. "In the drawer. By the bed. The ivory carving."

Kaspar looked up. She gestured for him to stop what he was doing. He lifted his head but did not remove his fingers from her quim. His eyes had gone dark, and his forehead was sheened with sweat. She could see her own fluids shining around his lips. He said, "I have used such carvings before, Your Grace. Will you allow me to demonstrate for Arno?"

Camille breathed, forcing her heart to slow its gallop. Slowly, her desperation receded. "You will work together," she said.

Kaspar bowed, his forehead touching her knee. "I am yours to command."

The duke had given her the ivory cock in a fit of scorn. She had never used it, from anger at its source and from not wanting to be seen by her maids. Now, it was a further weapon against her husband, providing for her what he did not.

Kaspar took the carving from its drawer and extracted it from its layers of linen wrappings. It looked larger than she remembered, even cradled in Kaspar's giant hands. "Arno," she said. "Fetch the oil in the red bottle."

Arno knew to look in the carved cabinet where her maids kept her bath and massage oils. He then went to the fire and poured heated water from the copper kettle into a bowl, to warm the oil. He carried bowl and bottle to her, and she removed its stopper, a spiral of red glass twisted with blue. "Lay the stopper on the linen," she said. In the meantime, Kaspar warmed the ivory cock in the water, as well.

"Arno, perhaps you could apply the oil to me, inside and out," she said. "Kaspar, then show us how you have seen one of these used. Arno will pay close attention, and perhaps take a turn if he finds himself intrigued."

"And you, Your Grace?" Kaspar asked, with the barest hint of humor.

"I hope to be otherwise occupied," she said.

Kaspar said, "If you will permit me, Your Grace?" He climbed onto the bed and knelt beside her. He laid the ivory cock on the coverlet and pressed her shoulders, encouraging her to lie back in her nest of pillows. "I will hold the bottle for now," he said. Arno gave the oil to him and slid onto the bed. He placed his hands on her knees, pressing them apart so he could slide closer. Camille could hear his rapid breathing. She looked up into his face and saw his eyes were wide and dark.

He was afraid, she realized. He was not thinking of what he was doing now, but of what would become of him once she and Kaspar and Sylvie had escaped. He needed encouragement. She signaled Kaspar with her eyes.

Kaspar used his free hand to gently rub Arno's bare shoulder. He leaned over and kissed Arno's cheekbone. "Stroke her as you would stroke the petals of a flower."

Arno said, his hands still cupping her knees, "Would you like that, Your Grace?"

"Yes," she said. She let her knees fall open another fraction. "You may pour the oil as you wish."

Kaspar tipped the bottle over her belly. It trickled onto her abdomen and down like the touch of fingers, trickling into the creases between her legs and slicking her mound.

"Now his hands," she said. Arno cupped his hands as if to receive an offering, and Kaspar bathed his palms in oil.

"Gently," Kaspar said.

Camille wasn't sure what he meant by that, but the thought evaporated as Arno laid his hands on her, one hand cupping her mound and the other pressing into her lower belly with a tender pressure like two bodies joined.

She was already swollen from their earlier attentions; Arno's finger nudged between her lower lips, and her breath caught. "Two fingers," she said. "Spread the oil deeply within."

Arno obeyed, his breathing rough but his fingers gentle. Closing her eyes made the sensation too intense. She focused on the ivory cock Kaspar was warming against his chest. Then he bent low and their eyes met. "Now, Your Grace?"

At first she could not speak, only nod. She swallowed and said, "Now."

Arno moved aside, though he still held her thighs apart. Kaspar oiled the carving, knelt between her knees, and eased its rounded head inside her. When her breath rushed out, he sheathed it fully in her passage. Her bodily tension was such that the stimulation was sweet to the point of pain. She could wait no longer.

"Quickly," she commanded. Kaspar gave her short, harsh thrusts with a twisting motion that in moments had her back arching off the bed, straining with her whole body toward her climax. Soon she could strangle her cries no longer as she shuddered in release, gasping with each fierce spasm.

Arno leaned to Kaspar and kissed him, at first gently and then hungrily. Camille might have wondered at it, had she not been so limp with fatigue and afterglow. She held out her arms, and was soon surrounded by their warmth and comforting bulk. Each kissed her in turn, a brief, warm pressure. She slept then, deeply, and woke to find Kaspar kneeling beside the bed, dressed again and weaponed, waiting for her to awaken.

"Your Grace," he said. "Sylvie is here. I have sent Arno for a few small items, and to dress in ordinary clothes."

Sylvie wore only a robe, her long hair escaping from a messy braid, her cheek creased from her pillow. "Madame," she said. "What is this that Kaspar tells me? We are to bring the stable-boy with us?"

"Yes. He offered his services of his own free will. You are to tell him, for me, that I have need of him now. He is to bring the horses, and a pack mule, and all necessary supplies for them. You recall I mentioned the breeding barn as a good hiding place before we can set out. He will know the best ways to conceal us there, and will be useful in other ways, as well."

"Other ways—madame—"

"Do not forget yourself, Sylvie. You knew I might not get immediately with child."

Sylvie flushed. "Yes, madame. I will do as you've ordered. I worry, however—"

"I will worry for all of us."

As soon as Sylvie had dressed and slipped out to find Henri, Kaspar draped Camille in a hooded cloak. "Could you run while wearing it, Your Grace?"

She tested the drape, then gathered up swaths of fabric. Beneath it, she wore a riding habit with a man's jacket to conceal her shape. She felt confined, but she could move. "I will do what is necessary," she said, as Kaspar shrugged on a shirt over his knife harness and fastened its ties up the front. He looked different with his hairless chest covered: bigger and more solid. Arno came back into the room, pushed up Kaspar's sleeves, and strapped on wrist harnesses for a pair of short-bladed knives, while Kaspar gave him what seemed to be a long catalog of instructions, delivered in so low a murmur that Camille could not discern his words.

She turned away from their colloquy and cast a final glance around her rooms. She might never return here again. She might be caught and killed on the journey. If she could not unseat Michel, she might die while facing him. It ought to be better, she reflected, to know one might die while in the midst of action, better than by being passively led to the block, but she could not muster any pleasure at the thought of simply avoiding execution to die in some other way. Dying was dying, and she did not want to die. She'd just begun to have a stirring of hope that life could be better.

Arno removed his nondescript soft cap and came to kneel before her. She kissed the top of his head and drew him to his feet, tugging his head down to kiss each of his cheeks then, formally, his mouth. She said, holding his gaze, "I do not want you to die for me, Arno. You will take care."

"I will, Your Grace," he said. "I should go now, when I will not be remarked."

Camille took his hand and folded his fingers over her signet ring. It looked like a doll's jewelry in his enormous hand. "You will do well," she said. "You may go."

After Arno had gone, Kaspar slung the larger of their bags across his massive shoulders. He reached for Camille's smaller bag, but she forestalled him. "I would prefer your hands be ready for weapons," she explained, taking her own bag herself. "We cannot stand on ceremony for the entire journey, not without drawing attention to ourselves."

"Very well, Your Grace." Kaspar laid a hand on her shoulder, guiding her toward the concealed door used by her maids. Camille's heart sped up. She was truly leaving.

She had not traveled these corridors since her youth, when she'd snuck all over the palace for assignations with Maxime. The servants' paths seemed smaller and darker now than they had then, and unnaturally silent as her riding boots tapped the scarred wooden flooring. The walls between these corridors and the chambers beyond were, by design, thick enough to conceal sounds as loud as rattling carts of porcelain dishes, so she did not need to feel nervous, but logical thought didn't ease her mind. The air felt close, thick with the reek of burning tallow candles. Their smoke lodged in her throat.

Kaspar's voice startled her. "Thérèse will not come to make up the fires for another hour," he said. "Until then, these corridors are usually deserted."

"And the paths leading outside the walls?" she asked. Even as a young girl, she had not slipped out of the palace at night, thanks to the guardianship of the eunuch Jarman.

"Those paths are less safe," Kaspar admitted. "Sometimes they are quite busy with guardsmen and courtiers returning from the Dewy Rose, paid companions going back to their homes, and the like. I will guard you, Your Grace."

Camille wished she could guard herself; she chafed at the need for circumspection. It felt cowardly, and she'd had enough of being a coward. She hadn't been brave enough to confront Michel; she'd had the opportunity, but done nothing to take advantage of it. Next time, she told herself, she would not be so cautious. Next time, she would work from a position of strength.

Kaspar led her on a direct route to the palace's main rear entrance. At the door, he reached to readjust the hood of her cloak. Camille brushed his hand away. "I am not a child," she said, more sharply than she'd intended. Kaspar inclined his head, then loosened his right-handed sword in its sheath. He pressed his ear to the door before easing it open.

Darkness and cool air rushed in, carrying a rich scent of damp earth and crushed grass. Camille inhaled deeply, feeling the outdoors like a tingle of freedom on her skin. She fought a sudden urge to run full tilt into the starlight and roll in the greenery. Instead, she tried to steady her breathing as she stared beneath Kaspar's massive arm and into the darkness. Distantly, she heard voices, resolving into a rumble of male ribaldry. Three men? Four? She heard a distinctive jingle—a chain-mail hauberk—and shrank back.

Kaspar tugged her forward. "Come. We must be out before they enter."

Camille let him pull her out the door and to the left, staying in the wall's shadow. A stretch of open grass, punctuated by a few sleeping cows, might as well have been a moat; they would easily be seen crossing it. The rear boundary wall reared beyond. In the illumination cast by their lantern, the shadows of four guardsmen loomed black against the wall's gleaming white marble.

"Hold still," Kaspar murmured, pressing her into a crouch next to the palace wall. Her dark cloak would melt into the dark granite, she hoped. He let his bag slide off his shoulder, next to her, and stepped into the light.

Trembling, Camille watched from beneath the hood of her cloak. Eunuchs were forbidden to venture outside the palace alone, and though she'd bent that rule before, there was no guarantee the guardsmen would do the same. If they decided to imprison Kaspar for the night, she could still make her way to the breeding barn alone, but retrieving Kaspar would be difficult, and delay their departure significantly. If the guards decided to escort him back to her chambers, and found her gone, it would be a disaster.

"Ho!" the smallest of the guardsmen called. "Kaspar!"

Worse and worse. Camille recognized the voice—Léopold, one of Michel's personal honor guard, who reported directly to him. He stopped in the middle of the graveled path, hands planted on hips. "What's amiss, eunuch? Searching for your manhood among the cowpats?"

"'Hap you can find it with them catamites at the Dewy Rose," another said, and belched. A third guard cuffed him on the side of the head and murmured something, which led to a brief scuffle between the two.

Ignoring the byplay, Kaspar said, "I'm in search of Vilmos. Have you seen him?"

"Fucking His Grace, most like," Léopold said, his perpetual sneer audible in his voice. "I'd leave his service first."

The fourth guardsman spoke. "Better fucking His Grace than losing his ballocks."

Kaspar said, his tone cool, "Better without ballocks than buggering His Grace's filthy arse."

If Kaspar provoked them into killing him, Camille would kill him again. She closed her eyes as insults began to fly faster and more foully, soon succeeded by the meaty smack of fists on flesh; the crash of the lantern being dropped; the thumps of large bodies hitting the ground; grunts and curses and panting. After a few minutes, she opened her eyes and found that two of the guardsmen were dragging Kaspar off Léopold's supine form. The last guardsman doubled over in the grass, vomiting.

"You'd better be off before Léopold comes to," one of them said. Camille recognized his voice: Rodrigue, another of Michel's honor guard. "Eugène, you, too. You can't afford any more trouble. Weren't you due on duty at dawn?" Eugène cursed and sprinted for the door into the palace. Camille winced as the door slammed shut behind him.

"Thanks," Kaspar said.

"You'd better be off to Her Grace, in case Léopold takes it into his head to make trouble," Rodrigue said, bending to hoist Léopold over his shoulder. He snagged the fourth guardsman by the sleeve and then shoved him toward the door. "If I see Vilmos, I will let him know you asked after him. Take the lantern, will you?"

"My thanks, again." Kaspar stood watching as Rodrigue and his drunken companion maneuvered Léopold through the narrow door, thumping his head against the wall more than once in the process. Then he wiped his sleeve across his face; in the lantern light, Camille saw a dark stain of blood beneath his nose.

Slowly, she unkinked her back and stood, propping one hand against the wall. Kaspar looked in her direction and snuffed the lantern. She heard his shoes crunching on gravel, then a *clank* as he set the lantern on the ground, next to the door. Camille took a deep breath and joined him. Softly, she said, "Thank you."

Kaspar said, "Léopold might be trouble."

"Then we'd best hurry."

His hand took hers in the darkness, and as he led her to the rear gate, Camille felt a rising joy. Soon she would be free.

CHAPTER SIX

Henri would have danced all the way home from the bathhouse if he had not been so utterly exhausted. He'd worked all morning, spent the afternoon alternating mortal terror with lust, then labored in the stables well into the evening, all before his exertions with Nico at the baths. And he had to be up before dawn to exercise the horses before the heat of the day.

No replacement had been bought for Poire after the old fellow, the duchess's childhood pony, had keeled over in the field last summer. Henri usually slept in Poire's empty stall, down at the end of the row. He kept his blankets there, and his extra shirt, except now he was wearing the shirt and carrying his filthy one in a sack. He felt so clean that he was reluctant to put it on again for work in the morning. In the morning, though, this wondrous night would seem like a dream. He hoped. One had to return to ordinary life sometime, and it would be easier if he didn't think too much about what he might be missing.

Henri lifted the bar across the stable door as cautiously as he could. None of the senior grooms slept here, not anymore, but they would hear a crashing noise from their cots in the next barn, where the duke's hunters ate their heads off and occasionally sauntered around the paddock. Henri's—the duchess's—horses were in prime condition. He kept them that way for her, because even if she never rode them again, she might see them, and he did not want her to be disappointed. Besides, he loved his horses.

He bolted the door again from the inside and padded down the aisle fronting the luxurious stalls. Slices of moonlight silvered the floor. Tonnelle whickered, so he stopped to pat her shoulder and let her nuzzle his hair. "Why are you still awake?" he asked softly. Of course she did not answer. Guirlande was awake also, blinking at him sleepily over the barrier inscribed with her name in fading gilt. Henri pulled her head down to his and pressed their foreheads together, breathing in the familiar smell of horse. He wanted to talk to her, to say aloud all the amazing things that had happened to him today, but not only would it be silly, but someone might hear. He must never speak, or even think, of what had happened today with the duchess. It might mean her death, and it would certainly mean his.

Henri yawned and began to clamber over the barrier marked *Poire.* Halfway over, he gasped and tried to go backward, but the dark figure he'd glimpsed grabbed his shoulders and yanked him into the straw.

He landed on something soft, but was immediately flipped

over and pinned. Straw poked hard into the back of his neck as his assailant's forearm pressed into his throat. Henri tried to suck in air and the pressure lessened. Abruptly, the figure let go and backed away.

"You startled me," she said, as if it had been his fault she'd tried to strangle him.

He recognized the voice: Sylvie, the duchess's maid who had fetched him that afternoon. "Oh," he said dumbly, shaking from head to foot.

"You shouldn't have come back so late," Sylvie said. "I've been waiting for over an hour." She dusted herself off with one gloved hand and unsealed her dark lantern. She wore snugly fitting riding leathers, a man's shirt and tall boots. His eyes widened. Her figure was slender, her hair concealed beneath a cap; if he'd seen her from a distance, he might not have recognized her as a woman. Perhaps that was the point. A lone woman wandering the stableyards at this time of night might run into unpleasantness.

"Waiting for what?" Henri asked.

He was unprepared to be clouted on the shoulder. He barely ducked in time to evade the worst of the blow. "Such is the loyalty of a stableboy!" Sylvie hissed. "You've forgotten already! Madame will be very disappointed!"

Henri sat down in the straw. He hadn't intended to sit, but there he was, sitting, his fingers clenched around prickly handfuls. "Her Grace?" he whispered.

"Yes, fool! Did you not say you could help her to escape, if there was need? Well, now there is need! For her, and she goes *nowhere* without me, and we will also have a guard, one of the eunuchs. And she says—*she* says—we must have you. Though I can't see you'll be much use. The eunuch and I can take care of the horses well enough, if we take it in turns to guard her. But madame must have what she wants. So you must come with us."

Henri blinked. *"Now?"*

Sylvie grabbed his shirt, hauled him upright, and shook him. "I did not come here for my health, idiot boy! Prepare your things, we are leaving tomorrow."

Wildly, Henri calculated in his head. He needed a stick and some dirt to make any complex computations, but even without that he knew already he didn't have enough money to feed himself on a journey of any length, much less the duchess and her retinue of two as well. Nor would he be able to earn sufficient funds along the way, not for so many. "It won't be enough," he said, trying to make her understand. "I will gladly give it, all of it, but it won't get us far. What will we do when my money runs out?"

Sylvie flung up her hands. Freed, Henri scrambled away from her. "You are deluded," she said, with patently false patience. Henri didn't ask what that meant. He could guess.

"Where are we going, then? We won't need money there?"

"I do not want your pathetic coins," Sylvie said. "All is prepared, sufficient funds are made portable, and I have already sewn jewels into garments. It is a place to hide that we need.

You can hide us, can't you? Only two of us, myself and madame. The eunuch will come to fetch us when it is safe to depart."

Henri said, "In the town there are more people. We could hide in their midst."

"No. Too many people know her there. Madame told me of the breeding barn—you can take us there. I will take care of protection. You need only distract the duke's searchers."

Of course. He should have thought of the breeding barn first, himself. "It's lucky Guirlande is near her time," he said. "I would never be let go otherwise."

"I'm glad you approve," Sylvie said, giving him a withering look. "Didn't I tell you to get your things?"

It all proved to be much easier than Henri had thought it would be, so easy that he felt sure things would soon go wrong in ways he did not expect. Unless his luck had changed. He'd heard of people being cursed to have boils, or impotence, or to vomit frogs. What if he'd been cursed to have good luck? He smiled to himself at his own foolishness, and Sylvie thumped the back of his head again. She seemed to like doing that. He strongly suspected she had a little brother, or perhaps three.

Shortly after dawn, Henri led Guirlande, Tonnelle, Lilas, Tulipe and a pack mule called Tigre down a path skirting the duke's landscaped forest. His heart lifted with the clean scent of fog rising off the grass. The day would be hot again, but for once he would not be out in it, not enough to matter. The mares always ran free in the paddock for the few days until the appropriate stallion, or stallions, was chosen and brought. By that time, he and the mares would be gone, and the duchess with him. He sighed. And Sylvie. And a eunuch. Assuming they weren't caught and killed first. He decided not to think about that possibility. He might frighten the horses with his own fear, and someone might truly notice something wrong.

Despite his worries, he saw no one while hiking to the breeding barn, not even a gardener or huntsman. The walk took more than an hour. The barn was far enough that no stallion screams would reach the main palace or any of the outlying courtiers' houses. It was not so far that Henri felt bad about loading Tigre with four sets of tack, carefully bundled. If they were truly to go on a long journey, he would not abuse the horses with cheap, ill-fitting saddles when they had their own.

When he arrived at the breeding barn, it felt deserted. He could not call out names in case of listeners. Perhaps the women had not yet arrived. He turned the mares into the smaller paddock, close by, and unloaded Tigre before turning him out, too. Still no sign of anyone. His heart, which had calmed with routine, began to pound faster again, and the back of his neck crawled. He stacked Guirlande's saddle atop Tulipe's, slung the bridles over his shoulder and carried it all into the tack room, using the key he'd been given that morning along with many dire warnings from the chief groom.

Once inside the darkened room, he stopped, sure someone was there. He could hear breathing and smell the faintest scent of roses. He stepped forward, inhaled deeply and relaxed. He bent and set the tack on the nearest bench. "Your Grace," he said quietly. "I've brought your horses. Shall I bring them in, so you can see them?"

"Henri." She came out of the darkness, dressed in a man's long jacket over her riding habit.

Henri bowed, face to the tiled floor.

"You needn't kneel to me," the duchess said. "Stand up."

His heart thumping, Henri stood. He ducked his head and saw straw sticking to his shirt. Did he dare brush it off? Would she think that disrespectful? Or was it more disrespectful to leave the straw on his clothing? He hazarded a glance at her face. She was smiling.

"Will you be my loyal servant, Henri?" she asked formally.

"If—if you would have me, Your Grace."

The duchess came closer. She laid her gloved fingertips on his cheek. Henri felt hot blood course into his face. She said, "My loyal stableboy."

"Yes, Your Grace." Hesitantly, he looked into her face, hoping she would see his loyalty. Their eyes met, and held.

A light clatter of boots from outside the tack room broke the stillness. Dizzy, Henri stepped back. "I must hang the tack properly—"

The duchess vanished, stepping back into the recesses of the room. Henri whirled to face the door as Sylvie strode in, still clad in her male garb. She carried a dark heap over one arm. Wisps of blond hair had escaped her leather huntsman's cap, but her expression did nothing to soften her sharp features. "Boy!" she said. "Leave that now." She thrust out her free arm and pushed him into the wall.

The push was gentle and Henri swiftly recovered his balance. He wished he could bring himself to fight a woman. Sylvie's roughness already wore thin. "The tack—I—"

"Take that off."

"Off?" Henri looked around himself, wondering what she meant.

"Off, off, stupid boy! Those filthy clothes! I will not have you offending madame! At least you don't stink, not more than any other man. There are some in the palace who stink far worse. Take them off!" She shook her bundle at him, and the aroma of cedar floated over him. "If you do not hurry, she will find you like this!"

"But—"

"Quiet. Use your small brain for your buttons."

The duchess did not speak from the darkness, and Henri would not reveal her presence without her permission. He summoned strength from the knowledge that she could trust him, and said to Sylvie, "I haven't any buttons."

Sylvie made a noise that sounded like a cat coughing up. She tossed the clothing onto the bench and began unlacing the neck of Henri's shirt. Her fingers accidentally touched his collarbone, the side of his neck, his upper chest. Her fingers were hot and rough. If he'd had time to think beforehand, he would have expected a smooth, icy chill. Curious, he breathed in her scent of lavender and leather. Her breath smelt sweetly of aniseed. She didn't seem as frightening, up close, but he still didn't dare defy her.

"Arms up," she demanded, intent on her task. "Hurry."

Henri obeyed. She yanked his shirt over his head and cast it on the floor. Before he could stop her, she began worrying the knot of his pants. Henri screwed his eyes shut and let his head thump back against the wall. He wasn't sure what to do with his hands. In a moment, he would be *naked*. In front of the duchess. *And* Sylvie. What was he supposed to do about that? He wouldn't strike her. He should grab her busy hands and push them aside, then run away. If he ran, though, she would bully him forever. Worse, the duchess would see him run.

His pants fell off his hips and puddled around his ankles. He bit back a protest. He was embarrassed to find that his cock was growing hard. If Sylvie looked, she would see.

Like the bathhouse, he told himself. *Like the——* It was no good. In the bathhouse, he removed his own clothes, and everyone else was naked as well. In the bathhouse last night, he had... This wasn't fair. "Give me the clothes," he said to Sylvie, suddenly angry enough to be brave.

Sylvie stepped back from him. He was free to move, if he dared. He didn't dare. She said, "Not yet."

"Why are you doing this to me?" Henri asked.

"For madame." Sylvie looked him up and down. "Everything I do is for madame." Henri attempted to speak. Sylvie planted her hand over his mouth. "You may think you are loyal to her, but you are only a boy. You cannot understand. I will give you something you can understand."

Gracefully, Sylvie dropped to her knees and pulled off her huntsman's cap. Her hair held its elaborate structure for a moment, then collapsed, drifting down her back and shoulders like a dream, catching glints of light from the open door. Henri couldn't look away. He wanted to plunge his hands into the glossiness, more gold than he would ever see in his life. He preferred dark hair, but there was something to be said for blond as well.

He reached for her hair, then froze. Sylvie looked up at him, her eyes narrowed. After a long moment, she said, "I will permit that." Before his fingers could reach her, she leaned forward and ran her tongue along his cock.

Henri gasped. His touch on her hair became a death grip.

"Be still," Sylvie said. She thumped his hip with her fist. "Pay attention."

Eyes wide, Henri nodded. He was definitely paying attention. When her mouth touched him again, he strangled his own cry. He'd been curious about this—had imagined this. His imaginings were nothing to the real details, to the teasing licks and nips and scrapes like random sparks from a bonfire that twitched the nerves in his arms, his legs, his neck. He could not steady his breathing. When her fingers tugged back his foreskin, and her lips closed over the head of his cock, he whimpered like a kicked puppy, and at her first suction, he thought he would cry with ecstasy.

Sylvie's hand pinned his hip against the wall. She leaned back a fraction. "I said to be still."

Henri couldn't speak, but he made a noise she took as assent. *Please don't stop,* he thought. He imagined the duchess before him, her long dark hair streaming down, silver glints in it catching the light, her eyes smiling up at him... Sylvie's lips closed over his cock again, and he pushed away his fevered imagining in horror, burying it deeply. He should not presume. It would never happen. He must never think on that again.

He looked down at Sylvie, concentrating on her satiny hair between his fingers, on the scalding wetness of her mouth. It wasn't difficult. Everything she did felt so astonishingly *good*. He couldn't tell what sensation would happen next, or where she would choose to bestow it. He couldn't tell how long it had been going on. He didn't care, so long as it kept happening. Even if it was Sylvie, who hadn't been kind to him. He forgave her everything, for this.

Sylvie's hand had been firmly holding the base of his cock, to position it to her liking. Now her other hand cupped his balls and her thumb rubbed over the delicate skin. "Oh," Henri said. He wanted to ask her to keep on doing exactly that, but realized in time that Sylvie would likely not be amenable to his requests.

Sylvie pulled her mouth free. "You are paying attention?"

"Yes." *Oh, yes. Go back to sucking. I'm getting close. Please, more. Faster.* The air was cold on his damp cock, and he shivered in mixed pleasure and pain.

"Good." She fondled his balls again, and he bit his lip, trying not to cry out. She said reflectively, "I adore to see a man look like this. Like so." She drew her fingernail along the length of his cock, and it felt as if she'd done the same to his spine. "You would do anything, would you not? You would do anything to have my mouth draw out your final pleasure?"

Henri's breath caught. Was this a trick? "Not—" he gasped.

"Not *what*, boy?" She flicked her finger against his cock. His hips lurched forward in response.

"I wouldn't—if it would hurt *her*—Her Grace—"

"So you say. But you would say anything just now, would you not?"

"No. I *wouldn't*." Henri struggled, and pulled himself free of her grip. The duchess might be watching, but it didn't matter. He would not be bullied in this. He had sworn to the duchess, mere moments before, and he had sworn to her in his heart long before. "I—I liked what you did, but—but you can leave now." He closed his eyes. He looked ridiculous, he knew, his cock iron-hard and reddened, his trousers tangled around his feet. If he took a step he might trip over them. "I risked my life for her, didn't I? What else do you want?!"

Sylvie made a disgusted noise. "I suppose I won't get anything more eloquent than that from a stableboy," she said. "And do not let it be said I fail in anything I set out to do." Her hand snaked out and grabbed his leg. "Madame would not be happy if I left you unable to concentrate on your work." She squeezed his shaft, dragging her tongue behind her hand.

Henri was too confused to fight her; and a few moments later, he was lost again to sensation. It didn't even upset him when Sylvie said, some time later, "Now! Finish now!" and he obeyed, coming so fiercely he thought he would fall to the floor.

Sylvie laughed, wiping his seed from her mouth. "You are a stupid boy," she said, "but good for a half hour's entertainment. Now put on those clothes."

CHAPTER SEVEN

Henri was only a boy after all. Only a boy, and a stableboy at that. Camille had no reason to care what he did with her maid or with anyone else, if it did not affect her safety, and she knew Sylvie would never allow any harm to come to her. If it was not for her, Sylvie would not have survived childhood. She had further proof: Sylvie might easily have betrayed her already, any number of times. She suspected, more than suspected, that Sylvie was in love with her, or at least imagined she was in love, because she did not know Camille and could never know her. Camille could not allow anyone to know her fully. That was too dangerous.

Camille had enjoyed watching Sylvie pleasure the boy. She had been jealous, it was true, and conscious of feeling guilt, but she hadn't been able to look away from his face, impossible had she been the one kneeling before him. He was so open in his pleasure, so…clean. She tried to imagine him accepting such a service from her, when he still thought of her as his duchess, not as a mere woman. He would likely kneel and beg her never to mention such a demeaning act again. Camille had never thought it particularly demeaning, but then how would she know? She and Maxime had only once reached the act of oral pleasure. The duke had never asked it of her; presumably, he had skilled concubines for that duty. Sylvie must have learned the skill outside the palace, and practiced it there, as well. Otherwise, Camille would have known every detail. She should be glad the girl had liberties which she did not, instead of feeling jealous of her freedom.

As if summoned by her thoughts, Sylvie came into the barn, looking like a well-kept page. Without preamble, she said, "Madame, are you sure we need the boy?"

"He is trustworthy."

"We could have come here on our own," Sylvie pointed out. "It's useful that he draws attention away from us, but once we leave this place, he will be a hindrance."

Camille stared down her nose. "He will be in charge of my horses."

"Kaspar and I—"

"You and Kaspar are to protect *me*. That is easier than caring for my horses, and requires less skill."

"Madame! You have been swayed by—by—" Sylvie flapped her hand, in what Camille chose not to see as an obscene gesture.

"You forget yourself," Camille said coldly. "I am responsible for all this. Not you."

Sylvie's lips tightened and she bowed, short and abrupt, before she hurried outside. Camille sighed. She should not have let the girl even begin to argue with her. That was Sylvie's failing, and Camille's comfort. She grew weary of hearing nothing but, *Yes, Your Grace.*

Henri returned to the duke's stables in the afternoon to fetch one of the stallions. The stallion would not be traveling with them but, as Henri pointed out, he had to follow the usual practice to avoid suspicion. Camille requested that a Warmblood from the mountain region, named Rhubarb, be brought; she'd intended him for Guirlande. Camille sent Sylvie, still in her man's garb, to purchase supplies, Kaspar with her. Wearing a hat, shirt and jacket, Kaspar was far less conspicuous than in his everyday uniform, and might not be remarked. Camille remained behind, wracked by tension and doubt, and wishing she'd had Henri bring her horses inside, so she could at least renew her acquaintance with them. To be so close and have to postpone their reunion still further was painful. She refused to fear that they might not remember her. She tried to read a book of mythological poetry, but it could not hold her attention. She found her sketchbook in her saddlebag, and a stick of charcoal. She sat near the entrance to the tack room, drew horses and reflected.

She would not have been missed yet. Her husband had seemed bent on an all-night debauch, from which he never rose before afternoon. Then he would require soothing of his inevitable headache with brandy, followed by the ministering of his concubines. Now that she was nearly free of him, her fear was tempered more strongly with scorn, and a sense of relief.

She drew him beneath the raised tail of a stallion, being shat upon, and laughed to herself at her childishness.

Camille had never loved her husband. Her father had chosen him, the younger son of a neighboring duke, to seal a treaty and contribute a large influx of cash and property to the privy purse. The young Michel had been handsome, and vigorous in taking his pleasure. He'd had an intensity that had sometimes given her sexual pleasure, as well, which was more than she'd expected of an arranged marriage. For some time, he'd tried to please her, or at least seemed to do so. He'd let her speak in council, and sit in judgment several times a week. He'd elevated one or two of her recommended courtiers to baronetcies, and agreed to consider her recommendations regarding taxation and the tithes received from Maxime's protectorate.

She had hoped to arrive at a place of contentment with Michel. She'd been willing to compromise, and had thought she would be able to convince him to do likewise. He came from the same world of politics and courtiers in which she had been raised. She'd thought he would understand her desire to make their pragmatic marriage benefit the duchy. She hadn't expected she would gradually lose opportunities to speak with him at all, or that he would so quickly embrace the idea that he was the sole ruling power in their partnership. From seeing her own mother, she ought to have known this would happen. Her mother, though, had been the younger daughter of an earl, not the sole heir of a duke. Camille had foolishly thought this made a difference. To Michel, however, she was first and always a woman, and his possession.

Even then, Camille might have tried to love Michel, or at least feel affection, if he hadn't gradually revealed a casual brutality toward his servants, and toward hers. She hadn't realized at the time, but she now suspected Michel had somehow engineered the death of Jarman, who'd been her chief eunuch guard since her childhood. He'd died mere days before she'd agreed to marry. And Michel's callousness had grown worse after the death of her father, when there was no longer anyone whom he cared to impress. She had first found a concubine in his bed—two of them, in fact—the night of her father's funeral. Camille had not refused Michel, now the new duke, her favors—she had bound herself to him by law—but soon his sexual technique could not reconcile her to her intense dislike of his arrogance and selfishness as well as his infidelities.

Gradually, she lost power. He'd taken over one of her days in court, then another, then another, at first saying he did so to give her more time with her horses, then implying that her womanly softness led to poor decisions. She'd argued with him and superficially won, only to find that he rescinded her verdicts. He'd sent away Casimir, the eunuch guard who'd been with her since her adolescence, ostensibly to offer him an early release from his indenture in return for good service, but in fact removing her staunchest protector and confidant. The day came when he'd forbidden her to ride out with the palace guard, because, he said, it gave the appearance of her having more power over them than he did, and if she was seen to enjoy herself with them, who was to say she had not taken some of them for lovers? She could not be seen to be unfaithful. It would put the succession in jeopardy.

The charcoal snapped in her fingers. Camille set her drawing down. Both pieces of the charcoal were too short now to use comfortably. She snapped each one again and again until she was left with a handful of bits the length of her smallest nail, then ground each one thoughtfully underfoot, reducing it to powder.

She folded her small pile of underthings again, wrapped them inside a linen towel, and slid the package into one of her saddlebags. Her sketchbook followed, and the volume of poetry, and a flat box of cosmetics and other items necessary for disguises. Sylvie would be offended. Packing was her task. Camille didn't care. She couldn't sit idle and wait. Once her own saddlebags were packed, she began conditioning the tack the horses would wear. Henri had brought her own saddle for Guirlande, she noted, which looked as perfect as if it had been in use every day. He appeared to be scrupulous about tending both leather and metal, but a little extra care never hurt. Besides, she loved the smell of oil and leather, with its overtones of horses and freedom.

Her mind went to Henri. She wanted him again. Her body vibrated with craving. She could have Henri; she need merely command him. But did he truly want her? Or had he fucked her before because he felt it was necessary to save her life? And how could she know the truth? She might ask him for sex, and he might comply, but what if he only pretended to want her? Would she then be like the duke?

She told herself it didn't matter, so long as she had Henri. Even a partner who felt pity for her was better than the duke. But she found it difficult to make herself believe the lie. She had sensed a sweetness about Henri. Even while dominating her, he had treated her with tenderness. It was that she wanted, only more. She wasn't sure if a relationship of equals was even possible. Even aside from their relative status, she was twenty years older than he, and she had no idea how to go about such interaction. She'd never had an equal, except perhaps Maxime, and him only briefly. It would be terribly unwise, in her current situation. She should never even consider putting herself into such a vulnerable position, ever again.

Henri had youth, comely features and long eyelashes. Even in ill-fitting and dirty clothing, he moved with grace. Given the chance, he could easily catch the eye of a rich lady of the court, who could keep him in style. Lady Cornaline, for instance, or the young widow the Countess Ramier. Camille snarled and twisted her polishing cloth in her hands. An instant later, discipline took over and she set to work again.

Perhaps an hour later, Camille heard hooves approaching, a horse at a gallop. She ran to the doorway, bridle in one hand and cloth in the other, determined to see. She'd left most of her fear behind in the palace. From a distance it was clear there was no danger; Henri rode Rhubarb bareback, jumping him over a small bush here and some plant clippings there, letting the stallion burn off some of his energy. Camille found herself smiling. The boy's seat was not just secure, but a thing of beauty.

He saw her from across the paddock and cantered up to the barn door, grinning hugely. He had no idea, Camille knew, how lovely his smile was; he had no trace of vanity. After knowing so many preening courtiers, she felt this was one of his most attractive traits.

"Your Grace," he said. "He's glorious! Would you like to ride him? He's well-mannered." He flushed. "Oh. He's really yours, isn't he. You can ride him whenever you wish."

Camille hung the bridle and cloth on a hook, and picked up the man's hat Sylvie had given her as a disguise. With that and her loose jacket, from a distance she ought to be safe from curious eyes. She now knew she'd hear another horse's approach, and any guards would come in a group. After quickly covering her hair and pulling on her gloves, she walked into the yard. The mares and gelding were far across the pasture, too far to go to just now. She would visit with them later. Now, she would ride. Her heart beat faster with excitement. "Give me a hand up."

Henri gingerly held out one hand and extended his foot, to give her a step. He blushed furiously. Camille hoisted her habit's skirt in one hand and in a few moments was astride a horse, for the first time in four years.

She gloried in the minute shifts of muscle beneath her, in the hum of living power along the stallion's skin. The scent of horse rose up around her. Laughing aloud, she clasped her arms firmly around Henri's slender waist. She could feel his muscles shifting, too. His smell reminded her of mulled wine. "Glorious!" she agreed.

Henri glanced at her over his shoulder. "Where would you like to go, Your Grace?"

"There's a stream nearby. You know it?"

Henri brought the stallion to a walk, then a trot, then a brisk canter. The high grass flicked her boots like tiny whips. The stallion's hooves crushed out the blissful scent of spring. Camille felt the strain in her long-unused riding muscles, but didn't care. So long as she was riding a powerful horse bareback in the sunlight, nothing could be wrong with the world.

In a few moments, Henri said, "Your Grace—"

"Yes, Henri?"

"I—I—"

"Why don't we gallop him the rest of the way?" Camille said, when it was clear no more words were forthcoming. She clapped one hand onto her hat, to make sure it didn't fly off at the greater speed.

"Yes, Your Grace."

Camille caught the green smell of the stream a few moments after the stallion's head lifted with interest. She had ridden by the water many times when she'd still been allowed to ride, some days splashing in the shallows, some days jumping the water's width. It had been her haven even before that, when she'd leave her lessons, saddle her pony, Poire, and sally forth with only a single eunuch to guard her. Today, it looked different; trees larger, streambanks smaller. After dismounting, she strode through tall grass and clouds of wildflowers to gaze down at the water. It slid over algaed rocks slick and shiny as her most precious emeralds.

Henri tied Rhubarb to a bush and quickly checked the horse's legs and feet. Camille smiled to see him taking such care. He turned before her smile had faded, and blushed. Since that one timeless moment in the barn that morning, he seemed to have rediscovered his nervousness. He bent over his boots, scrubbing them with a fistful of grass, then sat and yanked them off, possibly as a delaying tactic.

"Walk with me," Camille said.

"Yes, Your Grace."

"Henri," she said, eyeing him. "You needn't say *Your Grace* as part of every sentence you address to me."

"Y-yes." He looked determinedly at the ground as they walked. He'd abandoned his boots in the grass. Inspiration struck. She caught his arm, and he looked at her.

"We will be on the road for some time. Will you help me take off my boots? I would like to walk in the grass until it's time to return."

His eyes widened, then he nodded. "Of course, Your Grace."

In her mind, Camille sighed. She found a rock on which to sit and, mindful of Henri's attention, gathered her skirts in both hands, pulling them to her knees. The russet braid twisting along her hem just brushed the tops of her boots. She pointed one toe and Henri dropped to his knees. His broad palms, long squared fingers and reddened knuckles looked coarse and masculine next to the filigreed gold inlay on the heel of her boot. Camille imagined his hand on her bare foot, encompassing it, stroking, the roughness of his skin rasping her delicate arch; she leaned forward, pressing her boot into his grasp.

Henri fumbled with the strap across her ankle, pinching the filigree buckle between two fingers as if afraid to break it. Camille rotated her ankle, so she could nudge her toe against his knee. He glanced up, blushing, then looked down at the grass. "I'm sorry!"

"You have nothing to be sorry for," Camille said briskly, then regretted it, for she sounded like his mother. She swallowed and said, "You need not unfasten the buckle. It is for decoration. Just grab the heel and pull."

Henri took a deep breath and began to work the boot off her foot a bit at a time, his gaze intent on her toes. Camille closed her eyes. She wasn't sure if he was too afraid to yank the boot off as Sylvie would have done, or if he simply wanted to prolong the moment. Camille had every intention of prolonging the moment. Subtly, she tugged her skirt higher, baring a bit of her silk stockings.

Henri didn't notice what she'd done until he'd pulled her boot entirely free of her foot and glanced up; then he reddened all the way to his ears, and hurriedly bent to the second boot. He removed it more quickly than the first, rose, gathered both boots together, and asked, "Would you like a hand up, Your Grace?"

Camille tugged off her gloves, one finger at a time, and tucked them into her jacket. She held up her bare hands for

Henri to grasp, palms upturned. He looked at her hands, then to her face. He seemed about to speak. Camille waited. He took her hands and pulled her to her feet.

She didn't let go of his hands when his grip loosened. "Henri," she said. "If you do not want me, tell me now."

His hands moved restlessly in hers. "You don't have to do this, Your Grace," he said, in a rush. "I will do my best to protect you. You don't have to give me— I don't expect you ever to—" He took a deep breath. "It doesn't matter anymore, if you become pregnant."

Camille couldn't bear it. "Stop." She tugged on his hands, pulling him closer to her, until his bare dirty toes dug into the grass a handspan from her own feet. For her, she supposed, every seduction eventually had to become command. "It is not your duty to protect me, Henri. That is Kaspar's duty. Your duty is to care for my horses and to care for me, in whatever way I require, whether that includes providing me with an heir, or not. Can you do this?"

"Yes, Your Grace," he whispered. He lifted her hands to his mouth and pressed his lips to her skin, more fervent and seductive than any courtier's kiss. "I'm not fit for you—"

"You are what I command," Camille said. He looked frightened. Had she sounded like the duke? She forced a smile. "I have not asked you to fight an army of barbarians, have I? It is a simple thing. I want you to be with me when I require it. If the duty is too onerous, you have only to refuse me now."

"Are you sure that it's me who should—"

"Will you do this for me?"

Henri didn't hesitate. "Anything, Your Grace." He kissed her hands again.

Camille realized she still didn't know how Henri felt about this new duty. Was he truly willing? Did it matter, so long as his actions felt true? She'd spent most of her life without trust. She could get along without it now, so long as she did not have to do so alone. She would replace her fear from the past two decades with sensual pleasure, taken at her own command and no one else's. It would have to be enough.

CHAPTER EIGHT

One day into the escape, it seemed like an ordinary journey, perhaps to a horse fair. True, the back of Henri's neck itched unceasingly, and he could not stop himself from flinching whenever other travelers passed them. Her Grace had told him to flee if he saw any of the palace guards, but of course he would never abandon her like that; he would have to at least try to defend her. Sylvie might not like him, but she would need his help, until the eunuch guard, who covered their retreat, caught up to them.

Aside from the danger of being captured and killed, this journey was pleasant for Henri. Rain pattered on the hood and shoulders of his cloak, and he marveled at how dry he remained beneath its protection, and how warm from the spring chill. He'd never had a wool cloak before. He didn't really think he should have one now, since a boy and his tutor would be unlikely to pamper their groom, but Sylvie had insisted, and now he was glad of it, because his new clothes would be soaked otherwise, like the cuffs of his shirt and Tulipe's hide. Perhaps she was right; if the boy whom Sylvie acted was an aristocrat's son, then his servants might be better dressed, especially a higher level servant like the tutor who was the duchess's disguise. Though Sylvie made him feel clumsy and stupid, he was glad she was with them, to take care of things like disguises.

He wondered how Sylvie would disguise Kaspar when they met him tomorrow at the inn. A traveling mercenary? A merchant? Someone's grandmother?

He also wondered how well the eunuch could ride. Henri had surprised himself by feeling possessive of the horses. He'd given Lilas to Sylvie, so he could lead the gentler Tonnelle with the pack mule, and found that he could not stop himself from watching her and noting any awkwardness in her seat. She needed to be more giving with the horse's mouth, and less insistent with her off leg. He was sure Sylvie would not like him to say so, and perhaps his duchess would not, either. His job was to care for the horses and school them as needed, not to instruct his betters. He supposed it didn't matter, so long as it was clear Sylvie was not used to riding sidesaddle. That would give her boy disguise away immediately.

These thoughts could not long distract him from the duchess.

He swallowed a lump in his throat when he recalled her reunion with Guirlande in the early hours of the morning. She'd stood in the muddy paddock for several minutes with her arm flung over the mare's withers and her face pressed to the mare's neck while rain streamed down over them both. Sylvie had moved to draw her inside, but Henri had stopped her with a hand on her arm. "We'll all be soaked soon enough," he said.

He looked ahead, to the voluminous cloak on Guirlande's back. His duchess's seat was perfect in every way; he could tell merely from the way Guirlande walked, confident and balanced, perfectly in hand. He was glad the duchess rode astride. A sidesaddle would be sacrilege for one with such a seat. It was the first thing he had admired about her, and the thing he had most grieved for when the duke had forbidden her riding. As a boy, he had seen her ride before he had known she was the duchess; it made him more comfortable to remember that. In that one thing, he was not her equal but he thought he might at least share her feelings. He had been exhilarated riding with her, just they two, the day before. When he'd seen her wind-blown hair and reddened cheeks, the shine in her gray eyes, he had wanted to kiss her.

He found himself staring at the column of her back, then at her booted calf pressed to Guirlande's side, not the same boot as yesterday, but a much plainer one with a square toe that looked more like something a man might wear. It was lucky her feet were not tiny.

He swallowed hard, remembering her bare feet in the grass. Her feet were long and elegant, with blue veins tracing along their tops, and long toes that arched as they dug into the ground. Her feet might arch like that if he—

A tree branch slapped his face, dunking cold water down his collar. Henri sputtered, covering his clumsiness by glancing back at Tonnelle and Tigre, the pack mule. They followed placidly, unmoved by the rain. He adjusted the lead rope anyway, then rose in his stirrups for a few strides to stretch his legs and rearrange himself within his snug new leathers. The duchess might want him to give her pleasure, but that would not include the intimacies he dreamed of, intimacies of more than the flesh.

Someday, he would see Nicolette again, or find someone like her, whom he could love and caress with all that was within him. The duchess could never be that woman for him. He might admire her with all his heart, but he had his place in the world. He must remember that she had once offered him gold. To her, he was only a passing fancy. Another kind of servant.

By the time they reached the inn, called The First Swan, Henri's cloak had surrendered to the weather and he was wet to the skin. He removed the cloak to tend the horses—no one paid for grooms at an inn when they had their own. When he had finished he was cold to the bone, but the horses and mule were dry and warm and fed.

The duchess had directed him to eat in the common room after much argument with Sylvie about whether it would be safer than having food sent up to their room. The duchess had won by pointing out they could survey the inn's patrons.

When he slipped through the common room's door, a wall of heat and stifling odors pushed at him. Immense hearths blazed at opposite ends of the long room, one bordered by old men in chairs, the other surrounded by a kneeling, shouting group playing at dice. Tallow candles flickered and dripped in a central chandelier of beaten iron, lighting clusters of scarred, heavy wooden tables. Men played cards in one corner and some game involving pegs and a board in another. A group of whores had engaged the third corner, chatting brightly, fondling and teasing their potential clients. In the fourth corner, a panting couple partially obscured by a cloak-rack revealed that their business had progressed beyond the negotiation. Henri looked away quickly, inhaling the scents of roasting lamb and unwashed humans and molten tallow and acrid woodsmoke.

He could not immediately locate Sylvie and the duchess, until he remembered they would have shed their cloaks upstairs. In the corner nearest the whores, he caught sight of Sylvie's boyish cap bent over a tall mug, with the duchess's soft, pouchy hat next to it. Even remembering her disguise, Henri still winced to see the false gray beard she wore. It hung down over her chest and looked the worse for being rained on throughout the day. The beard did provide an admirable distraction from her womanly shape, or what remained of it after Sylvie had performed her magic with strips of linen and scraps of leather.

Henri was glad Sylvie hadn't taken it into her head to dress *him* as a girl. Of course, she had warned him that their disguises would change over the journey, so perhaps he was not yet safe from that fate.

He made free with his elbows and fought his way through the crowd to their tiny table. He pulled off his cap and ducked his head. "Greetings, my masters," he said, in case anyone was listening.

Sylvie looked up at him and said, "You're wet, boy."

The duchess gestured for him to sit on the stool between them. A trio of the whores shouted and clapped for attention: there would be a performance. At the moment, Henri's only appetite was for food, but in the crowd and sudden rush of orders for drink, he couldn't get anyone's attention.

The duchess threw one arm over Henri's shoulders and pulled him against her heavy scholar's robe, which smelled of wet sheep but, he fancied, also of her. He shifted his stool and leaned back against her bosom, remembering the false beard when it scratched his neck.

He would look like a man's catamite. He gasped and tried to sit up, but the duchess did not release him. Sylvie chortled behind her hand. Henri peered at the duchess from beneath his lashes. She was smiling; he could see the crinkles at the corners of her silvery eyes. He sighed and relaxed against her. It was his duty, and she was warm, and he wanted to be close to her however he could.

By the time the whores' entertainment progressed from lurid songs to dancing, Henri had obtained bread, a bowl of shredded roast lamb and a dish of cooked greens with onions. He devoured it all. A tavern maid brought them a flagon of red wine, coarse enough to bring tears to his eyes and hot sunlight to his stomach. Soon his fingers had regained their flexibility and his hair began to dry in the close warmth. Someone played a pipe and numerous men beat time on the tables with their hands and tin mugs. Henri was too sleepy to watch. The noise blurred when he closed his eyes and leaned back against the duchess.

She dragged her gloved hand through his hair, touched his cheek, then wrapped her arm firmly around his waist, tugging him even nearer than before. She leaned close to his ear and murmured, "Watch, Henri."

Her hot breath tickled against his skin; he shivered and obediently focused on the three whores. Two of them danced with each other, hands joined. Neither wore a tucker in her bodice, and he could see the dark edges of their nipples peeping in and out with their movements. He paid more attention. Occasionally, their breasts bumped together, and he could tell this wasn't accidental. One of the women, the skinny one with dark curls and brown skin, wore a lazy grin as she taunted the audience and teased her partner. The other, a plump moon-pale woman with a squint, looked almost savage as she tried to get closer and her partner retreated. Henri wasn't sure if that was part of the show or not. He felt as if he was watching a private argument between lovers.

The third whore had taken over a table. She moved slowly, deliberately, balancing on one foot and taking positions that revealed glimpses of her bare legs, then her breasts spilling from her bodice, then the curve of her round bottom. She was very beautiful, even with her pockmarked face. Then she held out a hand and a slender man joined her on the table, to rowdy cheers. The two embraced, kissing openmouthed and roving their hands over hips and buttocks. Watching, Henri felt their touches like phantoms on his own skin.

The duchess's arm tensed around him. Her other hand rested on his leg. She wore gloves to conceal her feminine hands, but Henri still felt the heat of her skin. She squeezed the muscle on the top of his thigh, once; lightning shot up toward his hip.

He didn't dare look at Sylvie to see if she'd noticed. He feared if he moved or looked at the duchess, she would push him away.

On the table-become-stage, the slender man loosened his partner's bodice, tugging the laces first with one hand, then the other while she leaned backward with perfect balance, arms behind her, proffering her breasts. Henri leaned toward them, his palms aching to cup her bosom in his own hands, and taste her skin with his tongue.

A firm hand on his belly sucked out his breath, pulling him backward. The duchess mouthed his neck, her lips soft and damp amidst the scratchy horsehair beard. A warm shudder rippled all the way to his toes. He tipped his head to give her better access, and she said into his ear, "Watch them. Aren't they beautiful? They want each other. They are truly lovers."

Henri wasn't sure if he'd really heard yearning in her voice. He dragged open his eyes and stared. The woman's bodice fell open and, just as he had imagined, her partner caught her breasts in his hands and laved them with his tongue. Her fingers tangled around his neck, then yanked off his cap. Long hair cascaded past his shoulders, and he arched, thrusting his chest against hers.

The duchess worked Henri's jacket loose. She dragged her hand from his belly to his breast, abrading his nipple against his damp shirt, an almost-pain spiking in his chest. Her teeth scraped against his neck, then her tongue laid a wet trail beneath his chin and down the thin skin over his throat. His mouth watered with his desire to kiss her, to mark her lower lip with his own teeth. Her other hand clenched and un-clenched on his thigh, each squeeze shooting more blood into his cock. He could not distract himself from the sensations by touching her in return. He looked up at the performers.

The woman pushed the man's coat from his shoulders. It fell to the table beneath them. She laid hands on his chest and rubbed, dislodging his shirt and revealing a band of red cloth. She bent her head and mouthed him there, leaving wet marks, and squeezed him roughly. He threw his head back and placed his feet wide; she thrust her thigh between his legs, and he rode down on it, rocking to the speeding drumbeat of hands on tables. Or *she* did. They were both women. The woman in the skirt unwound the red chest restraint, letting it trail down to the floor, and with each layer removed, more of the second woman's lush bosom took shape. Henri could almost feel it forming inside his grasping hands.

The duchess's hand circled on his belly, a soothing motion until she traced a single finger down the line of his swelling cock. He couldn't breathe. Someone would see. He didn't care. She had to touch him again, just there, or he would shake himself to flinders inside. His lips formed a plea; as if she'd heard the words in his mind, she trailed her gloved finger up his cock, then outlined his shape with two spread fingers, and rubbed his length with her thumb. The seam of her glove caught his cock's head and he gasped. "Watch them," the duchess murmured in his ear.

The women on stage twisted against each other, the trousered woman sliding and grinding along the other's thigh, one hand plunged down the back of her partner's skirt, kneading her buttocks, the other flicking against her partner's stiff red nipple. Both cried out, not in practiced sequence: ragged, breathy cries, rising and falling, audible in the abrupt lack of music and drums. Then the music began again, more loudly.

The duchess gripped him firmly with her whole hand, slowly squeezing his length, then again, faster yet still tortuous; not nearly as quickly as Henri would have stroked himself for relief. His neck arched and the back of his skull cracked against her collarbone. The performers' cries reverberated in his own head, noise he couldn't let free. His hand twitched toward the buttons of his fly, involuntarily. The duchess's free hand clamped atop his. "Undo them," she said in his ear. "I want you to come."

He felt her words like the caress of a tongue. His fingers fumbled in one-handed haste. She plunged her gloved hand inside, the thin goat leather rubbing him like some strange foreign skin, searching out and shaping and finally grasping, pulling him toward relief. Fluid leaked from his cock's tiny mouth. She used her thumb to spread the liquid over the head of his cock and slick her glove, easing her motion. The table hid her hands; he hoped it hid enough. Everyone watched the performers, tacitly ignoring the weakness of their fellow voyeurs.

"Watch," the duchess said. The performers subsided onto the table. The trousered woman fluttered her partner's skirt above her waist and knelt between her knees, bending to kiss and lick at her cunt. The drumming began again, then the pipes. He felt his hips jerk in reaction to the hard pressure of the duchess's thumb. Tears welled in his eyes; sweat spilled behind his knees. He no longer cared if anyone saw. She bit the corded muscle on the side of his neck and stroked his cock again, slower, as if soothing. "Let me know that you like this," she said. She brushed the tip of her tongue inside his ear.

He could not resist her. He rolled his head to the side and moaned into her neck. "Please," he said. "Just, just—"

"You are mine. Feel what I am doing to you."

Henri closed his eyes and felt. He clamped his lips shut over his own cries. In moments, a burn like alcohol shot down his spine and he spurted into her hand, writhing back against her as each spasm wrung his muscles.

He was hers, he had no doubt. But now he would go to sleep in the barn. No matter what they did together, no matter how good it felt, she could never be truly his.

CHAPTER NINE

In their narrow inn bedchamber, Sylvie shot home the door's bolt, then shoved the washstand beneath it; a wise precaution, given the rowdy crowd downstairs, whom Camille could still hear through the floor. The room wasn't as plush as the rooms in the ducal palace, of course, but it was cleaner than she had expected it to be. The only inns in which she'd stayed before had been between the duchy and the king's court, and all of those had catered to the nobility. This one normally housed merchants, some of them wealthy, and a wide variety of travelers of varying social status. She'd seen a few scruffy men downstairs, but had no idea if they were poorly dressed because they couldn't afford better or because of hard travel. They'd certainly behaved as if they had status, commanding the presence of the tavern maids with great frequency before the whores' show had begun.

This room was furnished with a single bed, wide enough to accommodate two if they were not wary of touching. Hooks on the wall took the place of a wardrobe. The table was large enough to hold a single tray and nothing else. From her seat in the room's only chair, Camille watched Sylvie's round bottom as she bent to add their saddlebags to the barrier against the door. It was a good thing the man's coat Sylvie had worn earlier fell to midthigh, or someone might have spotted her disguise. That telltale would never have occurred to Camille before the show she'd seen in the common room earlier that evening.

Surreptitiously, she wiped her hand along her dark scholar's robe. She still fancied she could feel Henri's hot, solid cock in her palm, though she'd never touched it skin to skin. She'd reduced him to moans in a public dining room; he'd come all over her hand. She'd had to borrow Sylvie's napkin to clean them off before Henri went to sleep in the stable. She hadn't come, but making him do so had made her burn. She fairly hummed with the power of it.

If she went out there now, he could take her in an empty stall, she gripping the edge of a manger, he pummeling her from behind.

She was losing her mind. Midlife came upon men sometimes this way, but from where had her own sudden lusts arisen?

Apparently satisfied with their safety, Sylvie divested herself of her short sword and belt knife, laying them atop the washstand. She nudged the chamber pot with her foot and said, "Madame, I do not think we should leave this room tonight." Disapproval tinged her voice as she added, "We have already risked enough, letting others see us in the common room."

She'd done it to defy her fear, and once she'd distracted herself with Henri, she'd been successful. Lifting a brow,

Camille said, "Do you think a lecher with his catamite will be confused with an errant duchess?"

Sylvie frowned. "That is for madame to say."

"Sylvie," Camille said. "I am no longer the duchess, you know. Not on this journey. The duke will have declared me dead, or worse."

"We've heard nothing of that, and we would have heard tonight," Sylvie said. She knelt at Camille's feet and tugged off her boots, then her stockings. She looked up. "I am sorry I cannot offer madame a bath."

"You need not apologize for things I know very well I cannot have," Camille said. She stood, and Sylvie unknotted the belt of her scholar's robe, tugging the fabric from Camille's shoulders as she turned. Beneath, she wore a simple linen tunic and pantaloons, worn almost as soft as the silk she preferred. If not for the bindings around her breasts, she would have been more comfortable than in her own apartments in the palace.

"Sit, madame," Sylvie said. She loosed Camille's hair and massaged her scalp for a few moments before dabbing oil on the glue that secured her false beard. Camille closed her eyes, enjoying being tended. It was a pity Kaspar was not here. He could have helped with the other part of her that needed tending.

Once the beard was off, Sylvie laid it carefully aside, ready to be reapplied in the morning. She bent close and wiped Camille's face with lotion and a soft cloth. Camille felt her soft breath on her cheeks.

Sylvie said, "Madame?"

"Out with it," she said. Sylvie rarely hesitated to speak her mind, and Camille allowed it; she wanted and needed her honesty.

Sylvie gestured for Camille to stand. She loosened the neck of Camille's tunic until it fell around her waist and unfastened her breast bindings. Focused on her work, she said, "The boy could not have disguised you as I have."

Amused, Camille said, "There is no reason for you to be jealous."

"He is beneath you."

"I would like that, yes." Camille smiled and licked her lips.

Sylvie jerked free the leather placard that transformed Camille's curves into flatness. Camille sighed and tried to rub at her sore breasts, but Sylvie fended her off. "I am not finished."

It would not do to say she wanted to be left alone to finish undressing herself. Also, it was not true. "Perhaps when you are finished, you could massage me." Ruefully, Camille explained, "I have lost my strength for riding, and find my muscles are a bit stiff."

"Of course, madame. But that will not stop you from thinking."

"I said nothing about—"

"You cannot hide from me, madame. You are worried, and rightfully so. We sat in plain sight downstairs, after arriving with so many fine horses—the rain will have helped to distract observers, if we are lucky, but I still think—"

"Enough! I require your assistance." Camille wished Sylvie

had kept her mouth closed. She had not needed to reiterate the risks they'd taken. Camille had quite enough nervous energy already.

Sylvie said, "I will of course be glad to massage you, but I think a more thorough distraction might be in order." She unwound the remainder of the breast bindings, pulled the tunic over Camille's head, then herself cradled Camille's bosom in her palms.

Disconcerted, Camille looked down at her breasts over-flowing Sylvie's small hands. "Sylvie—"

"Please, madame. Let me show you that I can take care of you as well as that ignorant boy." Her touch changed. One moment, it was the careful yet neutral touch Camille felt every day of her life; the next, warmth and deliberate friction of Sylvie's rough-ened skin, never so well cared for as Camille's own.

Camille's breasts were so tender, both from the day's con-finement and from what she'd done to Henri, that Sylvie's caress blushed warmth down to her belly. She had never thought she could feel such a sexual hum from a woman's touch. Perhaps once she'd betrayed Michel for the first time, with Henri, each subsequent betrayal grew easier and more pleasurable. Had it begun this way, for Michel? No. She refused to believe she could be like Michel in any way.

When Camille said nothing, Sylvie lifted one hand to her face, stroking her thumb over her cheekbone. Camille swal-lowed. "You are afraid I will make you sleep on the floor," she said, with a quick glance at the single narrow bed.

Sylvie stepped back, letting her hands fall to her sides. She said, "I am skilled, madame. You would not be sorry."

"I thought you preferred men," Camille said.

"Men are different," Sylvie said. "My first lover was another girl."

Camille thought of saying that she'd never had a woman for a lover, then decided she would sound foolish, and possibly insulting, as if she was considering this only for novelty value. Though her true reason might be considered insulting, as well; Camille felt guilty. She knew, had known for several years, that Sylvie loved her to a degree that Camille considered infatuation, and was loyal to her own detriment. In return, Camille had never protected Sylvie as well as she should have; more than once, as she'd lost power in the court, one of Michel's favorites had pressed his attentions on the girl, solely because he knew that Camille lacked the power to strike back. That Sylvie had escaped being abused spoke more of Sylvie's fighting skills than anything Camille, her ostensible protector, had done. And now Camille had taken up with a stableboy whom she hardly knew, instead of the girl who'd served her since the age of sixteen.

Sylvie deserved better of her, even if all she could give was flawed. She could easily guess what reward the girl would prefer. Camille took Sylvie's slender shoulders in her hands and pushed her toward the bed. Sylvie braced her feet. "Let me show you," she said. "You can trust me."

"After," Camille said, to retain control over the situation. She pushed again, and this time Sylvie went, until the backs of her knees hit the bed's edge.

Sylvie said, "Let me take off my boots."

Camille sat next to her on the bed, considering what to do first. It would be all too easy to let Sylvie lead, but unwise if she wanted to hold on to her authority. She wanted to make Sylvie come undone with pleasure, Sylvie who was never at a loss. She couldn't afford to let go, herself.

This would never have happened in the ducal palace. Events were ordered there. Every single person in the palace had their proper place and role. It had taken Camille a vast effort to think of how she could move differently than the world's plan. In her old world, the duke commanded her at his will; her eunuchs served her safety and her pleasure; Sylvie and the other maids served her physical needs. Yet her eunuchs and Sylvie had helped to save her life. Now Camille would serve Sylvie's pleasure, and Sylvie hers.

Sylvie half turned toward her, an odd expression on her face, and Camille realized it was shyness. Sylvie, shy. She looked like Henri, so young and trusting. She looked like everything Camille had lost, everything she could only touch in this way.

Camille took Sylvie's face in her hands and carefully kissed the girl's forehead, then each of her cheeks, then her mouth, a moth's fluttering. Before she could draw back, Sylvie leaned forward and kissed her, an openmouthed nudge with the briefest flicker of her tongue's tip. Camille rested her hand on

Sylvie's shoulder, holding her in place, and responded with a slightly deeper kiss.

Sylvie's mouth felt small to Camille, and softer than a man's. She liked that she was not abraded by stubble, at the same time that she missed the rough sensation. While they kissed, Sylvie's hands slid down to her breasts, and lightly squeezed them; that felt good, but unlike Henri's urgent touch. Something intangible was missing, like a scent or a vibration in the air. Or—not missing, but nearly so. Camille concentrated on the specific shape of Sylvie's mouth, on her taste, on her petal-soft skin. After a few minutes, she was able to settle into enjoyment of the subtler pleasures of a woman's kiss.

Sylvie was not so distanced. Camille could feel it in the urgent grasp of the girl's hands, in her rapid breathing when Camille kneaded her shoulder or her arm.

It felt good to be in control. She pulled open the throat of Sylvie's shirt, leaned in, and pressed her mouth to Sylvie's pulse point, lightly sucking. The vibration of Sylvie's moan hummed against Camille's lips, so she continued her exploration while her hands joined Sylvie's in removing her boy's shirt. It was frustrating to have that done, only to have her fingers bump hard against the leather and bindings that hid her bosom.

"Let me," Sylvie said. Her normally agile hands fumbled as she ripped at the linen, tugged out the leather busk and scrabbled the whole assemblage into a pile on the floor. Camille managed not to laugh. She pressed Sylvie back onto the feather mattress, shifting their position until they lay full-length.

Camille propped herself over Sylvie and looked at her. Sylvie's pupils had gone wide and dark; her lips were swollen from their kisses, and her cheeks and throat showed the blood rush of arousal. Camille cupped one of the girl's small breasts in her hand, sweeping her thumb over the nipple and gently squeezing the soft flesh. It was firmer than her own breast, the nipple longer and more pink than brown. Sylvie's eyes fluttered closed, her lips parting. It was fascinating, as if she could look in a mirror and see herself aroused by a mysterious other. Camille straddled Sylvie's hips and set to exploring her breasts, feeling another rush of satisfaction each time Sylvie's breath caught. Eventually, she gave in to curiosity and bent to capture one of Sylvie's nipples between her lips.

"Madame—" Sylvie gasped. Her fingers convulsed on Camille's shoulders.

Taking this as encouragement, Camille rolled the nipple between her lips. It was hotter than she'd expected, hotter than Sylvie's lips or the skin of her neck. Experimentally, Camille squeezed, careful not to use her teeth. Sylvie's back arched, and she moaned. Camille's belly went hollow at the sound, so she continued the torment. When she settled in to suck hard at Sylvie's nipples, she felt an answering pull in her own womb.

She traced Sylvie's ribs, caressed the thin skin over her jutting hip bone, then worked her fingers beneath the waist of her riding leathers, hinting at things to come. Remembering what she'd seen in the common room, she shifted to press her mound against Sylvie's thigh, undulating her hips with each sucking pull of her lips on Sylvie's nipple. Her linen pantaloons had come untied and slid down to her hip bones; Camille took a moment to shove them off before pressing herself against Sylvie again. Soon her skin was slippery with sweat.

In her mind, the noise from downstairs transformed into the steady drumbeats of the performance she'd seen. Camille imagined herself and Sylvie laid out on a table, men peering closely, talking amongst themselves and commenting on her actions. It wasn't the same as being watched by the duke. These men did not know her, knew nothing about her except that she was an instrument of pleasure. She had to do well, to impress them; her livelihood would depend on it.

She replaced her mouth with her hand and kissed Sylvie's soft mouth again, tasting the inside of her cheeks and sucking her tongue. Sylvie responded enthusiastically, sliding her hands down Camille's back. She hooked her leg over Camille's hip and ground upward, yielding new and extremely pleasant friction of Camille's bare quim against Sylvie's leathers.

Her imaginary audience would be pleased, but restless. Camille rubbed against Sylvie one last time, then sat up and unfastened the leathers, peeling them down over Sylvie's bony hips. Camille was startled to find no pantaloons, but then again, where would she hide them? She already carried a handkerchief there, to simulate a cock. Camille used the handkerchief to tease Sylvie's breasts and neck.

Sylvie snatched the handkerchief and tossed it on the floor. "Please, madame, hurry."

Camille gazed down at her sternly. "I will proceed at the pace I choose."

Sylvie's eyes widened, and for a moment, Camille thought she would protest. Then, slowly, she lowered her eyes and turned her head to the side. Her breathing sped up, and her tongue flicked her lips. She said, "You may punish me if you wish."

Camille wanted to smack Sylvie's round bottom. It was clear Sylvie would enjoy it, or she would not have requested it. But Camille had not struck a servant since she'd been a willful teenager, and the implications, even under these circumstances, made her feel dizzy. She could not strike this girl, even in play. She drew a deep breath, her eyes on the pulse beat in Sylvie's throat. "Take off your leathers." Obediently, Sylvie wriggled them down to her knees. Camille pulled them the rest of the way off and studied Sylvie's quim. Luxurious golden-brown curls sprang at her touch. She thought for a moment, then said, "You will remain silent, no matter what I do."

"Yes, madame," Sylvie breathed, wriggling beneath her hand.

Camille combed through Sylvie's damp curls, trying to regain her equilibrium. Sylvie laid her hand atop Camille's, half lacing their fingers together, and guided her hand. Camille smiled. "You are a very impatient girl."

Sylvie smiled back at her, laying her free hand over her own mouth.

Camille traced one finger down Sylvie's slit, over and over, each time pressing a little harder. When she bent close, she could see the tiny droplets of wetness clinging like dewdrops. Camille smeared the fluid with her palm, then pulled Sylvie's lips apart. She blew on the hood of her clitoris and was surprised when Sylvie stiffened and shuddered. She had intended to kiss her there, but this was more entertaining; Camille blew a directed stream of air this time, cooling the hot flesh her hands had exposed. Sylvie grabbed at the air, then the blanket. Camille nudged her middle finger into Sylvie's quim and thrust it like a tiny cock, alternating her other hand and her breath to tease Sylvie's clitoris.

Camille's arousal grew as Sylvie's breathing changed to gasps. Her own wetness trickled down between her thighs, slicking them as she shifted position. Camille settled in next to Sylvie again, pulling the girl's leg firmly between her own and teasing herself with twitches of her hips. She slid another finger into Sylvie, then another, gasping a little herself when Sylvie's inner muscles gripped her tightly and pulled. "Be still," she said. "I forbid you to come yet."

Sylvie drew in a long breath. Camille withdrew her fingers. She didn't think Sylvie would be able to resist climax for very long, but she could tell from the heat in her face that the command had excited her. Camille waited a while, idly teasing a curl, then leaned close to her ear. She said, "I am going to make you come. I want to hear you now," and slid her fingers back into Sylvie's quim, this time squeezing hard with her thumb.

Sylvie's moan seemed wrung from deep in her belly, and startled an answering gasp from Camille. Sylvie clutched desperately. Camille rubbed and thrust, driving her toward climax, panting with effort.

When Sylvie peaked, Camille felt the flutters on her fingers, the taut inner contractions and gush of wetness that echoed her final, whimpering cries. Camille was unable to look aside or pull away or do anything but stare in wonder at Sylvie's face as she rode her climax. When Sylvie relaxed into the mattress, Camille almost could not bear to look at her. Her eyes were damp with tears which she could not explain.

She should not have done this. She could not let Sylvie see the same vulnerability she'd just seen, but to refuse would be a terrible insult. Camille's heart tightened in dread.

Then Sylvie reached for her, and Camille went into her arms. She was good at control. She would simply hide her face.

CHAPTER TEN

Sylvie woke to the scent of sex and a sore jaw. She lay on her stomach, partially hanging off the narrow bed, her nose smashed into the very corner of a pillow. She squinted one eye open and was confronted by a heap of gray-streaked dark hair, just visible in the dawn light. The duchess, her mistress. Now in more ways than one.

"Mercy," she whispered, remembering. It was a great pity that madame had not enjoyed herself more. Oh, she had found pleasure in the act—Sylvie had made sure of that—but it was clear she would not become an inveterate lover of women, or even one like Sylvie, who found women equally as interesting as men, and sometimes yielding greater intensity of emotion.

Sylvie sighed. Madame might have been so different. A mere hint from her, and Sylvie would have submitted to being tied, gagged, blindfolded, smacked, whipped. From such as the duchess, it would have been ecstasy. Sylvie shivered at the thought. Given the chance, Sylvie would teach her to love all those things. Yes, a great pity that madame could not forget how the duke had so often treated her. That was at the root of it. If not for him, madame might have enjoyed a great many things that were now tainted.

Twisting her hair into a rough knot, she held it firm with a pair of quills from the scholar costume while she hunted up a cloth and washed. She had tooth powder, but her brush was buried in the saddlebags; she improvised with her finger, then spent a few moments massaging her jaw. She had done yeoman's work for madame with her mouth alone.

The chambermaid would be along soon. She would not know that a man and a boy had rented the room the previous night, so there was no need to resume their disguise just yet; if necessary, she had a story prepared, that they were two whores hired by the tutor, and the poor boy had been sent to sleep in the stable with the groom. If any had seen madame's performance in the common room the night before, no one would doubt this story. Sylvie dismantled her barrier from the night before, lifting the saddlebags rather than dragging them, so as not to wake the duchess. The washstand was more difficult, but she worked it gently from side to side until it no longer blocked the door. The duchess slept on. Sylvie went to sit next to her on the bed, admiring the long curve of her spine into her lush bottom, and the strong tendons at the backs of her thighs. She thought about stroking the length of her, then instead snuggled back into bed, draping her arm over the duchess's waist, the tips of her fingers just brushing the top of her depilated mound. It might be her last chance to be so intimate.

Knuckles rapped the door, startling Sylvie from a half-doze. Before she could leap from the bed, the door opened. Sylvie tried to look bored and satiated, and failed miserably, because instead of a maid, the stableboy stood in the doorway, gaping.

"Shut the door!" she hissed, tumbling from the bed. She found her leathers on the floor and tugged them on, leaving the waist open. Henri at least had the wits to obey orders. He fell back against the closed door, staring at the bed. She rolled her eyes. Did he think madame was his alone?

"Jealous?" she asked, with heavy irony.

"Not...exactly," Henri said. His gaze swept to Sylvie's breasts. He stepped forward, then turned back and shot the door's bolt. "I didn't think the door would open."

"I opened it for the chambermaid," Sylvie explained.

"But, wouldn't she see—"

"I was prepared with an explanation for her," she said. "I do not have to explain myself to *you*."

Henri straightened his back and said, "Her Grace does not have to explain herself to anyone." She might have respected him more for this if she had not also seen the swelling in his trousers. He lusted for madame. She doubted he could distinguish true love and loyalty from his boyish cravings.

The duchess stirred then, and sat up, pushing her hair from her face. Sylvie noted how Henri's eyes went to her bare breasts before he looked to her face. It was clear where his interest lay—on a woman's chest.

The duchess said, "Stop your bickering. Henri, is there danger?"

"No, Your Grace." He took another step closer. "It's raining, very hard. The bridge on our road is underwater. The other grooms told me we should stay another night here."

Sylvie breathed a sigh of relief. Pursuers would also be hampered by the flooded bridge.

"We should be safe," the duchess mused, "if we don't leave the room without our disguises. I hope Kaspar is wise enough to wait and catch up to us later."

Sylvie waited for her to dismiss the boy. Perhaps he could fetch water, and she could help her with her ablutions. Instead, the duchess said, "Henri, come here to me."

Sylvie did not intend to protest, but she must have made some sound. Madame gave her the look which made most of the court's women quail. Sylvie stepped aside, and tidied the clothing they'd dropped to the floor, and trimmed the wick and lit the lamp. She glanced back, though, when the boy reached the duchess. He dropped to his knees beside the bed; she laid a hand on his head, rustling his hair, dislodging a bit of straw. Sylvie's lip curled.

The duchess said, "Today is a good day to begin your other duties. Afterward, you may fetch our breakfast."

"Madame!" Sylvie said. She would fetch their breakfast. She certainly was not going to remain here and watch the boy desecrate the duchess. The eunuchs were one thing. They were her property and her privilege, and were forbidden pleasure for themselves. Sylvie knew the boy was different. She could tell from the unnecessary caresses the duchess bestowed on him, the hint of indulgence in her tone, undetectable to any but her.

"Perhaps you would like to join us," the duchess said. It was not a request. Sylvie did not want to do this, but...but. She had wanted the duchess to punish her, and the boy was her instrument. For madame, she would yield, and she would make the most of it. And she would show the boy how he should behave when the duchess made a simple request. Perhaps she would even make him scream; that would provide her with additional entertainment.

She swung her hips as she walked over to the bed, letting her thatch peep from the gaping fly of her riding leathers. She pulled the quills from her hair and shook her head, letting her hair fly in a wild cloud. "What is your will, madame?"

The duchess uncurled, rose from the bed, and stretched, taking Sylvie's eyes captive. "I will clean my teeth," she said. "You will strip Henri. He looks well in his new clothes, but I would like to see him out of them."

"In whatever manner I choose?" Sylvie asked, noting the boy's nervous expression.

"Don't be rough," the duchess chided. "You wouldn't like that, would you, Henri?"

"No, Your Grace," he said. Slowly, he stood and sat down on the bed, careful to keep his back to the wall. Sylvie advanced again, as predatory as she could manage; she had considerable practice at intimidating males, even having them beg for it. She was rewarded by his widening eyes.

He wore his new boots, a pair of riding leathers much like hers, a loose shirt and a dark livery jacket fastened with decorative frogging in the same color. The dark clothes did not lend him maturity. He looked more like a young boy playing dress-up in his father's uniform. Madame deserved a thousand times better than he. Though to be fair, he was not the swaggering sort of male whom Sylvie despised. She did not find him entirely unlikable. Therefore, and because it would please madame, she would make an effort for him.

The duchess rummaged her silk robe from a saddlebag and wrapped it around herself. She settled into the chair, propped her feet on Sylvie's saddlebag, and uncapped the tooth powder. "Proceed," she said. "I will join you later."

Sylvie made her decision and knelt before Henri, splaying her knees. His eyes traveled down her bosom to the apex of her legs. Sylvie grabbed one of his boots and pulled, stretching backward in ways she knew he would appreciate. A flush heated his cheekbones. She took more time with the second boot, curling her hand over his calf and squeezing then, when the boot was off, pulling his toes and running her thumb over the arch of his foot. He leaned back on his elbows, giving her an eye-level view of the swelling along his leg. The leathers would constrain him. Good.

Sylvie stood, grabbed the front of his jacket and tugged him upright. In bare feet, he was still slightly taller than she was. She unfastened his jacket quickly and draped it over their pile of saddlebags, then untucked his shirt. It billowed over his hips, hiding his bulge from her eyes but not from her thoughts. She said, "Perhaps you should face madame." With her hands on his shoulders, she encouraged him to turn.

The duchess had finished with her teeth and was brushing her hair. It crackled against her silk robe, dark against the pale gold. She smiled at them. "Thank you. Please continue."

Sylvie captured Henri's upper arms and pulled them behind his back. He made a noise, but didn't fight her. His eyes were on the appreciative duchess. Sylvie took a moment to test the shape of his muscles; hard labor had given him definition that she could feel through the tissue-thin linen of his shirt. If she'd had anything with which to tie him, she might have given the duchess a lovely view. As it was, she spent some time biting the cords of his neck, for the pleasure of feeling him arch back against her, and displaying himself for the duchess's pleasure.

Henri was breathing hard when she stopped, reached over his shoulder and loosened the ties at the neck of his shirt, shoving it off one shoulder. His shoulder and arm were marked by bruises she hadn't noticed back in the breeding barn. Sylvie stroked his skin with a single finger, and he shivered. She pulled the shirt over his head, trailing the fabric over his nipples, teasing his chest and neck.

He leaned back against her, hard, the muscles of his back pressing into her bare chest; he rolled his shoulders, and her nipples hardened. "Little slut!" she hissed. "I did not give you permission to—"

"Oh, leave him be, Sylvie. You liked it, didn't you?" The duchess tapped her hairbrush against her leg and raised one brow. Sylvie bit back a remark, tossed Henri's shirt to the floor and plastered herself to his back. She traced the waistline of his leathers and his hip bones, noting with satisfaction that he rose on his toes each time her hands crossed his fly. He didn't stop writhing against her, though, taking every opportunity. One day, she would have him tied, and he would beg for her to give him release while she remained perfectly cool, but for now, his hard body did feel good. She could only imagine the picture they must have made for the duchess. It was too bad this room had no mirrors such as adorned the ducal palace.

She could not see, but she could feel. She slid her hand lower and dug her fingers into the meat of his thigh. His breath caught. She rubbed herself against his rear, the leather pulling at her thatch. She hummed without intention, and sensed his grin, felt his puff of laughter. Retaliating, she used her other hand to firmly stroke his erection. It thickened and lengthened beneath her hand; she felt for its head. Teasing there with her mouth, just under the edge, had been particularly gratifying back in the breeding barn. She couldn't get a good grip on him now. His leathers were in the way. She undid his buttons and maneuvered his cock free.

Henri's head fell back against her shoulder as she massaged his foreskin against his shaft, and Sylvie smiled. "You are too easy," she said in his ear, dipping her tongue inside. He didn't reply, only gasped. Perhaps he had no defense.

"Madame," Sylvie said. She circled her thumb, gathering his droplets of moisture and glossing the head of his cock. He shuddered, and she pressed to his back more tightly. "How should I use him? Or is he to be yours now?"

The duchess licked her lips. Her fingers tightened on the handle of her hairbrush. "Henri," she said. "Will you fuck Sylvie? I would like to watch. You may refuse."

Sylvie shouldn't have been shocked. The two of them had been giving her a show all along. Would madame allow her to strike him if he refused, or was she too besotted with his girlish eyelashes? She realized that she would be angry if the boy said *no*. She would like to continue performing for madame. Her cunt trickled as she imagined it.

Henri covered her hand with his, holding it in place. "I would like that," he said. He drew her hand away from his cock and turned to face her. "Is that all right?"

He did not at all understand how this game was played. If only madame would allow her to properly instruct him. Probably he could not understand the subtleties even if taught. Sylvie gave him her most sultry smile. "By all means," she said. She walked backward to the bed, tugging him by the hand. His cheekbones were red and, she was amused to note, the tip of his nose. He could not seem to lift his eyes from her breasts. She took advantage of this, tripping him when they reached the bed, and wrestling him down on top of her. He did not fight. In moments she was stretched on the bed, legs splayed. Henri straddled her outside leg and looked down at her.

"Sylvie," he said. "May I kiss you?"

She wasn't sure how to answer. She'd never been asked permission before. Under ordinary circumstances, she would have refused, but madame was watching, and his breath was sweet.

She grasped his shoulders and pulled him down to her, wanting the pressure of his chest against her nipples. His cock thumped into her belly and she rubbed against it as he captured her mouth, sweet and gentle as a girl at first. He was not yet twenty, a mere babe. Though only a few years older in years, Sylvie felt decades older in experience. She dug her fingertips into his scalp as they kissed, and she felt his moan against her tongue. She opened her mouth wider, sucking him in, not doing battle but sharing a simple pleasure. She had to admit to herself that his eagerness was contagious.

Henri settled into her, flexing his hips, his hands gripping the sheet on either side of her head. Between kisses, he panted. Sylvie dragged her nails down his back, then dug her fingers into his buttocks, first through his leathers, then shoving them down to reach his skin. She couldn't reach far enough to touch his scrotum. She worked one hand between them and captured his shaft, pulling her mouth free of his. "Up, up!"

He rose to his elbows, planting a messy kiss on her cheek. "I am up, can't you tell?" He grinned at her.

Sylvie smacked his buttock with her free hand. "Get the pillow. I want to be comfortable. And take off your leathers." She glanced at the duchess as she spoke. Her robe had fallen open to the upper slope of her breasts. Sylvie could see the rigid points of her nipples beneath. The duchess's hands were knotted in her lap, and she watched with parted lips.

Sylvie wriggled out of her own leathers, making a show of it. The pillow elevated her hips to an inviting angle. Henri did not take the hint. He dropped his riding leathers on the floor, his eyes on the duchess.

"Your Grace?" he asked. "Would you like to join us?"

"In a few moments," she said.

Sylvie thought she looked melancholy. They would have to perform well, for her. "Henri!" she barked. "Come here and fuck me. Or have you forgotten where to stick your cock? It goes in this hole, here." She gestured with her hand, then held her labia open.

After a moment's hesitation, he grumbled, "Orders, orders, orders. Will nothing make you leave me alone?"

"No," she said. "Stop malingering."

After climbing onto the bed, Henri pressed her knees farther apart with his hands. He spent a few moments looking at her cunt, one hand absently smoothing his erection. Sylvie slid one finger into herself, rubbed inside for a delicious moment, then pulled out and smeared the juices, teasing her labia and clitoris. Knowing madame watched, she smeared her nipples as well. She was already close to coming, barely able to stand her own touch.

Henri leaned down and kissed her again, deeply, before he steadied his cock and pressed the head inside her. He stretched her delightfully. "More," she said, lifting her legs and clasping his hips. "Give it all to me."

He eased inside her and she hummed at the lubricious sound and feel. His pubic bone bumped her; he groaned and rotated his hips, grinding into her clitoris. Sylvie squeaked in surprise at the jagged stabs of near pain; she hadn't caught her breath before she was abruptly climaxing, shallow contractions that shuddered across her skin, leaving her starving for more. "More, damn you!" she gasped. "Fuck me!"

They both sighed as he pulled out, and groaned when he filled her again. Sylvie licked her fingers and played with her nipples as Henri thrust. The bed creaked. She tipped her head back and closed her eyes, hoping the duchess was well entertained. She no longer had the concentration to spare for anything else; her whole attention spiraled down to her cunt and the wet sliding of Henri's hard, hot cock.

Her first orgasm had taken the edge off. She breathed deeply, holding the second away from her for as long as possible, wanting to outlast Henri. But when he showed no signs of flagging, she determined to wring him dry. On his next thrust, she tightened her inner muscles, holding him in for a long second before releasing him. After the third time, he did not fully withdraw. He pressed his face to the side of her neck, sobbing for breath, and pumped his hips in short, savage bursts. Sylvie gripped him inside each time. She grabbed his buttocks. A tiny climax like a wave of heat flowed across her skin, then another, and she could not stop her moans. She wasn't there yet, hadn't had the full body tremors she craved. "Faster," she growled. "Harder!"

She was ready to scream when Henri froze in her arms, then began to jerk in long spasms. His semen seemed to scald her cunt; hot liquid ran down her inner thighs. She clamped down on him and he groaned deeply; then her own climax took her, sunbursts against her eyelids, and she could only shiver and whimper.

Her arms felt heavy and limp as wet laundry as she patted Henri on the buttocks, feeling munificent now that she'd bested him. "I hope you have saved something for madame," she slurred. "I believe she is ready for you now."

CHAPTER ELEVEN

Camille's knees trembled as she crossed the room to the bed. Sylvie, limp and satisfied as a cat, pushed Henri out of her way and sat up. She smiled at Camille and licked her lips. "I fear there is not room for both of us here, but I will fetch the chair."

Uncharitably, Camille did not want to face Sylvie just now. The girl might enjoy being commanded, but Camille felt dirtied, not least because she'd been so aroused by the result. It wouldn't do to let Sylvie know of her feelings, however. She leaned forward and kissed Sylvie's mouth, then her forehead. Sylvie smiled at her again and slid off the bed, gesturing for Camille to take her place.

Henri propped himself on one arm and held out his hand. Camille placed hers in it and laced their fingers together. She met his eyes, sleepy and satiated, and flowed into his arms. They stretched out together, shifting and sliding against each other, their legs overlapping, her breasts rubbing against his chest. Camille curved one arm around his ribs and flattened the other against his chest, resting her fingertips over his heart. Henri lifted a hand and moved toward her, but stopped abruptly and pulled back. Her belly went cold. There'd been no kiss between them yet. She shouldn't allow it, but he'd kissed Sylvie, and she craved that pleasure for herself. She leaned forward and kissed him for the first time, as carnally as she could manage, as she and Maxime had once kissed.

Henri made a sound in his throat. He cupped her head in his hands, tilting her to a better angle, and dipped his tongue into her mouth. She felt another small moan escape him; she echoed. He pushed her silk robe out of the way and curled his fingers around her breast. He kissed her again, then murmured, "I need—a moment—" His eyes closed. Camille closed her eyes as well. When she was sure he slept, she snuggled as close as she dared. She could give him a few moments to doze.

Sylvie touched her shoulder. "Madame? Is he *sleeping?*"

Camille nuzzled Henri's neck. "I believe so."

"I will wake him for you, the ungrateful wretch."

"No, it's better to let him have a little rest first, or his performance will suffer," she said. She looked back over her shoulder at Sylvie, blowing a strand of hair from her mouth. Perhaps Sylvie could be useful in preventing her from becoming too involved in Henri. "I want you to be with us, as well. Will you do that for me?"

Sylvie scowled. "You do not have to ask. I will do whatever you wish, always." She adjusted the chair, drawing it closer to the bed. With her hair wild down her shoulders and her pert features, she looked like a fierce tree spirit bent on seducing the entire mortal world.

When performing with Henri, Sylvie had been different

than the night before; more confident and brash, more like the Sylvie Camille had thought she'd known. She wasn't sure where the tender, intense girl had gone, or if she would ever meet her again, or even if she wanted to meet her again. The place they'd been together was too dangerous; Camille had thought too much, been unable to find the freedom she needed while attuning herself so closely to Sylvie. She didn't really want to know Sylvie's deepest self, when the Sylvie she liked was a saucy brat who enjoyed controlling others.

Camille twisted her torso and grasped Sylvie's hand. "I want you to enjoy this," she said. "I thought you enjoyed yourself with Henri."

"Oh, I did, madame, you may be sure of that." She added grudgingly, "He is…well, he is still not worthy of you, but he is a fine diversion. I do not think he will betray you if he can help himself."

"Praise indeed," Camille said. "Come here. You are so small, I think you will fit close to me."

"Perhaps if you shove that great oaf against the wall," Sylvie said.

Henri woke when Sylvie yanked on his leg, and peered blearily at them before his eyes abruptly widened in comprehension. "Did I sleep long?"

Camille smiled. "Perhaps you should lie back and rest for a time." With her straddling him, there was room for Sylvie on the outside.

Sylvie bent down and kissed him, mussing his hair. "If you

were mine, I would not be so kind," she said. "Men were put on this earth to work for our pleasure."

He grinned, even as he blushed. "I'm happy to oblige."

Camille rested her hands on his chest, making a circle with her palms. "Sylvie, perhaps we should prepare him for his labors."

"Feet first," Sylvie said, clambering off the bed, then climbing back at the bottom. She dragged his feet into her lap, squirming until one of his heels pressed into her mound. Leaving her to it, Camille turned back to Henri. When she nodded that he was to begin, he reached up and fondled her breasts, occasionally twitching as Sylvie did something to his feet.

Camille had not touched herself while she watched Henri and Sylvie, and now her previous arousal, that had built and built, rushed back in on her. Every nerve kindled, the pit of her belly squeezing. She fluttered her fingers over him as he stroked and squeezed, brushing her quim against his scrotum and the base of his cock. Youth was an advantage; he was already filling and stretching. She bent over him to join their mouths, sighing with satisfaction as her breasts compressed against his chest and slid in their mingled sweat. He wrapped his arms around her and stroked her back, while she trapped his head between her forearms. She loved the hungry way he sucked at her lips and tongue and tasted the corners of her mouth, the spot beneath her nose, the end of her chin. She could not remember ever being kissed as thoroughly.

His attention on her seemed so encompassing, Camille could lose herself in him, or perhaps she was finding herself, the person deep within who rarely saw the light. She could not think of the duke while Henri tried to meld his body entirely with hers. She could only think of what Henri did to her skin, and the desperate grasping deep within her. She would have to take him inside her soon, or scream. She glanced at his face, dazed with passion, and wished she hadn't. He felt too much, and she could see all of it. She closed her eyes.

Tingling sensation flared on her rear, and she realized Sylvie had begun to massage her buttocks, pushing her more firmly into Henri's thickening erection. Camille murmured her approval and bit the strong tendon on the side of Henri's neck. His hips surged, nearly dislodging her from her seat.

Sylvie's strong hands worked on her lower back and sides, urging her up and forward. Camille reared up, bracing herself with one hand near his head, and captured Henri's cock in the other. He turned his head to the side and licked at her fingers. She pressed the head of his cock against her opening and twisted her hips, determined to enjoy every fraction of his entrance. She drove her quim onto his cock in breathless increments. Once she had taken all of him, Henri grabbed her hand and sucked her fingers into his mouth.

Camille wanted to bend close to him and feel more of his skin, but her current angle was too good; the upward curve of his cock bumped her favorite spot inside her quim, and while upright she could work herself against him with abandon. As if she'd sensed Camille's desire, Sylvie shifted position, pressing her soft warmth against Camille's back and pinching her nipples at maddening intervals. Henri's hands gripped her hips, sharing her motion rather than forcing it. His ragged breathing came close to sobs of effort as he fought against thrusting upward and disturbing the rhythm she'd set.

She sped her riding. Heat fluttered beneath her skin. She dove deep into her body and peaked, her belly muscles wrenching and flinging her outward again. A series of cries she could not control escaped her; she rose to her knees, her quim suddenly too tender to be touched, and held herself there as her climax tore through her. Sylvie held her around her waist, a safe mooring that kept her from flying apart.

When she opened her eyes, Henri was still hard, and laughing. "You're so beautiful!" he said. "So beautiful when you come."

Camille clamped down on an unexpected urge to weep. She wasn't beautiful, and had done nothing beautiful in her life; but she couldn't say so to this innocent boy. She touched his face with her palm, fed his cock into her again, and said, "Take your pleasure, Henri."

The attentions of Henri's cock and his hands on her breasts, and Sylvie's hands on her clitoris, gave her another climax before Henri's, but this one was not so shattering. Once they'd all squirmed together on the narrow bed, she was able to regain her composure enough to ask after Sylvie's completion.

Sylvie chortled. "Oh, madame, I am quite able to take care of myself."

Someone rapped on the door, and Sylvie scrambled free. "If it is the chambermaid, I will send her away." She picked up

Camille's robe from the floor and slipped it on, then tossed the crumpled blanket to hide Camille and the slumbering Henri. She lifted the door's bar and peeked through the opening. Almost immediately, she opened the door wider, grabbed Kaspar and hauled him inside, slamming the door behind him and rebarring it. He wore riding leathers and a long, oiled coat, with a hat pulled low over his eyes, and brought in a scent of lightning and rain.

Camille bolted from the bed. "Kaspar, what is wrong?"

His brow creased. "Your Grace, you asked that I meet you at this inn." He glanced meaningfully at Sylvie. She took off the robe and passed it to Camille, who slipped it on.

Sylvie didn't seem to mind being nude. She said, "We were not expecting you—the bridges are out, and we cannot leave today."

Kaspar smiled wryly. "The bridge from the ducal seat to this village was still open this morning, though it was washed with water from end to end. I didn't think it wise to wait and be trapped on the wrong side. It was safer on foot, I think. I weigh much less than a horse, or a wagon and ox." He glanced at the bed. "I see you've had plenty to occupy yourselves."

Camille noted with interest that he would not have made such an amused comment back at the palace, before he'd been intimate with her. She ignored the remark. "If you passed the bridge, so might pursuers."

Kaspar grinned and touched his hip, where he wore a blade. "They did not pass the bridge."

Camille felt the blood drain from her face. "You fought? With whom?"

"Yes, Your Grace. Two of the duke's guards, Claude and Francis. I wounded them sufficiently that neither could pursue us farther, and their report back to the palace should be significantly delayed."

"Thank you for letting them live." The palace guard belonged to the duke, but over the years she had ridden out with many of them, and supported them in equestrian competitions. She wasn't sure she was ruthless enough to have any of them killed. "I don't think it's wise to stay here too long. We should leave this afternoon. Is there another inn?"

Sylvie had originally chosen this village. "No, there is not. We could alter our disguises, perhaps."

Kaspar said consideringly, "There is a brothel. I passed it on the way here. This is a coaching stop. They would have rooms for customers."

"Their customers are trapped here as much as we are," Sylvie pointed out. "Their rooms will be full."

"Not necessarily," Kaspar said. "I can bargain with them. I know of this brothel."

Camille said, "We don't want to spend all our money here, when we've barely begun the journey. There is no place we can discreetly sell the jewels. Unless either of you had time to find that out, before we fled?"

"I didn't mean to pay them with money," Kaspar said. "You know I have special skills, Your Grace. It seems a shame not to use them at need."

Camille didn't like the idea of separating their party yet again, but she sent Kaspar out regardless, to negotiate with the brothel keeper while Sylvie, back in boy disguise, paid the bill for his "drunken" tutor. Kaspar returned a bare hour later with four gilded tokens. "Their discretion is legendary," he assured Camille. Having no useful alternative, she did her best to remain calm as Sylvie packed their saddlebags and Henri readied the horses. She hoped the brothel bore little resemblance to the duke's eroticized chambers.

Soon their small group was ensconced in a brothel larger than the one in the ducal seat. Camille had expected a plain and sturdy building like the inn, but this place clearly intended to entice travelers with more than its human amenities; also, she recalled, the taxes on the business and its premises would be lower here than in the palace district. It helped to remember that an establishment of this rank would employ only highly trained and well-paid professionals. She'd seen the licenses pass through the courts, and once arbitrated over a pay dispute between a cadre of women who'd learned a special skill overseas and wished to be additionally compensated each time they performed, in order to recoup their time and travel expenses. She'd ruled in their favor. The brothel where they worked had more than doubled its profits as their fame spread. She wondered what had become of them in the years since.

A woman greeted them at the door. She was tall and willowy, gowned in velvet the color of charcoal, which set off her pale skin and long, wheat-colored curls. Her skirts swept the polished marble steps with a weight that reflected expert tailoring, and cuffs embellished with tiny flecks of crystal trailed elegantly over her hands. Camille would never have taken her for a prostitute. Of course, she hadn't seen many. Her father and Michel both tended to obtain their concubines from sources other than brothels. Usually some debt was involved, a debt that could never be quite repaid. The loyalty of the ducal concubines was thus ensured by more than mere gold.

The woman led them through a grand entrance hall to a flight of stairs. A pair of muscular young men took their bags and carried them away, as smoothly efficient as servants in a aristocratic house, even if their flattened noses and scarred faces would have looked out of place in elaborate livery.

Upstairs, the central wing seemed devoted to a series of rooms intended for small gatherings. Through the occasional open door, Camille saw couches and thick carpets and sideboards gleaming with every kind of glass bottle. "Where are the bedrooms?" she asked their guide.

The woman turned. Her expression didn't change. "In the west wing. You, however, will be staying in the east wing. That is reserved for guests who will be staying longer than a night."

The furnishing in their lavish suite were far from tawdry, and though odd, their very distance from the palace's rich style reassured her. Sheepskin rugs scattered the floor and the two large beds. The beds' head and foot fixtures were constructed of slats, like fencing. The curtains and wall hangings were woven of wool in the bold geometric patterns favored by shepherds, who worked their looms in bare huts all through the winter months. Instead of wardrobes, shelves had been built of the same fencelike slats, and a blanket-lined manger sat at the foot of each bed to hold their saddlebags. Sylvie slung her leg over a large replica of a ram, complete with fleece body covering and real horns attached to its carved wooden head. She settled onto it as if it was a hobby horse, gripped one horn in each hand, and said, "Madame, I think I am in love." She planted a kiss atop the ram's head.

Henri sat on a high stool and hooked his feet through its bars. He remarked, "I don't think I want to know the specialty they offer here."

Kaspar laughed. "It's not what you think. Aristocratic lords and ladies like to play at being shepherds and shepherdesses. Rustic pleasures are supposed to restore a man's potency."

Of course he would know about such things, Camille thought. He served as both her guard and her sexual servant; he'd been trained for both duties. She remembered her mother's eunuch who had guarded her as a child. After her mother's death, he'd gone back to his home duchy and opened a brothel there, becoming rich on the proceeds and leaving all to the young man he'd trained as his heir. Camille had once wondered if the two had been lovers, but how could that be possible?

Camille went to Kaspar and quietly said, "You do not have to do this for me. We have money."

He shook his head. "No, Your Grace. All the money in the

world would not be enough. The brothel keeper wants my services for the night and nothing else. It's the price we must pay for silence and protection. We would be sleeping in the street, and it's still raining."

"She will not harm you, will she?"

"He," Kaspar corrected. A curious smile lifted one corner of his mouth. "No, he will not harm me."

Camille raised her chin. "Are you still bound to me?"

Looking shocked, Kaspar sank to his knees and kissed her feet before he said, "Always, Your Grace."

She could not let Kaspar serve a man she didn't know as if he was a slave or a whore, with no protection. "Then you will do this, but I will witness it."

In the end, she and Sylvie and Henri were all escorted to a narrow room furnished with tall padded stools, occasional tables to hold refreshments and viewports that might have come from a ship at sea, except for the scrim of golden cloth that hung over each, concealing it from the other side. Henri drew his stool close to hers and took her hand. Sylvie made herself comfortable, swinging her legs, and Camille considered asking her what she expected would happen, but decided against it, not wanting to appear either nervous or ignorant.

The room's attendant said, "Please do not speak while in the viewing chamber, or you might disturb the participants. Any disruption is forbidden."

"I wouldn't dream of interrupting," Sylvie said, grinning. She wore her boy's clothing, but her hair fell down her back.

She seemed determined to enjoy herself, no matter what. Camille considered her answer, and finally nodded. Glancing at her, Henri dipped his head as well. The attendant offered them wine, then departed.

Camille felt cold with apprehension, and very glad of Henri's warm fingers laced within hers. Kaspar had insisted he would not be harmed. She should trust his word, but she'd been betrayed so many times in her life that it was difficult to trust even her own servant.

Henri leaned over, his lips close to her ear. She couldn't help smiling at the tickle of his breath. "Madame," he murmured, and she smiled more broadly, squeezing his hand.

She pressed her lips to his ear in turn. "Camille," she whispered.

He blushed and shook his head.

"Later, then," she said. She turned to the room on the other side of the viewport.

Like this one, the room was longer than it was wide, and nearly bare of furniture. Single beeswax candles burned in individual wall sconces, their light flickering over an eye-blurring mosaic floor of black-and-white squares. A black velvet chaise stood across from the viewports, against the far wall. Three matching chairs, with the plainest, smoothest structure Camille had ever seen, were lined next to the chaise. A fourth velvet-covered chair, this one expansive and luxuriously cushioned, was shoved in the far corner. There were no wall hangings or curtains of any sort, except for the cloth that concealed their viewports.

In the middle of the room stood a frame in the shape of the letter x, taller than a man and wrapped in black leather. Leather straps dangled from its several crossbars, as well as something that glinted in the candle flames like metal. She'd never seen its like.

A door opened in the opposite wall, and a tall man walked in, wearing a richly brocaded flame-orange robe. An attendant followed him, then Kaspar. Kaspar wore only a silky black loincloth. He stood aside as the man in the robe, presumably the brothel keeper, removed his robe and dropped it over the attendant's arm. Beneath, he was entirely naked, his tea-colored skin sleek and his chest and limbs pleasingly muscular. Camille studied him; he appeared to be a whole man, with the beginnings of an erection, but his only hair was the tight curls on his head. He also seemed to lack a foreskin and most bizarre of all, his lower abdomen bore a tattoo of an octopus, its wavy limbs curling toward his cock. The brothel keeper walked to the center of the room and stopped near the frame. This close, Camille could see the old sword scars on his chest and arms. He'd been a soldier.

The attendant gave Kaspar two velvet bags before he departed. Kaspar solemnly hooked them to his belt. He approached the brothel keeper and said, "Master Fouet. Do you give yourself into my hands?"

"I do," Fouet said, his voice deep and rich. He bowed to Kaspar, then straightened. Kaspar reached into one bag and drew out a strip of leather. He collared Fouet's neck and fed the tongue through the buckle. Camille shivered, remembering the duke tugging on her own jeweled collar. Henri put his arm around her, and she calmed enough to notice that Fouet's erection lengthened as he rolled his neck, obviously appreciating the binding.

Next, Kaspar withdrew a leather blindfold, with padded flaps to muffle Fouet's hearing. Fouet put this on himself, adjusting it to his liking, then holding out a meaty hand. Kaspar led him to the frame and strapped him there, legs splayed and arms stretched to the side, his wrists enclosed in padded metal cuffs. Kaspar brought out thinner strips of leather, wrapping them snugly and decoratively in various places: between Fouet's toes and down the arch of his foot; around his chest, compressing the nipples; between his teeth; and, last, constricting his cock and balls.

Their view was profile. Camille clearly saw Fouet's erection rising like a kite, in fits and starts. Astonishing. In a like situation, she would be terrified. She glanced over at Sylvie, and found that she was watching with a lustful half smile. Of course she would like seeing a man tied. She had never made any secret of her views on the male sex, and how they would benefit from chastening.

Except Fouet had willingly done this. He had actively given himself to Kaspar. Why? She could not imagine trusting anyone so much. She had to breathe slowly and carefully to fend off panic.

Kaspar circled the frame, examining his work while he rummaged in one of the velvet bags. Fouet's head moved, as if trying to ascertain his location. His chest moved more rapidly. Fear or anticipation? Camille jumped when Kaspar's hand licked out, slapping a narrow leather paddle on Fouet's buttocks and thighs until the skin looked ruddy and tender. Sweat trickled down Fouet's back, and his cock protruded through a gap in the frame, rigid and shiny as metal. Camille glanced at Sylvie, who leaned forward on her stool, clenching her fingers into her thighs. Henri was watching Camille, not Fouet. Camille straightened until they no longer touched and looked back through the viewport.

Kaspar had retreated some distance from the frame. Now he lifted his hands and clapped them sharply together. The door opened. A woman entered, dressed in a long skirt, with a dark leather harness constraining her breasts. She carried a long drum beneath one arm. She glanced at Kaspar, then took the cushioned chair, settling the drum between her knees. She played a quick roll. The sound echoed from the bare walls and floor.

Kaspar removed the bags from his belt. He laid the empty one on the floor, well to the side, then pulled loose the black ribbon tie of the other. Before he reached inside, he called out formally, "Master Fouet! You have chosen the single-tail. Nod if you still accept this."

Camille found she was holding her breath, as if she were watching a play. Fouet nodded firmly, then propped his forehead on a crossbar. She heard Sylvie sigh.

Kaspar could not actually be going to whip the brothel keeper. What pleasure was there in pain? What would she do if there was blood? She'd been sick, once, when the duke had whipped a servant who displeased him, and that had been with a cane, not long whips like the ones rippling from Kaspar's hands and coiling on the floor. The duke had often threatened to whip her and mar her skin. She covered her mouth with her hand. There was a hum, a pop of leather hitting flesh, twice rapidly, and a man's moan.

Then Sylvie was there, arms wrapped around her from behind, while Henri held her from the front, his cheek pressed tight to hers. Sylvie murmured in her ear, "Madame, madame, Kaspar will give him pleasure, not pain. He will barely mark him, you will see. Look, look, and you will see."

Camille had said she would witness, and she would keep her word. She looked past Henri's ear and controlled herself. Kaspar flicked his wrists in sequence, barely moving his arms. The single-tails crossed but never tangled, plunging toward their target as smoothly as hawks to prey, over and over again, laying a perfect pink pattern from his shoulders down the backs of his thighs. The drummer kept a steady beat. Fouet gasped and moaned with each stroke, his powerful buttocks and shoulders clenching and unclenching. Sweat dripped from his hair.

There was no blood, though the whips left faint welts on his skin. Camille pointed to Sylvie's stool with her chin. She directed Henri to turn in her arms so he could watch as well, resting her chin on his shoulder.

Kaspar's whip strokes were lovely to watch when she knew Fouet felt pleasure. She wondered how long he could endure.

She was not sure how much time had passed. The drumming, the snap of the whips, Fouet's deep groans, all blurred into a timeless haze. She only slowly became aware that Kaspar's pace had increased, as had the volume of Fouet's voice.

Suddenly, Fouet jerked and shuddered in his bonds, his cock bobbing fiercely, though his binding prevented him from ejaculating. Kaspar's strokes, and the drumming, rose to a crescendo. Camille's pulse sped up. Then Kaspar's strokes began to slow and soften, at last fading away. The drum stopped. Fouet slumped in his bonds. Kaspar lowered his arms. He was sweating almost as much as Fouet. He gave each whip a final flick and coiled it neatly in his hand. "Master Fouet," he called. "Are you satisfied?"

Fouet nodded weakly. Sweat trickled down Camille's back beneath her dress, and she wished she could sag as Fouet did. Kaspar took his time stowing the whips, then went to loose Fouet's bonds, beginning with the gag strap. Kaspar said something, too softly for Camille to hear, and ran his thumb along Fouet's rigid cock. Fouet replied. Kaspar smiled. He turned and called, "Sylvie! Are you willing to provide one last service for our host?"

Sylvie grinned widely and slid from her stool. "For such a man, I am willing to entertain for the rest of the night!"

She could have him, and welcome. Camille wanted only to bury herself in Henri's strong body and forget the past few days. Unfortunately, to do so would reveal her weakness when her authority was all she could cling to.

"I shall sleep alone," she said when Sylvie had departed. "Go to Kaspar, Henri. He is to teach you to use a knife. He may as well begin tonight."

Henri bowed his head. "Are you sure, madame?"

"Go," she said.

When he had gone, she drew a long, slow breath, then another. She glanced into the room beyond the viewport and saw Master Fouet kissing Kaspar, one hand clearly visible on the eunuch's hip. Camille watched closely, wary of coercion, but Kaspar seemed to lean into the touch; then he laid his hands on Master Fouet's chest and gently pushed him away.

Camille could hear the brothel keeper's voice only as a low rumble, but Kaspar's lighter reply carried easily. "Yes, I'm sure. I have promised myself to another."

Master Fouet said something else, and clouted him on the shoulder, in what looked like a comradely blow.

"Don't worry, Karl. Sylvie will surprise you. Go to her. I want a bath."

Camille watched them exit the room. Did Kaspar mean that he'd promised himself to her? The duchy's law forbade eunuchs who were sworn to service from forming any sexual attachment. She'd thought that law essentially meaningless, meant to protect the masters and mistresses of eunuchs from being manipulated through their desires; what could a eunuch do involving sex? However, she'd seen this very evening that there was more to sexual congress than one body thrusting into another. Kaspar might have all manner of sexual relationships. The most obvious object would be Arno. She remembered the tender kiss she'd once seen them exchange, and her certainty grew. Kaspar and Arno had served her so long and so well, they deserved a pleasurable reward. She would think on it as she lay alone in her bed.

She did not sleep for many hours. Again and again she saw the whip flicker through the air, and twice she woke with a start, as if a whip had cut her skin. She woke again in the early hours, trembling, her chest cold from sweat. She could not remember what she had dreamed, except for a vague impression of being trapped, bound; also, something had blocked her throat. She'd been unable to speak.

Sylvie was not sleeping in the room; she must still be with Master Fouet. Camille took out her sketchpad, and drew horses until the morning came.

CHAPTER TWELVE

Days passed, the rain stopped and the flood receded from the bridges. When travelers resumed their journeys, tales of trouble in the palace traveled with them. Henri spent every spare moment collecting rumors, hoping to find something useful before their journey began again. The duchess had gone mad and been confined to a dungeon. The duchess was dead, and had been for years. The duchess had gone mad from her barren state, fled the palace and tried to amass an army of peasants to overthrow her husband and rip him to bits. Rumors of her success at this were varied. One consistent rumor, however, said that the duke had repudiated her and their marriage, declaring her insanity the same as death. He was now negotiating with a neighboring duke for his fourteen-year-old daughter, or for a princess of a tiny mountain kingdom who possessed an army of eunuchs and bare-chested women warriors, or planned to elevate a lowly concubine to be his consort. Or was it two concubines?

Some, mostly women, blamed the duke for failing to get a

child on their hereditary ruler, and believed Camille had gone forth in disguise to find a worthy sire for her heir. Some feared she'd been killed; others ventured to say she should have killed him instead.

The duchess refused to comment on any of the rumors, but she spent many hours planning the next stage of the journey with Sylvie and Kaspar. From now until they reached Maxime's coastal protectorate, they would travel lesser roads. For the next few nights, they would camp in the forest. Kaspar would become their hired guard and the duchess would play a widow, mother of Sylvie, who would keep her boy disguise. Henri would remain their groom, a role he would have no trouble playing.

Henri would miss the comfortable brothel, and all that he'd experienced there. He'd been taken out of his daily round of work for the first time in his life. While there, he'd only visited the horses, not cared for them himself. He would have been saddened by this except that the duchess had accompanied him, feeding rounds of carrot to Guirlande, her favorite, and letting them all bump their heads against her chest. Every smile she gave the horses gave Henri a thrill of pride and tenderness.

He'd seen little of Sylvie after that first day. She'd become fast friends with Master Fouet, and even been offered a position before they'd departed, but she would not leave the duchess while she was still needed. Also, she said, she wanted Kaspar to teach her to handle a single-tail.

Kaspar had been busy with Henri for much of the time there.

As they rode away from the brothel, Henri glanced back at the fenced side courtyard, remembering his first lesson in weapons. Kaspar had laid a knife across his hand. Henri looked down at it. The blade was thin as a whisper, the metal faintly scarred from sharpening. The hilt was wrapped in blue pigskin, marred in one spot, where Kaspar must have pried off the duchess's seal. Henri said, "It looks like what it is. Something to kill."

"You might need to kill for her," Kaspar said. "Are you willing? I'll tell you now, you won't know if you *can,* not until the moment arrives—but are you willing?"

Henri closed his fingers over the sleek suede hilt and hefted it. The blade had barely any weight. He could thrust his arm forward with sharp death protruding from his fingers, and his punch would be deadly. He imagined a hazy figure flying backward as if from a horse's kick, limbs flopping, blood spilling from the mouth—and Henri, holding a bloodied blade, standing over the collapsed body, watching life leach from its eyes. He shook himself and looked at Kaspar. "I don't know," he said. "I am willing to kill to defend her. If she ordered me to kill on command...I don't know."

Kaspar said, "I doubt it will come to that."

Henri balanced the knife across his palm. "What about the duke? Does she— Do you think she would have him killed?" He didn't think she could order a death, but how well did he know her, really? Her father and husband both had ordered many. He knew she wanted to take power for herself, not for its own sake, but so she could be safe from the duke. Henri feared the only way to prevent the duke from taking revenge was for him to be killed.

Kaspar didn't seem very upset at the thought of the duke being killed. "You wouldn't be the one doing the killing, if Her Grace needed it done," he said. He patted one of the long daggers at his hip.

He hadn't thought that far. "Have you——" He stopped. He wasn't sure how much he wanted to know. Had Kaspar killed? Had he killed at the duchess's command?

Kaspar rested his meaty hand on Henri's shoulder for a moment. "Her Grace has never asked me to kill for her," he said, "but I would do so in less than a heartbeat. It is my duty to protect her, to the point of my death. Killing for her is a small thing, in comparison."

"You would even kill the duke, if she asked?"

Kaspar's face turned savage, and Henri took a step backward. "If you knew the duke, you would not ask that question. I have witnessed what he's done to Her Grace. The only thing that's kept me from falling upon him with my bare hands is knowing I would die soon after, and Her Grace would be left alone and unprotected."

Henri took a deep breath. "I'll do my best."

Kaspar nodded. "Good. Now, have you fought before?"

"With my fists," Henri said. "Not since I was a boy, though." Kaspar smirked. He amended it. "Not for a few years. I can wrestle, too. I'm not bad at wrestling." It was a popular pastime among the younger grooms.

"You know how to fall?"

"I think so."

"Then give me back the knife for now, and we'll begin there."

When not teaching Henri the basics of sword and knife, Kaspar spent their visit being treated like the king. He was given his own chamber, and two pages to provide him with baths, delicacies, massages and anything else he desired. He'd come to the duchess twice each day, of course, to see what she required, but each time she'd sent him away, spending her time with Henri instead.

Henri shifted in his saddle to ease himself as he thought of how they'd spent that time. She'd begun to teach him the art of massage, demonstrating on his body; when Master Fouet had heard what they were doing, he sent one of his own masseurs, a squat, hairy man whose hands turned muscles to liquid. Henri had practiced his new expertise on their last evening, spending two hours alone with the duchess, reveling in each soft moan he squeezed from her lips. She had fallen asleep from his ministrations, so they hadn't been able to couple, but he'd slept in her bed, and for him it was almost enough; she'd slept so sweetly and deeply.

The duchess had spent one evening in the brothel's baths being scrubbed and steamed and trimmed and shaved, and most importantly, having her hair dyed dark to aid in her disguise. Henri had spent the same evening in an observation room. The pair he'd watched had included a young woman guest, perhaps Sylvie's age, and an older man, one of Master Fouet's senior prostitutes. Their activities consisted solely of the man's kissing and licking his partner's cunt and clitoris, in a seemingly endless range of techniques. She climaxed at least seven times that he could see, and perhaps more that he couldn't. He hadn't even realized a woman could experience such a thing; he'd never managed so many climaxes in a row even when he'd newly gained his manhood and could think of nothing else; no wonder she had paid for this service alone. Henri had watched with all of his attention, and later pondered how he might broach the subject with the duchess, for he could think of no better way to serve her.

Also, he really wanted to see if he could make her come seven times in a night. Or more. He wouldn't mind having her at his mercy in such a way, just for a little while. No matter how many times they fucked, she always kept him at a distance. He knew it was the way of the world—he was not her equal and never could be—but he hadn't realized how wearing it could be, to feel like a convenience.

The morning of their departure from the brothel, Henri slipped out of their rooms before the duchess could summon him, and cared for their horses and mule himself. It felt good to remind himself of who he truly was, and the animals' affection for him didn't hurt.

Being on the road again was strange. Henri felt years older than at the journey's beginning. They camped in early evening, to give him time to care for all the animals before dark. The duchess, to Henri's surprise, helped him, and the work went more quickly. Sylvie gathered deadwood for a fire, and heated water for washing and tea; as twilight fell, they ate bread and cheese and fruit, and drank two bottles of wine from wooden cups.

The duchess curled in a heap of blankets near the low fire and opened her sketchbook. Henri thought of lying near her, then saw Sylvie capture Kaspar's hand and drag him toward the denser trees. Curious, he followed. He knew they'd seen him, but neither protested. After a few steps, Sylvie stopped and waited for him to catch up.

All three of them wore their cloaks against the spring chill, and to Henri, only their faces were visible as lighter blurs. As they went farther from the fire, even their faces faded. Henri tripped over a tree root and stumbled into Kaspar's bulk. Sylvie caught his arms; he recognized her small hands.

"We may stop here, I think we will not disturb madame," Sylvie said.

Kaspar sighed. Henri had noticed he often sighed when Sylvie was involved. "What do you want? I don't have the single-tail, and I won't have you tangling it in these trees and spoiling the leather."

"I wanted to thank you," Sylvie said. "You kept us safe, when I could not. Also, I enjoyed myself with Master Fouet."

"You may thank me by letting me have my rest," Kaspar said. "If you have so much vigor, why don't you play with Henri out here, while Her Grace and I sleep? Besides, what do you think you can do for me, girl?"

"I'm not Sylvie's toy," Henri said.

Talking over him, Sylvie said, "I am not a fool, Kaspar. What do you think Master Fouet and I spoke of, those nights we spent together? I know there are ways a eunuch can be plea-sured. I can't imagine you don't know them yourself."

"Really?" Henri said, before he could stop himself. "How?"

Kaspar said, "I'm not your toy, either, Sylvie."

"I only wanted to be kind. Why must you always be so awful to me?" From her tone, Henri could tell Sylvie was pouting.

"I gave you Master Fouet. That ought to keep you for a few months."

"Are you jealous? I have had madame now, and so has Henri. Do you think we are taking your duties away? Or is it that you miss Arno? I miss him. He is much nicer than you."

Henri wondered if Arno still lived, and felt pity. How strange that, at the beginning of this adventure, he'd feared the eunuch guards more than anything else, even the duke.

Kaspar said, "Arno is no business of yours."

"You *do* miss him," Sylvie said. "You should tell him so, when next you see him. Madame would not mind."

"Sylvie, your nose must be too long, as I'm sure you didn't mean to poke it into my business."

Henri heard a boot crunch on leaf litter, then a rustling, and he guessed she'd embraced Kaspar. Kaspar did not push her away until a moment later. Henri wondered what his expression might have shown. He considered walking back to their camp-site.

"Perhaps we can take your mind from what is none of our business," Sylvie said. "You would enjoy giving a gift to madame, wouldn't you, Kaspar? Henri, come here."

"Me?"

"Is there anyone else standing here in the dark? And why do you always question me, when you know you will like what I do?"

He wasn't sure why. He didn't always like the way she treated him, but he did like sex. Henri stumbled forward until he collided with soft warmth. Hands grabbed him, Sylvie's small ones and Kaspar's huge paws.

Sylvie said, "Just be still. You want to help Kaspar, don't you?"

Henri felt the puff of Kaspar's chuckle on the top of his head. The eunuch slid his hands down Henri's back until he could squeeze Henri's buttocks. Henri rose onto his toes; Kaspar's fingertips passed dangerously close to his scrotum. Kaspar said, "Sylvie, you have no shame." He reached lower, and then did close his fingers over Henri's balls. He traced and pulled on them gently. Henri's riding leathers were quickly too tight.

Sylvie pressed close to his back, trapping Kaspar's arms between them. Putting her arms around his waist, she pushed her hands beneath the edge of Henri's leathers and delicately squeezed. She unbuttoned his leathers, drew out his cock and pulled on it. Henri choked. Sylvie and Kaspar were tugging in opposite directions, and he thought he would fly apart. Sylvie ringed his erection with her fingers, one hand beneath the head and the other at the base, and said, "Dear Henri, you are such fun. Don't worry, we'll send you to madame soon."

Henri gave in to the present moment. Kaspar was laughing. Henri had never heard him laugh aloud before. Kaspar went to his knees behind Henri, dragged his leathers down farther and set to licking his scrotum as he rolled it between palm and fingers. Sylvie sank to her knees as well, pressing kisses along his shaft before closing her lips over his crown and sucking.

Henri clamped his hand over his mouth to muffle his groan. He panted, belly heaving, for several moments before he could say, "Stop. Please. Stop."

Sylvie pulled her mouth free with a smacking sound. Kaspar gave his buttocks one final squeeze, stood up and clapped him on the shoulder. "Go to her. Don't trip over…anything." He began to chuckle again as Henri retreated, yanking at his leathers and pulling them up as far as they would go.

Henri flipped his shirttails over his erection and stumbled into the firelight. The duchess was sitting up, a blanket around her shoulders. "Henri?" she said, then looked at him more closely. The corner of her mouth twitched. "Come here," she said.

For a moment, Henri wished someone would take him seriously. If he hadn't been so desperately aroused, he might have asked that she tell Sylvie to leave him alone, even though he really ought to deal with Sylvie himself. He couldn't always hide behind his duchess. Now, however, he sank down next to her. She lifted his shirttail, then lifted a brow.

Henri swallowed. "May I—what would you like?"

She looked him over, knees to face. Her expression didn't change, but he could tell she was thinking. At last she said, "Stroke yourself, as you like to be stroked. Close your eyes. Pretend I am not here."

"Yes, madame," Henri whispered. He closed his eyes and let his hand drift down and cup his cock's head. He squeezed and pulled, remembering Sylvie's mouth on him, then gripped below the head. He could relax a little with the more indirect stimulation. He stroked down, then up, rubbing his foreskin against his shaft, shifting to two hands when he needed more stimulation, working his fingers along the prominent ridge that ran beneath. From time to time, he nudged the edge of his thumb beneath his foreskin, flinching in pleasure as his calluses brushed his tenderest skin.

He remembered Kaspar's tongue on his scrotum and reached down as his balls drew up, close to spilling. He cupped them in his hand and stilled his grasp on his cock, breathing deeply.

The duchess touched his shoulder and he startled, his eyes flying open. She said, "Fuck me now," and tugged her skirts up around her waist. She leaned back onto her elbows and beckoned, her gaze soft and her cheeks flushed bright with desire.

He hadn't wanted this to go so quickly. He hadn't had a chance to tell her what he wanted. He could not argue, however, either with her or with his insistent cock.

Henri pushed her knees apart and pressed the head of his cock just within her cunt, shivering all over as her wet lips grasped. Her inner muscles pulled; he gave up teasing himself and thrust. Not deeply enough. He hooked his arms beneath her thighs and lifted, driving more deeply into her with a long sigh of satisfaction. He held there, his cock trembling in the caress of her wet inner skin, then leaned down and kissed her lips. Her hands went to her breasts, pulling at her nipples. When he straightened, she said, "Fuck me."

Henri pulled back, then slid into her more deeply, his eyes fluttering shut in pleasure. He had to withdraw entirely and breathe before he could speak. "I'm glad to do this," he said, in a rush. "You don't have to order me. I—I don't like to be reminded that you can order me."

The duchess looked up at him in surprise. "It isn't orders." She touched his arm. It gave him courage to speak further.

"You know that can't be so," Henri said. "Not really. No one would ever believe it. But if, in private, when we're together—"

"Henri—" she said.

He sensed pity for his ignorance and couldn't stand it. "You think it's impossible to forget what I am. It is, if you won't even try."

The duchess looked at him searchingly, for a long time. At last she said, "I am always the duchess. Pretense is a mistake."

Henri closed his eyes for a moment. He said, "Then maybe you could just ask me for what you want. Not because you think it's right, or because you think I'll like it, but because you want it, too. And I'll try to do the same."

"And what do you want right now, Henri?" the duchess asked.

Henri couldn't have what he truly wanted, so he told her what he knew she could give. "I would really, really like to fuck you now, and maybe you could keep playing with your breasts so I can watch."

She smiled faintly. "I think I will be satisfied with that. And...and I would also like it if you once called me by my name."

Henri's heart seemed to stop. He bent close to her, passing his lips along her cheekbone on the way to her ear. "Camille," he breathed.

CHAPTER THIRTEEN

Once, it had not been so difficult for Camille to open her own desires to another, even though most of her trust had been based on lies. She'd been eight years old when her father had conquered the coastal duchy and killed its duke, establishing the lands and their valuable harbors as a protectorate of his own. The next year, he'd come home, bringing young Maxime with him to groom him as Lord Protector and, incidentally, keep him away from any groups needing a focus for rebellion. He had also hoped to instill in the boy a great loyalty to himself, as he had no son of his own. He took great care when telling Camille this, reminding her that she had no need for jealousy. As she could never be a man, it was his duty as her father to find a male ally for her until she married the man who would be the next duke.

At eight, Camille had understood that palace intrigues happened, and wars, but she saw the surface results more than the interior motivations, and when her parents bothered to speak to her, she believed what they told her. The truth she knew the was that her father had eliminated a dangerous, piratical duke who endangered them all by angering their neighbors. The pirate had refused to negotiate, so her father had killed him. The duke's wife had been killed in the fighting that ensued. This left Maxime fatherless as well as motherless, so her father would now take care of Maxime instead. Because Maxime was a boy, he held greater value than she did, despite her being given much greater privilege. He could never become duke, so at least she did not have to think of him as a brother. She could not hate him; he had no father or mother, and even his dog was dead. To be angry with her father would be punished as childishness. So she reserved her anger for a place inside her belly, where it would live until, one day, her future husband would release it.

She hadn't seen much of Maxime in her day-to-day life. He was always there in the palace, but his schooling was different from hers, and he took his meals with his tutors. Most of the time, she forgot about him. Her life revolved around lessons in deportment and foreign languages and riding. She had no more and no less attention from her father than she'd had before Maxime's arrival; she had always known she was less to him than his favorite concubine. Her mother lacked interest in Maxime just as she had always lacked interest in Camille, preferring to spend her time with her coterie of aristocratic ladies, gambling at cards and dice for high stakes, which sometimes included the favors of her eunuchs. For the remaining three months of the year, she would travel to the king's court, garnering gossip and new styles to bring back to the duchy with the spring.

Her mother died of a sudden attack when Camille was eleven, and for the next year and more, she had no room in her life for anything else than grief; not grief for her mother, but grief for the mothering she'd never received. She was then sent away to court for two years, to attain the requisite polish for a prize in the marriage auction. She considered herself lucky that her period of official mourning had prevented her from going earlier, for attendance at court would take most hours of her day, and she would only be able to ride in the early mornings. The girls and women of the court were friendly to her at first, but she soon learned this was because of her father's recent wealth, obtained from the lands of Maxime's father, whom he had slain. Once they knew her better, and learned she had more time for horses than fashion, they eyed her askance, as if at any moment she might put on boy's clothes and ride away like a girl in a ballad. The boys of her own age smirked while they bowed to her, and behind her back made ribald comments about riding astride.

She returned home to find her father preparing lists of prospective husbands for her. Maxime was not among them. Though he was not her friend, he was still more familiar to her than the young people of the court, and she found she looked forward to seeing him again. While she was gone, Maxime had grown tall and beautiful. She began to watch for him in the corridors, and to schedule her riding when he would be riding, too. The women of the palace had noticed him as well, but Camille knew she would have him in the end. They might give him their bodies, but she would not be distracted by courtiers, footmen and eunuchs.

Maxime was only a year older than she, and it didn't take long before he watched for her, too. Their first conversations were brief, relating to their relative health, to their schooling, or the merits and flaws of their current horses; they spoke of nothing her accompanying eunuch and Maxime's accompanying manservant would find exceptionable. She preferred to speak of horses. One day, Maxime spoke to her of the sea instead. It was as if he saw her for the first time, and she him. Camille basked in his fervent gaze and begged him to tell her more. He asked about her new foal instead, staring into her eyes as she spoke. No one had ever listened to her so closely before. No one had wanted her to speak.

Gradually, their conversations grew and shifted; Maxime spoke of his lessons in government, and encouraged Camille to do the same. In whispers, he would then tell her of how his parents' duchy had been governed, and how it had differed from that of her father. His mother had shared equally in the duties of state, something no one spoke of anymore, save Maxime. Women had also served as guards and soldiers; there were no eunuchs, except those who'd fled persecution else-where. Camille found the differences intriguing, and in some cases wondered why her father had not done the same. This led to her first real questioning of things as they were. She began to secretly plan, in her mind, what she would do with the duchy, were she the duke.

One winter day, she spent the morning planning a ball to celebrate her sixteenth birthday, her first official appearance among the highest of the land. Prospective suitors from six duchies would attend including, though she did not know it then, her future husband. Maxime would also attend, wearing her father's colors, a fact which he probably disliked though he had learned by now to show nothing of his true feelings. Camille was learning much the same as she observed the intrigues of her father and his own suitors.

That particular day, it snowed, accumulating so fast during the morning hours that her daily ride would be unwise. Unwilling to give up her few precious hours of privacy, she slipped away from her guard and escaped to the stable. She found Maxime there waiting. He, too, had escaped his guard, or managed to bribe him; she knew he bribed his guard when he sought the sexual services of the palace maids or seamstresses. Camille fought her jealousy by wondering what it would be like to have such freedom for herself.

Maxime leaned confidently in the corner alcove where buckets were stored, arms crossed over his chest, booted ankles crossed. He was black-haired, and even then had needed to shave twice in a day if he had to attend an evening event. Camille wondered if the hair on the backs of his hands was wiry or soft, and how the hair on his head would feel in contrast.

His long locks curled on the back of his neck and trailed invitingly down his forehead. His eyes were dark, rich brown, unreadable, his teeth when he smiled almost unbearably white and straight.

Camille had hoped he would be there, even though she hadn't really expected it. For a moment she wondered if she might be dreaming. However, the knee-weakening fantasies she'd entertained through many nights bore no resemblance to this reality: the small sounds of horses shifting their weight, their smell mingling with that of manure and stale winter hay; the crunch of straw beneath her boots as she slowly walked toward him.

"I thought you'd find me." Maxime's deep voice thrilled in her throat, her chest. As she came closer, she fancied she could feel his body heat. He'd slung his jacket on a hook, and she could see, at the open throat of his loose shirt, an intriguing wisp of black hair. Was he hairy all over? His belly and legs, too? What would it feel like to touch? Did he like being hairy instead of soft and smooth? She wanted to ask him that and many other questions. He would laugh if she did. He might laugh if she touched him as she wanted to touch.

Maxime did not laugh when she laid her hand on his forearm. She could feel the heat of his skin through the thin linen. Her fingers curled as a shock like velvet traveled up her arm. Maxime said, "What do you want, Camille?"

His use of her name gave her another small shock. Her father addressed her by her title, everyone else by her title or as

Mistress. She didn't think her father would allow Maxime this liberty if he knew. She smiled, trying not to show her nervousness. "Maxime. I want to be alone with you, of course."

"I don't think you know what that means. You only have your eunuchs, after all."

Actually, she didn't, not in the way he meant. Jarman the eunuch guarded her, but did not perform any of the other duties she'd heard rumored, not with her. She'd never dared ask for those services, when she knew her father would find out. If Jarman did not speak, then her maids would do so. When she was betrothed, of course, it would be different; Jarman and Casimir, the younger of the two eunuchs, would prepare her body for marriage. But until then, her father believed the teaching they could provide was too dangerous. If she came to rely on them, she might lose all taste for relations with the real man who would be her husband.

She said, "Maybe I don't know what I want. Do you want me to leave? Do you have someone else waiting for you?" She lifted an eyebrow. She'd spent hours practicing the expression in the mirror, and knew it was maddening.

Maxime matched her expression, though without the lifted brow. "You are going to be trouble for someone," he said. "Too bad it isn't your father."

"Let's not talk about him right now."

"No talking? All right." He grabbed her shoulders and pulled her toward him. Excitement surged through Camille, culminating when his open mouth swept down on hers. Their kiss was wetter and more slippery than she'd imagined; she was surprised by how much she liked that, how the slide of his tongue seemed to shiver all the way down between her legs. He was large and solid and warm, and he smelled delicious. He tasted forbidden.

As they kissed, she stood on her toes, digging her fingers into his shirt. He controlled her head with his hands, turning her so he could penetrate more deeply with his tongue, thrusting in slowly and slickly for an interminable time. She squeezed her thighs together, applying pressure to the swelling tissues of her quim. She moaned and felt a damp trickle down her leg. When Maxime's hand closed over her breast, she jerked in surprise then clamped her own hand over his, so he wouldn't stop.

Maxime kissed her neck and the soft skin under her jaw, tasting her with his tongue, murmuring, "You do have some juice in you, don't you? I'd love to feel that juice. I could stick my finger up in you, make you cry like a wild hawk in the clouds. Have you ever done that? Have you ever put your finger inside your cunt?"

"Oh," Camille breathed, letting him back her against the wall. He spoke things she had not allowed herself even to think. Forbidden, it was all forbidden, and thrilling down to the marrow of her bones.

He opened his mouth against her throat and sucked. His hands coasted down her back and clenched on her bottom, gathering fistfuls of her split riding skirt. He hauled her against him, against something hard, and made a gasping sound. "Yes," he said. "That's so good. Feel that? Feel how hard I am? I want to put that inside you. It would feel good, I promise. You would moan and twist and cry for more, so I'd go in even more, and shove and shove until I was all the way in, and then I'd ride you until you screamed." He thrust against her, and she moaned as her belly knotted with need. "Oh, I want to fuck you."

"Please," she gasped.

"Please stop or please fuck you?"

"Please fuck me." Camille jerked back, breathing hard. She'd never said the words before. Her quim overflowed with cream and her nipples burned and ached inside her jacket. Her mouth felt loose and wet as her quim. "No," she said. "Don't, we can't."

Maxime groaned and let her go. "Damn it." He turned his back, shoulders heaving as he gasped for breath. She caught a glimpse of his male flesh poking out the top of his riding leathers and was astonished by how fat and shiny it looked. *That* was supposed to fit inside of her?

"I didn't mean to—"

He turned back toward her, leaning one arm against the wall. His face was red. "Damn, I don't think I can wait." He flipped open the buttons of his leathers one-handed and his cock bounced out, slapping against his belly. Black hair curled all around it, hiding its root from her eyes. "How about watching? Will you watch me?"

Camille could not look away from the hugeness of his erection. She licked her lips. "You don't understand. I never—not ever—"

Maxime paused. "Really?" He grabbed his shaft and pulled it

once, end to end, groaning. "The old bastard never lets you have any fun." He pulled again. "Well, now's your chance. Last chance. Stay, or run."

Camille wanted to touch his cock for herself, trace the blue veins in the reddened skin, but couldn't make herself move. "I want to see," she said, backing away until she found a bale of straw on which to sit. "Maxime, I liked the rest. The kissing, and the... what else you did. It was even better than I imagined. I'm just not ready this time. It's too much. Can we—will you show me more, later?"

"So long as you understand it's just fun, we've got all winter," he said, hauling on his cock twice more. There was a swelling at the top, like a mushroom's cap, or a helmet. Fluid eased from its tip. He smeared the fluid over the helmet and down his shaft, then spit on his hand and added that. "Watch this. You can do it for me sometime. Then you can do it with your mouth."

Camille balled her fists in her lap. Pictures flashed rapidly through her mind, images of what he'd described, before his hand moved again. He fondled the helmet for a few moments, gasped, then used both hands on his whole cock in rapid succession, pulling his shaft away from his body and letting it thump back against his belly. His shirt darkened with sweat. Camille stared, entranced. She could smell his sweat and something else, muskier. She hadn't realized a man's sex had its own scent, as hers did. She pressed her hands down against her quim, breathing rapidly. Maxime pumped faster, faster. He threw his head back and groaned with each stroke. Suddenly, his body tensed and his cock began to jolt, spewing thick white liquid. "Oh, fuck," he said. "Fuck, fuck, yes."

Camille writhed against her fists. She felt huge between her legs, overflowing, soaking her underthings and dampening the front of her skirt. She stared at Maxime's juddering cock and imagined it rammed against her, into her. She needed it, needed something, before she burst. She ground her fist into her quim. She couldn't breathe. Her breath came in jerks. Her quim convulsed, washing her with sweetness. "Oh," she moaned. "Oh, that's so good." When it was over, she and Maxime stared at each other in dazed repletion.

After that, Camille knew what she wanted to happen, but unfortunately, the opportunity didn't. A new tutor came for Maxime to teach him advanced mathematics, and a new riding master to perfect his technique in the subtle skills of the ring. Camille, too, convinced the new riding master to teach her in the evenings, but by then Maxime had returned to his mathematics. For almost a year, they met only in the corridors, taking every chance to brush against each other as they passed, and exchange hot glances. She could barely speak to him without thinking of his cock jerking in his hand. A few times, they were able to steal hurried kisses, hiding in closets and curtained alcoves and, once, a wardrobe. It wasn't even close to enough. Alone in her bed at night, Camille tested herself with her fingers, biting her lip against any sound that would wake her maids, and imagining herself taking Maxime's huge cock in her mouth, or her quim. On more than one occasion, she spent their brief times together whispering her fantasies against his rough cheek, making him pant.

At the ball celebrating her seventeenth birthday, she and Maxime performed the stilted opening dance, not daring to get too close to each other. Maxime slipped her a bit of paper as they parted. She went to the retiring room as soon as she could and, in private, unfolded the paper. It read, *the library*. She tossed the paper quickly into the fire and went out again for the next dance.

"They tell me you have an interest in riding," Lord Michel said. His hand rested on the small of her back, faint pressure through her layers of gown, bodice and chemise. His gloved hand held one of hers, pinching a little too tightly; she could see the shape of a bulky signet ring and at least two other rings bulging the white fabric. She wondered how he kept his gloves clean, when he did not always have a maid nearby to unobtrusively exchange stained ones.

She was glad when their turn came, and he had to release her to move down the row. She didn't much like him; he had little conversation and seemed extraordinarily dismissive of almost everyone. At least he was not too old, and had all his teeth, and did not spray droplets of spittle when he brayed a laugh. She supposed his blue eyes could be handsome, if they ever showed any kindness, and his gaze was so intense that it incited twisting in her belly. When she went to her next partner, she did not think of him again, except once, when she felt his eyes on her from across the room.

Camille was expected to be on display for the length of the ball, but she had sent her maids to sleep early, so they would not know when she returned. The ball ended at two. She shook the guests' hands as they departed, until her fingers were swollen and aching. She did not see Maxime at all.

Nevertheless, once the last guest had gone, she gathered up her lacy skirts and slipped into the library, lit for the night with a single lamp turned low. Deep alcoves for the window seats were covered by long curtains. She chose one near the long chaise and tucked her feet up, folding her skirts carefully out of sight. She arranged a tiny gap in the curtains and waited, heart thumping.

Maxime came in as the clock struck the half hour. Before Camille could lift the curtain, a woman entered. She pushed the door closed and giggled. Maxime whirled at the sound. Camille's eyes widened. It was Madame Visser, the widowed daughter of the minister of finance. She had three children.

She said, "Meeting Her Grace here, are you? Shame on you. If I tell His Grace he'll make you a eunuch. What a waste that would be."

Camille bit her hand. Her chest felt cold from shock. Maxime's shoulders stiffened. Camille willed him to deny it. He said nothing.

Madame Visser said, "There's a price for my silence. My

bathmaid says she's had you a few times. Is it true that you're...prodigious?"

The moment stretched. Maxime would refuse, and her father would find out. He couldn't kill her, but what would he do instead, to punish her for choosing her own partner? What might he do to Maxime, whom he did not intend should marry his daughter? Would he truly castrate him? Maxime took a deep breath. "You may be the judge of that, my lady," he said. He took the widow's hand and pressed it to his bulge.

Madame Visser gasped and massaged him. "Let me see it," she demanded.

"Let me see your teats," Maxime countered. He stripped down her bodice, sliding his hands into her corset and extracting what little of her breasts was not already exposed. Camille gasped, clapping her hand over her mouth. Madame Visser had a metal bar pierced through her right nipple, with a tiny emerald dangling from each end. Maxime sucked one end of the bar into his mouth and she instantly groaned. He walked her backward to the chaise. They collapsed onto it, full-length. The back of the chaise faced the door; from her window alcove, Camille had a perfect view.

Madame Visser rolled her shoulders against the chaise as Maxime suckled her. She roughly pinched and pulled her other nipple and held Maxime's head with her free hand. "Yes, yes, yes," she chanted. Camille stared as Madame Visser lifted one leg entirely and hooked it over Maxime's back. He yanked up her skirt and ground against her.

Camille was growing wet. Surely she shouldn't be watching

this, shouldn't be enjoying it. Maxime had been forced into this. As Camille watched, Madame Visser fumbled his formal breeches open and tugged out his cock and balls.

"You beauty," she crooned, running her hands over his thick length. "How long is it?"

"I've never measured, madame."

"I could wrap a piece of notepaper around this prong, and the edges would never touch," she said, urging him off her. "I shall have to ride you. Lie down for me."

Camille wanted to scream. She had never particularly noticed Madame Visser before, but now she hated her. She'd forced Maxime into sex; she didn't have to humiliate him as well.

Maxime braced one foot on the floor and held Madame Visser's waist as she lowered herself onto him a bit at a time. Camille found herself watching with held breath. Maxime's cock was truly large. It was shocking to see it be swallowed up, a fraction at a time. She glanced at his face; his eyes were open, watching Madame Visser's breasts, but his jaw was clenched. When she had managed to take about half of his length, she began to move up and down, impaling herself deeper each time, letting out little cries at each stroke. Before many minutes had passed, she was groin to groin with Maxime. She rocked back and forth now, groaning out, "You brute, you big brute. Don't thrust. Don't you dare. I'm going to come." Camille couldn't help but be aroused now. She couldn't stop imagining herself in the other woman's place. Except she would be nicer to Maxime.

Madame Visser keened as she climaxed, then slowly stretched her arms and back. "Don't move!" she said. She rolled her hips, then grabbed the back of the chaise and lifted herself off. She stared at his still-hard cock, shook her head in amazement, and giggled. She pulled down her skirt and began fastening her bodice. "If only I had a measuring tape. But, oh, I suppose that will have to keep me for now. I must go. My father will be wondering why I haven't returned, and I must kiss my children good-night. Consider your secret safe with me. Another time, perhaps?"

"Of course," Maxime said, heavily sarcastic. "Another time." He climbed to his feet, his cock bobbing, yet appearing graceful all the same, and bowed as Madame Visser hurried out the door. As soon as the door closed, he sat down, hard. "Camille?" he whispered.

Camille flung open the curtains and threw herself at his feet. "Thank you, Maxime! Thank you. She was terrible."

"You *were* here," he said, and poked his cock with his fingertip, watching it bob. "At least this was useful, for once." Gingerly, he wiped the wetness from his erection with his shirttail. "She must have followed me. I'm so stupid!"

Camille fetched a decanter of water and a napkin, which Maxime used to thoroughly wash himself. She said, "She could have seen either of us, any time in the past few months. She didn't even let you—Maxime," Camille said, tentatively reaching out a hand. "Can I—will you let me help you?"

He glanced at the clock. "I'm almost out of time," he said. "I won't be able to do anything for you this time."

"I don't care," Camille said. "Tell me if I do it wrong." She licked her palms and grasped his cock in both hands, as she'd seen him do so long ago. She kept up a steady motion while she licked and sucked at the head.

"A little harder," he begged, after a while, so she sucked until her cheeks hollowed. His helmet rubbed against the top of her mouth and he groaned, then groaned again. "I can't—I'm—fuck!"

Camille choked and spat, but she was laughing, too, amazed at her own power.

"Next time," Maxime promised once he'd recovered, pulling her to her feet and kissing her. "I'll show you what it feels like when I lick your cunt. I want you to know why I did that for you."

She'd clung to that promise until a week later, when her father sent Maxime away first to swear his fealty to the king and then to travel on to the coastal protectorate and be instructed in its rule. It was months too soon. She suspected her father had at least guessed at her interest. Camille hadn't seen Maxime since. A few years later, he had written to her through Lord Stagiaire, hoping to continue their discourse as adults, but by then she had married, and foolishly had not replied, thinking it disloyal to Michel to maintain a friendship with another man, one with whom she'd been intimate.

She'd been a fool. She was a fool no longer.

CHAPTER FOURTEEN

Henri had been spoiled on the journey so far. After three nights sleeping on the hard ground and only cursory washing, he was pitifully grateful to stop at another inn, even if only to meet with a courier from the duchess's loyalists in the palace. They'd like as not be fleeing in the middle of the night.

This time, he wouldn't be sleeping in the barn; his new disguise was as Sylvie's older brother. He made sure to call her "little brother" at every opportunity, and once or twice thumped the back of her head with his forefinger, if someone on the road was watching, or if he felt he had enough escape room. Kaspar, with distracting noise and hilarity, played their father, and the duchess his silent, unobtrusive wife. Henri had even disguised the horses and mule as best he could, cropping their manes and obscuring their fine lines through a mixture of poor grooming and judicious applications of mud and tree sap. He hoped no one would notice the tack; he'd removed all embellishment early in the journey, to make the saddles look as if they'd been bought second- or thirdhand, but a trained eye would recognize their quality.

Despite their disguises, Henri felt uneasy on the crowded coastal road. He thought Sylvie might feel the same, given that she was distracted enough not to murder him for his teasing. Kaspar's playacting included carrying a massive ax, just the sort of thing to clear fallen trees from the road, but clearly chosen as a dangerous weapon. They all knew that if the loyal courier could find them, the duke's spies could as well. The duchess alone appeared unmoved by their first venture into society in many days. But then, Henri reflected, she almost always appeared unmoved.

The village they reached at the end of the day held a blacksmith's hut and shed, five shabby houses and a single inn with three rooms to let, one of which already held a peddler, his apprentice, his burly dog and his pet monkey. A family such as they pretended to be would not pay for two rooms when one would do. There wouldn't be room for Kaspar to practice knifeplay with him, an exercise Henri had grown used to on the road. He resigned himself to a night sleeping on the floor, listening to Sylvie's snoring and the constant *whisht* of Kaspar honing his blades while he guarded the door. When Sylvie took over the watch in the early morning hours, she generally trod on Henri as she passed, just as a matter of principle.

A third traveler, a man of perhaps fifty with sleek boots and a fashionable haircut, arrived as Henri and Sylvie lugged their saddlebags upstairs. The duchess conferred with Kaspar a moment longer, glancing at the traveler as she headed for the stairs. Neither made a signal of recognition that he could see, but Henri noted, his neck prickling, that the traveler seemed arrested by her long dark hair, caught back by a short scarf.

Sylvie slung a saddlebag at his rear. "Hurry up," she growled, in her near-perfect imitation of a young boy's cracking voice. The sooner they were out of sight, the sooner Kaspar could sneak out to watch the road.

But before he went, Kaspar arranged to have supper brought up from the inn's kitchen.

Watching him leave, the duchess said, "He's a better man than my—former—husband, and a better mother than I would ever be."

Henri crossed his fingers and jerked them over his shoulder, to avert bad luck. She might be pregnant with his child at this very moment. The duchess saw his gesture and raised a brow at him. Henri lifted his chin. If she bore his child, she would not bear the burden of it alone.

Sylvie interrupted, barging into the room with an armload of clean linens. She and Henri made the bed, then she helped the duchess out of her riding boots and brushed her hair. Henri sat on the floor, watching them, turning a hoof pick over and over in his hands. Tired and hungry, no one spoke, until the duchess took the brush from Sylvie's hand.

"Go and help Kaspar," she said.

Henri got to his feet, but she shook her head. "No, Sylvie will go."

"Madame, you will have no protection."

The duchess straightened her back. "If anything happens we don't expect, bring word. Go."

Looking mutinous, Sylvie took her time assembling her costume and putting together a sandwich of bread, cheese and meat. When the duchess at last pointed her chin to the door, Sylvie went, letting the door slam behind her.

Her boots clattered down the stairs. Henri would have argued with the duchess, reminded her that Kaspar and Sylvie saw protecting her to be their duty, and that she should let them get on with it as they saw fit. He should have argued, but Sylvie was gone, and only they two were left. He scooted along the floor and leaned against her leg without speaking.

She tangled her fingers in his hair, rubbing his scalp. Henri let his head loll. He closed his eyes. It would be easy to fall asleep at her feet. She stopped, though, and grasped his shoulder. "Don't you want to sit up here?"

Henri wanted his dinner more than he wanted sex. On the other hand, he'd barely touched her since the day before. He sat on the bed next to her and took her in his arms. The bed had a mattress stuffed with horsehair that made it hard as rock; they might as well have slept on the hard ground, and the ground hadn't been as redolent of past visitors as this bed. He'd prefer clean straw to this. He supposed it would be all right once they got going.

The duchess laid her head on his shoulder and sighed. Perhaps she didn't want sex right now, either. Henri hesitated, then kissed her hair.

His heart nearly jolted from his chest when someone pounded on the door. It was not the rhythm indicating their contact. "I'll send them away," he said.

The duchess opened her mouth, closed it and pressed her fingers to her lips. She pointed to Henri. He would be the one to speak for them, if necessary.

The pounding stopped. A maid would not have knocked. Henri opened the door a crack and saw the traveler from downstairs eyeing him expectantly. Sick apprehension churned through his belly, and his scalp pulled tight with fear. The traveler held a sword. He pushed the blade farther through the doorway, forcing Henri backward. He opened the door with his shoulder, entered and kicked it shut, all without lowering his blade.

Purple gems clustered on the sword's protective hilt. Henri could see the etched crest on the blade, just below. This was a courtier of the duke's. If not for the blade, he would have struck him without warning. As it was, he couldn't approach without being skewered. He carried a knife now, at the small of his back. He could almost hear Kaspar's patient voice: his knife wasn't suited for throwing; he would need to be closer.

Behind him, Henri heard the duchess slide off the bed to her feet and step forward. She was going to speak. The courtier would know her. Henri did not search for courage. It shot into his throat and out his mouth before he could think. He said, "What do you want? Who are you?"

The courtier stopped. He did not lower his sword. "I am Lord Belette," he said. He smiled. "I am wondering who you might be. I recognize the lady, of course." He inclined his head the barest fraction. "Your Grace. Or should I say, Your *former* Grace."

Henri couldn't manage a laugh, but he threw out his hands as if no longer afraid of the sword. If he reached just a bit more, he could grab the blade and perhaps wrest it from Belette's grip. "You see, Marie, it's easy! If you can take in a man of status such as Lord Belette, the bumpkins of these towns will be completely satisfied!"

The sword's tip pressed into his belly and Henri sucked in his breath. Belette said, "Move away from her. Slowly."

Henri didn't dare glance at the duchess for help; it would seem, rightly, as if she commanded him. Nor did he want to show too much fear and appear guilty. He blustered, but didn't move. "Sir! What are you— I shall call the innkeeper—"

Belette prodded him with the sword. "No one will care if I kill you," he remarked. "Stop protecting her, and I will let you go free."

"Protecting—no, sir! She is not who you think she is. She is merely a whore! The newest attraction at Master Fouet's establishment, along the road. We are on our way there."

It was clear Belette had heard of Master Fouet's. His sword lowered a fraction. Henri's fear surged again when he said, "I heard a rumor that Master Fouet already had such an attraction. And recently."

Henri managed to sound indignant. "She is inferior, sir, to my Marie. I have it on Master Fouet's authority that creature will serve only as understudy once we've arrived."

The sword lowered farther, and Belette abruptly stepped to

the side, peering at the duchess over Henri's shoulder. "It is an excellent likeness."

"More so, when she is properly dressed," Henri said quickly. "Master Fouet will provide the proper costumes, to suit all tastes."

Belette took a step closer. Henri stepped back, then wanted to hit himself for not standing his ground. Would a pimp stand his ground? His reaction had been instinctive. Belette said, "Her Grace is older. Her hair is turning gray. Though your Marie is older than she looks at a distance."

"Men do not want reality mixed with their fantasies," Henri said boldly. "And how many clients will she have, who have really seen the duchess?"

"I have seen her," Belette said. "I have stood across the room from her, and watched her on His Grace's arm. She is very regal. It is a pity she is barren, and thus useless to the succession. The duke will have to replace her. Your Marie might be out of fashion sooner than you think."

Stung, Henri said, "That will be my problem, not yours."

"Perhaps you would let me sample her."

Before that moment, Henri had not known he could be possessed by jealous rage. Before words could erupt, or he could attack Belette, the duchess shouldered him aside. Hands on hips, she surveyed Belette up and down. "A bit poncey," she said, in a voice higher pitched than her own.

Heart thudding painfully in his ears, Henri said, "He's a court flower, lovey. You've seen them before." *Don't,* he thought. *Please, Camille, don't do this.*

"He's more poncey than any of them I seen," she said. "I don't think he can sample anything in a dress."

"Marie, don't be rude to the gentleman," Henri said desperately. "I'll see him out. You need your rest."

The duchess threw a glance at him over her shoulder. "I won't have this poncey bastard saying I'm no good," she said, then returned her gaze to Belette. "Bad for business. You know that." She tossed her hair and began gathering her skirt in her hands. To Belette, she said, "Come on, then, my lord. Let's see what you've got."

"You've got too much sauce, my girl," Belette said. "Her Grace would never be so coarse."

"Well, I'm not Her Grace," the duchess said. "You're not man enough for her."

Belette lifted one corner of his lip in an unattractive snarl. "Your opinion is singularly worthless, tart. Get out, pimp."

"Oh, no," the duchess said. "My protector stays here. We don't know nothing about you. You could be claiming all manner of things that aren't true." To Henri's horror, she clambered onto the bed and, on all fours, yanked up her skirt. "Get on with it. Or can't you get it up?"

Henri stepped between her and Belette. "I don't want him soiling you," he said. "You're right, Marie, he could be the fake. At least you're an honest fake."

The duchess snorted, even as Belette grabbed Henri's arm and dragged him to the side. Henri twisted free only to freeze when she said, "I'll handle him, Master. Won't take but a tick."

Belette tossed his sword across the end of the bed and ripped open the fall of his pants. "Insolent, the pair of you," he snarled. "She wants it, she'll have it."

Henri's hands clenched into fists.

The duchess hadn't moved, or acknowledged Henri's attempted defense. "Just get it over with," she said wearily. "Master, he won't get out of here until he's satisfied, so we might as well."

"Out of my way, pimp," Belette said.

Henri backed slowly away, until his shoulders thumped into the wall. He clenched his fists behind his back, so Belette wouldn't see. His body felt like one giant knot, and if he could have, he would have killed Belette then, dragged him off the duchess and pummeled his face to pulp. Instead, he forced himself to watch as Belette hurriedly stroked himself to firmness and grabbed the duchess's breasts.

No.

Henri lunged, grabbing Belette's shoulders and slamming him into the door. "Pig!" he growled, and rammed his fist into Belette's gut.

The duchess shouted. Gradually, her words came through. She was demanding her fee.

"A crown!" Henri shouted, shaking Belette by the shoulders.

Belette choked and sneered. He dug into his waist pouch and flung the coin on the floor. "If her pussy's anything like her tongue, I'd do better with a cow in the field."

Henri squeezed his forearm against Belette's throat, his scalp prickling with rage. "Bastard," he snarled.

The duchess's fingers dug into his shoulder. "Master! I talked to him. He hasn't paid for that yet! Ten crowns a go with conversation, you promised!"

"Ten crowns!" Belette choked. "That's ridiculous for an old hag like her!"

"That's the price," Henri said. He could barely see the man's face through a red blur. "Pay up."

"I haven't got ten crowns on me! I pay on credit."

"That's what they all say," the duchess said darkly. "Shake him down, master." Henri heard a clink; she'd picked up the sword and rested its point on Belette's belt buckle.

"Gladly," Henri growled. After a rough and thorough search, he was shocked to find that Belette spoke the truth. Remembering his knife, he used it to cut through Belette's belt. He shoved him aside as his pants sagged and stepped back, letting the duchess menace him with the sword. "Maybe you should take it out in trade," he suggested, enjoying the way Belette paled, and the duchess smiled.

"Think I will," she said. She stepped closer, dropped the sword's point to the floor, and efficiently kneed Belette in the groin. As he doubled over, retching, she handed Henri the sword and said under her breath, "Get the magistrate. They'll hold him as a debtor until he can get someone to vouch for him."

Henri gave the sword back to her. "Keep this, just in case," he said.

He reached out his hand, wanting to touch her, but she

quickly stepped out of his reach. Belette had curled on the floor; she aimed a kick at his kidney and said, "Go on, I've got better things to do than look at this cheap son of a bitch."

Henri hesitated, then inclined his head to her, as formally as he knew how, and went to do her bidding.

CHAPTER FIFTEEN

Sylvie rode Lilas down a wagon track, reins in one hand, sandwich in the other. When she found Kaspar, he would probably laugh at her for being so disgruntled; after all, the duchess's will was their duty. If she wanted to fuck the stable-boy while she waited for the courier, they should be ready to strip off his clothes and shove him into the room.

Sylvie sighed. Perhaps it was different for the eunuchs. Perhaps they equated sex with simpler things like eating and sleeping. They wouldn't see anything wrong about madame wanting to eat her dinner in private. Though it was not the same here as in the palace. She was not safe. Wasn't it also their duty to keep her safe? Freedom was very unsafe. She didn't like it when madame took her safety into her own hands.

She spotted Tonnelle tied to a branch and placidly cropping its leaves. Sylvie tied Lilas nearby, remembering to let them stand head to tail as Henri had taught her, so each horse could brush flies from the face of the other. Why did the boy always have to think of madame's horses? He treated them like they were his children. The thought of Henri having children—if he'd planted his seed in madame's belly—she growled as she rummaged out pistols from her saddlebag, and fought her way through tangled brush until she found Kaspar's hiding place. He'd settled cross-legged behind a bristly hedge, in which he'd broken branches to have a clear view of the road. Sylvie made noise in her approach so he wouldn't accidentally kill her, and said, "Madame says I am to watch with you."

"She does, does she?" Kaspar gave her a brief, ironic glance, then returned his gaze to the road. "Try not to draw any attention. If the courier isn't who I hope, I'll need you to run and warn them."

If that had been the plan all along, madame and Kaspar must have discussed this between them, without involving her. Did madame not trust her? Because she did not look at her with calf eyes, like the boy? She moved a little farther back, concealing herself behind a clump of wild roses and slinging her pistols' belts across her chest. There were no convenient rocks or fallen trunks on which to lean. She unfolded her legs and bent over them, stretching the tired muscles in her thighs and back while pondering who Kaspar thought might be their courier. Arno? True, Arno would be most loyal, but his role in their escape and afterward had been dangerous. She would not be surprised if the young eunuch was dead. Kaspar would know this. It wasn't like him to express hope for something unlikely.

Unless she had been right, when she teased Kaspar about having feelings for his partner. It seemed unlikely. The court eunuchs were forbidden any sexual activity except in the service of their master or mistress. She couldn't imagine Kaspar breaking that law.

She had not known Arno well, even though he'd been in the duchess's service nearly five years. He'd always deferred to Kaspar, his mentor, just as Kaspar had deferred to his own teacher, Casimir. Except...Sylvie remembered the day madame had instructed her to fetch Henri to the palace. Arno had not been pleased when madame had sent him away for the afternoon; he worried the duke's guards would catch her at it and kill her on the spot. Sylvie had thought for a moment that he might actually protest. Kaspar's face and bearing had been more controlled. He'd taken the younger eunuch's arm and led him from the room. When Sylvie had returned from her errand, she'd found them together, sitting side by side on a bench, so close their thighs touched, though they weren't looking at each other. She remembered thinking it odd. There had been another chair, across the room. Perhaps the chair had been too far for casual conversation. Perhaps.

Sylvie watched Kaspar, speculating. It was better than thinking of the lumpy ground digging into her buttocks.

The light grayed. She fingered the flint and steel in her jacket pocket as the sun set, thinking they could pretend to be ordinary travelers stopped for the night, that is if no one noticed their lack of bags and supplies, all of which resided at the inn.

She sighed. Kaspar wouldn't want to expose them to possibly unfriendly eyes like that. He was more paranoid than she had ever been. She might be paranoid, too, if someone had tied her down and cut off her balls.

The moon cast enough light to see shapes. Concentrating on the dim bulks surrounding her, she almost missed Kaspar's swift and silent movement. Sylvie tensed and tried to funnel all her attention into her ears. She could hear hooves plodding in the dust, and the scuff of boots. Brush crackled, then Kaspar pounded into the road. "Arno!" he said.

Sylvie tripped when she scrambled after him. Cursing under her breath, she disentangled her sleeves from the roses and eased a thorn from the soft flesh at the bottom of her thumb. Then she flinched as Kaspar's ax sailed through the hedge, cutting a path for Arno and his horse. "So subtle!" she exclaimed, when she had her breath back. "I don't think anyone could have failed to hear that."

A large hand slapped her shoulder, staggering her. "I never thought I'd be glad to hear you haranguing!" Arno said.

"I never thought to see you alive again," Sylvie confessed, grasping his forearm. Her fingers could not encircle it.

He replied, "I'm surprised I've lived this long myself."

With Kaspar leading Arno's horse, the three of them tramped back to Lilas and Tonnelle, and then back to the inn. Arno, Sylvie saw as they drew near the lamplit stableyard, was dressed in the clothing of a farmer. A good choice. His size would be noticeable, but his hair had grown out enough to show beneath his hat brim, and its disarray contributed to the impression of a yokel, someone who might easily have been encountered along a country road at night. She decided they would pass him off as a friend from their home village, met by chance earlier in the day, who had only now consented to stay in the inn, after they had fetched him from his campsite. Sylvie embroidered further on the story as she went upstairs, leaving Kaspar and Arno to care for the horses. She would need the explanations ready in the morning, when they produced Arno at breakfast.

She hoped madame had finished with Henri. She did not intend to spend the night in the corridor.

At the door to their room, Sylvie froze, touching her pistols beneath her cloak. The air wasn't right. She should have heard sounds from within, breathing and rustling, but she heard nothing. Heart thudding, she opened the door. Even as its stale scent blew over her, she knew the room was empty.

After controlling her breathing, Sylvie lit the candle. Two sets of saddlebags were gone, and madame had left a note pinned to the counterpane. As if any family such as they appeared to be would abandon a fine steel pin! Sylvie tucked the pin safely inside her jacket and brought the note over to the light. She was glad all over again she'd taught the duchess a simple cipher. They'd spent so many hours in practice, Sylvie could read the contents without needing to scratch out the pattern with a pen.

It read, *We have fled. Belette is imprisoned. Meet us on the road.*

Bring the mule. In a more hurried hand, she'd added, *Safe. Give courier time to rest first.*

Kaspar and Arno burst into the room as Sylvie finished reading. "The horses!" Kaspar hissed. "The horses are gone!"

"And madame and the boy," Sylvie said. "We are instructed to wait here until Arno is rested, then meet them on the road. They were discovered by Lord Belette."

"That foul— But what happened?"

Sylvie shrugged. "It says he's in the local gaol, unless there is some other prison nearby. Perhaps madame found a way to discredit him."

"I'll find out," Kaspar swore.

"Not tonight, you won't," Sylvie said. "First we need Arno's news. It won't do for him to bring it all this way and not pass it on."

"I don't believe I can sleep until I've told all. I have swayed Vilmos," Arno reported. After looking to Sylvie for permission, he sat on the bed, his shoulders slumping with weariness. Kaspar sat beside him, resting a giant hand on the nape of his neck, gently rubbing. "To be truthful, he didn't need much swaying. Vilmos was a friend to Lord Maxime when they were boys, though he was supposed to be a spy for the old duke. He still corresponds with Lord Maxime when the tithe reckonings go out. If Her Grace and Lord Maxime send the word, he will confine the duke."

"It can't be that easy," Sylvie said. "What of the duke's guards?" She swept off Arno's hat, knelt and began tugging at his right boot. Kaspar promptly went to work on the other. "Be still," she commanded, when Arno tried to stop them.

Kaspar set Arno's boot and stocking aside and said, "It would be easy for a servant of the chamber to be a villain. Think on our own service, and tell me it's not true."

Arno added, "Vilmos has been working to suborn some of the guards. Most of them know Her Grace well, from accompanying her on rides, and she always rewarded their extra service to her. The duke skimps their pay. They haven't been happy with the way Her Grace has been treated. The duke's courtiers won't need to know he's been confined, not at first. Vilmos can hide it from them. He's done so before, when the duke was indisposed, or busy with his concubines."

Sylvie sat back on her heels, Arno's boot still in her hands. "This begins to sound less impossible," she admitted, "but it is for madame to decide. We will follow her in the morning. After we have visited Lord Belette. I thought we were rid of him when he lost his money in the canal scheme. We must make sure he does not return to the ducal palace prematurely."

Kaspar bowed. "*I* must make sure."

"I will help you," Arno said, his expression mulish. "You will not go alone."

It took only a moment for her to understand their meaning. She would gladly kill Belette herself, if only the eunuchs would allow her to usurp their duties with weapons. However, Her Grace would not agree, and Sylvie would not keep such a secret from her. She said, "There will be no killing. Madame would not like it. Now, we rest." Kaspar gave her an ironic look. "If that plan agrees with you, Kaspar? Since you are in charge."

Arno said thoughtfully, "I suppose his death would be tied to Her Grace, no matter if she had no hand in it. The king might trouble her over such a thing."

Kaspar sighed. "Very well. Luckily for Belette, I have other concerns at the moment." He bent and kissed Arno's bare foot.

"Don't!" Arno said. "It's forbidden!"

Sylvie stood, dropping the boot on the floor. "I think he means, *don't stop,*" she commented.

Arno pulled his feet away, but Kaspar would not let go of his ankle. "If you don't want me to do this, then why did you kiss me when we last met? I doubt you were lost to passion. You knew what you did, and you did it where Her Grace could see." He glared at Arno. "I thought you were dead! I thought I would never see you again! What would I do then? Well? Do you have an answer?"

"I won't stop you," Sylvie said, more to Arno than to Kaspar, who was paying no attention to her. She'd never seen the eunuchs kiss before. That could be entertaining. It was too bad she'd missed it last time.

Arno said, "But Her Grace. We are sworn to her. We are forbidden to—"

"Kaspar, close his mouth," Sylvie said. "Arno, we neither of us want to hear this bilge. I don't think madame would, either. After all she has endured from the duke, do you think she would grudge you? Her most loyal eunuchs? She did not leave you behind for the duke to slaughter, did she? Do you think she would accuse you now and have your guts drawn? She would never. You insult her."

Kaspar stood up and folded his arms across his chest. "We are no longer in the palace," he said. "We have the freedom to be together. I love you, and I thought you loved me. And you protest?"

Despite his great size, Arno looked to Sylvie like a puppy just dragged from its mother's teats. He said, "I thought— I thought—" Kaspar stared at him but did not speak.

"And I thought Henri lacked intelligence," Sylvie said. "I am going to find a place to sleep. You two may argue until dawn for all I care."

"You can't, Sylvie," Kaspar said. "I need you to guard the door. Though I would be glad if you would *close your mouth* while you did."

"I can—" Arno said.

"You can't guard the door, because you will be busy with me," Kaspar said. "Am I mistaken? If I am, tell me now."

This grew quickly more interesting, Sylvie decided. She seized a blanket and pillow from the pile in the corner and made herself a seat, her back against the door. If the eunuchs didn't provide sufficient amusement, she could always clean her pistols.

"Kaspar," Arno said, standing up. "Can we truly— I didn't think—"

"I'll show you," Kaspar said.

"I've never—"

"He'll *show* you," Sylvie said impatiently. "Take off your clothes."

Kaspar cast her a look meant to wither. Sylvie arranged herself more comfortably and made a dismissive motion with her hand. Kaspar sighed, then leaned forward and kissed Arno on the mouth, cupping the left side of his face so he couldn't see Sylvie.

The two eunuchs moved against each other, slowly and sensually. They'd been trained to this, Sylvie knew, trained to pleasure their mistress or master both physically and visually, but Sylvie watched closely enough to see the small signs of emotion in their actions: Kaspar's palm curving tenderly around Arno's skull, Arno's eyes fluttering closed and his quick nuzzle at Kaspar's throat before joining their mouths once again. They moved closer, shifting their bodies, gradually melting into each other. She found she was not impatient to see more. She would relax and see where they led her.

"Good?" Kaspar asked, leaning his forehead against Arno's.

Arno unfastened Kaspar's shirt. "I know this part," he said, and pressed his hands flat on Kaspar's chest, over a strap of knife harness. "I was hoping, once I arrived, you could massage me. It was a long journey."

"This will be better," Kaspar said. He lifted Arno's hands away from him and removed his weapons. "You undress, too," he said, when Arno didn't move.

"I was watching," Arno confessed. "I've seen you so often before, but it's different now."

"That's important," Kaspar said. "Always remember this is different. This is for us."

Arno removed his shirt with no further argument, then hesitated at the tie to his pants. He glanced at Sylvie, startling her from her dreamy observations. "Please," he said, and nothing more.

"I wouldn't mock you," she said, surprised. "Don't be ashamed. What have you to be ashamed of?"

"Let me," Kaspar said, loosing the tie of Arno's pants, then his long drawers, letting them fall to the floor. "Now you," he said, putting Arno's hands to the knot at his own waist.

It was strange, seeing men naked together but their cocks limp. They'd both been circumcised, like Master Fouet, except without his great handfuls of balls. Their empty sacs curled delicately behind their smooth shafts. Sylvie wished she could fondle them; they looked soft, easy to suckle and pet and roll between the fingers. They might not come erect, but such caressing would be pleasurable to them, she felt sure.

Kaspar encouraged Arno to stretch out on the narrow bed, then wedged himself in, his chest pressed to Arno's. Sylvie wanted a better view, but reluctantly decided it would be rude if they noticed her. She concentrated on their soft murmurs and sighs, and the slick sounds of kisses. She could see Arno's hand, resting on Kaspar's shoulder. Gradually, his hand moved lower, and caressed his partner's rib cage, tentatively at first, then more firmly. Then his fingers went taut and stiff. Kaspar, she surmised, had done something very pleasant that was out of her view. She was annoyed she could not see. It was very unfair.

As if he'd heard her thought, Kaspar turned his head and said, "Sylvie, do you have the oil Master Fouet gave you?"

"Of course I do," she said. "What will you give me if I let you have some?"

Kaspar rolled off the bed and towered over her. She was surprised that his cock was indeed partially erect; upon brief reflection, she supposed it would have to work that way, or he might not be able to piss. How fascinating. "If you let me have some, I won't smack your bottom."

Arno sat up. "Nor I."

Sylvie sighed. "That is even more unfair than not letting me watch. If I give you some, you must both smack my bottom at some later date. I insist."

"I'll do so gladly if you will just *get the bottle*."

"What are you going to do with it?" she asked, and rose to find the bottle wrapped in her extra shirts.

She could hear Kaspar's impatient breathing behind her, and she smirked. He was so easy to annoy. Arno said, "Yes, love, what *are* you going to do with the oil?"

There were sounds of passionate kissing. Sylvie whirled just in time to catch Kaspar's hand sneaking down to the crease between Arno's buttocks. So Master Fouet had told her truly; eunuchs might not have balls, but the small organ inside their anal passage could take a similar part, if properly stimulated. She waited until they stopped kissing, and Kaspar held out a hand.

Sylvie put the bottle in it. "May I watch more closely?" she asked. "I'm really very curious."

"Kaspar!" Arno pleaded.

"Out," Kaspar said. He grabbed her arm and her saddlebags and marched her to the door. "Guard from outside. Clean your pistols."

Sylvie pouted, but did as he asked. "You both owe me," she said. "I will not forget. And do not think you can both spank me at once. It is one at a time or—" The door shut in her face.

"Hmph," she said. She slumped against the door. It was too thick to hear much. She would have to arrange another opportunity to watch, at some later date.

Her mind drifted to a morning she'd spent with Master Fouet. He'd taught her how to pleasure him with her fingers and tongue in ways she'd never before attempted. She hadn't liked the idea at first, having had a poor experience with her own rear passage once, but had lost all inhibition once she saw how big, muscled Karl Fouet gasped and whimpered at the lightest pressure from the pad of one finger.

She'd been intrigued by his control, as well; without any sort of cock restraint, he could prevent himself from ejaculating for a ridiculous amount of time, not once but many times in a row. It didn't stop him from reaching a peak. Sylvie had nearly come herself, watching him shiver in intense pleasure for minutes at a time. It had almost been like fucking a woman.

Afterward, she'd lain in her favorite position atop his chest, tracing her fingers along his upper arm, examining each line of defined muscle, each visible vein and each scar, while his fingertips pressed patterns up and down her spine, not soothing patterns but ones that pushed her arousal higher and higher. She said, "I would like to do that to you again. It was most rewarding."

Fouet chuckled. "Tomorrow, perhaps. You'd like me to have the strength to give you your pleasure today, little lioness, am I right? I'm a mere old man. What you did for me is enough to stir a eunuch to pleasure."

"Truly?"

"I have seen it," he said. "I have done it. I loved a eunuch once, in my youth. He'd fled the court of your duchess's father, and brought his skills to the house where I first learned my trade. He taught me that the balls matter, it's true, but rubbing that one spot can have a similar result, if you don't mind there's no true jism. He didn't, and I didn't. He would scream. It was...what did you say before? Rewarding."

Sylvie lay thoughtfully for a moment. "Did you offer this to Kaspar?"

"I did. He refused me." Fouet lightly smacked her rear. "I don't think he refused me for duty's sake."

"I think he loves," Sylvie said. "Perhaps I will write to you, later. I will tell you if his love ended happily."

"I would like that," Fouet said. He smacked her again, a bit harder, with his cupped hand. Sylvie shivered at the popping noise. "You like this, I believe?"

Her belly was already going liquid. She hooked her thighs to either side of his hips, then squirmed against him until her cunt spread wide against his sweat-slick skin, over his octopus tattoo. "Strike me again," she said. "Make it last."

"You are a joy," Fouet said. He slapped one cupped hand to her right buttock, then another to her left, jolting her cunt against him.

"Harder," she breathed.

"Not yet. You told me to make it last, little lioness."

She took two breaths before he spanked her again, finally beginning a slow rhythm. She breathed deeply, letting each stroke flow through her, spreading from the initial sting down her legs, up her torso, out to the ends of her fingertips, and finally prickling her scalp. Her skin began to grow hot. Before it reached the point of pain, he varied his stroke, taking care to spread the heat from her lower back to her upper thighs.

Because Fouet struck steadily, at just the right pace, intensifying speed or force just when she needed more, the flow of sensation never stopped, circling back on itself with each stroke until she was so awash in tingling heat that she could no longer distinguish the individual blows. She was dimly aware of moaning, a distant low sound that she couldn't stop. The sound might have come from someone else. She floated inside her own body. She didn't have the concentration to press her cunt against him anymore. She didn't need to; the blows of his hands did it for her. The contact was not enough to make her come. Fouet kept her balanced on a high peak, and just when she thought she could take no more, he would force her higher, until the moans she heard turned to sobs. Her skin felt on fire wherever he slapped. Eventually she did begin to come, first prickles chasing across her skin, maddening her, then a feeling

like cramps that made it hard to breathe. Fouet changed his
blows to squeezing and massaging her tender skin. That, finally,
shoved her into a series of almost unbearably pleasurable con-
vulsions, recurring at intervals for several hours. She could
not remember much of it. The whole experience had been
oddly out of time, even out of her body. Their other encounters had been good as well, but that had been one of the most
intense experiences of her life.

She wondered what Kaspar and Arno felt now. Perhaps,
tomorrow, she would ask them. And then she would write to
Fouet.

CHAPTER SIXTEEN

"Please don't do this." White-knuckled, Henri gripped the reins of Tulipe and Guirlande while the duchess knelt on a pile of dead leaves, snipping through her hair with a pair of nail scissors.

"Don't be foolish," she said, fisting another hank of hair and sawing at it. The scissors were too short to be efficient.

"Madame," he said. "You don't have to—"

"It's only hair, and right now, it marks me."

If she would show some emotion, Henri would not be so worried. And, he confessed to himself, if Sylvie were with them instead of with Kaspar, he would not feel so helpless. Sylvie was a woman, too, and might be able to comfort the duchess in some way, or reassure her, or something that she would not accept from Henri. All he could do was press his shoulder to Guirlande.

Another handful of strands sifted to the ground. Henri felt their phantom traces between his fingers. The duchess said, "The wind will take some, and the rest we will cover with leaves. Then we'll both change clothes before we go back on the road."

"Camille——" Henri said. "I am worried that you——"

She looked up at him, one eyebrow lifted. "You have a mistaken idea of my fortitude." *Snip.*

"I'm sorry," he said. "If I could have stopped Belette from touching you——"

"Don't be foolish," she said again. "You also seem to have a mistaken idea of your place."

Henri flinched and looked down at the toes of his boots. She obviously did not want to discuss what had happened with Belette, nor would she accept anything from Henri, at least not right now. He dared another glance at her, from beneath his lashes. Her hands were steady as she cut her hair. She did not look as if she needed anything from him. If she did, would he be able to tell? Frustrated, he lifted his hand to his mouth and chewed on his knuckle. After several minutes, she said, "Henri."

"Yes, madame."

"I'm fine," she said. "I am cutting my hair so I will look different than at the last stop. I am not losing my mind."

"No, madame."

She sighed. "You may look at me. You did nothing wrong. You did rather well."

"I let him——"

"*I* let him," the duchess said. "It was necessary. I do not regret it."

"Yes, madame."

"Now forget it. I have done so already."

"Yes, madame." Henri turned to Tulipe and scratched beneath the animal's forelock. "Did he bruise you?"

"I will recover. You need have no thoughts of revenge on Belette," the duchess said. "I'd prefer you to stay alive and useful. Dead, you're just a corpse."

"Yes, madame." He looped the horses' reins around a branch and sat cross-legged in the leaves, watching her and trying not to think. Thinking of what she said and did not say would send a devil loose in his head.

When the duchess finally stopped cutting, her hair barely reached past her ears. It looked as if she'd hacked it with a dull knife. He tried to hide his dismay, but must not have succeeded, for she smiled at him wickedly and held out the scissors. "Tidy it up for me."

Henri couldn't help but grin back. He'd liked her mischievous smile and wanted her to smile like that again. He set to work, cupping her warm nape or chin in his free hand to hold her head steady, trimming more carefully than he usually did with his own hair. In truth, it was easier to be tidy while working on someone else. When he'd finished, he leaned forward and gently kissed her lips. He'd clipped her hair close to her skull, letting it feather over her forehead and onto her slender neck and the sleek shape of her ears.

"I have prickles down my dress," the duchess remarked. "I suppose I must endure them until we can have a bath."

Tentatively, Henri said, "Cutting your hair was your own idea."

"That's true. It's my own fault." She pushed herself to her feet, rummaged in her saddlebag and brought out the crushed hat she'd worn at the very beginning of their journey. "Come, give me a leg up."

Though Henri felt that the duchess with short hair was more distinctive, not less, than before, their day's ride proceeded without incident. Perhaps her hat drew the attention, instead. They were remarkable mostly for not being merchants or drovers on this road. Once, they had to wait at the side of the road for a flock of geese to pass. Tulipe was nervous from their loud honking and the random flapping of their wings, but soon the drover's two spotted dogs had chivvied them on their way, leaving a trail of sticky excrement, more solid and stickier than other bird guano. Henri added extra foot and fetlock grooming to his mental plan for the horses that evening.

Ox-drawn wagons dominated the traffic, some piled with bundles to the height of two men. Once, they passed a wagon laden with glass bottles of distilled liquor, drawn by a team of six mules, that Henri guessed was worth more than the yearly payment for an entire set of grooms and stableboys. A guard with a crossbow rode on the front seat with the driver, and another dangled his feet off the wagon's tail. The drivers would lift a casual hand as they passed, but none appeared to take any undue notice of two dusty people on two dusty horses.

Henri fell into the state of extra awareness he reached when schooling the animals in the ring, when his vision narrowed and his world became the constant subtle communications between his body and the horse's. Tulipe was more skittish today than usual, and he devoted himself to using the horse's mood as an exercise, almost forgetting that he rode beside his duchess. He thus didn't notice three riders exploding from the forest until Tulipe reacted to them.

The two riders in front held swords. Henri's first instinct was to urge Tulipe into a gallop, but he settled back abruptly when he saw the third rider sweep a short, recurved bow between him and the duchess, a viciously tipped arrow nocked and ready to kill.

Henri's second thought was here was his chance to save his duchess, but he had no idea how. His knife was for close fighting, the duchess wasn't armed, and he had no skills except riding, roughhousing and rudimentary knifeplay. Tulipe would obey him, but no matter what he did, the arrow could still find its mark. The duchess had said he was not to endanger himself, and he did not think she would want Tulipe to be wounded, either. Or the archer could just as easily kill her instead of Henri. His heart pounded at the mistake he had almost made. Still, it would take time for the bowman to reload. If he shot at Henri, the duchess might escape. He shifted his weight in the saddle. Before he could cue Tulipe, the duchess said, "No."

Henri forced himself to relax and lower his hands. He remembered then that she carried jewels and money. Not all of their supply, but perhaps enough to satisfy the brigands, whether the duke had sent them or not; if they had been bought once, they could be bought again. He and the duchess would not need much more money; they were almost to their destination, and soon Sylvie and Kaspar would catch up to them and replenish their funds. The duchess would think their lives a worthy exchange. But what would the brigands think of the jewels? If the duke had *not* sent them, would it seem suspicious, two nondescript travelers carrying such plunder? Perhaps he and the duchess could pretend to be merchants, or bankers, dressed this way as a disguise.

His tentative plans proved to be irrelevant. "Give us the horses or you die," the lead rider demanded. He was a big man, heavily bearded and, like all three of the brigands, wearing a mask bound over his eyes and nose.

"No!" the duchess said.

Henri grinned in reflexive agreement—never the horses!—then his belly went cold with horror. He should have spoken up immediately, said they had money. Except then the brigands might have demanded the money *and* the horses. Did that matter? There were other horses in the world, much as he loved them. There was only one duchess.

The lead brigand rode toward the duchess, blade held out. She backed Guirlande with consummate skill, keeping a distance between them. The brigand said, "Now, lady, we could use some nice mounts like these."

Henri opened his mouth. She cast him a warning glance, and he closed it. "I am sure you could," she said. "However, they are mine."

"You wouldn't like to die in the road, would you?"

"You can't shoot us both," she said. "The survivor would make quite a lot of trouble for you."

The archer said, "Want to bet there'd be a survivor?"

Henri thought furiously. He could rear Tulipe and perhaps distract their horses, allowing the duchess to run, but that would expose his horse's belly to both swords and arrow, and they might cut her down as she ran. How could he use his knife? Kaspar's single-tail would have been of more use right now. He sidled Tulipe left, then right, trying to draw their attention away from the duchess. Maybe that would be enough, a distraction so she and Guirlande could run.

"Don't move!" someone shouted.

Henri froze. Casting his eyes to the trees, he recognized Lilas first, the small figure on her back second. Sylvie held a long-barreled pistol in each hand. The brigands were easily in range of her shot, and he did not doubt she could hit anything at which she aimed.

The first rider wheeled his horse to face her, while the second took over menacing the duchess. "There are three of us, if you haven't noticed," he called.

A shot ripped the air. Henri quickly controlled Tulipe. Guirlande barely flinched. The archer had lost his bow, and was clutching at his shoulder. Sylvie dropped her spent pistol, seized another from her belt, and shouted, "Two of you. I would go now, if you wish to live."

The brigands knew when they were beaten and fled. Henri soothed the horses while Sylvie exclaimed over the duchess's hair. He heard the words, **"Arno is saf**e," and saw the duchess's posture ease. When Sylvie reclaimed Lilas's reins, he said to her, "Thank you."

"You owe me now," she said, with a sidelong grin. "Will you repay me when I ask?"

"I will," Henri swore. He held out his hand, and when Sylvie took it, he brought their joined hands to his lips and kissed her knuckles. "Her Grace would have wept to lose Guirlande."

"I would not weep, but I would grieve," the duchess said. "I would grieve more to lose either of you." She sighed. "It was foolish of me to refuse them, but I could not stop myself. Let that be a lesson to you, Henri, not to let your heart rule your head. If not for Sylvie, we might be those corpses I spoke of."

"I see I cannot leave you for an instant," Sylvie said. "It is too bad we cannot report those ruffians to the magistrate."

Henri bowed his head. "I'm sorry I couldn't protect you, madame." As his relief faded, he felt angry with himself for his inability to help, and frustrated with his own impotence. His hands began to shake.

"I will not leave you again," Sylvie swore. Neither of them mentioned that the duchess had ordered her to stay behind with Kaspar.

"Let's move on," the duchess said finally. "Kaspar and Arno will meet us at one of two inns. The first is not far, is it, Sylvie?"

Henri had never seen an inn with a signboard as large as that of The Escaping Mermaid. Instead of hanging out into the road, it stretched the length of the building, from the edge of the roof down to the tops of the windows. The board, he realized, told an entire story.

A mermaid swam among a cloud of brightly colored fish, her long hair swirling around her breasts, artfully concealed by real pink shells applied to the board. Then the same mermaid was shown trapped in a fisherman's net, her hair tangled with its strands. Finally the mermaid was free, swimming from the torn net, one hand clasping the pink shells she'd used as knives. The end of the sign trapped her there. Did she ever find her true home and true self again?

Henri also wondered if her bare breasts would really stand upright like that while she swam, especially considering their prodigious size, but decided he didn't care, the picture was lovely. Also, he noticed that the depicted water of the ocean must be quite cold.

"Ouch!" he exclaimed, grabbing for the back of his head.

Sylvie withdrew her hand. "Wake up! Take care of the horses!"

Henri took his time with the horses, at first telling himself that Tulipe and Guirlande needed extra attention after their frightening afternoon, but at last admitting he was the one needing to be comforted. Long after he'd finished grooming them and sponging quantities of mud from Lilas's fetlocks, he stood in Guirlande's stall, one arm slung over her withers and his nose against her neck.

Eventually, she turned her head and nipped at his hair and jacket, and he went to the bucket by the stable's door to feed them each a carrot. When he was finished, the bucket was empty. He wasn't ready to go inside yet, and be rejected by the duchess when he offered comfort. At least the horses understood how he felt about them. Henri picked up the bucket, swung it thoughtfully for a moment, and headed to the rear of the inn, where he guessed the kitchen might be located.

The kitchen was actually a separate building, connected to the inn by a covered walkway. As he drew closer, he saw wooden shutters folded away at each support pole, probably for when the weather was bad. Henri ducked under the roof and saw the kitchen's door was open, propped with a brick. He heard voices from within, hurried, quiet, but audible in the walkway when they hadn't been in the innyard. "I tell you, it is her!" a woman's voice said. "I've seen the coins!"

"Don't be silly, Blanche. You are too much of a dreamer."

"And you are a fool, Charles. There is a reward! We could be rich!"

"We have enough. Why are you never satisfied? Why must you— Oh, never mind. We will discuss this later. Finish the supper, we have new guests."

A burly man with a mane of gray hair stomped out the door. Henri ducked back behind a shutter until the innkeeper was gone, his heart pounding. They should flee, but that would convince the woman of their guilt, and she might call down pursuit. They needed to stay here, for at least a few days, waiting for Kaspar and the second eunuch, Arno. Or they could proceed to the second rendezvous, but that was too close; they could easily be found there if the woman raised the alarm. She had to be convinced she was wrong, and Henri must take care of it himself.

"Hello?" he called, making a racket with his boots. He poked his head into the doorway.

"Yes?" Madame Blanche looked agitated, her fingers prodding at a bowl of dough. She was small, barely as tall as Henri's heart, but with the buxom shape of a much larger woman; Henri was reminded of the mermaid painting, then realized with a shock that her face was similar, as well, though she was much older, perhaps a few years older than the duchess.

"I've come from the stable," Henri said. "I thought you might have some more carrots for the bucket? I'm afraid I took the last of them, for our horses." Hesitantly, he smiled, knowing he needed to make her like him.

She looked up for the first time, and for a moment didn't move, her eyes fixed on his face. Henri shifted his feet, and she abruptly looked down at her bowl again, saying, "I send the scullery boy for that bucket every day. You—our guests—don't need to concern yourselves."

Henri felt his smile fading. "I'm sorry. I was just trying to be helpful. We've only just arrived." He said, more firmly, "My mother and brother and I. If that was your husband I saw leaving, he helped us."

She nodded, said, "No, Charles is my brother. I am Madame Blanche," and turned out the dough from the bowl, vigorously kneading it on a flour-strewn board. "Your mother, is she?"

"Yes, ma'am."

"I heard she had no children," Blanche remarked.

"You know my mother?" Henri asked.

"I know of her. I do not think you are her son, nor your brother. The three of you look nothing alike." She paused. When Henri said nothing, she split the dough and formed it into long pans in the shapes of mermaids.

Henri set down the bucket. "Please don't tell anyone."

"Tell them what?" Blanche said. She wiped her hands on a towel and propped them on her hips. "Well?"

Henri didn't have to work to look shamefaced. "We wanted to stay in a respectable place," he said, "and your sign, with the mermaids, it's so beautiful. I chose to come here, when the others wanted to sleep by the road, where no one would ask us to—" He risked a glance at her face.

Blanche looked more puzzled than belligerent now. "What would they ask you?"

"They would ask our favors," Henri blurted, "and Marie is so weary—she wants to retire. We are on our way—you are a woman, even though you're respectable, can't you understand what it's like for her? To always do what a man wants of her, and never have anything for herself?"

Blanche's lips parted. "You are saying—"

"We are not respectable," Henri said, blushing furiously at the lie. "We worked—we worked together in an establishment. For gentlemen. And at the last inn, there was a man—he made Marie— Oh, I cannot tell you. Please, keep our secret. If you let us stay here tonight, I will—I will do anything you want me to." He looked at her, cautiously. "I will do my best to please you, if you only let us stay."

He took one step closer, then another. There was a table between them, but he extended his hand. He did not have to pretend it trembled. "Please."

Blanche stepped around the table. "You poor boy," she said. "Such horrible things you must have been made to do!"

Henri lowered his gaze. "I will never go back."

"I hope not," she said. "I would like to give you some better memories?" She took his hand in hers and squeezed it. He felt no thrill from the touch, but no horror, either. He would just have to do his best to make her think he felt true desire, and perhaps it would eventually become true. At least this stranger would hold him in her arms, and allow him to hold her.

Henri took a deep breath, lifted her hand to his mouth and kissed it lingeringly. "Oh, lady, thank you. I will try to give you memories of me you will never forget."

CHAPTER SEVENTEEN

Soon after their dawn departure from The Escaping Mermaid, Arno and Kaspar met them on the road, leading the pack mule as well as their horses. Tonnelle looked to be in good condition, and Arno had ridden a sturdy, even-tempered gelding named Pivoine whom Camille remembered as being more of a stylish jumper than his looks would indicate. Camille rode over to Arno and laid her fingers on his arm. Pivoine sidled; she made a mental note to help him with his riding when she had a chance, but now was not the time. "You did well," she said. He met her eyes for a moment, then glanced at Kaspar. He seemed embarrassed. Camille eased away. Perhaps she shouldn't have touched him. She said, "I would like you to report to me as we ride." Sylvie had passed on his news already, but she needed details.

"Of course, Your Grace," he said.

Camille asked after her former husband's guards, the courtiers and the townsfolk. What did they think of her disappearance? Had anyone discovered the truth? How did this change their feelings for the duke, or did their loyalties remain the same? How many seemed unhappy with the duke? Were there murmurings? What of visitors to the court? Had the king sent an envoy? All these things would be important when she came out of hiding. She didn't want to incite a bloody rebellion, though; her people would be killed. No matter how "bloodless" a coup one attempted, lives were always lost, and if she sacrificed her people needlessly, she would be a failure.

She was pleased to learn Annette the midwife had been one of Arno's informants, and had offered her help. She had no rank and little power, and surely could do little enough to topple the duke from his position, but she did care what happened to her duchess. Camille was warmed by the knowledge.

After she'd finished questioning Arno, she ignored Henri's hopeful glance and rode on alone, thinking on the facts she'd gained. Her disappearance had not been noticed by the duke for the first several days, though it was obvious to her maids and to those of her husband's guards who sometimes accompanied her. There was talk among their fellow guards, with the palace staff and in the town. The duke's indiscretions could be ignored while he had a wife in residence, but without her the appearance of impropriety was greater. Even that might have been overlooked, had he not become so unreliable in matters of finance and diplomacy. She might truly be able to gain support for herself and push him aside. If she could bring Maxime to her side, then they would control the greatest portion of the duchy's trade. She need fear nothing, then.

She straightened in her saddle and lifted her chin. It was time to resume being the duchess. At their first stop today, she changed into finer clothing than she'd worn so far on the journey, a split skirt and bodice in rich green, with a jacket of brown leather and a scarf hiding her hair. Both her eunuchs flanked her, providing a barrier between her and the world. It wasn't that she felt safer under their guard. It was more that they were an integral part of the woman who planned to negotiate with Maxime. Camille had been someone different these past days on the road, but she needed to remember, as they approached Maxime's seat, what it was like to be a symbol.

Maxime lived in the great castle of his ancestors. It perched on a titanic mound of earth overlooking jagged gray cliffs that were riddled with caves and home to thousands of screaming seabirds. From the castle's towers, Camille had been told, one could see the goats living on barrier islands at the edge of the bay. She didn't think Maxime spied on the goats. He watched the ships coming to harbor all along his stretch of coast, taking note of each one's point of origin, size, cargo capacity, draft and armaments. Every captain who dropped anchor within his sight came ashore and rendered tribute, a tithe of which traveled overland to the ducal palace every month. Given the size of his tithe, Camille could not quite imagine the scale of harborage and other fees he likely extracted; if she were Maxime, she would never report her entire income to the duke. That income would doubtless include smuggled luxuries as well, items that in the rest of the duchy were heavily taxed, everything from distilled liquors to purple silks to rare, foreign breeds of lapdogs.

The day was hotter than it had been for some time, and she'd felt it wise to give the horses and mule a rest before climbing the castle hill. She could use a little time to collect herself, as well. This grove of scrubby trees with its well and water trough had been designed for that purpose. Camille readjusted her headscarf, then pulled it off entirely. The cliff road leading to the castle was a busy one, but her cropped hair should help her elude recognition. If not, well, she no longer cared very much. She was weary of hiding, it was too difficult to disguise both Kaspar and Arno, and as soon as she appeared in public with those two at her back, her aristocratic position would be obvious.

She glanced at Henri, who was letting the horses graze, and Sylvie, who drank from her water flask. It might be better to pass those two off as her servants alone and have them housed as such. She could not afford distraction while negotiating with Maxime, and perhaps he would be disturbed that she considered these two youngsters to be more than servants. He might think she'd gone mad, or become so helpless she needed the crutch of reassurance at every juncture, or simply that she'd grown as debauched as her husband. Or perhaps she should stop worrying what Maxime would think. Her household was none of his business. Given what she knew of him, his was likely more debauched than hers.

Their negotiations should be her main concern. Though she hadn't seen Maxime in more than twenty years, she had read documents of his writing in that time, especially his court documents. He was intelligent as well as savvy and manipulative. Camille had some of the same qualities—she wouldn't have recognized them in his writing otherwise—but she hadn't had daily practice in business and diplomacy for two decades, either. She had only two decades of close observation, of thought rather than action.

Maxime would not have the same knowledge of her as she had of him. Her journals of court proceedings were not published, and of course lately there had been none. Her letters to him—usually to thank him for a particular item he'd sent—had always been confined to brief news of her horses. Recently, she hadn't written at all.

She wondered if he kept a mistress. She knew he'd never married, and she couldn't imagine him celibate. Sylvie might be able to seduce Maxime, or allow herself to be seduced by him. Would that be of use? Camille stopped, horrified at herself. She was not Michel; she would not abuse Sylvie's service in that way. Would the mere fact of her asking seem to Sylvie like a command? If Sylvie voluntarily made such a move, that might be acceptable; or would her intervention disturb what Camille hoped to accomplish? Perhaps it would be necessary for her to seduce Maxime herself.

Camille's body liked this idea. Every thought she had of Maxime eventually linked to sex. It might have been years in the past, and they might have never once coupled, but he'd been her first great passion. He'd been the first to truly arouse her, body and mind, and the last until she'd met Henri. Maxime had made an immeasurable impact in her mind and body. Or, rather, the idea of him had. From the initial spark of their few encounters, she'd dared to use him as fuel for her fantasies. Her body had ignited, and she'd become someone new. She wished that new person had never married Michel. Even then, however, her fantasies had sometimes sustained her, providing her a place of refuge.

She would not be meeting a fantasy creature, though. She would be meeting a mature man, and a wise one at that. She remembered how he'd seen through her in their youth, to desires she had not yet articulated, or that she'd barely known she had. She doubted this skill had dulled over the intervening years. Maxime was dangerous. She should fear him as she did the duke, or more so, because she actually cared for Maxime's good opinion of her. She wanted to meet Maxime again, and reestablish the connection she remembered between them. She desperately needed a friend. Even more, she needed an equal in whom to confide.

If, as she hoped, Maxime's sympathies lay with her rather than with the duke, she would have a chance. If she had misjudged him, or he'd changed out of all recognition…well, she hoped his memories of her would be enough to let her die quickly, and that he would spare Sylvie and Henri. She feared Kaspar and Arno would die in her defense, and hoped to create no opportunity for them to do so. Perhaps she could persuade Maxime to take them into his service, employing them as guards on a ship or at the harbor.

Such thoughts might weaken her. She had to stop fretting and focus on her present duties. More likely than any of her fantasy fears was that she would see Maxime in the flesh and realize she felt nothing.

Her stomach cramped with nerves. "I think we'll rest here a little longer," she said, and led them farther from the road, letting the grove block their presence from casual view. "Henri, unsaddle the horses and let them roll. The mule, too. Arno will help you. We'll want to be fresh when we appear at Lord Maxime's door."

"I'll brush them after," Henri said, stroking Guirlande's neck before he loosened the buckle on her girth.

"Sylvie, watch the people," Camille said. "You can see well enough from here, can't you?"

"Yes, madame."

"I'll watch, too, but two sets of eyes are better. We might need to know who comes to see Maxime, and why." Camille took charge of the saddlebags, extracting sandwiches from the last inn before propping them into comfortable seats. She handed the first sandwich to Kaspar, who settled himself at the best vantage point, a bow across his lap.

Camille noted, first, that while some travelers came from the same coastal road she had ridden, others came from the southeast. The town was there, she recalled from her map, not the inns and supply yards of the harbor settlement, but the permanent residences of the artisans and builders and others under Maxime's protection. The road from the town to the castle, and from the town to the coast, appeared well-kept and well-traveled. Maxime had gone so far as to sink cobblestones into the road's surfaces, to save wagons becoming mired in mud. She wondered if the roads from the surrounding farms to the town were cobbled as well. From her studies of the duchy, she did not think any of the roads had been so in Maxime's father's time.

The people traveling the road seemed content, though of course there was the usual shouting at others for blocking the road or yelling at recalcitrant oxen or mules. No one took notice of Camille and her group, other than in passing, as if it was completely unremarkable to see travelers lounging in the trees. Camille didn't see any others beside the road just now, but that didn't mean it didn't happen. As noon grew near, she suspected there would be drovers pausing to eat their lunch and give their animals feedbags. She took another bite of her sandwich. Henri finished with the horses and came to sprawl at her feet, one arm flung over his eyes. She took a wrapped sandwich and tossed it onto his belly, smiling a little when he startled.

"Madame," Sylvie said. "I don't know where all of these people come from. Look there! That bird in the cage, it's like a rainbow!"

Camille had heard the whole world met at seaports, and here was her evidence. She saw more dark-skinned people than pale, some so dark they appeared almost like shadows in the bright sunlight, others of various skin shades from olive to brown, and a few paler than Camille, their skins freckled and tinged red by the sun. They wore an array of clothing styles, from pants and boots to long, flowing robes with sandals to a group in billowing trousers and short collarless coats with high-heeled wooden sandals that rattled on the cobblestones. Some looked completely foreign except for their clothing and manners, and some groups were mixed beyond her determining their origin.

One wagon bore Easterners, the first she'd ever seen beyond a single ambassadorial group in her childhood. A tiny man with a long braid down his back drove their wagon, guarded by a giant eunuch who wore little more than a loincloth and leather straps. Behind the driver, on a padded bench, rode an elderly bearded man clothed head to foot in brocaded yellow silk. He occasionally cast a glance to their cargo, neatly stacked boxes wrapped in burlap and tied with red ribbons, which Camille suspected held porcelains. Maxime had once sent her a special box along with the tithe. Packed in the straw had been a single cup, eggshell-thin, adorned with a scene of boats on a tree-lined river, each line delicately feathered in blue paint. The duke had taken it from her, later, and broken it in his hands.

Camille stood up, brushing crumbs from her skirt. "It's time to go," she said.

Maxime's castle was built of local green-and-white stones in alternating layers. The stripes of color, the fanciful finlike crenellations, and the spiky observation towers along each wall made her think of gaudy fish in a bowl or of a cake with icing sculpted of meringue. It was larger than she had expected, she saw as they drew closer; larger, in fact, than her own palace. How had her father conquered such an edifice? Trickery? Treachery?

The first wall was no taller than a horse, and built of the same white-and-green stones as the castle. A brightly polished bronze gate, dense with reliefs of fish and octopuses, stood open directly in front of them.

Maxime waited just beyond the gate to greet them, unarmed, wearing a long, bright blue coat embroidered with black and green and gray sea creatures, his fingers encased to the knuckles in gold filigree sheaths, a thick gold band twisted around his throat. Thumbnail rubies studded each of his earlobes, gleaming brilliantly in contrast to his dark hair and beard. With his loose trousers and shoulder-length hair whipping in the sea breeze, he looked magnificent, and a bit wild.

Camille and Guirlande led the way to the gate. Before she could even dismount, Maxime bowed low, giving her a good view of his strong shoulders and back. "My lady Camille," he said, after he straightened. "Your Grace, you and your entourage are my welcome guests." Then he smiled, his teeth blinding white in his dark beard, his eyes settling on her like a touch.

Camille restrained an answering smile and inclined her head. "My thanks to you. These are my retinue, Sylvie, Henri, Kaspar and Arno."

Maxime cast a quick, shrewd glance over her party, and did not remark that she hadn't needed to name her servants. He understood her message, that she considered them more than servants. "I will come to you at your rooms in a short while, if I may."

A herd of Maxime's stablehands—both male and female, she noted in surprise—appeared when he clapped his hands, taking the horses to the stables ringing the castle's inner wall. Other servants, these liveried in blue shirts and mostly male, descended from staircases all around the courtyard, extracted their belongings and faded through doors. Maxime himself escorted them to a huge suite, just down a corridor from his own, then departed while more of the male servants, and perhaps the same ones again, fetched portable tubs and began to fill them with steaming water. None of them had blinked at being ordered about by Sylvie; however unconventional she presently appeared, she was prompt and skilled in her duties. Henri unpacked their saddlebags while a maid snatched dirty clothing from his hands, to take away to be washed. Kaspar scouted the entrances and exits to the room, Arno trailing him. They were all busy and cared for. She could let go her responsibility for them, for now.

Camille slipped into the corridor, escaping the bustle. Oil lamps flickered, each flame enclosed in rippling colored glass that cast blue and red and yellow patterns on the white stone walls only to vanish into the dark green sea of the floor. She wanted to find Maxime; their formal greetings had not been enough. Her heart longed for his familiarity, a reminder of a time when she'd been young and hopeful. She wanted to hear more of his voice, wanted to touch him, if she could do so in a way that would not reveal weakness. After that, she thought she could manage to speak to him coherently. She shut the door and caught her breath. Maxime stood a few steps beyond, leaning against the wall.

"Thank you for welcoming me," she said.

"And I welcome you again," Maxime said, though his tone and facial expression conveyed no emotion that she could discern. His teasing glances at the gate might never have happened. "Come, let's go to a more private room."

He led her to a chamber almost empty of furniture and brimming with light from a series of tall, open window slits. Camille took the only chair, a spindly bamboo confection padded with a white pillow striped in shades of olive and yellow. A bamboo table stood empty in front of her. Maxime settled into a padded window embrasure, the afternoon sun at his back, lining his broad form in gold but utterly shadowing his expression from Camille's eyes. He didn't immediately speak, so she didn't, either; she was unwilling to give up any advantage when so much—the duchy, her life—depended upon her success in wooing Maxime to her side. His greeting had been cordial, but that had been in public. Camille suppressed an urge to cast a glance over her shoulder at the closed door.

Someone tapped lightly. "Come in," Maxime said. A flurry of servants carried in long-handled silver spoons, tall and narrow silver goblets and a tray bearing a bucket-shaped silver container, all of which they arranged on the table. One of the servants spooned ice from the bucket into the goblets. He presented a goblet and spoon to Camille. She held it cautiously, the cold metal beginning to sweat into her palm.

Maxime tasted his ice as soon as it was given to him. "It's not poisoned," he said. "Have things grown so bad at the ducal court that you'd fear that of me?" He glanced to the open door, dismissing the servants. The last one pulled the door shut behind her. Maxime added, "Of course, you did come to me, which you have never done before. So, unless you have an extraordinarily slow-burning lust—"

Camille swallowed cool, sour lemon ice. "Don't be flippant. You cannot pretend you don't know every movement inside this protectorate. You were dressed for my arrival."

"Perhaps I am always so splendid."

"Splendid you may be, but waiting at the gate?"

He inclined his head to her. "You were hardly subtle in your arrival. You rode up to the front gate with your face clearly visible. Everyone in the protectorate will know by nightfall that you are here, and news should reach the ducal palace not long after. The duke will not like your betrayal. Michel could easily blame me for your defiance. How will he take vengeance on me and my people, Camille? Had you thought you'd be risking me as well as your own life?"

If Maxime feared her husband, she would eat the table, and the ice bucket as well. "You're sitting in a castle, with dozens of ships at your command."

"Eighty-seven," he said. "But that doesn't mean I wish to use them for defense. The purpose of ships is to make money and friends."

"You might have me for a friend," Camille said. "I am a valuable friend to have."

"And what am I to you? Do you want me for your friend?"

"Yes," she said.

"You haven't seen me in more than twenty years. You should not be so sure," he reminded her.

Camille put down her goblet and straightened her back. She captured his gaze. "I have chosen you now."

Maxime grinned. "Thank you. I'm relieved."

She couldn't stop her frown at his unexpected words. "Relieved?"

"I worried that Michel might be a better fuck than I am."

She laughed before she could clamp her hand over her mouth, which she suspected was Maxime's intention. "I never knew you to have such doubts."

"Perhaps I'm growing old." More seriously, he asked, "Why did you leave him? Why now, after so long?"

"Does it matter?"

"It does to me." He leaned forward, elbows on his knees, so she could see his face. His dark eyes intensely studied her face.

Camille looked away. Bright, lightweight hangings draped the stone walls, lively with schools of fish that glimmered with gilt thread. It was easy for him to ask, in this open, sunny room. Her own throat strangled her; she was not sure she could answer. This was Maxime before her, who'd been given truncated power and made something of it, while she'd taken greater power and scattered it to the winds. She was ashamed to confess her failure to him, and her weakness, and her stupidities of twenty years. At last, she said, "I feared for my people if I died."

Maxime sat up abruptly. "Are you ill?"

"No. No. Michel——" She stopped. Swallowed.

He lifted a hand, forestalling her attempt at speech. "You are saying he wishes to be rid of you?"

His calm tone gave her courage. "I will not let him have my duchy."

"Good." He paused. "I should tell you I've tried to be informed about your continued health, but of late it's grown more and more difficult. I confess, I was relieved to hear you had left the palace. The most alarming rumors have traveled down the coast."

"It couldn't be helped," Camille said, "but I am sorry if the news distressed you."

"*Distress* is a mild word for what I felt. Ever since I knew you'd fled, I asked my couriers to seek out word. I hoped you would come to me."

"Couriers," Camille said wryly, knowing he meant spies. "And what did you intend to offer me?" She watched his face carefully. Maxime's lips looked succulent within his closely trimmed dark beard, and she remembered what it had been like to kiss him. She forced the memory away. Now was not the time for remembering how he'd made her feel.

"A place of safety and, if you wish, advice and supplies for a return journey," he said. "There are things I would like in exchange, if that's permissible."

"There are things I cannot give you. *May not* give you, or I will be in no better circumstances than when I left the ducal palace."

"You needn't fear. You have power over me, as well."

Camille swallowed more of her melting lemon ice. "It's not the same. I am a duchess, but also a woman. If I'd been allowed to rule my duchy when my father died, none of this would have arisen. But the king did not permit it—my father did not want it—and here I am. I have decided I must take this power for myself, now, while I can. That must come before any payment you request of me. Will you trust me to keep my word?"

"Better you than Michel. What of the king?"

"I intend to see he recognizes the wisdom of my decision." Camille had no alternative, if she wished to take power and keep it. It was one more challenge in a series of them.

Maxime said, "Allying yourself with me might not help your arguments with the king. This protectorate was always an uneasy companion to the realm, richer and more varied than the other duchies. He might not want to see me restored to power over my own lands, and that is my price for helping you. As you have no doubt guessed."

"He will see the wisdom of it, and Lord Stagiaire will plead my case," she said. "You might be able to help, with a suitable donation to His Majesty's coffers. I've always suspected you did not send your true trade figures to my father, or to Michel."

He snorted. "Ah, yes, gold is a better lubricant than most would think. I think I deserve a kiss, for even considering a sacrifice such as that."

"Buying kisses? I thought you had no need to buy them."

"Then perhaps you might kiss me freely, Camille?"

"You are attempting to distract me," she said, though in truth the mere word *kiss* had been sufficient to do so.

He smiled slowly. "Would it help if I removed my clothing?"

Camille sputtered with laughter. "Later, Maxime."

He sighed dramatically. "Have you thought it through, about the king? It would be a pity to bring Michel down and fail to gain the king's support."

"Once the thing is accomplished, the king will have little choice. He will not want to destabilize the realm."

"What if he decides the duchy is more stable under his protection?"

"The law forbids—"

"Laws can be changed. You know that."

She'd hoped the other dukes would not take kindly to the king seizing power, and support her as the less dangerous alternative. But Maxime was correct; additional assurance would be a good idea. "Do you have any suggestion, to help win the king to my cause?"

Maxime startled her again when he said promptly, "My aunt Gisele." He drank from his goblet. "She's been my envoy to court for the past five years, and is a formidable strategist. We'll consult with her."

Camille felt a wash of relief, and had to work to keep her spine from weakening. Until his answer, she hadn't known what to expect from Maxime, beyond his basic desires. Those desires still drove him: reclaiming his father's power, and holding it. Those desires, now, weren't far from her own. What she hadn't known was how far he would go to meet his desires. Her fears in that area were much allayed. He hadn't suggested making war on the king; he'd proposed an indirect method. She approved. "And if we succeed?"

"I would like two things. The first is my title, and the right to my duchy. I imagine you knew that already. We can work out the trade agreements later in detail. I would even be willing to continue tithing to you, for a few years, as part of my gratitude."

She would be happy to meet all those requests, and more besides, though it wouldn't do to say so now. "And the other?"

He smiled slowly. "Surely you can guess. It's been a long time, but I never forgot what I promised to you."

Camille's heart began to hammer. "I remember you said, all those years ago, that what we did was only for amusement. I do not require you to keep any promises made then."

"I do not want to keep my promise out of sentiment. I think we should be together, at least once, as a part of our negotiations. It is harder for bodies to lie than words."

"I do not think that's true," Camille said. How could anyone know what lurked inside the mind of another? How could the actions of bodies provide a reason for trust? She had lied many times with her body, more times than she could count. Sometimes she had lied to her husband, and sometimes to herself. Beyond conscious deception, even the simplest lusts could lead one astray, creating fantasies of emotion. Henri's image crossed her mind, but she pushed it away. He was not yet twenty, and infatuated with her. It was true she was also infatuated with him, but when he grew older…well, he would not want to stay with her as she grew wrinkled and bent. It was pathetic to encourage her ridiculous passion for a stableboy.

Maxime set his goblet on the table. "So you refuse me?" He rose from his seat, and she rose from her chair.

This had nothing to do with Henri. It was negotiation, and necessary. "I didn't say that."

Maxime held out his hand, big and broad-palmed. She remembered his palm cupping her breast and rubbing against her nipple as vividly as if it were happening now. She laid her hand in his, thinking he would lead her down the corridor to some other room, but instead he drew her close and nuzzled her neck. Her body melted. They might never have been apart. Did she truly trust him, or did her body's lust rule her mind?

"You smell delicious," he murmured against her throat. His fingers tickled her bare nape and his breath sang over her skin. She could feel his lips move within his softly bristling beard, then the soft touch of his tongue. She shivered.

"This could all be much simpler if you would only marry me," Maxime said, combing his fingers through her hair. She could feel his muscles shifting against her. "I notice that you did not ask me."

Camille looked away. "You forget, I am already married.

Michel may say he's cast me off, but only the king can dissolve our marriage."

"Unless one of you is dead," he mused, stroking his thumbs over her cheeks. Camille fought the desire to melt against his hard body. "I would kill him for you, if you asked."

"No, you would not," she said. "First, I will not ask. Second, my eunuchs would win the privilege, should the king require the duke's execution." The thought made her feel ill. Much as she hated Michel, she could not see herself putting a period to his life, even indirectly. It was not a trait of which she felt proud—being a ruler required difficult decisions—but she could not change and remain herself. If it was a womanly weakness or otherwise, she accepted that about herself. "It will not be necessary to kill him," she said. "I have a plan." When she did not elaborate, Maxime drew back enough to stare down into her face. Camille said, "You do not need to know."

"I don't." A pause. "Very well. If you are to trust me, I must trust you."

Camille smiled at him. Her cheeks felt stiff. "Thank you. I should go. I must tell my servants where I've gone." Otherwise, Kaspar and Sylvie and Arno, and probably Henri as well, would come after her, intent on rescue.

Maxime sighed, a hot gust against her ear, and stepped away from her. "And then?" He looked more cautious and less confident than when she'd first arrived. He watched her face intently, his breathing slightly faster.

Camille made her decision. "And then I will come to you, and we shall finish what we began all those years ago."

Back in their spacious quarters, Sylvie insisted that she have a bath, scrubbing Camille herself and washing her hair, a much less onerous process than before she'd cut it all off. Camille allowed herself to be tended in silence. She wasn't yet ready to discuss her meeting with Maxime, and she especially did not want to discuss what she planned to do with him tonight. Dreams were one thing, especially youthful dreams, but now she was an adult, and knew what she was about. She still lusted for Maxime. She knew he would be an excellent lover. And she knew that she did not intend to rekindle their old romance. She was about to fuck Maxime to seal a bargain, nothing more.

Sylvie anointed Camille's limbs with a flower-scented cream and dressed her in a clean gray gown that was only slightly crumpled from its long journey in a saddlebag. On her way out of the main room, Henri looked as if he wanted to speak, but Camille smiled at him benignly, pretending not to notice.

Maxime stood outside the door, twirling a rose between his fingers. He'd unfastened the neck of the bright blue coat, revealing a gleaming white silk shirt with lace at the cuffs and throat, sharp contrast to the dark chest hair curling from his open collar. He held out the flower. "For you."

He'd been much less gallant as a boy. Though she tried to tell herself he was manipulating her, the gesture of kindness made her heart tremble. She took the rose from his hand, bringing it to her nostrils, taking the opportunity to look down instead of into his eyes. She inhaled; the rose smelled rich as incense. When the petals brushed her lips they tasted of sea salt. She tucked it into her bodice. "Shall we go?"

Maxime grinned and seized her hand, leading her down the corridor to his own suite of rooms. Camille vividly remembered watching him hurry away from her, while she watched from a doorway until she could be safe from prying eyes. She'd never hurried with him. They'd always arrived and departed separately from their rendezvous. Whoever found the sanctuary first would wait, panting with anticipation, adolescent lust and fear of discovery. This was better; she felt almost a sense of conspiracy between them.

Maxime glanced over his shoulder as he pushed open the door. "I feel as if I'm a boy again," he commented wryly, once they'd entered the room and shut and bolted the door. "I'm not usually so maladroit, dragging my lovers by the hand."

"Still plural?" Camille said. "You have not changed all that much."

Maxime cupped her face in his hands, trapping her hand against his chest. Camille couldn't resist shifting into his touch, uncurling her fingers against sleek silk. She was close enough to inhale his scent; her body loosened in remembered pleasure. Maxime lifted her face with fingers beneath her chin, until she had to meet his gaze. He said, "You are even more lovely than I remember. The way you've cut your hair makes me want to bite the back of your neck like a stallion."

A thrill raced through her at his words. She'd loved the way he always told her exactly what he wanted, and what he hoped she might want. The familiarity comforted her. She moved back a little, forcing him to loosen his hold. "You do not need to flatter me."

"I never flatter. With a cock like mine, I need never say a word." He grinned and fluttered his brows.

Camille almost laughed. She raised an eyebrow, instead, and reached down to trace his cock through his silk trousers. Her hand slid on the fabric as if it were oiled. Her mouth watered, and her quim dampened. Her palms ached to touch him.

"There are lacings," Maxime informed her, arching his pelvis into her grip. "You could untie them."

"Then you would escape," Camille noted, massaging him more firmly. She gripped his buttock with her free hand and dug her fingers in, gladly moving closer again when Maxime dragged her to him for a deep kiss.

He still kissed as he had, fervently thrusting his tongue, but now his beard added new stimulation she thought would drive her mad, a velvety bristling coursing over her skin, from face to toes. The barest thought of how his beard would crush against her quim made her wet. She wanted to shove him to the floor and let him burrow beneath her skirt, but he wouldn't stop kissing her mouth, her chin, her throat, her mouth again, until there was no world but their mouths, sliding together and pressing and tugging. She didn't fear showing him her hunger. He'd known it already.

Maxime's hands fumbled loose enough buttons to touch her bare skin. His nails skated down her spine and his hot touch spiraled on the upper slope of her rear. Her own panting grew loud in her ears, gradually replaced with Maxime's rough voice. "Give me your juice, I need you so hot you can't think, squirming on my prick, your juice spilling out and dripping on my balls, your cunt sucking me all the way in," he said in her ear, between nips on her earlobe. He gripped handfuls of her flesh, squeezing with almost-pain that stabbed deep within her quim. This wasn't measured or considered. It was lust, driving out all fear and doubt. Camille embraced it as she embraced Maxime.

His silk coat wouldn't rip in her hands, and she couldn't locate its frogged fasteners until she realized they were the off-center lumps digging into her breast. She had not put on drawers; her thighs slid in her own wetness. "Fuck," she said, struggling to strip him while he held her too close to freely move.

"I'm trying," Maxime said, chuckling madly. He sucked on her neck between phrases and rubbed his chest against her breasts. "I want to fuck you on that table. I want to fuck you against a wall. I want to fuck you on the floor. I want—"

Camille gave up on the coat and ripped the laces on his trousers, moaning as his erection swelled out and she could rub herself against it. Her hands shook violently.

"Oh, fuck," Maxime said. "Don't do that. Don't—"

"If you don't hurry up—" Camille said.

"Bed." Maxime lifted and tossed her onto the thick, soft

mattress. Camille squirmed on the silken coverlet, shoving her dress completely off her shoulders and down to her knees. Maxime leaped onto the bed next to her and yanked her dress the rest of the way off, then tore at his coat.

Afternoon rays of sunlight filtered through the silk canopy, bathing them in sunset colors. Camille had meant to take control, to leisurely have her pleasure with him. Instead, they scrambled and grabbed and devoured each other as if the intervening years had never happened, or as if each intervening year had been its own separate pain. "Kiss me," she demanded. "Kiss me now."

She'd forgotten how big he was, his size inescapable when he sealed his side to her bare skin, one arm flung across her belly, the other cradling her neck while they kissed, messily and desperately. His muscular upper arm was nearly as big around as her thigh; his leg, flung over both of hers, was a dense, comforting weight. She felt enveloped in his familiar heat, so much more than she had ever experienced of him before. She wanted more still. She buried her nose in his neck, breathing him in. She rubbed her palms against his ribs, marking herself with his scent. If only she could be with Henri like this, free to lose herself in the madness of passion.

"You're so soft," Maxime said, grasping her more tightly. He lowered his head to her breast, kissing the upper slope, the outer side, the very edge of her areola. "I was fascinated with you. I dreamed of you for years after. Sometimes I dream of you still. Did you think of me? Did you think of me after I was gone?" He sucked her nipple into his mouth, hard, and Camille cried out.

"Yes," she confessed, clutching at his head, her hips bucking into his hard cock. The words ripped free with each hard pull of his mouth. "You were the first. When Michel—when Michel hurt me—I remembered you, and what you did for me. Maxime—it's too much. Stop. Stop."

He withdrew slowly, gently licking her nipple, then a circle around it. His hands shaped her sides, then the curve of her hips, then her thighs, pulling them apart. "I want to kiss your cunt. I want to suck your juice into my mouth and lick it out of you with my tongue. I'm going to fuck you with my mouth until you scream, and you will never think of him again."

"Do it," Camille gasped. "I want to be here, now. Forget it all."

"You'll forget everything but me and your cunt." Maxime's beard brushed her labia, the touch almost imperceptible, phantom sparkles of sensation that drove her to arch against the grip of his hands.

"More!" she demanded.

His tongue traced her slit, prickling the stubble that had grown there in recent days. Her thighs quivered. She closed her eyes; a tear of frustration seeped from one corner as he delicately teased apart her lower lips, flicking delicately, keeping her on the edge of sensation. "I need to come!" she said, knowing he knew it, too, and would not deny her.

Maxime bent lower, effortlessly lifting her thighs over his shoulders and pressing his chin into her quim. Camille grabbed handfuls of coverlet and threw her head back. He said, "Once, now, for you. Or maybe twice," he added, on a breathless chuckle, before peeling her open like a fruit and suckling until she cried out. The scraping of his beard was every bit as potent as she'd imagined, almost too intense for her, until he distracted her with a finger in her quim, rotating inside. Her orgasm was upon her before she could take a breath; her vision whited out while she jerked and shuddered around his finger, against his mouth. Maxime coaxed her down with gentle laps of his tongue, slowly easing away. "Better?" he asked, as her hands went lax.

Camille's muscles were still trembling. She wanted more. "Shall it be your turn now?" She stretched, breathing deeply to regain control, then reached down and stroked his head.

Maxime looked down at her thoughtfully, then at her quim. He rubbed her with the tip of his nose. "You're not as limp as I'd hoped. You might not give me my title. I'm going to make you come again. With two fingers inside you this time, and sucking on your clit. Perhaps I can make you come twice in succession. Or even three times. I'm sure I could manage that, if it would please you. Then you'll be delectably relaxed for when I fuck you into the mattress. Since you'll probably be too tired for me to come more than once, I want to fuck you for a very long time. It wouldn't be fair for me, otherwise. You wouldn't want me to feel cheated, would you?"

"But, Maxime—"

"You haven't screamed yet. I really do require that to show

your good faith. I want you to know that I always keep my promises." He rubbed one hand up her belly and squeezed her breast. An aftershock pierced her quim, and she moaned. He slid his finger farther inside of her, pressing up and stroking. Her breath faltered. "Say yes."

"Yes, Maxime," Camille said.

"Tell me about your servants," he said. "We will need their help to take the duchy."

"I am aware of that," Camille said. She drew a shaky breath and caught Maxime's wrist, pushing his hand away from her. "Did you think I had not made plans of attack? The duke's chamber servant is poised to imprison him at need."

Maxime let her push him away, but then curled himself over and around her, graceful as a cat for all his size. He splayed one hot hand over her belly and nuzzled the nape of her neck, occasionally licking and kissing her bared skin, which sent shivers all through her. She thought he had dropped the subject until he said, "Vilmos certainly has reason to betray Michel, after what your father and Michel's did to his family. Michel's a fool to keep him so close."

"He likes to gloat," Camille said, the words bitter on her tongue. "My eunuch, Arno, is also of that family."

"*Is* he? That is good fortune, then. Vilmos was always kind to me, you know, when I lived in the palace."

"I never saw you together."

"We were very discreet," Maxime said. "Did you know that his family's treason involved siding with my family, when my parents were killed? Vilmos's grandfather spoke out against it."

Ashamed, Camille realized she had never thought to ask. She had known only that the treason lay in the past, and that Vilmos had done nothing himself. "I thought to reward Vilmos with a position," she said. "Steward or chamberlain."

"He is well-educated," Maxime noted. "He would make an admirable chamberlain."

"I will consider it," she said shortly. She did not want Maxime to feel he could direct her actions.

"And the others? The servants you brought with you?" Maxime asked.

"Kaspar guards my life," Camille said, "as will Sylvie. She is my spy, as well. I rely on her for many things."

"And Henri?"

"My groom," Camille said.

"That's all? You brought a groom on your escape?"

"I would not have escaped so quickly on foot," Camille snapped.

Maxime held up a hand. "I am hardly one to protest your bringing along a lover. It's good to have that release available to you."

Camille almost protested: Henri was more than easy release to her! She turned her face away.

Maxime touched her bare shoulder, cupping it in his palm. Gently, he asked, "Is he your confidant?"

"No. He is a boy."

"Youth need not lessen his value to you."

"Perhaps." She turned onto her back and drew Maxime's

hand from her shoulder, twining their fingers together. She could distract as well as Maxime could.

Or perhaps not. He ignored her gaze on his cock and asked, "How long has he been your lover?"

"He's not my lover."

"You've never fucked him? Passed time, then—"

"I have," she said. She had to force out the words. "I used him. I tried to get with child. He is not my lover."

"He looks at you as if—"

"The boy's infatuated."

"Enough so to accompany you all this way. What could he hope to gain?"

"He has asked for nothing." Except, perhaps, too much of her thoughts, and only with his eyes.

Maxime said, "If Henri is not required for your plans any longer, then perhaps you might leave him here when you go. He's a comely lad, and I could use a trustworthy Master of Horse. There are foreign breeds that would fetch incredible prices, if I only had someone with knowledge of horses on hand."

"He will return to the duchy with me," Camille said flatly.

Maxime lifted his brows. "Very well, then." He paused. "I really would marry you, you know."

"I've told you that would be...difficult. No, I cannot marry you."

"A liaison, now and again? It can be your tithe to me." He pressed a kiss to the inside of her thigh. "Don't forget how very large a cock I can bring to the bargain."

Camille chuckled. "I begin to worry about your preoccupation with your cock."

He licked the curve of her belly and lightly brushed her skin with his beard. His big hand squeezed her thigh and she moaned. "Of those who are great, much is required." He kissed her still-tender quim. "I'm sure it will take me hours to be sufficient unto your needs."

CHAPTER EIGHTEEN

"It's time," Sylvie said to Henri. "You have had your luncheon, and you have promised I could have my way with you. We have been in this castle for two days. I am tired of waiting." Also, if she *once more* saw him moping near madame's door, waiting for her to return from yet another meeting with Maxime, she would have to tie him up for purposes of murder, not fun.

"Oh," he said. "Yes." He did not sound the slightest bit apprehensive. That would never do.

Sylvie cracked her palms together. "You will kneel when you acknowledge me!"

Henri jumped at the noise. "Stop it, Sylvie! I'm not in the mood for your games!"

She planted her hands on her hips and advanced on him. "You will put yourself into the mood," she said. "*You owe me.* Or do you break your promises so easily?"

"What does it matter? It's all just fucking, in the end. Why can't we skip all that—that—" He flapped his hand in the air.

"Nonsense?" she suggested. "Was it nonsense when Kaspar flogged Master Fouet? You saw something laughable in that?"

"I didn't say it was nonsense!"

"You were thinking it. On your knees. This is what I want. You will give me what I want. Yes?"

"Yes." Henri sighed and knelt on the floor at her feet.

"Show a little more enthusiasm," Sylvie directed. "Perhaps you could kiss my feet."

Henri leaned over and studied her boots. "Are you going to take your boots off?"

"No."

"May I take them off?"

"No."

He sat back on his heels. "Sylvie, this game might be fun for lords and ladies and—and you—but I've spent my whole life having people order me around. It isn't the same for me. If I wanted someone to hit me, I could go back to the duke's stable."

Sylvie frowned. This wasn't going according to plan. Things between them had changed too much over the course of the journey, and she could no longer treat him like one of her short-time paramours. Truthfully, his genuine reluctance was only frustrating her, and not in a way she enjoyed. "We will try something else."

"I could take my clothes off," Henri said hopefully.

"First, we will go elsewhere. This corridor is not private. You may get up."

"I'll try," he said, with a crooked grin.

Sylvie smacked his rear, not too hard. "Impertinent."

She'd inquired of several servants about the various wings of Lord Maxime's labyrinthine monstrosity of a castle, and places where two visitors might play unnoticed. She'd considered the small wine cellar where the most valuable vintages were racked, but it was visited too often, as was the cool room where cheeses and milk were stored, and the laundry facility, and the extensive baths. However, a helpful valet had told her of a much more appropriate tower room.

Lord Maxime clearly partook of specialized pleasures, judging by his X-shaped rack, the padded leather benches and the leather cuffs bound together by shiny chains. Matching human-size bronze statues stood in the corners: mermaids and mermen with their arms trapped in tangles of seaweed and bound by their own wild locks of hair. The walls were hung with brocaded green drapes atop slatted bamboo mats that both hid ringbolts and muffled sound. There was a padded chair with arms, large enough for a couple to amuse themselves upon without injuring their knees or elbows. Most tempting of all was a large table, comfortably padded with layers of goosedown beneath leather, with iron loops along each side, to allow for a variety of positions. She'd found no paddles or whips; he likely kept those wrapped or cased in his own chamber. It didn't matter. Henri would not experience those toys properly.

Sylvie appreciated the look on his face as he stepped through the heavy wooden door. She needed both hands to close the door behind him, and lever down the bar. By the time she turned back to him, he was straddling a bench meant to mimic the breadth and curve of a horse's back, his hands on his knees, and he'd mastered his face. He'd learned some control from madame. Sylvie wasn't sure if she was glad about that, or sorry.

Sylvie dusted off her hands and examined him. She thought he'd grown taller since she'd first brought him to madame, and his shoulders looked broader, or perhaps he simply no longer cowered. With the proper haircut he'd had from Lord Maxime's valet, and new clothing that didn't hang on him, she didn't immediately expect to find manure adhering to his boots. His eyes still betrayed his softness. Perhaps he would never lose that.

"Undress," Sylvie said.

Henri swung one leg over the leather horse and unbuttoned his jacket. "What are we going to do?"

"You would have liked being caned," Sylvie said. "Truly, it's exquisite."

"No, it isn't," he said darkly. He hung his jacket on a hook, sat on a low bench and attacked his boots. He looked up at her, a sudden eager light in his eyes. "If you'd like me to bring you off with my mouth, I could do that. I watched at Master Fouet's. I could do all sorts of things."

Enthusiasm was always a thrill. Sylvie appreciated the little shiver across her skin at his words, then denied him. "Perhaps later. Today, I will tie you up and bind your cock and balls so you cannot come until I wish. You will like that very much."

"I will?"

"Yes, you will, or I will know the reason why." Sylvie reached into her belt pouch and removed a neatly folded leather strap. "I must put this on you before you begin to like it too much."

Henri set his boots on the floor in the corner. "What's that?"

"Weren't you watching, when Kaspar bound Master Fouet?"

Henri shrugged, and unbuttoned his shirt. He thumbed open his leathers on the way down, revealing curling hair. The casual way he did it made Sylvie's palms ache, to reach inside the leathers and touch him. "I was watching madame."

Sylvie said, "And so you remain ignorant. This is a harness for your cock and balls. I must bind those to my will, too. It is a simpler harness than Kaspar used, but serves much the same purpose. I should really shave you before I strap this on—"

"What?!"

"—but I don't think madame would like it. So I will be careful not to pinch." She dangled the strap between two fingers.

Henri tried to step toward her to get a closer look, stumbled on his leathers and sat down hard on a bench. "That thing doesn't hurt, does it?"

Sylvie smiled at the note of apprehension in his voice. "I would not say it *hurts,* exactly." She tucked the harness into the waistband of her leathers and removed her jacket, hanging it carefully on a hook. She secured her hair in a tighter knot and popped loose the top buttons of her shirt. As she was not wearing her breast bindings or a corset, Henri would have tantalizing glimpses of her bosom. When she turned to him again, he stood naked, hands at his sides, looking nervous.

She advanced on him. "You are here of your own free will?" she asked. "Tell me truthfully, Henri."

He took a deep breath. "I am," he said. "I might be crazy to trust you, but I do. You haven't hurt me yet."

Sylvie couldn't resist smiling. She always felt a rush of delight when a man gave himself into her hands, trusting her with his pleasure. She would do her best to give it to him, more pleasure than he'd ever known. Or, at the very least, different pleasure. He would learn how far one could travel, when one was not afraid.

"Hold your cock for me, then," she said. He was already swelling, enough that he would be sensitive. She cupped his balls in her own hand, careful not to handle them too much as she looped the strap beneath his scrotum and fastened it above the shaft of his cock. "Let go," she said, adjusting him within the strap and refastening it, slightly tighter. "Do you feel it?" she asked, a matter of form, as she knew he would feel the beginnings of constriction.

"Yes, but what happens when——" His cock hardened as she watched.

"Now you see?"

"Yes," he said, restlessly shifting his hips. He looked at her from under his long lashes, a look of mixed acquiescence and trepidation and arousal.

"It will be better still," she promised. "Perhaps you could lie on that table."

Sylvie took her time binding him in place. She loved the smell of leather and its smooth, rich feel; she loved the security of a leather tongue sliding home through a buckle. She gave each a small tug as she finished, for the satisfaction of it. Henri's legs were bound open, of course, for easy access to everything from his cock down. After a little thought, she bound his wrists at waist level, away from his body, but not so high that his muscles would be strained. He was inexperienced at this game. A little would go a long way.

After she'd bound him, she stepped back and settled into the chair, leaning against one of its arms and dangling her legs over the other. Henri's head turned to follow her. "What are you doing?" he asked.

"Making myself comfortable," she said, studying her handiwork. His muscles were well-defined for one so young, especially in his thighs and shoulders. All that riding, she supposed, and shoveling manure. His thighs flexed as he tested his bonds, and she said, "Wouldn't it be nice if madame were here?"

Henri tensed.

"You would let her bind you, wouldn't you? I would."

"It isn't like that," he said, his voice strained.

"She might enjoy binding you. Running her hands along your arms, shoulders to wrists. Your hairs rise as she passes. Your fingers move to grasp her, but too late! You are captured. You are subject to her will, to her pleasure. And her pleasure is your pleasure. You like to make her gasp and moan. She likes the same. Does she call out your name? Do you call hers?"

Henri's breathing sped up as she spoke. "I'm not going to tell you."

Sylvie did not tell him that reality was not at issue here. She spun the fantasy at length, idly swinging her leg, occasionally unbuttoning another of her shirt buttons, until Henri would not look at her anymore, only at the ceiling, while his belly heaved with his rapid breathing. He was hard now; the harness would squeeze him like looped fingers. Except the harness would not, could not stroke him as he longed to be stroked. She could smell his arousal mingled with leather and lemony wood polish; she inhaled the scents like sweet perfume.

She finished describing how and where madame might desire to lick him, waited a few moments for the ideas to sink in, then went to him, trailing her hand along the table's surface between his legs. His muscles twitched as his body strove to meet hers, like a plant reaching for the sun. She outlined his leg with her fingers, not quite touching. "Can you feel that?" she asked. The hairs on his legs had risen, and she brushed her fingertip down his calf.

"Please," Henri said.

"Oh, so you are ready for the teasing, are you?" Sylvie walked closer to his upper body and flicked his nipple with her nail; his shoulder tensed, bringing his pectoral muscle closer to her fingers. "I can amuse myself for quite some time this way." She rested one hand in his hair and lightly scratched his scalp, which she knew he liked, and said, "Madame might want me to prepare you for her. She would be waiting, watching us, perhaps smoothing the cream around her cunt—"

"Fuck, Sylvie, you're killing me!"

"Oh, hush. You are not nearly ready to burst yet."

"Please don't say *burst.*" Henri rolled his shoulders against the padding and shifted his hips. "How long do I have to stay here?"

"Until I free you, of course. Where would be the fun in letting you do as you wish?" Sylvie traced the shape of his ear and teased inside with her smallest finger. "You men, always wanting to rush, rush, rush."

"Not always," he protested.

"Mostly," she said. "Tell the truth."

"Depends what you mean by *rush,*" Henri said, gasping when she pinched his earlobe between a fingertip and nail.

"Perhaps you could tell me," Sylvie said. She flicked his cheekbone with her finger and trailed her nail down his chest. He shivered.

"Tell you——"

"Explain to me, how you would not rush. If you had an entire night with madame, and nothing to do but please her. Perhaps first you could tell me where this would happen."

"I don't know if that's right. She might not want——"

"This has nothing to do with madame. You are not her slave. Even if you were, your thoughts are your own."

Henri looked directly at her. "You won't tell her? What I say?"

"I would never hurt madame," Sylvie reassured him. "How many times must I tell you?" She poked him in the belly. There wasn't much give. She patted him with the flat of her hand, then rubbed in a circular motion, watching his erection tighten further. "If you must know, I won't hurt you, either. Because madame cares for you."

That statement had sounded more sentimental than she'd intended. Sylvie flicked the tip of his cock with her nail and, grinning, watched his reaction.

Henri said, "One day I will tie *you* down and see how you like it."

Sylvie rubbed her thumb against his balls. "I would like that very well," she said. "Now, tell. Where would you like to make love to madame?"

"Will you let me go if I tell you?"

"Perhaps. What would you do first? With madame, not with me. We shall discuss our own imaginary encounter after."

Henri flushed. "Will you keep touching me?"

"I see you begin to understand this game. Of course, I could leave you here, and touch myself instead," she suggested.

Henri's flush deepened. "Maybe some other time," he said.

Sylvie leaned over him, letting her breasts come close to his chest without touching. She could feel the heat of his skin, and he looked down his nose, trying to see down her shirt. "What are you and madame doing? Close your eyes."

Henri closed his eyes. "We'll go riding," he said.

Typical, Sylvie thought. They were both mad for horses. So mad Henri could not even have a simple fantasy that did not include them. Clearly, he needed tutoring in that area.

"We'd have to ride to get to the place I want," he said.

Not so bad. Sylvie liked realistic details, herself. They gave the fantasy that much more intensity and poignance. Idly, she circled his nipples with her fingertips, wondering if anyone had ever bitten them before. She would do that later, and see how he reacted.

"It's not a real place," Henri explained. "It can't be anywhere I've been before. Everywhere on the palace grounds will remind us both what I am. She wouldn't be able to forget that I'm not—forget where I came from."

Sylvie brushed her thumbs across his nipples and was rewarded by his caught breath before he went on.

"We'll ride into the hills to a cottage I own, and then we'll take care of our horses together. Her horses love her, you know, and she loves them. I'll have a paddock, so they don't have to be tethered. They can roll in the grass and sleep under the shade trees. Maybe fruit trees."

Sylvie rolled her eyes, but he couldn't see her. "What's inside your cottage?"

"The bedroom's at the back," Henri said. "She'll close the door behind us, and shoot the bolt. Then she'll come to me and I'll unbutton her coat." He described undressing her in great detail, including the texture of the cloth and how her skin looked as it was revealed, then moved on to caressing. His level of detail was obsessive. Sylvie began to be more interested. She stroked his hip bones and upper thighs.

"And then?" she asked. "Perhaps you join her on the bed."

"No," Henri said thoughtfully. "First, she would sit on the edge of the bed, and I would kneel between her feet."

"What would she say?" Sylvie asked.

"Don't kneel to me."

"And you?"

"I'd say I want to kneel, and then I would press her knees apart with my hands, and kiss her at the top of her cunt. I'd take care of her, I'd be careful not to scrape her with my cheeks. I'd lick her skin, she's so soft, or maybe by then she wouldn't bother to shave herself, she'd be able to do whatever she wanted, and I'd rub her hair against her skin with my nose. And she would lie back on the bed and let *me* do whatever *I* wanted. I would taste every little bit of her, like that little hood that hides her clit, I want to slide the tip of my tongue under it and press down and it would take a while, because she tries to hide things, but then she would make that *sound,* the sound I like best, or maybe an even better sound I've never heard before. I'd go slow, until she begged me for more."

When he stopped speaking, Sylvie took a moment to come out of her trance; she'd been remembering her own night with madame, and now her breathing was almost as unsteady as Henri's. She bent over him slowly, giving him time to anticipate, and gently brushed her upper lip across the tip of his cock. "Look at me," she said, before licking his moisture from her mouth. A vein in his neck was throbbing, and when she bent close to his cock again, she could see his pulse beating in his shaft.

"Like this?" Sylvie asked, letting her breath warm the head

of his cock. She nudged the tip of her tongue beneath his foreskin, gently abrading, shivering at the noises he made. She braced her palm on his hip bone and continued, grinding in with the heel of her hand when he tried to arch into her teasing.

"You're hurting me," Henri gasped, his breath coming in hard sobs.

"Am I really? I'll stop."

"I can't tell! Sylvie! Stop—no! Don't!"

She would have laughed in triumph, but it was difficult with her mouth full. She pulled her lips free of his cock's head and licked her lips. "Now I am having fun," she said. "How long shall I hold you here, I wonder?"

"You are not nice at all," Henri moaned. "Take that fucking strap off me!"

"Perhaps I shall deliver you to madame like this. I can go and fetch her."

"Don't!" He gasped as his erection tautened, which Sylvie had not thought was possible. "She's—she's busy with *him!*"

Sylvie sighed, washing his skin with heat and following her breath with the lightest touch of her fingers. "True. We would not want her to look foolish. Perhaps you could wait until she is finished with her duties."

"No!" Henri banged the back of his head against the padding, once, twice, three times. "I'll make you sorry, Sylvie!"

"You promised to submit to me," she noted.

"Fuck!" He banged his head one more time, and then bit his lip. "Fine! Do what you want!"

Sylvie grinned. "That is all *I* want," she said, and gave his shaft a squeeze before unfastening the strap. "Now I will make you come so hard you will mark the ceiling. There, isn't this fun?"

CHAPTER NINETEEN

Someone pounded on the door. "Hurry up in there, you're wanted!"

Henri pried his eyes open. It felt close to the evening meal; he was mildly hungry. He was no longer bound—he quickly checked—anywhere, though he still lay on the padded table. Sylvie was curled next to him, mostly clothed, her head pillowed on his shoulder. She stretched, knocking her elbow into his jaw, and said, "Shall we let this importunate person in? Madame might need us."

"I'm naked!" Henri protested, struggling to free himself from Sylvie's grasp.

"She certainly needs you naked quite often," Sylvie remarked, giving him a shove. His feet hit the cool stone floor. "Get dressed. I will answer the door."

Henri ducked behind the big chair and scrambled into his clothes while Sylvie called, "Yes, yes!" and walked to the door, buttoning her shirt as she went. She threw the bolt, yanked it open, and then fell abruptly silent.

Henri peered over the back of the chair. A bald woman stood in the doorway, her scalp completely decorated with blue and white and red designs; tattoos, he realized. She wore a loose, billowing shirt in deep orange, a curved dagger at her belt and brown leather pants to the knee. Below, her feet were bare, exposing more swirling tattoos. She was the tallest woman he had ever seen, as tall as Lord Maxime.

Henri noticed he was holding his cock and hurriedly stuffed it into his pants, his fingers stumbling on the buttons. The tall woman stared down her shapely nose at Sylvie and said, "I'm Captain Leung. Lord Maxime wants to see the boy."

Sylvie said breathlessly, "I want to lick your skull."

Leung lifted her brows. "Perhaps later. The boy?"

Henri grabbed his boots and stepped out. "Here I am."

Leung looked him up and down. "You?" Her eyes crinkled at the corners. They were a startling, mossy green, like sunlit water, contrasting starkly with her honey-colored skin.

"Yes," Henri said, meeting her gaze. Her lips shifted into a small, toothy smile.

"I am not a boy at all," Sylvie said, but was ignored.

"Put your boots on," Leung said. When Henri had finished, she took his arm and escorted him from the room, down a flight of stairs, across a landing to yet another staircase, and down three corridors before a final flight of stairs leading downward. Leung was intimidating in her silence, but didn't seem angry or cruel. Her bare feet and minimal weapons reassured him further. If she could kill him without any help, it wouldn't matter how he tried to defend himself. He was sure she didn't intend to harm him.

Leung gave Henri a little push at a doorway carved all over with octopuses. "Lord Maxime is in there." She turned and strode lithely back up the stairs.

Henri caught himself on the edge of the door and took a deep breath. Lord Maxime could not have known what he and Sylvie had been doing. What possible need could he have for Henri? Unless the duchess was with him here, and had requested his presence; but then why say he was wanted by Lord Maxime?

Henri pushed the door open. Steam curled out. A laundry room? No, baths. In the cellars? He entered the room, which flickered with oil lamps behind colored glass, red and gold and sunset orange. On a second look, he saw the glass had been blown into the shapes of bulbous octopuses with bronze tentacles, or bright bubbles encircled by bronze dolphins. The walls were irregular, curving stone, pocketed with carved niches for the lamps, the floor decorated with chips of red and orange stone. The air smelled of water and minerals and smoke. He put these things together and understood. This was a cave, and it held hot springs.

It also held Lord Maxime, mostly naked, lounging on a stone couch carved from one wall, a red towel draped over his loins. "Welcome, Henri," he said. "I advise you to strip down and have a scrub over there." He indicated with a wave of his hand. "Then perhaps we can soak together."

"Thank you, my lord." What else could he say? Despite his nudity, Lord Maxime was still much larger and stronger, and trained as a warrior. Henri wasn't sure he had a choice about staying.

Hoping his body bore no marks from Sylvie's entertainment, Henri laid his clothes on a wooden bench that already held pants and shirt and jacket, and a little dish full of jeweled earrings. Lord Maxime normally wore plain clothing, he noted, not like the embroidered coat he'd worn to greet them. Henri tucked his boots beneath the bench with Lord Maxime's, and went to the area where buckets of steaming water had been set out. The floor was warm beneath his feet, nearly hot.

"There's soap on the shelf," Lord Maxime said. Was he kind to offer, or implying that Henri smelled of the stable and offended his nostrils? He padded over to Henri, the towel flung over one massive shoulder. He looked powerful as a mastiff. Henri kept his shoulders straight, though his body wanted to cringe. He found the soap and a cloth, and held both out to Lord Maxime. He might be the guest here, but he couldn't forget their relative ranks. Lord Maxime should wash first.

"Thank you, Henri," he said. "You must call me Maxime. I am sure Camille would not want you to bow and scrape to me." He dipped the cloth in a bucket, rubbed it with soap and captured Henri's wrist.

Henri twitched in surprise, but held still as Maxime cleansed his forearm. He hadn't been hurt yet. Maxime's hand felt pleasantly warm and didn't squeeze painfully; the rough cloth felt good on his skin. It was clear he intended to wash Henri, as if they were equals. Turning Henri's wrist, he stroked the inside of his arm, then up to his bicep and the tender pit of his underarm. Henri jerked involuntarily; Maxime smiled at him, but did not let go of his wrist. He continued to wash Henri's shoulder and the side of his neck, a thoughtful expression on his handsome features. When he let go of Henri's wrist, Henri did not flee. The duchess would not flee.

After lying sleepless for several nights, worrying over what Camille had done when confronted by Lord Belette, Henri had finally decided that her direct attack had been the best strategy possible to them. He would not have done it; he had been too afraid. He thought she had been afraid, too, but her fear had not ruled her. Instead, she'd channeled her fear into Marie-the-whore's defiance. She'd been so successful, she'd distracted Belette completely from his original beliefs, and she'd prevented him from following them any farther.

Of course, Henri reflected, it had taken him days to understand the full beauty of her solution, instead of the seconds she'd had to both plan and act. His seduction of the innkeeper at The Escaping Mermaid had been paltry by comparison. He would have to work to aspire to the duchess's skills. He had vowed he would begin as soon as he could, to make himself more useful to her. This seemed to be a good time to emulate her methods, and see where they led. He crossed his arms over his chest and asked, "Why did you have me brought here?"

Maxime answered casually, "So we can talk. You realize that I do not love Camille?"

Henri's muscles tightened. "It is none of my business whom she loves." Maxime knew, then, about what Henri did for his duchess. Had she told him? Had they discussed Henri and laughed? Why would they have bothered? Surely, he wasn't that important. The thought made him angry. He strove to keep his anger from his face.

"I am sure she does not love me," Maxime said, though Henri had not asked. He didn't sound mocking. He moved a little closer, close enough for Henri to be grateful he didn't smell of the duchess. He began to scrub Henri's chest, in a circular motion that Henri recognized from when he groomed horses. It was soothing, more so than it should have been; was the air drugged? He could feel the heat of Maxime's hand through the cloth, though the abrasion made him want to shiver. Maxime grasped Henri's shoulder with his free hand and scrubbed a little harder, gentling when he crossed Henri's nipples; now he did shiver, though he tried not to show it. Henri did not normally desire men, but the Lord Maxime had an extraordinarily seductive touch. Henri could easily see how the duchess had been attracted. It was difficult for him not to be envious of such easy charisma.

Maxime said, "Camille and I, we had an appetite for each other when we were young. Now we've met as adults and the appetite is still there, but it's quite different for both of us."

"She can do as she likes," Henri said. He knew that the duchess had fucked Maxime since their arrival, but he did not want to hear Maxime say so. He especially did not want to hear Maxime explain why the duchess wanted someone of her own age and station, instead of a stableboy.

Maxime said, "She will not marry me, but you will stay with her, won't you?" Henri blinked, for a few moments sure he'd heard the opposite. Maxime continued, "It's you she needs."

Henri snatched the soapy cloth from Lord Maxime's hand. "Where is Her Grace?"

"I left her sleeping in my rooms. Later, she is to meet with my aunt."

Henri swallowed down rage. He had no right to be jealous. Camille had known Lord Maxime before he was even born. "Why have you called me here, if she needs me but fucks you?" If she needed him, she had clearly not needed him recently. He had not even slept in her bed since their arrival at the castle.

"Because she came to me for help."

"Help her, then. I have no money or soldiers." He added bitterly, "I am no threat to anyone."

"That isn't why I wanted to speak with you," Maxime said. "You care for her, don't you?"

Henri went cold. "I am Her Grace's—" He wasn't sure what he was, or how he could say it.

"—lover," Maxime said. "I am glad."

"Glad." He felt as if he rode a bucking horse that twisted a new direction each time he took a breath.

"Yes. I may not be called a duke, but I know what it's like to rule. One needs loyalty. And more, one needs a safe harbor.

Camille and I cannot be that for each other. The danger is too great that we will fight each other for dominance. And also...it has been many years. We have both changed. There is another whom I want to keep by me. I believe that Camille wants *you* to stay by her. She has not said this to you?"

Henri shook his head. "Of course not."

"Of course she would not," Maxime mused. He paused. "I will help you, if you like. If she is happy and cared for, all our lives will be much better, don't you think? Her duchy will be the stronger for it, and then I need no longer fear for mine."

If he was sincere, the exercise might be useful. As he pondered, Henri set to washing Lord Maxime's muscular shoulders and chest.

Henri knew he had no skill in politics but, he reminded himself, he often had a good sense of people's motives. He'd known Sylvie didn't hate him personally even before she'd proven it; he'd known he could manipulate the innkeeper at The Escaping Mermaid. When he asked himself whether he could trust Maxime's motives, he found that he did. He thought Maxime was telling the truth. If he couldn't trust his own feelings, then he had nothing.

He wasn't sure he wanted to be noticed by anyone as powerful as Lord Maxime, but it was too late, he had already been noticed. He'd set himself on this path by not refusing Camille's orders the first time she'd summoned him. And, he reminded himself, what *he* wanted wasn't as important as what she wanted. She might not say it, ever, but he, too, believed she needed him in some way, even if only for sex. Until now, he'd had little more than that to give her. If she'd chosen Maxime over him for that reason, he would have...he would find it difficult, very difficult, to let her go, but he would have done so for her sake. He would have, wouldn't he? But if he didn't have to give her up...if he could also become more worthy of her... He shouldn't get ahead of himself.

"How will you help me?" he asked.

"I will show you how to act as her equal, at least in your personal dealings."

He liked the idea of bettering himself. He could do it, he knew he could, given this chance. "Is that possible?" Henri asked.

"We will make it possible. You must be able to accompany her wherever she goes, even to the royal court, if necessary. You must understand how a court works, from the inside, and help to guard her from plots, and support her in her wishes. To do this, you must learn to act as a courtier acts. That, I can teach you."

"Then I will try to learn."

"Very good. We will have a soak and then begin your education with a meal, in my chambers."

CHAPTER TWENTY

Camille woke in need of a long, languorous stretch. The ache between her legs reminded her of Maxime's vigorous presence, and she turned to look for him, sensing as she did so that she was alone in his suite of rooms, sprawled naked across piles of green silken covers that spilled to the floor amid the litter of their clothing. On a table next to the bed stood a white porcelain pitcher and a matching cup. Camille poured herself cold water and drank. She wasn't sure how long she'd slept, but it felt like morning. The room was lit by a single lamp on the mantelpiece. It seemed deathly quiet without her retinue; so often she'd craved solitude, but now it unnerved her, after so many days in the close company of Sylvie and Kaspar and Henri. She wondered where Henri was now.

It didn't matter what Henri was doing. She had no need of his services just now.

She'd been left alone and unguarded in Maxime's most private space. A pile of leather-bound books, each holding a tasseled silken marker, tipped drunkenly on the floor next to the massive, carved wooden bed. He'd left his red-and-black lacquered portable writing desk on a bamboo stand nearby. The desk wasn't locked, and held several unanswered letters in different languages. He'd begun drafting a document outlining the reasons she would rule the duchy well. Clearly, he did not consider her a threat to his privacy, and meant to make good on his promises. She selected a dressing gown from Maxime's wardrobe—rich green silk—and ventured into the corridor. He'd left a maid stationed there, a plump dark-skinned woman who laid down her embroidery, stood and bobbed a curtsy. It looked strange, given that she wore loose, gathered trousers and a long tunic, and bore a sword at her hip. Perhaps she was not a maid, or like Sylvie, only partly a maid. She had the air of a guard. "Your Grace," she said. "How may I serve you?"

"Do you know where Lord Maxime has gone?"

"To the springs, Your Grace." At Camille's questioning look, the guard explained, "There are caves below the castle. Some of them contain natural hot springs."

Camille considered. She did want to wash and eat. It was unnecessary to find Henri before she did these things. "I will have a bath here," she decided. "Also a tray. Then I am to meet with Lady Gisele. Will you escort me to her?"

"Captain Leung will come for you," the guard said. Camille decided not to ask who Captain Leung might be. Presumably, he was another guard, but of higher status.

After Camille's bath and meal, a tall shapely woman with a shaven head entered the room. Her scalp and bare feet were completely covered by colored tattooing, her pale eyes outlined in dark kohl. She carried a long dagger in her belt, its sheath made of carved wood, its designs so tiny and intricate Camille could not decipher them. She bowed to Camille, from the waist like a man, and said, "Your Grace? Are you ready to speak with the Lady Gisele?"

Leung had the cool, deadly air of both a warrior and a commander, skills which Camille envied. "I am, thank you," Camille said.

She strolled with Captain Leung through several green and white striped passageways, through a small, sandy courtyard filled with guards, both male and female, practicing wrestling, and up a short staircase to a tower room filled with padded divans in shades of cream and buttery yellow, bamboo tea tables and potted plants, some large enough to be called small trees, others draping vinelike from the walls and ceiling. During the walk, Leung regaled her with a tale of alien splendor, taxation and retaliatory acts of piracy, which had apparently taken place two centuries ago. On another occasion, when less preoccupied, Camille might have been lost in the tale, which included a wizened old woman commanding hundreds of ships while holding a little flat-nosed dog on her lap. She determined to ask for the tale again when next they met. Camille had learned that the captain was commander of her own ship and Maxime's right hand; she would see her again, and often. She would appreciate finding out how Captain Leung had reached such a position and how she kept it in a profession dominated by men.

Lady Gisele had not yet arrived. Captain Leung swept a hand at the divans, more graceful than any courtier. "Please sit, Your Grace. I believe I will find her above, in her conservatory."

Camille chose a divan that faced both the door through which they'd entered and an open alcove. Leung parted a bead curtain and vanished up the stairs, while Camille pondered how she might lure Captain Leung to her own service. It did not seem likely. Her duchy did not possess a seacoast.

Out of courtesy to an elder, Camille rose when Lady Gisele entered the room, closely followed by Leung. Gisele's head only came to Camille's shoulder, and she was as comfortably rounded as a bear in the autumn. Her eyes and mouth smiled. Her gray hair, however, had been tied back in a short military queue, and the hilt of the dagger she wore was scarred with age and rough use. The plump hand she extended to Camille was marked by myriad small scars and one jagged white line that vanished into her sleeve. "Your Grace," she said.

Camille inclined her head. It was best to be honest with one's allies. "I am sorry, my lady, for your losses at the hands of my father."

Gisele shook her head sharply. "You were a child. My sister and brother-in-law— No, we shall speak of it another time. What matters now is how you will take back your duchy, and how you will hold it." She smiled. "And, of course, when you give to my nephew the ducal authority he already exerts."

Captain Leung said, "Your Grace, I am not a citizen of the protectorate, but Lord Maxime has earned my loyalty. Is it agreeable to you if I attend this meeting, as well? I would like to pledge myself and my ship and crew to your cause."

"I would be in your debt," Camille said. "I must ask if you agree with the possible risks."

"I do," Leung said. "I would risk much more to see a woman on the throne of your country, who would deal fairly with the queen of mine. But I suppose a duchy will have to do, for now."

"Shall we sit?" Gisele asked. "I will call for refreshments."

As they drank tea and ate small pink-frosted cakes, Camille related all that she had learned from Arno about the current state of the duchy. She did not see any alternative except returning to the ducal palace herself before ousting Michel. This was only partly for her own satisfaction. She needed to be in place as soon as he was removed from power, so the king would have no time to appoint a man of his own choosing.

Lady Gisele said, "Your Grace, if you had an indefinite amount of time, I am sure you would not need to confront the duke. As well as your eunuch's report, I have heard from my couriers. They have seen evidence of support for you in every town and village which they've visited."

"It's my absence that has given me power," Camille said wryly. "Most are reassured by thinking someone waits in the distance to ride to their rescue. It's easy enough to imagine me in that role, like an armored knight of old. I fear, though, that as time passes they will lose hope. I must take the palace as soon as I can, and show my people what real benefit they will derive from my rule."

Gisele nodded, once. "Then that is what we will do."

The afternoon passed quickly in plans, for Camille discovered that not only was Lady Gisele the protectorate's envoy to the king's court, she commanded the protectorate's defense forces, of which Captain Leung was sometimes a part; the discreet use of mercenaries neatly circumvented restrictions imposed on the protectorate by her father. Maxime dealt with all matters judicial and economic, consulting with Lady Gisele on the guards only to keep apprised of their status and her decisions. Camille felt as if she had fallen through a mirror to the other side of the world. She'd known women had a greater place in the protectorate, but it had not seemed real to her until now.

After she had left Lady Gisele and Captain Leung, Camille took Gisele's advice and went to walk alone in the rose garden. The bushes bordered a long spiraling path, the flowers' colors and scents gradually darkening and deepening as she approached the garden's center. The more she walked, the more she calmed. Her thoughts grew clearer and more defined. By the time she reached the sun-warmed stone bench nestling within a lush wall of garnet-colored roses, she felt as if she'd woken from a long sleep. She inhaled the peppery sweetness of the roses and the warm, soft odor of loam, all of it seasoned by a hint of the sea.

If she concentrated, she could catch echoes of voices beyond this courtyard. Small green-and-yellow birds settled onto the rosebushes and monotonously exchanged a few short phrases.

Camille closed her eyes. Here she could simply exist, feeling the world around her like a blanket of sensation. All too soon, however, her fears crept in, prickles of inadequacy and failure. She remembered the expression on Lord Belette's face when he'd thought her trapped: disgust and scorn, which had not altered whether he thought her duchess or whore. She'd been cold at the time, her rage and anger trapped behind a shield of ice, but now those emotions rushed in, a molten tide in her belly. How dared he? How dared he, a scheming courtier and failed investor, try to hinder her escape for his own paltry gain? How dared he treat her, or any woman, like chattel?

She remembered his hands on her, crushing into her flesh, and shuddered. Now that it was too late, she wished she had accepted Henri's embrace, once they'd been free and safe. She craved his physical comfort now. If only she could take it, without him realizing how much she needed it, and him. Perhaps when she had defeated Michel, she would feel strong enough to show weakness to Henri.

If, that is, Henri remained with her. Would he return to the duchy with her, travel into danger, or would he prefer to remain here? Without realizing it, she'd become convinced of Henri's attachment to her, but she had been wrong before, most notably wrong about Michel.

Feelings, personal desires: those were dangerous. Even when shown to a boy of no status. He might not betray her, but her feelings could betray her into all manner of folly. Especially now, when she needed to keep her mind on her work.

A cool calm flowed over her with the decision. She could—would—step back from Henri, and the tangle he caused in her mind and heart. Logic and practicality would carry her through the dangerous waters ahead. She'd had a pleasant respite, but it was time to return to her true world.

CHAPTER TWENTY-ONE

After a long day of wrestling and knifework with Kaspar and Arno, and lessons in etiquette from Maxime, Henri welcomed Camille's invitation to join her in the hot springs. He hoped it meant she'd relented about his taking part in her plans. He hadn't had a chance to be alone with her in days, and had not shared her bed since they'd arrived at Maxime's castle. It felt strange to be alone with her now. He felt strange. Different. He closed his eyes, listening to her bathe.

The sound of trickling water stopped, and his eyes flew open at the lack. He must have dozed off, for now Camille stood directly in front of him with a soapy cloth in her hand. The colored light from the lamps flickered in her eyes. "Sorry," he said, struggling to regain his balance. "What did you need?"

Camille touched his shoulder. "Sit still," she said, as if he would run away.

"I thought you wanted—"

She pressed her lips to his. Henri let her kiss him. By the time his hands obeyed his will and lifted to her sides, she'd drawn away from him and was soaping his chest. He let his hands fall. "You shouldn't do that. I can wash myself."

"I may do what I like," she said. "Be still. Close your eyes."

"But it isn't—"

"I did not ask your opinion." She paused. "If this is unpleasant for you, I will stop."

Henri shook his head. His brain ached, from the unlikelihood of what she did, but his flesh liked it all too well. Her hand with the cloth hadn't ceased moving over him as they spoke, and his skin was coming awake. He could almost imagine she washed him out of tenderness. Her touch felt tender, but he wasn't sure he could trust that. He could interpret anyone else better than her. Sometimes, he felt as if he was separated from her by a wide river.

She swept the cloth over his belly, then crouched and washed his thighs, her free hand braced against him for balance. He wondered if she knew how to bathe someone because she had been bathed so many times. Water trickled over his skin, tickling until she stroked it away. He was tired enough that his cock didn't harden, even with her face so near to it, and even though he looked down to see her breasts hanging loose and the sweet curve of her hips and the soft swell of her stomach, where he so loved to press his mouth. He felt warmth instead of sexual arousal, warmth every place her fingers touched. She pressed a kiss to the inside of his thigh and he felt a different warmth, wetter and more thrilling, but still distant and dream-like. "You can do that again," he suggested.

She said, "When I've finished." Then she returned to washing him, handling his cock and balls gently. He'd forgotten how small her hands were. He stared at them as if he'd never seen them before. He'd sucked those fingers into his mouth, and she'd allowed it. Before he could grow too attached to her manipulations of his soapy cock, she wiped off the foam and moved up to his belly.

Henri remembered when she had massaged him at Master Fouet's brothel, instructing as she did so, but after a time her voice had trailed away while her hands kept up their smooth swirls over his back. The oil she'd used had smelled of fir trees. He'd never be able to walk in a forest again without thinking of her hands on his body.

He'd enjoyed doing the same for her, because for once he'd been allowed to touch her as much as he liked, for as long as he liked, learning every inch of her. He loved finding the softest, most hidden parts of her: the crease where buttock met thigh, the patch of skin just below her earlobe, the underside of her clit's hood, the thin skin covering the bones of her feet. He'd been able to use his hands to tell her his feelings, safe from appearing foolish because she couldn't translate.

He was sure if he tried to tell her how he felt with words, she would never let him finish speaking. Worse, she might dismiss his words. He knew her better now than he had at first. Open emotion made her uncomfortable. So he spared her his passion and tenderness as much as he could, except when they fucked. Then he couldn't hide anything.

He wondered if she knew how he felt. She was so clever, he

couldn't imagine she didn't know. Except he would never be able to tell; she hid everything, her face usually as smooth as her profile on a coin. He'd learned to watch for the subtlest signs, drawing on his experience with observing horses, who couldn't talk to him. He'd often watched her and wondered how she managed to be so contained. He'd wondered if others couldn't see how she felt, if that meant she couldn't feel her own feelings, either. He'd imagined he could be the one to teach her, and thought of a thousand ways he'd like to do so.

It was only a dream. He'd spent his life being satisfied with what he could get. If he kept on that way, he'd be happier. He'd already achieved a modest ambition, for his duchess to know how he respected her. He should be grateful she allowed him to serve her. She would probably give him the cottage he longed for, if he asked. He was grateful. Only…he couldn't stop himself from wanting more. Everything she did had a reason. He wanted to know what those reasons were. He wanted to know her dreams and her feelings. He didn't want to be pensioned off somewhere, always wondering what might have become of them.

He wanted a connection with her, and for her to say that the connection was there. He wanted confirmation that he meant something to her. Maybe, to Camille, he was like the eunuchs, who, until they grew too old and were freed from their duties, were like slaves. Henri had sworn himself to her, tacitly giving her leave to treat him like that. He'd done it out of his own free will, thinking he could somehow change her life and his. He had only himself to blame. He wasn't a child, to change his mind when things became difficult.

If she didn't need him, then he should leave her. Except it wasn't that simple. He felt sure she needed someone. Everyone did. And she had no one.

Camille cupped the back of his neck and pushed down. Henri squeezed his eyes shut as she poured water over his head. Maybe she didn't think twice about washing him. Maybe it was like grooming one's horse. Did he come before or after Guirlande in her affections?

He was very tired of trying to understand the workings of her mind. If she would just let him love her, everything would be much simpler. He wondered if she knew how.

Young as he was, he'd had a mother, and a grandmother, and for a brief while, a sister, and had loved and lost them all. Camille had lost her mother when young, but her father had been a cruel lord, and had married her to the present duke. He did not think there had been much affection between her and her father or her husband. She sometimes treated Sylvie with exasperated indulgence that never even hinted they'd once fucked; and he was sure it had never happened again. Fond as she was of the eunuchs, she treated them as servants. Maxime swore she did not love him. What of Henri? Compared to all those others, he was only an eyeblink, a momentary convenience.

Camille's hand, strong from riding, squeezed the last of the water from his hair. He didn't lift his head, afraid to let her see his eyes. She smoothed her hand over his neck and back, as she might stroke Guirlande. Silence stretched. Would he ever find the courage to speak to her of his feelings?

She said nothing and he didn't think she ever would. Or ever could. She wasn't only a duchess. She was damaged. She had been damaged before he was born, probably. It was ludicrous to think he could make a difference to her. This was not a fairy tale. He didn't possess a magic cock.

He remembered one of the duke's hunters, a chestnut whom the duke had struck repeatedly in the face with his crop. Henri hadn't seen it happen, but all the grooms and stableboys knew. The gelding had been useless after that, so skittish no one could approach without him rearing in terror. Finally, weeks later, the head groom had slit the animal's throat. Henri had been ten. He still remembered how he'd hidden in the loft and wept. The duke would have done much worse to Camille than to the gelding.

Tears scalded his eyes and he angrily dashed them away with his hand. She wasn't a terrified horse, she was a duchess, and she wasn't alone anymore. She shouldn't settle for less than her due. She shouldn't be alone. "You should marry Lord Maxime."

Silence. Then, "No." She moved away from him, sitting on the bench just beyond his arm's reach.

He couldn't look at her while he said these things, while he destroyed the little he did have with her. "Think of the alliance you could make."

"Because that worked so well the last time," she said.

"He'll fuck you however you like, whenever you like. And he won't shame you."

"I would ask a bit more than not being shamed," she said.

"Would you? You don't seem to want anything more."

She lifted her chin. "You know nothing of what I want."

He never would, unless he did something about it. "You haven't *told* me what you want, have you? I'd do anything you wanted. Anything. But you don't want anything from me except my cock."

Her bare feet brushed the stone floor when she rose and moved away. She paced. That meant she was upset. Not enough for it to show on her face, but enough for him to tell. "You have never yet refused me."

Henri tried to explain. "You haven't taken anything from me. I've given. Over and over. But *you* won't take. You won't…" It hurt him to be shut away. He couldn't make himself tell her.

Silence. "I do not understand."

"I might as well be making love to your statue in the town square."

Stiffly, she said, "If I do not satisfy you, you need not fuck me."

He had to look at her, and turned. She stood with arms wrapping her chest, her head high. "It's you who needs to be satisfied! There's more to fucking than bodies!"

Camille's voice remained steady and cool. "What do you want from me? Shall I make myself vulnerable to you? Tell you all my sorrows? Allow you to bind me? It is all the same to me, Henri. It would change nothing."

He blew out his breath to stop himself from shouting again.

"I don't want that," he said. "I just want to be with you. And I want you to be with me."

"I am right here."

He shook his head. "No. You're not. You're always thinking about anything but me and you. You feed me apples and let me bump my head against your chest, but you won't let me care for you."

"I did not ask you to care for me."

He felt his shoulders slump. "Then why do anything at all? Why bother?"

Silence. When he looked up again, Camille was holding out her hand to him. "Come and sit with me," she said.

Henri went with her, because his bare wet skin was cold. He deliberately did not look at her naked body as he helped her into the hot pool. He slid in across from her, sinking down to his shoulders and letting his head fall forward, his wet hair hiding his eyes.

He should have gone back to Nico, or someone like her, of his own station, who understood there was more to life than power. Someone who admitted that human beings needed each other.

Camille said, "How will it help me, to take from you?"

Henri stared into the water. "Don't you feel alone?"

At least she didn't pretend to misunderstand him. She said, "What does that matter to me? It is what people see that's important. If they saw me as weak, how would I rule? That is even more vital now. No one will abandon the duke for me unless they see I am a better bargain."

She had good reasons for what she did. Henri still knew she

wasn't right. How could he explain what he knew? "You're good at hiding your feelings," he said.

"But?" She didn't sound like she would take his answer seriously.

Henri made himself look at her, her shorn hair and strong features and lovely silvery eyes. "I think it poisons you from within," he said. "If you keep everything inside you, good or bad, there's no room. It festers. You may not notice at first. You may be able to keep walking. Until one day, it's too much, and you need a surgeon. Except you don't have one. You didn't need him, so you sent him away. Or—no. A fine horse, when you leave it in the stall, all day, every day. It has nowhere to go, nothing to do but stand and watch all the other horses coming and going. Its skin begins to twitch, and it chews the manger, and its eyes roll, and its feet rot."

She watched him without speaking until, embarrassed, he looked away. He said, "You can't tell me you're perfectly happy. Not and tell the truth." He chanced a glance at her. She was listening. He continued, "Don't you understand? I won't tell anyone! Not ever!"

"Henri—"

"Can't you forget to be wise and powerful for even a moment? If you needed to remember again, I would tell you." Inspired, he added, "Like Guirlande. You give yourself to Guirlande, and she gives herself to you."

Camille laid her hand over his lips. He was astonished she'd let him speak as long as she had done. She followed her fingers with her mouth, sinking her teeth into his lower lip in a near-painful bite, then pressing him open with her tongue. She meant to silence him, but didn't he believe his body could speak to her, as well? Even if she wouldn't listen.

He snaked his hand behind her, pulling her toward him. He almost slipped off the bench when she abruptly gave in and stood between his knees. He dug his fingers into the silky skin of her back as they kissed, fighting the need to breathe, because then he would have to pull away.

Her hands on his shoulders were gentle, her thumbs stroking over his skin. Henri pulled away from her. "No," he said.

"You want me," Camille said.

"I always want you," Henri replied. "It doesn't matter. It doesn't—" At a loss, he captured her face between his hands. "I love you," he said. "That's what I want to tell you. Even if you don't care, or won't let yourself care."

"You want to fuck me, that's all," Camille said. "You are a boy, you are confused, you can't understand—"

"How do you know? How?" Henri wanted to shake her. Instead, he took his hands away. If she said anything else, he feared he would weep. He scrambled backward out of the pool, struggling for control. He could feel her eyes on him as he awkwardly heaved himself out of the water. "I'm going to see your horses," he said. "You can come with me if you want."

Henri pulled on his leathers, buttoning them with shaking hands. He wasn't sure how to get back to the stables from here. He didn't care; he would find them somehow. He'd forgotten his stockings. He worked them under the lower edge of his leathers and sat to yank on his boots.

He heard water. Camille had climbed out of the pool. She would need help lacing her gown. He wasn't her maid, though. He wasn't anything to her. He shook out his shirt and stuffed his head through the neck. The sleeve was still twisted. He took it off again and turned everything to the right side.

"Are you ready?" Camille asked.

Henri finished putting on his shirt before he looked. She was wearing a long, loose robe with an open collar, the fabric striped in green and rusty orange and black. It must have come from the shelves near the towels. She didn't look like herself.

Henri didn't feel like himself. "Yes," he said. "Let's go."

They walked in silence. Henri followed the path Leung had shown him, until they could find one of the blue-shirted servants to give directions to the stables, which had been cut into the rock next to the castle's outer wall. He should have known already where they were. Instead, he'd allowed Maxime's servants to care for Camille's horses. He'd given them over. Well, he'd changed his mind. If he couldn't have Camille herself, at least he would have what he'd had of her before.

Carved wooden doors, this time decorated with a navy of sea horses encrusted in copper, guarded the stable door. Henri took a sealed lantern that hung outside and pushed the door open, holding it for Camille. Two stableboys slept on cots nearby; the dark-skinned one sat up, blinking sleepily, and Henri realized she was a girl, her long hair confined in many tiny, beaded braids. She opened her mouth, perhaps to protest, but Guirlande whickered eagerly. She smiled, waved them on and fell back onto her cot. The other girl never stopped snoring.

Henri went first to Pivoine, who'd been ridden longer and harder than the rest. The gelding was asleep. Gently, he touched his legs, feeling for unusual heat. Nothing. He was recovered from his journey. From an empty bucket, he could tell the stablegirls had given him a bran mash. He sniffed it and smelled molasses. Tigre's coat glowed, and his sparse mane had been braided with ribbons. Lilas and Tonnelle gleamed from careful grooming, from noses down to a sheen of oil on their hooves. Tulipe butted his chest with his nose, blew into his ear and lipped his hair. Henri picked a strand of hay off the horse's nose.

Guirlande whickered again, softly, in the tone she reserved for one person alone. Henri looked over. Camille's arms encircled the mare's head. Their foreheads pressed together. Her eyes were closed. The tense line of her jaw had relaxed. After a few moments, she moved one hand to scratch beneath Guirlande's halter, the movement of her fingers almost contemplative.

Henri felt as if he were choking. He patted Tulipe's neck and stepped out of the stall. "Camille," he said. She didn't respond at first. "Camille," he said, more loudly. She opened her eyes and turned her cheek against Guirlande's nose. "This is what I meant," he said. "What you're doing now."

Her eyes closed again. "I cannot," she said.

"Yes, you can." Henri went forward and took her into his arms.

CHAPTER TWENTY-TWO

Henri smelled of horses. Camille tucked her face into the crook of his neck and inhaled. Her chin dug into the muscle where his neck met his shoulder; she felt his cheek rubbing across her hair. Her scalp prickled as her hair caught on his stubble. He was murmuring as his hands slid up and down her back. She couldn't make out the words.

She shouldn't be allowing him this liberty, but she was tired, and it felt so very good to be held. Henri was right. She needed this. She'd come close to admitting as much to Maxime, but in the end it was Henri she wanted. And he wanted her. He hadn't been lying to her. She didn't think he was capable. After all, the horses trusted him. She was a fool not to heed them, the only beings who had never failed her.

She had to reply to him in kind. It was difficult to lift her own arms, and wrap them around Henri in return. Each fraction of movement flayed her to the bone; he would know that she wanted to hold him. But she had done more difficult things than let someone know she wanted him. She'd allowed the duke to touch her after his first betrayal; she'd displayed herself on command; she'd betrayed the duke in turn. She'd summoned a stranger to impregnate her. This, today, ought to be simple and easy. Other people did it every day.

She squeezed Henri's waist, nestling her hips into his. Guirlande's nose bumped her back, and she remembered they were standing in the middle of Maxime's stable. Straw prickled her bare ankles above her slippers. Two young girls whom she'd never seen before tonight slept a few strides away.

Guirlande snorted. Before she could bump them again, Henri stepped back, tugging Camille gently by the hand. "Careful of your feet," he whispered.

"Where are we going?"

"Don't know."

That was true in more ways than one. She should veer back to her original path. Someone might be looking for her by now. She had plans to make, things to discuss with Maxime and with Kaspar, and with Gisele. Thoughts of all that lay before her dragged like lead weights around her neck. But now, here, in the darkened stable, being drawn toward an illicit encounter with a boy whose only goal was her comfort and pleasure...she felt light, and almost new.

The sealed lantern, which Henri had hung outside Tulipe's stall, didn't cast its light this far down the aisle. She let Henri lead her into darkness made cozy by the warm, rich scent of horses' bodies and horses' manure. Horses shifted their weight in the darkness, crackling fresh straw. They passed several empty loose boxes and came to two doors. Camille ran her hand over the first. It was carved with a saddle and bridle. The second was marked by a bucket; probably a room to mix poultices and mashes. She could faintly smell molasses and cooked oats.

Henri chose the tack room. Appropriate; he'd first pledged himself to her in a tack room, back in the breeding barn. Then, she'd only meant to ensure he traveled with her, instead of remaining behind and being questioned by the duke's guards.

No. That wasn't entirely true. She'd wanted him to swear himself to her, of his own free will. No one had ever done that before. Even Sylvie had come to her because she had no other place to go. She'd wanted Henri to give himself to her. Then he would be hers, as well, all his bravado and tender glances and youthful optimism, as if having him would give her those qualities, as well. At the time, she hadn't even considered giving herself to him in the same way.

If she hadn't lied to herself so much, for so many years, she might have seen it sooner. Everything might have been very different. When had it all begun? Where had she first lost herself, and when? Who might have helped her, had she only asked? Mentally, she shook herself. She couldn't dwell on past mistakes, or they would devour her.

Camille followed Henri into the tack room, into the smell of leather and oil and polish. She let go his hand to push the door shut and found herself alone in near-total darkness; the barest hint of light shone beneath the door and through the cracks near its hinges. She could faintly smell Henri, sandal-wood soap and mineral residue from the hot spring, but could not see him, or even her own hand in front of her. She remembered a night ten years before, when she'd lain confined in the dark of her bedroom, her wrists bound to the bed frame, waiting for Michel to arrive and work his will upon her. Every tiny sound had made her flinch. She'd never felt more alone in her life. She'd been so glad to see him when he finally came, bearing a lit candle. The light had taken away her fear. She'd almost been grateful to him for it, until he spilled the candle's melted wax on the tip of her breast.

Henri crashed into something, yelped and swore. Yanked back to the present, she began to laugh. This was reality; this was what she wanted in her life. She wanted the chance to trip and fall, and then to succeed. She was free now. She had freed herself. She had a beautiful, virile young lover, who could curse with great fluency.

Henri bumped her arm, followed it to her torso and wrapped her in his arms. She continued laughing at her life's absurdity for a few moments, grasping at the front of his shirt. Finally, he kissed her, which also seemed funny. His stubble tickled her. His tongue slid into her mouth and she grabbed the back of his head, holding him closer, and they kissed and kissed and kissed.

When she came up for air, her back was pressed against a wall. She could feel the rough stone through her thin robe, and she luxuriously rubbed her shoulders against it, running one hand over Henri's cheek and jaw, holding on to his shirt with the other. "I don't know why I'm doing this right now," she said. "We should go back to our rooms, and lie down in comfort."

"You don't want to stop," Henri said nervously.

"No. It is far too late." Camille traced the length of his nose with her fingertip, then his lips. "What will become of us? There are no secrets in a palace."

Henri touched her face, tentatively at first, then with a more assured tenderness. His thumbs swept along her cheekbones. "I don't want you to be ashamed of me," he said. "Someone will know who I am and where I came from, no matter what we do or say. Maybe if I...if I didn't see you often."

"No," Camille said. "No half measures. You will live in the palace with me." When he said nothing, his hands stilling in their caresses, she asked, "You would do that for me?"

He said, very softly, "I'm scared. But...you give me reasons to try to be more than just a stableboy. That's the first thing I learned from you, when I was new to the stables and I saw you riding. I wanted to ride like you. If it hadn't been for that, I would never have schooled your horses, and you and Sylvie might never have seen me, and we might never have... You might never have chosen me."

Camille thought of what he'd said. She leaned forward and laid her lips against his forehead, then his mouth. "What we do changes more than we think," she said at last. "Even if we don't know it at the time. Having you in the palace will change the way the court sees me, and the people as well. I will have to make sure the change is for the better. I will give you a position, one that is neither aristocrat nor servant. Horsemaster, perhaps. Then we shall see."

"I'll do my best," Henri said. He kissed her quickly, then one of his hands trailed down her neck, across her shoulder and down to her breast, which he cupped in his palm. "I would like to have a place that couldn't be taken from me," he admitted. "So I wouldn't be afraid of everyone who… Maxime is teaching me," he confessed. "Because if the courtiers look down on me, they'll be looking down on you."

"Maxime will certainly help you," Camille said. "Henri, I do not intend to give him up. He is not the same to me as you are. I will tell you that, so you don't fear. But he and I share a past I want to remember, and I do care for him."

Henri fondled her breast and rubbed his cheek against hers. There was a long pause. "May I watch?"

Camille choked back another laugh. "You have been playing too much with Sylvie."

"And with you."

Camille sighed and relaxed into his caresses. "Play with me now. Only me. And I will think only of you."

Henri kissed her cheeks, the corners of her mouth, the softness beneath her jaw, each touch like velvet brushing her skin. His hands shaped her breasts and, soon, found their way inside her robe, traveling over her skin with feathery touches that cramped her quim with the need to have something inside. Henri's mouth brushed her nipple; then his lips closed over it, and he suckled hard. Her knees shivered and lost their tensile strength. Her shoulders met the wall again, and she gratefully took the support of stone at her back as he continued suckling first one breast, then the other, his fingers all the while grasping her hips, sliding over her ribs and tracing the spaces between with his thumbs, then sliding down again and kneading just above her quim, maddeningly close to her clitoris. Henri kissed her throat, his hips nudging into hers. She pushed back, opening her thighs to make a cradle for him. He thrust against her with a soft sound that she echoed. "Oh, please do that again," she said, and when he thrust again, she thrust toward him, as well, utterly fixated on the gliding friction and the acute pleasure each touch shot into her womb.

She fumbled at the buttons of his leathers and freed his cock. He moaned softly as she grasped his shaft and drew it to the damp folds between her legs, rubbing the head between her lips. "I want this inside me," she said.

Henri panted in her ear. "A blanket?"

"Here." She couldn't wait and didn't want to. She shoved her pelvis against him and rubbed crudely. It felt so dizzyingly good that she did it again and moaned. She could not stop her hips from moving.

"Oh, fuck," Henri said, thrusting back against her. "Let me—lift up—"

He gripped her buttocks and effortlessly lifted. Camille clamped her thighs on his hips, grabbing behind her for more support, then at his straining shoulders. "In," she demanded.

Henri shifted her weight, then shifted again, and she felt his cock squeezing into her quim's tight grasp. She felt as if he pierced her up into her chest, a stab of pleasure so intense she momentarily lost the grip of her thighs. She squirmed against him, catching a startled breath when he accidentally pinched her nipple against his chest. His shirt rubbed her skin harshly. She squeezed closer to him, wanting the roughness of it, which changed the angle of her pelvis. She gasped again as he groaned and slid more deeply inside her.

She dug her fingers into his back, his buttocks, whatever she could reach. The angle was exquisite, their connection so tight she could feel every minute shift of position and every nuance of his shape. Her fluids trickled out of her, slicking them both. "Yes," she said. "Yes, yes, please, fuck me now."

"Camille," he said. His voice sounded tight. He changed his grip on her and thrust. His forehead fell onto her shoulder. He thrust again, then again, the disarranged folds of his shirt rasping against her bare breasts. It was awkward. She couldn't maintain a grip on either him or the wall, and he couldn't thrust steadily. Because of this, each thrust and shift maddened her, pushing her toward a peak she couldn't get close enough to see. She didn't suggest giving up, and neither did Henri. They strained together for something unreachable. Camille was conscious only of her body where it rubbed and slid against his, most poignantly where they joined inside, and of Henri: his hands and mouth on her, speaking to her, his familiar and comforting smell, his body's protective embrace.

Henri's muscles shuddered beneath her hands. "Can't hold you much longer," he said. "If we turn—" He let her slide down his body to the floor. Camille cried out as his cock slipped free of her quim. "This'll be better," he said, grabbing her shoulders and moving her. She realized he was bracing his own back against the wall, to help him support her weight. She scrambled onto him, able to hold his shoulders now while he worked his cock into her. She was so tender and swollen now, each increment brought tears of pleasure to her eyes. "I want this to be good for you," he said, his breath coming in pants. "So good."

Camille breathed deep, then remembered. She didn't have to hide. When he thrust, she opened her throat and let her cries escape, one for each piercingly sweet penetration of her deepest self.

Henri's breaths sounded like sobs. His thrusting sped up, hovering her on the brink for a time that seemed like hours. All at once, he stopped, jerked, thrust once more, and said, "Come for me, Camille. Come. I want to hear you come. You're so beautiful—you feel beautiful to me—I love you so much—" He thrust, rapidly and fiercely, his pubic bone slamming into her clitoris. It was like racing down a hill, faster and faster. She could see her climax approaching, could no more put it off than she could stop breathing. She no longer heard his words, or felt any motion outside of her quim. She hurtled, closer, closer, and then flew.

She might have screamed. She wasn't sure. She was conscious of jerking in his embrace, of losing her grip on him and sliding half to the floor before he caught her. She trembled in his arms, whimpering with each fading spasm, until she felt his erection thumping urgently against her belly. She encircled his hips with her arms, slid to the floor and engulfed his cock in her mouth. Henri's cry was sharp and deep. Camille sucked him deep, as hard as she could, her fingers digging into his buttocks, licking her own fluids from his shaft. She used her hands to stroke his cock's base, quick and harsh, and sucked the head without finesse. Henri's hips bucked, and then his cock was jerking in her mouth, fighting against her grip. She swallowed, coughed and spat, then returned to him, stroking him throughout his climax and licking him clean.

Henri dropped to his knees and leaned his hot, heavy shoulder against her. Camille stroked his back and arm. His breathing gradually slowed. He said, "That was supposed to be all for you."

"It was," she assured him. "I simply..." She drew back from telling him she'd been afraid. "I wanted you to know you were right." She felt safe with him. Relaxed. At peace.

Henri put his arms around her. "I feel as if Tulipe and I had just cleared the grand gate of the palace and landed without a single stumble. I can tell you that, because no one else would understand."

The gate loomed in Camille's mind, the white ashlar blocks, the filigreed iron atop, the massive mahogany doors with their cranks and pullies. She imagined herself on one side, and the duke on the other, and suddenly felt very cold.

CHAPTER TWENTY–THREE

Two months passed in the castle by the sea, months of both pleasure and frustration for Henri. Camille spent her time planning her return to the ducal palace, and what would happen after, and how. Henri's role was smaller. He wore silk now, and fine linen, and bright wool as soft as clouds. He kept his hair tied back in a stubby queue he was forbidden from hacking off, though wisps continually came loose. Maxime made him put on a different style of clothes each day, insisting he had to wear them all as if they belonged to him, as if he'd never worn anything else. He liked some of the clothes, particularly the ones to be worn with boots—he'd fallen in love with having boots made carefully to his measure, instead of only approximately so—and even became used to sometimes wearing bright colors. It was much easier to keep colors clean when he wasn't shoveling manure. Some of the clothing, like the floor-length, billowing desert robes, were a terrible annoyance. He wondered how Camille managed her long gowns. Sylvie laughed aloud when he asked, and spent an afternoon drilling him in the niceties of wearing skirts. Then she moved on to posture, but Henri defeated her in that; his balance was splendid, and he could even climb stairs without dislodging several books balanced on his head.

Maxime dragged him into one formal room after another, directing him endlessly. "You have no doubts! You wear whatever you like! You belong at Camille's side! Act as if it is true, and it will be so." Then his expression would darken. "If you want to give up, of course I will gladly assume your role."

"I never see her, except at night," Henri grumbled. He sat in a heavy, carved dining-room chair, staring down an array of cutlery. Today he was wearing a short, padded jacket and snug knitted pants with low suede boots, all of it in drab brown. He looked and felt like a sack of turnips, except for his legs, which felt skinny and naked. He'd been glad to use the table to hide his crotch. He didn't want everyone in the castle to know on which side he tucked his cock. He hadn't minded so much Maxime's thoughtful gaze, then cheery smile, because he'd learned not to expect better from him, but he'd seen more than one maid giggling behind her hand as he passed.

"I barely see her at all. I'm left to imagine what you two are doing in my best guest room," Maxime said, shoving tentacle tongs in front of Henri. "That one."

"We never eat octopus," Henri pointed out. He picked up the tongs and demonstrated their use anyway. He knew hundreds of ways to physic a horse. This was much easier memorization.

It wasn't knowing facts that was hard. It was what those facts meant, and how they were meant to affect the way he behaved. He knew that was how he would trip and fall; he would know an answer, but use his answer in the wrong way. He wasn't sure if he could ever learn to *feel* like an aristocrat. He wasn't sure he wanted to be one, deep down, not where it mattered. But he had to at least learn to pretend, for Camille's sake, so he would not shame her. And for his own sake, so he would be able to hold his head high.

Maxime's next words confirmed his thoughts. "Doesn't matter if you use the tongs or not. You only have to know what they are, and not care that you know. Don't show you're proud of the knowledge."

"I *don't* care," Henri said. "Anyone could learn these were tentacle tongs. It's only rich people who care if you know." He held up his hand. "Yes, yes, I am pretending to be a rich person, as hard as I can." He changed his voice, imitating one of the more pompous grooms he remembered from the duke's stable. "If you can't pick up tentacle tongs, what good are you for anything?"

Maxime grinned. "Good, you're learning. They *pretend* they don't care, even though they really do feel it's a matter of life and death."

Henri paused, toying with a snipper intended for tea leaves. "Maxime, how do you know these things?"

He leaned back in his chair. It creaked alarmingly. "I've taken a few journeys," he said. "It's the only way to truly learn anything. You should try it. I will gladly put you on a ship to, oh, the Eastern Empire, and then you can see for yourself what it's like to watch everyone nimbly picking up grains of rice with two pointed sticks, while you consider eating with your fingers."

"Someday I will," Henri said. He added sarcastically, "I suppose you'd be happy to take care of Camille while I was gone?"

"Of course. How could you doubt me?" Maxime held up an eyeball scoop for use with whole baked fish. "Now, what's this one?"

When Henri had free hours in the afternoon, he would visit the stables. The two girls cared for the animals attentively, but the horses expected him each day, and he refused to disappoint them, since they wouldn't understand his explanations. He found he needed the time, however brief, to forget everything else and just be himself. When he returned to their suite in the evenings, he would have time to sit wordlessly with Camille for a few moments, while she was deep in conversation with Captain Leung, who would sail them up the coast, and with Maxime's aunt Gisele. Then Kaspar and often Arno as well would seize him and Sylvie and lead them away to practice with blades and bows and pistols. Henri hated the pistols; they were noisy and dirty and slow, and left his hands stinking of acrid powder; but he loved the bow. From using a sling as a child, he'd developed a sense of how to aim, and shooting at standing targets seemed like a game. Sometimes, he forgot that the training was so important to his future life in the palace.

He slept in the same bed with Camille. She usually wasn't there when he went to sleep. Often, he would wake in the wee hours to find her shedding a robe with more weariness than she showed before anyone else. Blinking sleepily, he would sit up and hold out his arms for her. Those were his favorite times. Camille would relax bonelessly into his embrace, nuzzling her face into his throat, murmuring incomprehensibly when he stroked her hair and rubbed the nape of her neck. He wanted to talk with her, but it was clear how exhausted she felt.

Once, he gave in to his long-standing desire and brought her to pleasure with his mouth. She enjoyed it, he could tell, and her soft cries when she came were sweet, but she fell asleep immediately afterward, her fingers going lax in his hair. He'd wryly reminded himself that he'd fallen asleep with his cock inside her, more than once, so he could hardly blame her. The one time she'd come into their bed earlier, her amorous intent was clear; he woke with her hand gently petting him.

Her thumb stroked his cock as if it was impossibly delicate, so lightly that Henri did not wake completely at first, but thought himself enmeshed in an erotic dream. When she curled her hand around him and stroked, he floated slowly to the surface of consciousness and blinked up at her. She knelt next to him, her breasts swaying gently with the movement of her arm, her face intent. Henri lifted his hand and touched her forearm, to let her know he'd awoken. Her eyes met his.

"I like to see you sleep," she said. "Then I know you are all my own."

"I am still all your own," he said. He let his hand fall to the sheet and stretched luxuriously among the silky linens. "Please, use me as you will." He fluttered his lashes, and was rewarded by Camille's soft puff of laughter.

She bent and licked him, lightly fondling, tracing the creases where his leg met his hip and the edges of his curling nest of hair. Gently, she combed her fingers through his hair, then tugged on it. She gripped some in her teeth and pulled that, then returned to licking. Henri's breath fluttered as he twitched with each new spear of sweet sensation and he said, "Help me, Your Grace! I'm being ravished by butterflies!"

Camille laughed against his cock, drew back and puffed her breath along its length. "It's rising," she said, in a tone of exaggerated surprise. "Why, Henri, it is escaping me!"

"Capture it quickly!" he said, arching his back to bring his cock closer to her mouth. She licked her lips and Henri moaned. "Please?" He lifted his arms above his head and grasped the bed frame. She liked that, he knew, because she always looked for a moment. It showed the muscles in his arms in some way that she found pleasing.

Camille sat up and scratched the backs of his arms with her nails, long strokes that made him shudder. His tensed muscles intensified the sensation. She followed her nails with her tongue, then licked down to the ticklish pits of his arms, then onto his nipples. Henri had never had anyone before her pay such attention to his chest for so long. His nipples hardened almost immediately, stabbing him with shards of almost-pain each time Camille's fingers brushed them. When she settled in to suckle them, he cried out in shock at how deeply he felt it. No wonder women liked this.

His eyes blurred with pleasure, and after a time he fell limp against the sheets, only his cock erect and straining. Camille pressed her lips around the head and sucked hard, one long pull. His balls contracted as if she'd hitched them up with her hand. His back arched off the bed again. "Fuck," he gasped. "Camille—more—I need more—"

Camille sucked harder, using her hands to enclose him where her mouth could not. Henri could not tell anymore if he was moaning or not. His entire world was her mouth, the mouth that smiled at him, the mouth that kissed him.

He came in her mouth, his hips wrenching uncontrollably. It was almost more than he could bear. Red-hot lightning sizzled down his spine with each jerk of his cock. When it was over, he could barely lift his hand to touch her hair. Drowsily, he asked, "What about you?"

Camille crawled up his body and snuggled into his arm. "Too tired and sore," she confessed. "But I wanted to see you come. Do you remember what you said to me, once?"

Henri thought back. It was still true. "You're beautiful when you come."

"Yes," she said, and kissed him, distracting him from his question, of why she might be sore, and if he might help her to feel less so.

During an afternoon a week later, Sylvie came to find Henri

in the stables. He'd spent a grueling day drilling appropriate greetings for a whole host of nobility, and regarded her approach irritably. She'd never put off her boy's clothing, and he could scarcely remember anymore how she'd looked in a dress. Of course, she was bossy no matter what she wore. He gave Tigre a last chunk of parsnip, stepped out of the stall and turned to her. Sylvie put her hands on his shoulders, stood on her toes and kissed him on each cheek.

Henri blinked. "I've done nothing," he said, wondering if this was a trick of some kind.

Sylvie crossed her arms and glared at him. "Madame is lying in her bed. She does not want olives, or any cheese at all, or even grapes."

"But she loves—" Henri closed his mouth. "She's…sick."

"I believe this to be your fault," Sylvie said. "Perhaps you could have waited until after we were on the ship! She will be ill for the entire journey!"

Henri did not hear the rest of Sylvie's tirade. He pounded out of the stables, found the nearest exit and ran up flights of stairs through a series of courtyards until he reached the staircase leading to their guest suite. By the time he flung open the door to their bedchamber, he was gasping for breath. Camille didn't look ill. She was fully dressed except for shoes, and lounging in bed with a map spread on the coverlet. Lady Gisele held a tray for her, which held a small black teapot and a single cup.

Henri caught his breath, clinging to a bedpost for support.

"Are you sure?" he asked. "We've done it? You're to have an heir?"

"We are," she said. "If you are wondering, I do not think the father can be Maxime."

Henri blinked. "I didn't care—you want this so much." In truth, he did care, because he wanted to be part of her, but it would be rude to show unnecessary jealousy, when he knew she had chosen him over Maxime some time ago.

Camille smiled. "I do not believe you. Now come here and kiss me."

Lady Gisele set the tray on a side table. "I'll return later," she said, and exited.

Once the door had shut behind her, Henri stumbled over to the bed and gently kissed Camille's mouth. "Are you all right?" he asked.

She looked away. "I am fine. Some foods taste strange to me, that's all."

He sat on the bed next to her and stroked her short hair. "Are you happy? I mean, this isn't what you planned. I'm glad I was able to—but—"

"You do not want a child?"

Henri thought about it. He'd taken care of a few babies, when he was still too young to be much use in the stables. They could be troublesome. What he remembered most, though, was their milky smell, skin softer than a horse's nose, and best of all, the warm limp weight of them in his arms. It didn't matter that she might be carrying the duchy's heir. This would be something of his, and hers. He felt a rush of love for a baby yet unborn. "If it's a girl," he said, "she should rule. Not the man she marries." Surely that would be possible? If he'd learned one thing from Maxime, it was that the world had room enough for everything.

"I don't think we need to worry about that just yet," Camille said. "There are at least seven months before we'll know. Also, I am giving Michel a prime chance to kill me when I ride in those gates."

Her voice didn't change, but Henri put his arm around her anyway. "I'll be with you," he said.

She looked about to protest. Henri held her. "Please," he said. "Let me." He took her hand in his, kissed her palm and then pressed their hands together, as if hiding the kiss from prying eyes. Camille sighed and laced their fingers together.

"I feel strange," she confessed.

"Ill?" Henri rubbed her back with his free hand.

"No. As if…I am two people. Which I am. There is some-one inside of me." She laid her hand on her belly. "I wondered if I would know, without any other sign. I didn't know. I felt nothing when it must have happened. But now, I think I do feel someone. I don't know how. Perhaps it's just fancy."

"Does it matter, if it's real or not?"

"I suppose not." Camille sighed. "Don't allow me to be mawkish. This is the heir to the duchy in my belly. I am fulfill-ing my duty by carrying this child. How I feel has nothing to do with it. It is necessary."

Henri listened solemnly, then kissed her cheek. "I'm very excited, though. That can be my duty. When your belly gets big and round, I'll still think you're beautiful, even if you don't."

Camille's pregnancy meant she needed to return to the ducal palace sooner than she'd planned, as she did not want her condition to be obvious to the duke, who might use it against her, and she didn't know how much her pregnancy would incapacitate her. She also decided to include Henri in more of her councils. He was present at the next meeting to discuss strategies, which took place in a windowless long room on the castle's ground floor. It was furnished with a single long table in the center, hard wooden chairs and a series of slanted map tables around the room's edges. It might have seemed cold, but the floor was thick with a random assortment of small carpets, and the walls hung with tapestries depicting the martial accomplishments of the Duchess Elisabeth, Maxime's grandmother.

He'd expected to feel cowed by being alone with so many aristocrats, but he discovered, more than that, he felt young, and inexperienced in battle. Those things weren't so bad. They would be cured in time. He sat close to Kaspar and Arno at the far end of the table, reminding himself to appear at ease, no matter how he felt. It helped to watch Camille, who was studying documents and did not realize he scrutinized her every move, and tried to spot the very faint pink mark he'd made with his mouth, now half-hidden by the collar of her shirt.

By the time Maxime strode in, trailed by his aunt Gisele and Captain Leung, Henri's pretense of relaxation had become truth. When Maxime passed him a cup of wine, he took it with aplomb, deliberately following Maxime's own little ritual of swirling the liquid, sniffing its bouquet and only then sipping. When he noticed, Maxime lifted his cup to Henri in amused acknowledgment.

Lady Gisele, looking rather like someone's kindly grand-mother (which she was—Henri hadn't been able to count the number of grandchildren in her herd), sat at the head of the table, Maxime to one side of her and Camille to the other. Captain Leung slid into a chair next to Henri, settling her cup in front of her. He smelled a flowery tea she favored, overlaid with a haze of gunpowder, a disconcerting mix. Leung spoke first. "One of the Lord Maxime's spies—"

"Couriers—" Maxime interrupted.

She flashed him a look. He held up his hands, palms out in surrender, and subsided into his chair, crossing his ankles. "The spy returned down the coast via the mail packet. Skeat passed easily as a fisherman, seeking out new markets. He had no trouble entering the ducal seat, and wasn't detained at any point during his visit. At first, he saw a general atmosphere of prosperity. The markets appeared busy and there was a good variety of food available, not much different from when he was last there, two years ago. He saw no violence in the streets."

"What did he have to report, then?" Camille asked.

"On Skeat's second day in the town, hundreds of farmers' wives and shopkeepers—almost all women, and even some pros-titutes—took to the streets and blockaded the palace entrance."

"With what?" Lady Gisele asked.

"Their bodies," Leung said. "It was ingenious. They linked their arms in lines. Skeat said it was quite a sight."

Lady Gisele made a note.

"And their demands?" Camille asked. "I did not arrange for this to happen." She appeared, to Henri's eyes, mildly disconcerted.

"They begged to know what had become of their duchess," Leung said, with an air of satisfaction. "Their leaders, a midwife and a bath maid, tied themselves to the gate. Others of the women brought them food and water." She paused and added wryly, "I am not sure how they managed the sanitary arrangements."

Camille said, "Annette."

Everyone in the room looked inquiringly at her.

"The midwife. I have met her. She counseled me on many occasions."

Henri blinked. "Your Grace—this is Annette who works in the Dewy Rose?" She had summoned a midwife from a brothel?

"Yes—she's very skilled. She had a wider range of experience than the woman who formerly served the palace women."

That was likely true. "I think I know the bath maid, as well." He could feel himself flushing. "We've...talked. Her name is Nicolette. She is very loyal to you, Your Grace. And she was once the lover of Annette."

Leung rubbed her hands together briskly. "Excellent. This information will make things simpler, later. If I may continue? I will reassure you now, neither of the leaders was harmed."

Henri breathed a sigh of relief. Camille said, "Please, go on."

Leung sipped her tea. "The palace guard would not attack women who had no weapons and showed no intention of using any. The duke's chamberlain reported the duke was ill and unable to command them otherwise."

Maxime said, "A ruse, to avoid the appearance of unchecked mutiny?"

"Possibly," Kaspar said. "Or Vilmos had already succeeded in imprisoning the duke."

Camille said, "There's been no word from Vilmos, but he warned Arno that sending word might not be possible. Has he been seen in the palace? Do we even know if he still lives?"

"Skeat was unable to get past the gates," Leung said apologetically. "The women's blockade lasted three days. He'd been instructed not to go in over the walls—besides being a bit too old for that, he might have been seen and questioned—and he worried that if he didn't catch the tide, we'd have no news at all."

"I didn't tell Skeat we'd sent Kamah as well," Maxime said. "She's the girl who returned last night. She made better time, since she had a fast horse to get her to the coast, and a cutter was waiting for her under cover of night. She told me, Camille, that she had no difficulty in liberating the gelding from his stable, and left him at the village of salt farmers. He'll be cared for there until she returns."

Camille glanced at Henri and said, "Preste," naming the horse. "What news did Kamah bring?"

Maxime said, "On the fourth day of the women's blockade, the group began to disperse naturally. They'd had no word from within the palace and were not attacked from without. The leaders vanished into hiding. Then a new group of men arrived, led by an old soldier, who happened to have served under my mother's command, before her death."

"This was not coincidence," Camille stated. A hint of displeasure colored her tone.

"Not in the least," Maxime said, with relish. "Karl was quite willing. In fact, you have met him, and he was pleased to learn you were nothing like your father or husband. He now uses the name Fouet."

Henri glanced around. No one else seemed startled at this news. Camille said, "You seem quite skilled in the art of insurrection, Maxime. Will I need to fear for my seat, once it is mine?"

"Unlike Michel, you will give me concessions in exchange for my goods," Maxime said. "Also, I don't forget that throwing endless problems against Michel's gates was your idea."

Kaspar said, "What problem did Master Fouet bring?"

"A collection of documents from towns and villages, all of which demanded the return of the Duchess Camille, with Karl given as their representative."

"The duke could refuse to see him," Arno noted.

"Not with a hundred armed men at his back. You might be too young to remember, Arno, but after Camille's father killed mine, he laid waste to a few carefully chosen areas of the countryside, to make sure his message was heard. Many fled to Camille's duchy and remain there today. Karl had little trouble in collecting men. Even better, those who didn't serve with my mother at least remembered her, and Gisele. They consider Camille the rightful heir to the duchy, not Michel."

"But what happened?" Henri asked.

"Kamah says the duke never appeared. He did nothing. When she left, they were still encamped outside the palace gates, exchanging friendly insults with the duke's guards."

Camille folded her hands on the table. "Then it seems likely Vilmos was successful. If he wasn't, well, we shall soon find out. I would like to sail as soon as possible."

Two days later, the last of the horses was slung aboard Captain Leung's ship. Watching from the dock, Henri bounced on his toes. He'd never been to sea before, though the coast was less than a day's journey from the ducal seat, if one wasn't picky about where one took ship.

Sylvie jabbed him with her elbow. "Be still. You are older than five."

Henri grinned at her. "We're going to sea!"

"We will likely drown," she said dourly. "Or be eaten by sharks. Or the tiny fish, who attack in flocks and shred the flesh from your bones."

"Those are only in rivers, Captain Leung said."

"Rivers run into the sea, and fish can swim along them," Sylvie said. "You seem insufferably pleased with yourself. It could wear on a person's patience. There might be an accident. Do you swim?"

Henri rose to his toes again, this time to try to see how Lilas fared as her hooves met the deck. He glanced over his shoulder at Sylvie. "She turned you down, didn't she? Captain Leung?"

"Not all of us are so lucky as you," she growled, and stomped away.

Kaspar strolled to Henri's side. "And she gets seasick as well," he said. "Won't this be a pleasant trip?"

Henri hoped he wouldn't get sick. He had plans for himself, Camille and the cabin they'd have all to themselves. Before he could reply to Kaspar, Camille beckoned him to her side. Maxime had just arrived, a vision of splendor in a knee-length coat embroidered all over with brilliantly colored birds and lizards. Henri looked askance at his tall boots, though, which were constructed from bright blue reptile hide and capped and heeled with gold foil. Practice or not, he didn't think he could wear such things and keep his face straight.

Maxime clapped him on the shoulder. "I have a gift for you," he said.

"Thank you," he replied. It hadn't once occurred to him that Maxime would do such a thing. "I'm sorry I have nothing for you."

Maxime folded Henri's fingers over a small leather bag and smiled slowly. He did not release Henri's hand. "Perhaps you might come to visit, later on, and give me a present then."

Henri swallowed, hard. "It's a promise," he said.

Maxime grinned, leaned forward and kissed him slowly. His beard felt soft against Henri's lips. Then he pulled away, and touched Henri's cheek, lingering. "Farewell. Take care of Camille."

Henri nodded. The little leather bag held something small and heavy. He closed his fingers on it. He couldn't remember the last time anyone had given him a gift.

"Farewell, Maxime," Camille said. She kissed him quickly, resting her hand on his chest.

"I would like to go with you," he said.

"We've discussed this," she said. "You're a man."

"I can't help that."

"If you're with me when I ride to those gates, no one will see me," she said.

"I think you underestimate yourself."

"Nevertheless. And I see you aren't dressed for a journey by sea. You knew I would refuse you."

"You can't blame me for making one more attempt," Maxime said. "Come, sweet, another kiss, and I'll let you go."

Henri glanced away, glad piles of crates mostly hid them from the other denizens of the busy docks. When he looked back, Maxime stood a pace away, his head bowed. Camille laid her hand on his hair. "I'll send word when all's finished, Your Grace."

"Farewell, Camille." He strode away. The boots looked more dignified than Henri could have imagined. He opened his hand and stared at the little bag.

"What did he give you?" Camille asked.

Henri tugged open the bag's drawstring and looked inside.

"A ring," he said. The heavy gold signet gleamed softly, impossibly smooth in his calloused palm. It bore a crest of a running horse.

"Will you wear it?" she asked.

Henri slid the ring onto his finger and closed his fist. It looked like it belonged there. "I will," he said.

"Come, then. Let's go home."

CHAPTER TWENTY–FOUR

The ship rocked gently at anchor, and Camille gazed at the shore as Kamah, the brown-skinned girl who served as Maxime's best courier, waded onto the sand, her boots hung around her neck. She would recover Preste and ride ahead, to warn Master Fouet of their arrival and then spread the word among the townsfolk. Camille both wanted and needed an audience for her arrival, to demonstrate that she lived and to ward off any suggestion of her being unfit to rule.

She'd spoken with Captain Leung many times on the journey. That morning, as they drank tea together near the ship's prow, wind in their faces, Leung said, "It's not your fault. Your husband would have acted the same with anyone in his power."

Camille said, "I suppose this never happens with women in your own country."

Leung smiled grimly. "Unfortunately, it does. I've traveled nowhere in this world where violence is a stranger."

"You do not think it makes a woman weak?" Camille could have bitten her tongue off for saying the words aloud, but she wanted—needed—to know what Leung thought. In her own way, she was a ruler as well, of her own small duchy cutting through the waves, with men under her command, and no outside authority to protect her.

Leung shrugged. "Does it make a man weak, to be wounded in battle? If you're asking, *Do I think you're weak,* then no, Your Grace, I do not. If you require proof, I cannot give you that. Perhaps the fact that you are here, and planning to confront your husband and take what is yours, should be enough for you."

Camille considered denying she'd asked the other woman for reassurance, but it seemed pointless when faced with the steady, knowing gaze of Leung's startlingly pale eyes. What she'd wanted, she realized, was to know she was not alone. Instead she said, "Perhaps one day you will visit me at the ducal palace, and we may speak further."

"I'd like that, Your Grace."

Camille turned her mind to her plans. Boats would carry her and her entourage to shore as soon as possible, and they would travel cross-country to the ducal palace. Camille knew better than anyone that appearance was the largest portion of the effect she must create for her grand return. All the advance rumors in the world would not help if, once she was seen, the people were disappointed. Many had seen her before, at least from a distance; her profile validated coins; she knew of at least three songs describing her physical appearance, and one very popular ballad that narrated one of her childhood accomplishments involving her pony Poire, a snake and a guard who hadn't kept his saddle. She decided to disregard the prevalence of female prostitutes who made a living from dressing in a style reminiscent of her. She supposed, once she was in power, that she could forbid the practice, but that would likely only make it more popular among its aficionados.

In public appearance before, she'd always been gowned in rich fabrics and dark, jewellike colors, her skirts heavy and sweeping, her sleeves elegantly close-fitting. If she did not wear a jeweled necklace or collar, the neck of her dress would be en-crusted with embroidery or beads. She'd looked, she realized now, much like her own statue, the rich colors alone saving her from the appearance of marble. When she'd stood as a symbol of the duchy, that had been appropriate. What was inside her had not been important. Now, however, it was her inner strength she wished to display. She'd thought long and hard on this over the course of the voyage, and decided that she needed to survey the clothing she had at hand.

Sylvie had brought trunks upon trunks onto the ship, until Captain Leung swore she would have no need for ballast. There was no room even in their spacious cabin to spread all the clothing out, so two grinning sailors hoisted the trunks on deck with an ingenious assembly of ropes and pulleys, constructed on the spot. Sylvie then directed a motley group of foremast hands, both men and women, in holding up the various dresses and riding habits for Camille's inspection. It was disconcerting and also amusing to view a russet riding habit, couched with gold satin cord in intricate swirling patterns, then to look up and find the neckline framed the visage of a grizzled, bearded sailor in a greasy cap. Henri, trailing behind her, would laugh outright at such sights, and exchange comments with the sailors about their tastes in gowns suited for climbing the rigging, lowering an anchor or surviving a storm. Camille watched the graceful gestures of his hands, accentuated by the heavy gold ring he now wore on his left hand. She remembered looking down at him, the previous night, and seeing his hand clasping her hip, the ring gleaming softly against her skin.

Henri had changed. So had she. None of the gowns looked any different from how she'd been before. She glanced at Sylvie, who leaned against the rail and nibbled on the end of a dry loaf of bread to ease her seasickness. Sylvie had done her best, but Camille had not asked her to prepare a completely new costume. She'd left her to pack as she normally did. At the time, thoughts of plots and confrontations had seemed more important than clothing.

She could no longer be a statue duchess. She would still need to draw the eye and, at the same time, be set apart. She must be recognizable as the duchess at first glance, and from a distance. Yet she did not want to remind anyone of the duke. Soon enough, of course, her enormous belly would clearly distinguish her from the duke, she thought with wry distaste, but right now her pregnancy was much less important than the appearance of strength and command. She was not only a vessel to produce the next ruler for the duchy.

Henri had wandered over to chat with Sylvie, offering her

a drink from his cup of water. His booted feet were braced wide, showing off his strong thighs and easy balance as he rocked with the ship's movement. Sylvie still looked pale and a bit uneasy with stomach distress. She wore the same pair of riding leathers she'd worn for most of their journey, though she hadn't bothered today to bind her breasts, so no one could mistake her for a man. Camille remembered Sylvie with pistols jutting at her hips, then the Lady Gisele with her curved dagger and unmistakable authority, then Captain Leung's shorn head and the red sash that exaggerated every movement of her hips.

"Thank you," she said to the assembled sailors. "Please pack the dresses back into the trunks. I have chosen."

"Madame?" Sylvie abandoned Henri and unsteadily walked over to the nearest trunk.

Camille pointed to a midnight-blue skirted coat made of plush silk velvet and trimmed in gold frogging and braid. It was intended to be worn with a riding skirt. "That one," she said. "No hat. A plain white shirt beneath, perhaps the one with lace at the cuffs. And are you able to locate the pair of riding leathers I wore on the journey?"

Camille was ready to go and full of energy as soon as she'd decided how she would present herself, but preparations took a little longer. Arno took over brushing her clothing and running a hot iron over her shirt while Sylvie washed Camille's hair in fresh water, dried it with a towel and applied subtle cosmetics to emphasize her eyes. Kaspar examined their store of weapons for perhaps the tenth time since they'd embarked, cleaning each of the pistols and testing the powder, honing the blades and burnishing each medallion that bore Camille's crest. Tigre had been left behind with Maxime, gifted to his stable-girls, but the horses they would ride to the palace had to be ferried ashore in a longboat, one at a time. Henri took that task, of course, blindfolding the horses to ease their nerves and then standing at their heads as Captain Leung's rowers shot the boat over the waves.

In the excitement and clamor of recent days, Camille had forgotten how tortured she always felt by waiting. She gazed over the ship's rail as Henri jogged up and down the beach, his hand at Tonnelle's halter, Tulipe loping alongside him like a dog. She went to the heap of gear piled on the deck, rummaged in a saddlebag and emerged with her sketchbook, now sadly crumpled around the edges. She braced it on the railing and began sketching the horses in motion. The activity calmed her until it was time to depart, and on the subsequent travel to the ducal seat, she occupied her mind solely with riding.

Just outside the town's borders, she halted the group and dis-mounted. Sylvie slid down as well, hurrying over to tidy her clothing and repair her cosmetics. Camille would rather have worked on the animals, but Henri directed Kaspar and Arno in that task, quickly unsaddling the horses for a hurried session of grooming, and wiping down the tack with soft cloths. As soon as Sylvie had finished with her appearance, and they'd swiftly eaten their lunches, Camille's stomach began to twist with tension. She would be on display soon. She couldn't remember the last time that had made her nervous. She'd been attending court since before she could walk. This was very different, though. This time, she was showing herself before the people whom she hoped would let her rule them. Before she mounted Guirlande again, she strapped a knife to her thigh.

Strangely, her tension eased as houses began to accumulate, denoting the town's outside borders. She'd not had the chance to ride out like this in years; she'd barely left the palace since Michel had sequestered her, and then only in a closed carriage. Riding in the open air, she inhaled the mixed odors of horses, baking bread, roasting meat and flowers that, to her, meant home. She'd left beleagured by a cold, heavy rain. Returning in summer, each house was adorned by extravagant tumbles of flowering vines, purple and red and orange and yellow blossoms glowing in the sunlight. She glanced at Henri, by her side, and smiled at him. He smiled back, and pointed out a house whose door was nearly obscured by towering rosebushes.

Kamah had done her work well. A young woman, her hair cropped close to her skull, waited for them a few streets before the palace, holding a banner painted with Camille's crest. She waved it joyfully as they approached. Henri rose in his saddle, his face alight. "Nico!" he called.

Her face lit. "Henri!" Then she saw Camille, and her eyes widened. "Your Grace!" She fell to her knees in the road.

Camille leaned from Guirlande's back and reached out a hand. "We haven't time for that. Can you run ahead and bring word?"

"Of course, Your Grace! I was— Yes." Nico seemed to shake

herself. She glanced among the horses, spotted Sylvie, blushed and looked back at Camille. "Your Grace, all is ready for your arrival."

"Thank you. And thank Annette for me, when you have a chance," Camille said.

Nico bobbed a curtsy and ran, the banner trailing behind her.

"What's that noise?" Henri asked, watching her run.

"A very large crowd," Camille said. "Come. They're waiting for us."

They approached the tall, smooth white walls of the palace, each one topped by a walkway wide enough for two ranks of guards. Camille could feel the walls' heavy weight pressing on her heart. Next time, she vowed, it would be different; she would see it as a place of safety and stability. For now, she ignored the iron lacework of the closed gates, in favor of focusing on Guirlande. The mare looked her best, and Camille would make sure that the mare's movement was as controlled and graceful as any of the king's ceremonial guard. The people watching, most of whom did not own horses, might not know what she was doing, might have no idea of the years of training necessary for Guirlande's intricate dance, but Camille knew. Her confident pride would reflect in her bearing.

Cheering erupted. For the barest second, she closed her eyes in relief, then smiled broadly and waved.

The duke's guard captain, David-Marie, rode forward from the walls at a measured pace. His saber hung at his side, but he made no move toward it even when he halted his horse a few feet from Guirlande. He rode a brawny gray gelding, young enough to still show some dappling across its rump. David-Marie did not appear to move in the saddle, but the gelding extended one foreleg and lowered its head in a bow. "Your Grace," the captain said. "Welcome home."

Camille inclined her head, inwardly sighing a little in relief. "Is that Sucre you're riding?"

"Yes, Your Grace. Son of Tonnelle," he said, tipping his head slightly toward the mare Kaspar rode. "You are well?"

She didn't dare glance to see if anyone else was close enough to hear. Then Lilas whickered, and she guessed a combination of Sylvie's indifferent control and the advancing crowd had combined to distract the smaller mare from the comfort of her companions. Camille leaned forward slightly, as if to speak in confidence. She almost felt the pressure of eyes on her growing more intense. Gently, making the gesture appear natural, she laid her hand on her lower belly. "I am very well indeed, David-Marie. Horseback riding does not seem to have had a deleterious effect on my womanhood after all."

She hadn't been completely aware of the tiny sound of the crowd, their shifts and murmurs and rustling clothing, until a more absolute silence fell. For a moment or two, it was like a blanket had been dropped from the sky, blurring all sound and movement. Then voices bubbled up, those who had heard her voice passing her words to those who had not. Or perhaps words weren't needed. Her gesture might have been enough.

David-Marie was smiling. His scarred forehead relaxed and his seat became entirely more natural as he moved his free hand from his thigh to Sucre's withers for a quick pat. "May I congratulate you, Your Grace?"

Camille nodded graciously. A cheer rang out, then another, and soon the clamor was enough to make her wince. To her relief, David-Marie had taken the opportunity to ride back to the gate and command the guards to begin cranking the wheels that would force open the heavy gates.

Tonnelle's white nose appeared at Guirlande's right shoulder. "Let us go first, Your Grace," Kaspar said. He wore his saber on his back, she noted, ready to hand. Arno, to her left astride Pivoine, had added a pistol to his arsenal, the curved wood grip protruding from the harness he wore over his blue silk shirt. Camille nodded infinitesimally, and the two eunuchs moved forward.

As she rode through the gates, she could sense Henri and Tulipe at her back, like warmth. Once inside, Sylvie discreetly angled to the side, to find Vilmos. Henri brought Tulipe up next to her. Camille said, "You will accompany me inside."

"I'm ready," he said.

"David-Marie," Camille called.

He turned back to her. "Yes, Your Grace?"

"I would like you to take our horses," she said. "Please see that they're cared for in their own stable. Rhubarb's handler will take charge of them there."

"As you wish, Your Grace. Do you require an escort?"

"I can find my own way through the palace. My guards will accompany me."

"Yes, Your Grace." As she dismounted and turned over her reins, Camille reflected that she normally found the endless repetition of her title to be, at best, a meaningless buzz and at worst, a grinding annoyance. But sometimes, the words were satisfyingly sweet.

"I'll lead," she said to Kaspar and Arno. "Flank me, as usual."

Arno safely holstered his pistol and drew his sword, taking up his familiar position at her left. Kaspar swept his sword to his forehead, then down to his side. "Henri, you have your knife?" he asked.

"Yes," he said. He stood at her shoulder, perhaps a pace behind. In his fine clothes, she knew, he looked nothing like a groom. Without the sapphires now studding his ears, the ring Maxime had given him and the gleaming golden wrist cuff, he might have been an upper-level manservant, an additional bodyguard or even a secretary. The jewelry marked him as something more, a courtier of some kind, though he wore no crest, or perhaps an ambassador who affected a humble attitude. No one, not even David-Marie, had blinked an untoward eye at his presence. Of course, David-Marie might very well have recognized Henri.

Camille led the way up a short flight of steps into the high-ceilinged entrance hall. The door fell shut behind Henri with a ponderous, inevitable *thud,* abruptly cutting off the crowd noise that had traveled over the walls and into the courtyard. Footmen stood at the doors of each audience chamber, and two guards flanked the wide central staircase, tall halberds planted firmly on the carpet. Camille swept forward without hesitation. Her legs felt long and loose without the concealing, hampering weight of skirts. Her boots made satisfying *thocks* on the marble that mingled with the tapping of Henri's boots and the jingle of the purely decorative gold spurs she'd insisted he wear. Kaspar and Arno, of course, moved silently as cats.

The sound softened when she stepped onto the plush blue and gold carpet. The guards did not move a muscle as she approached them, but she could sense the straightening of their posture and the sharpening of their attention. They would have reacted to anyone approaching, but her eunuchs were unmistakable, and even in trousers and with her hair cropped, they would know their duchess. Trusting Kaspar and Arno to stop when she did, Camille halted a pace from the two guards, close enough that to see her properly, they would have to turn their heads toward her. She said casually, "Please remain on guard," and led her entourage up the stairs. For two steps, she allowed herself to wonder if a halberd would pierce her back, then closed the fear away. It was more pleasant to concentrate on how easy climbing a staircase could be, if one were wearing snug riding leathers and comfortable boots.

The second pair of guards, at the top of the stairs, merely thumped the butts of their halberds on the carpet in salute as she passed. Camille almost smiled.

Henri had never walked through these hallways, and she glanced back to see his reaction. He looked nervous. She would have liked to touch his hand, but now was not the time. On his first visit to the palace, Sylvie had smuggled him through hidden corridors intended for servants and frequently used for assignations. The open corridors suited him better. Candles blazed here, perfuming the air with the sweet scent of beeswax. The candles smelled like home. She inhaled deeply but did not slow her steps. She did not think she could have slowed herself even if restrained. She felt light and fluttery inside, but strong, too. Everything looked cleaner and clearer, smelled and sounded sharper, as if a scrim had been yanked from her face. She ascended the staircase.

The duke's chambers were to the left. Camille turned sharply to hide her sudden distress. She'd always hated his suite. He'd summoned her there many times, as if she were a dog, to berate and humiliate her in front of the servants. He hadn't scrupled to hide his humiliation of the servants from her, either. That would change. She owed too much to Sylvie and Kaspar and Arno, and to Vilmos, not to reward them with better than the occasional cast-off clothing. It was yet another item to add to the list of changes she could spend her life making.

She stopped in front of the duke's door. She heard nothing from within. Henri touched her shoulder, then curved his fingers over it and squeezed. Warmth rushed through her blood. She opened the door.

Sylvie leaped backward. Luckily, the pistol she held did not go off. Camille recovered her breath and entered the room, trailed by Henri and the eunuchs. This central room of the duke's suite was empty except for them and the single, throne-like chair from which Michel preferred to make his pronouncements. Her spine stiffened and her muscles tightened. After a moment's thought, she realized she could smell the lingering odor of Michel's perfume, like a blow about to fall.

"Where is he?" she asked.

Sylvie lowered her pistol. "In his bedchamber. I would like to shoot him."

"No," Camille said. "That is not your task."

Kaspar cleared his throat. "I will be glad to take care of that problem for you, Your Grace. I can prevent him from bleeding onto the carpet."

She glanced at the others. "Arno, Henri? Will you also offer to murder my former husband?"

"If you ask it," Arno said.

Henri alone slowly shook his head.

"I will not stoop to murder," Camille said. "Is Vilmos within?"

"Yes, madame. And Marrine, that red-haired concubine. She helped Vilmos. They are waiting for you."

Camille straightened her shoulders. "I will go in alone."

"Camille—"

"No, Henri." Then she reconsidered. "No. You come with me." She wanted him to see this. She wanted him to know what Michel was like, and perhaps understand how she had become as she was.

"Your Grace—" Kaspar began.

"You will wait here. Henri?"

The audience room opened onto a narrow closet intended for a chamber servant. Camille pushed open the door and found Marrine sitting cross-legged on the cot. She looked different than the last time Camille had seen her, in the basement room; her hair was severely braided, and she wore an oversize shirt over a long skirt and sturdy boots. A musket lay across her lap. She set it aside as soon as Camille entered, and curtsied. "Your Grace." She did not look up, pretending, Camille thought, that they'd never met. And of course they had not; she had only seen Marrine be fucked from across a room. She had no idea how Marrine had felt about it at the time. It seemed she had not been entirely pleased, if the musket was any indication.

"Open the door," Camille said. Henri crowded behind her; she welcomed the warmth of his body at her back. Then she was standing in the duke's chamber, holding hard to her composure.

Michel stood with his back to the wall, staring at her with a supercilious smile in the midst of his carefully curled beard. He wore a lavish blue and gold robe of state over his formal tailored garments; his fingers dripped with jeweled rings, and he'd crowned himself with the ducal circlet. There was an odd stuffy smell in the air. Camille's eyes flashed to the water pipe in the corner, and back to the duke, this time noting his pinpoint pupils. He'd been indulging in drugged smoke. She wondered if Vilmos had procured it for him.

Vilmos, she noted, stood well to the side. He no longer wore the duke's livery, only a plain shirt and a pair of loose trousers like the ones Arno preferred. He inclined his head to her. "Your Grace." She nodded in response, not trusting her voice yet.

The duke said, "He's given up calling me that, the filthy traitor. After all I did for his family."

"You killed most of them," Vilmos remarked, staring straight ahead. "And castrated four of the boys. And would have done the same to me, had I not been a little too old."

"And too well-hung," the duke said. "Well, my whore of a wife. Is that the stableboy you've been letting fuck you? A poor substitute for your stallions, isn't he?"

Years of practice kept her face immobile. She hoped Henri would imitate her restraint. "You cast me off," she said. "I am casting you off, as well."

The duke laughed. In his drugged state, his laughing lasted long enough to make Camille's skin crawl, but she wasn't going to show her feelings to him. Never again would she do that.

"Will you kill me yourself?" the duke asked. "Or will your catamite do the job? Or your ball-less slaves?"

"I am not going to kill you, Michel. I am simply removing you from your position."

He rolled his eyes and leaned indolently back against the wall. "And do you have a writ from the king? For I know of no other way I can be removed. Have you been fucking the king, as well? Is that where you've been?"

"My father was duke here, not yours," Camille said. "It is my right to rule this duchy."

"You'd better get yourself a cock, first. Wait, I'll hack off the manure-shoveler's for you. You can carry it in your pocket."

Camille put out a hand, pressing Henri back. When she felt him relax, she said, "If your sanity is in doubt, of course you must be removed. The king will agree."

"Well, my ducal whore, I will not."

Camille drew the knife from its sheath. "Then you prefer to be castrated? I am sure Vilmos will help to hold you. A little more of that drug, and you won't feel a thing. Kaspar tells me the discomfort only lasts a few months."

The duke's face froze.

Camille held up the knife, studying it. "There is a retreat Lord Maxime told me of. It lies across the sea. Those whose minds have gone, or who have succumbed to addictions, might live out their lives there, if someone pays."

"You are a filthy bitch," the duke snarled.

"Your opinion matters little to me," Camille said. "I think that's all for today. You will be ready to sail tomorrow. Vilmos, will you ensure his cooperation?"

"Yes, Your Grace."

"And, Michel? I will have the circlet now."

He threw it at her. Henri scooped it from the carpet and held it out to her. Settling the circlet on her head, she turned her back on Michel and strode from the room. Henri followed.

Kaspar, Arno and Sylvie were waiting. "It's done," she said. "Kaspar, Arno, would you please help Vilmos with Michel? He will be sailing with Captain Leung tomorrow. I wish him to be alive when he reaches his destination. I will **not** have it said I murdered to rule the duchy."

Kaspar ducked his head. "Yes, Your Grace." When he moved, Camille stopped him with a hand on his arm. "Wait," she said. "Both of you. I would like to thank you, for all you have done for me and for the duchy."

"It was our duty," Kaspar said.

"A duty you were forced to perform. Perhaps you do it now out of choice, and love of me, but in the beginning you could not choose. I would like you to choose now."

Arno looked alarmed, Kaspar watchful. "Choose, Your Grace?"

"I set you free. I understand now that you must also choose to set yourselves free. I would like to make that easier for you. Perhaps you could each think on how you would like to be rewarded for your service, and tell me when you have decided. I will see it done." She paused. "Also, I plan to forbid the creation of eunuchs in future."

"Your Grace!" Arno said. He glanced at Kaspar.

"Thank you," Kaspar said. He hadn't moved a muscle as she spoke.

Camille smiled at them, feeling a rush of fondness. "And, Kaspar, Arno?"

"Yes, Your Grace?" Kaspar said, speaking for both.

"Perhaps tonight you will leave me to myself, and enjoy a room together. Sylvie, Henri, come with me now."

Camille felt as if she floated down the staircase and back out into the palace courtyard. She could shrug her shoulders and her remaining cares would catch the wind. There was work to be done, of course. Years of work lay ahead of her, even if she disregarded the child in her womb. At least she would have help in her labors, and she would find more. Lord Stagiaire should be summoned for the one, and Annette the midwife for the other. Vilmos might be glad of a higher position, and there were some among the court who might be wooed to her side; she'd spent the past weeks making a list. For now, she stepped through the palace gate, and received the cheers of her people.

CHAPTER TWENTY–FIVE

Camille had not ridden since the birth of their daughter, and Henri watched nervously as she pulled herself into the saddle. At least she no longer bothered with cumbersome habits. He was just as pleased to see her in riding leathers, if it meant she could better stay on the horse, and more easily get up again should she be thrown. Also, the leathers pleasingly molded to her exemplary curves. He watched as she settled into Guirlande's saddle and scooped the reins into one gloved hand. He felt silly after he had done so. Nothing had changed. She might have been born attached to Guirlande's sleek back.

Camille looked at him. "Perhaps you'd like to see me ride figures in the ring, to make absolutely sure?"

He could feel his cheeks flushing red. "I was only a little worried."

Camille's mouth quirked up, and she adjusted the red knitted cap she'd worn over her cropped hair, then tucked her scarf more securely into her buttoned jacket. "I suppose it's a small price to pay now, since you did not scream, drink excessively or weep during Aimée's birth."

"I didn't drink at all!" Henri protested, as he nudged Tulipe into a walk, following Camille's lead. He'd wanted to drink himself insensible as the hours stretched, but to do so would hardly have been fair, since the midwife Annette had forbidden Camille even wine, instead relying on walking, topical creams and massage to ease the worst of the labor. If Camille could endure, so could he. Now he was glad he had not weakened. He would not have missed his daughter's birth for anything.

To his relief, Camille kept Guirlande to an easy walk. She might have lost none of her skill at riding, but her muscles were no doubt weaker than they had been. She would need to build up slowly; it was a good thing their trip to the king's court to present Aimée was some months away.

After a short distance, Camille said, "You took good care of my Guirlande. She's responding to my very thoughts."

Henri grinned. "She's the finest horse I've ever ridden. You can hardly give me honor, when it was your schooling that made her so."

She glanced over at him solemnly. "I didn't ride Guirlande for years. You are as much to thank as I am. Did you never think of that?"

Henri blinked. "I— No. She is *your* horse."

"She is yours as well. I watched you ride her." Camille smiled, a fierce smile. "You have nothing to say to that, do you? You cannot be humble when you know your own worth."

For the first time in nearly a year, Henri almost addressed her as *Your Grace*. Adopting one of her gestures, he nodded at the compliment and cast his eyes between Tulipe's pricked ears.

Camille led him through a fallow pasture, dismounting to open the gate and close it behind them. Once remounted, she took the path leading down to the stream that would, some distance along, meander past the pastures attached to the breeding barns. Henri couldn't remember if there was any sort of bridge down this far. They were already nearly to the edge of the ducal lands. He'd never had reason to travel this far into land used for hay and hunting small game.

He brought Tulipe up beside Guirlande. "Where are we going?"

"Not far," she said. "I'm enjoying being outside."

The snow had almost entirely melted, but the brown grass was crisp, the sky steely, and the air sharp with chill. The horses' shod hooves sounded like a clock striking the hour on the frozen ground. Henri wore a quilted coat, scarf, hat and thin leather gloves, but his toes and fingertips were edging toward numbness. "The air smells nice," he said. The tip of his nose was icy.

He did prefer being outdoors to anywhere else. He just didn't like to remember his days of breaking ice on troughs and lugging heavy buckets of icy water, with his hands protected only by a wrapping of rags. The stables had at least been moderately warm, and he'd slept warmer still in the old pony Poire's stall, provided Poire was in a good temper. He'd spent many nights planning how he would heat his own cottage, as soon as he could save the money to buy it. Most times, he'd envisioned both a fireplace and a central stove, and had gone so far as to ponder ways to have heated water inside, as well, like in the bathhouse. It all seemed impossible then, so why not dream as wildly as he liked? It had become too dispiriting, though. When he'd grown older and begun to collect pay, one of his first purchases had been snug woolen socks.

There was a narrow bridge over the stream, a pleasing arch with handrails worn shiny from use. The horses' hooves echoed on the wood planks as they crossed single file. Henri looked over the edge and saw water flowing sluggishly, in places still crusted with ice.

On the opposite shore, the frosted grass looked almost like flowers in places. He halted Tulipe and waved to Camille, pointing at the ground. She looked down, a puzzled look on her face. "Rabbit holes?" she asked, after a moment.

"It's just pretty," Henri said. "Look, over there. By the rock."

"There *is* a rabbit hole," she said, adding absently, "Take care for Tulipe's footing." She leaned from her saddle and peered at the ground. Henri fidgeted. She was likely trying to think of something appropriate to say. Sometimes, the differences between them flew up out of the ground like startled pheasants.

Camille said, after some time, "The grass is smashed together, and the frost makes the clusters look like asters. Or perhaps marigolds."

"I've never noticed anything like that before."

"Nor have I," she said, glancing back at him. "It's lovely. Come. It's not far."

"We're going somewhere in particular?" He'd thought they were simply out for a ride. He hoped there was no matter of business to which she had to attend. She did enough work back in the palace, even from the nursery, sometimes. It was a lucky thing Aimée had him, and a host of nurses, to cosset and amuse her. Camille could cosset much more sweetly than he'd predicted, but was also more easily distracted by matters of politics. Henri had made it an ongoing, private quest to bring at least one of the finer things in life to her attention, every day, while not being so obvious he might seem critical. He admired and loved her ability to lead, after all.

Camille didn't answer, and he decided she hadn't heard. He brought Tulipe abreast with Guirlande again, and rode in silence. If he ignored the drip developing at the end of his nose, the cold air did have a stimulating effect. He might be happy to stay out in it all day, riding with Camille between long rows of straight, skeletal trees and past bare hedgerows alive with birds preparing to seek out their breakfast in the fallow fields. He couldn't see the rodents, but knew they had to be there. Once, he saw a gray fox's flaglike tail disappearing into bare branches, probably chasing one of the hungry rodents for his own breakfast.

"Are we still on ducal lands?" he asked. He hadn't noticed any marker, though they now approached a sturdy, black-painted fence. Camille dismounted, threw the gate's crossbar, and used her weight to ride the wide gate open. Henri took the opportunity to admire the fine shape of her rear in riding leathers.

"We're not quite on ducal lands anymore," she said, waving him through. She closed the gate behind them, but did not remount. "There's a stable up ahead, with room for four horses," she explained. "I need a little walk, to loosen up." She stopped and lifted her hand. "You're not to tell Sylvie I did too much."

"Never," he swore. Besides, Sylvie was too occupied with juggling Annette and Nico these days, and their upcoming journey to visit the Duke Maxime, to fret over Camille.

To keep Camille company, Henri dismounted as well. Tulipe immediately stretched his neck toward a clump of dead grass. Henri shook some life into his fingers and tucked his hands beneath his armpits. The ground burned cold through his thin-soled boots. He should have foregone their sleek style and reverted to his old sturdy ones, which were padded inside with scavenged fistfuls of warm wool.

He could think of a way to warm himself. Leaving Tulipe to investigate the available grazing, he walked over to Camille. He'd experienced many new things over the past months, among them musical performances for the sake of listening rather than dancing or encouraging the consumption of wine. There were breaks at intervals, which he sardonically suspected were intended to wake any of the audience who might be disturbing others with their snoring. For Henri, the breaks had become a favored time to escort Camille from the crowd, with the excuse that her pregnancy necessitated frequent visits to the retiring room. After that, however, obscure alcoves could be found in almost any grand house, where they could spend a few moments pursuing private amusements. He held out his hands to Camille now and asked, "Is it time for the interlude?"

She took his hands in hers and pulled him close. Henri fumbled his coat open, wrapping it partially around her to share his warmth, and rubbed his cheek against hers. He lipped at the bit of her earlobe that was exposed beneath the edge of her knitted cap. Camille wriggled her fingers between his coat and his woolen jacket, then up under his shirt. Even through her gloves, her hands felt cold, and he gasped and flinched while she laughed. Fighting back, he rubbed his cold nose along her neck, then nipped and sucked gently at the tendon where her neck met her shoulder, feeling her delighted shudder as she melted into his embrace.

Several minutes passed in this blissful fashion. Henri's toes were definitely going numb by the time Camille teasingly gave his cock a quick rub through his leathers, then pushed him away with both hands on his chest. She righted her cap, which he'd thoroughly dislodged. "We've loitered here long enough," she said. "Bring the horses and follow me."

Her eyes sparkled in a way Henri saw more rarely than he would like. He did as she'd bid him, tugging Guirlande and Tulipe along behind him as Camille set out across the field. He could just make out the shape of the stable she'd mentioned, and a smaller brick building sheltered by its bulk. Smoke rose from a chimney. Hot tea might be nigh, and a fire to warm his hands. He walked faster.

Piney woodsmoke in cold air was, to Henri, the smell of perfect comfort. He glanced at the cottage's closed door as they approached. No one emerged, and Camille did not go over to knock. "No one is here right now. Let's take care of the horses," she said. "There will be blankets in the stable."

She must have made prior arrangements. Henri wondered if she'd also arranged for food. A midmorning snack would be nice, along with hot tea, and then perhaps some mulled wine before the long, cold ride back to the palace. He unsaddled the horses while Camille produced blankets and a basket of grooming tools from a shelf. The combs and brushes and hoofpicks looked new, made of high-quality bright steel and satiny dark wood with brass fittings. Perhaps this had been one of the duke's hunting lodges. It seemed a bit small, and snug rather than ostentatious. Perhaps a previous duke had built the place.

Camille moved to Guirlande after she'd shared the tools with Henri, and they set to brushing and currying, not as thoroughly as would be needed that evening, but enough to stimulate the blood. Henri finished first. He eased Tulipe's foot to the ground and watched Camille's bare hands smoothing a satiny glow onto Guirlande's dark withers, before heaving a blanket onto her back and buckling it beneath the mare's belly. "Finished?" he asked.

Camille dusted her hands together. She'd tucked her gloves into the waist of her riding leathers. "Yes. Let's go in."

Her eyes were smiling at him. She was clearly as ready for refreshment as he was. He hoped there was already a pot of water on the fire.

At the cottage's door, Camille dug into a pocket of her coat and produced a key, its hasp chased in silver. Perhaps the interior was fancier than the exterior. She unlocked the door and pushed it open. Henri followed her into glorious warmth and the scent of woodsmoke and mulling wine. Thick, soft rugs in dark colors like jewels cushioned and warmed his cold feet. "No one's here?" he asked, after a quick glance around. Someone must have set the wine and spices to heat. Camille didn't answer; she was stripping off her coat, hat and scarf. The lower floor was a large single room, divided by furniture into several areas: a softly padded sofa, covered in brown leather, placed in front of the main fireplace; a plain table and chairs of heavy, polished wood grouped into a dining area; and a rack of cooking implements near a barrel-shaped stove, whose pipe vanished through the upper loft and out the roof. The back of the room was curtained off by a heavy tapestry in the same rich colors as the rugs, presumably setting apart a sleeping area. He spotted another possible sleeping area in the loft, that could be reached by a ladder. It was, without doubt, the most comfortable home Henri had ever seen. Had he never met Camille, he might have been happy in a cottage like this for the rest of his life.

Camille strode briskly to the fire and held out her hands to the flames while Henri investigated the pot of wine and spices, kept hot on the stove. He found a couple of sturdy stoneware mugs, filled them with the wine and brought one to Camille. He joined her by the fire, letting the fierce heat bake the chill out of his skin, and taking sips of the wine to warm himself from the inside.

After a time, he said, "I found fresh pastries under that dishcloth. You thought of everything."

"Do you like it?" Camille asked. She touched her mug to his.

"It's delicious," he said. "I wouldn't mind another cup. I can bring you another, if you want."

Camille leaned forward and kissed his mouth. Henri licked the taste of cinnamon and cloves from his lips. "This is my gift to you," she said.

"Thank you," he said, suddenly ripped from the commonplace and into solemnity. "What would you like in return?"

Camille laughed. "You don't understand."

"I don't always understand you," he said, feeling a little put out.

"Not my kiss. The cottage. This place is my gift to you. It's what you wanted, isn't it? If Sylvie lied to me—"

Henri couldn't speak at first. "But—but why?"

"I thought you wanted something of your own. Not part of the palace."

Henri swallowed. "Do you want me to live here?"

She smiled. "I'd rather have you within my reach. This can be a retreat. I would like to join you here sometimes, if you would permit it."

"If *I'd*— You really mean it. This place is mine. *Mine.* The stable, too?" Henri looked around again, in growing wonder.

"I could hardly make a place for you, and none for your horses," Camille pointed out. She set her mug on the mantel-piece and slid her arms around his neck. "I had no place to be alone for…well. I never really had a place to be alone. I didn't realize how much that meant, until I fled the palace. You were accustomed to it, weren't you, before you joined me? I worried that you would miss having somewhere to be yourself. And perhaps, someday, you might bring Aimée here."

Henri kissed her quickly on the mouth. "We will both bring Aimée here," he vowed. "Perhaps when she's old enough to play the game of running and screaming for no reason. The palace might not be the best place for that. The marble floors are better for sliding in your stockings."

Camille hugged him close. Henri held her with one arm, glanced into his empty mug, and tossed it onto the sofa so he could use both arms to hold her to him and rock her gently back and forth. "Thank you," he said. He tugged her over to the sofa. "We could be more comfortable here," he suggested.

Camille fit perfectly between his updrawn knees, her back against his chest, his back cushioned by the sofa's arm. He circled one hand on her belly and used the other to hold her hand. "I could fetch us more wine," he said.

"Then you would have to leave me," Camille said.

"Very true. I don't want more wine right now." He rubbed his nose in the hair at her nape. "I'm nicely warm already."

Camille tipped her head back against his shoulder, and he kissed her, somewhat awkwardly. She said, "Sylvie said there was more to your wish than the cottage itself."

Henri swallowed, hard. "Did she tell you when she learned all this?"

"No. I suspect she tortured it out of you. You really shouldn't let her tease you as she does."

Henri breathed a sigh of relief. "I don't let her. Not much. Not anymore. She has Nico and Annette to tease her now. I think she likes that better."

"I don't want to talk about Sylvie just now," Camille said. "Tell me about your wish."

"We've already done the riding part," he said.

"There's none of the other kind of riding?" she asked archly. "I'd thought better of you, Henri."

He kissed her once more. "No, no riding. If there's a bed behind that curtain, would you like me to show you?"

"There is a bed," she said. "I would never forget such a detail." She leaned back against him and squirmed.

Hastily, Henri pushed her from him and got up. He readjusted himself in his leathers, then held out his hand and pulled her to her feet. "Do you mind hurrying, then? I promised myself I would make you come seven times, and we have no one to tend the fire for us."

"I doubt we shall notice beneath all those lovely blankets," Camille said. She lifted the curtain, stepped through and let it fall. "Perhaps you could help me undress?"

"I'm sure I can manage," Henri said. He yanked her sweater over her head, then the thin shirt she wore beneath. Her breasts were loose, still full from pregnancy and nursing. He handled them gently for a moment, knowing she was tender, then moved on to the buttons of her riding leathers.

As they undressed, he explained, "I have many different versions of what happens next."

Camille stretched, naked, on the sheets, and wedged her feet under the puddle of blankets at the bed's foot. "We shall have to try them one at a time." She grinned suddenly, wickedly. "Henri, do you know another reason you need this cottage?"

"Tell me." He knelt on the bed, straddling her hips. He leaned down and kissed her neck.

Camille smiled up at him. She reached up and touched his face, tracing her fingertips over his cheekbone and his lips. "Out here, no one can hear me scream."

Henri felt his eyes widening, and his erection suddenly pained him with a sudden rush of blood. "Oh. I'll do my best, then."

"Henri?"

"Yes, Camille?"

"You need not be quick about it, either."

"Yes, Camille."

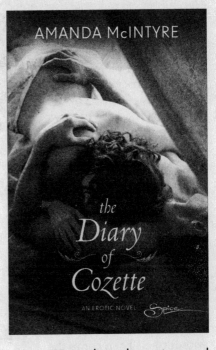

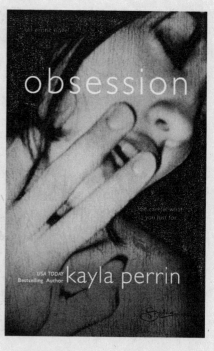